JENNY ESSENDEN

JENNY ESSENDEN

A Romance of the Other Woman

By ANTHONY PRYDE

AUTHOR OF
"Marqueray's Duel."

A. L. BURT COMPANY
Publishers   New York

Published by arrangement with Robert M. McBride & Co.

TO D. C.,

Without whose help this tale
could not have been written.

JENNY ESSENDEN

CHAPTER I

MARK STURT had not long returned from an expedition to the Southern Andes, and since he was of a contemplative turn of mind it amused him to stand behind a curtain in the recess of the balcony window and watch the dance going on to the tune of Offenbach's ingenuous Barcarolle. Andean rivers run with a swifter flow, and Pacific tides flood in with a stronger wash than that Mediterranean rippling, but for all that Mark liked the little lazy tune—liked it the better, perhaps, because it was steeped in the color and languor of European life. After the energetic wanderings which had taken him over the porphyry barrier of the Cordilleras and across the Chilian nitrate plains, it was agreeable to return to the leisurely ways of an English country house.

His reflections were tranquil and pleasant, and yet, though he was scarcely aware of it, they were tinged with melancholy. He was five and thirty, an age when a man begins, in odd moments, to contrast what he has done with what he once dreamed of doing. Sturt was, in modest measure, a successful man; he had realized some of his ambitions' and was in a fair way to achieve others. He was well in health and well off, staying in a pleasant house and among pleasant people; Charles Ferrier and his wife were old friends, and for the latter Sturt felt as warm a sentiment as a man can feel for any one in a life where the affections are habitually subordinated to the activities. But the dancing, or the tune, or some accident of his own mood touched him to a vague dissatisfaction. As happened to many men who were in their early twenties in 1914, the discipline of endurance and responsibility had made a middle-aged man of him in a few weeks, and he had never been able to go back as did many more and pick up the threads where he had dropped them: and now and again there stirred in him a regret, not for what he had lost, but for what he had never had. Offenbach's melodies are a cry to youth, and Sturt had done with youth. Or had he not, after all, altogether done with it? "Ces œuvres légères, où se mêlent subtilement la froide ironie et la griserie." But that sort of *griserie* is for boys of twenty. Happy boys of twenty, then! Say what one will, it is sober work to reflect that one will never hear chimes at midnight again.

A touch fell on his arm. His brother had come up the broad flight of steps from the garden, and stood looking over his shoulder into the dark splendor of flowers and jewels, and candle flames that sparkled, like stars reflected in black water, on black paneled walls. They were both tall men, but Lawrence Sturt was the taller and in every way the more remarkable, a figure difficult to overlook or to forget: they were twin brothers, but Lawrence might have passed for eight and twenty. There are no milestones on the primrose way.

"Pretty sight, isn't it?" he said in low, blunted tones that carried no further than his companion's ear. "Rather different from our last night at the base! Do you remember how the tent blew down and we had to dig for our instruments by starlight in the snow? Royal country that by night—all dark blue and silver. But one can't camp at fourteen thousand feet in the Andes in July—more's the pity!"

"I thought I saw you go into the garden with Miss Archdale. Have you deserted her?"

"On the contrary," Lawrence replied. "She fled from me on the terrace to fetch a scarf from her room. Why should it take her twenty minutes to fetch a scarf from her room?"

"Can't imagine. No wonder you pine for the Andes," said Mark, amused. "Arising out of that question— what had you been saying to her?"

"If you want to know, I was telling her our plans for Colorado. She was rather struck when I said you were coming too: wanted to know how long you would be away and what your constituents would think of your going off again. Has it ever occurred to you that she takes an interest in your affairs?"

"No, it hasn't. There she is with Mrs. Ferrier."

Lawrence Sturt followed his brother's long-sighted glance to the female figures framed in a distant doorway: their hostess, Dorothea Ferrier, a slender, fair-haired young woman with vividly blue eyes, and her friend,

Miss Archdale. "Trust you to know where she is," Lawrence murmured. "And on my honor I don't blame you! Dodo Ferrier sets her off: not that Dodo isn't a pretty woman too in her way, but she looks washed out by the side of Maisie Archdale—a fact of which the fair Maisie is probably aware. Women's friendships!"

"Do you mean that, Lawrence?" Mark asked mildly. He had learned long ago to accept his brother's point of view without protest, but, if he never quarreled with it, he was still occasionally mystified.

"Every word of it. Women are born actresses: they generally have twenty different motives for everything they do, nineteen of which aren't presentable. Oh, not Dodo so much! She's married and out of the running, and very fond of Charles Ferrier into the bargain, which leaves her free to be as natural as any woman can be. But the other is the fine social mask—Sappho up to date——"

"Sappho—?" Mark, who had been listening with half an ear, turned round to his brother. "Look here, old man, you oughtn't to say that sort of thing. It isn't decent."

"No, isn't it?" Lawrence shrugged his shoulders. "'Vengeance of Jenny's case, never name her'—is that your idea of decency?"

"After all one doesn't forget that Miss Archdale has no men belonging to her."

"Ah! I apologize. I forgot your personal feelings, my boy."

"Lawrence, don't be a fool! You know I haven't any."

"Not you," said Lawrence, pressing his arm. "Never look at her, do you? Couldn't tell me the color of her eyes? In point of fact I can't see why you hold off, for you could hardly do better for yourself. You ought to marry and now's your time. One of us is bound to carry

on the name, and, candidly, I don't think I was born to
figure as a husband and father. Whereas you, old Mark,
I think I see you with a little less hair and a little more
waistcoat, taking the kids—you will infallibly have half
a dozen of them—to Mass on a Sunday morning. Your
eldest son will carry on the business and step into the
family constituency, your second will go to Sandhurst:
I'm afraid I can't promise that the third won't be a *dé-
traqué* like myself. Come, own that the prospect at-
tracts you! And Maisie Archdale will do you down to
the ground: handsome, good family, good temper, any
amount of money, and no near relations. Probably she
has a devil of a will of her own but you ought to be
able to cope with that: you're not Arthur Sturt's son
for nothing. He had an eye for a pretty woman, too:
come now, haven't you?"

Sex was the one aspect of civilized life that interested
Lawrence Sturt, and it would be idle to pretend that he
was the less popular because in any male society, however
refined or respectable, his genial cynicism assumed com-
munity of taste. Mark's answering smile was rather
dry: it was difficult to resist Lawrence when he bade
one read the world in terms of French comedy: he was
improper but unaffected.

"After all, she might not have me. It is on the cards!"

"Rising politician—blameless record? Hang it, she's
got to marry somebody—she's three-and-twenty."

"And I'm five-and-thirty. Thanks!" Mark shook his
head. "You aren't so encouraging as apparently you
mean to be." Lawrence's unbelieving eyes irritated him
into indiscretion. "I don't want to marry any one, but
if I did it wouldn't be a woman who has already turned
down a dozen better men than I am."

"So that's it, is it? I fancied there was something of
the sort in the back of your mind."

"Something of what sort?"

"Oh! I understand well enough: sympathize, too, if it comes to that. She is too rich. It's a difficult position, and I can't see you competing with Forester's lovely uniform or Rudolph P. Hickson's railway shares. All the same it seems a pity, since you confess to the attraction——"

"Oh, shut up, Lawrence!" Mark Sturt broke into an impatient laugh: if at the back of his mind there lurked an assent, he was not going to admit as much even to himself. But he knew from experience that it would be idle to lose his temper with Lawrence, who would only become more and more placidly confirmed in his own opinion. Mark was not self-conscious enough to realize that he was confirming it at every step merely by arguing the point instead of letting the conversation drop. He did not know that he was in the habit of watching Miss Archdale or that he liked to think of her in relation to himself. "No! go your own way and leave me to mine. Heavens! what should I do with that lovely young lady? I couldn't take her to Colorado—or to the works. I should have to spend my life steering her through what Grayson-Drew calls the social vortex—if, that is, she would have me, which, as I'm not a duke, of course she wouldn't."

"No, wouldn't she?" Lawrence was flicking a rose leaf from the lapel of his coat. "My good Mark, I'm not so sure. It is precisely you fellows who refuse to compete——"

"Compete for what?"

Even Lawrence Sturt's Gallic candor died on his lips, for the speaker was Miss Archdale herself. She was alone, having apparently crossed the room on purpose to join them in the alcove: she came up to Lawrence with her slow easy step, but she was quietly watching

Mark. Dodo Ferrier in the doorway pressed her hands together with a little "Oh!" between mirth and distress: she wished Maisie would not do these odd things, which laid her open to misinterpretation! Somehow or other, however, she managed to escape comment as a rule.

"A penny for your—not your thoughts, Captain Sturt, they're probably too crude for publication. But for the end of your sentence: tell me, what won't your brother compete for?"

"Is this your apology for doing me out of a dance? Come back into the garden," said Lawrence, offering her his arm. "Then I'll tell you anything you like."

"Anything you like, you mean," said Maisie. "Then I should have to fetch another scarf." She turned to Mark. "You are not engaged, are you, Mr. Sturt?"

"For this dance? No," said Mark Sturt, startled.

"Then—may I have the honor?"

She curtseyed to him airily with her teasing faint smile and her sparkling eyes, direct and merry, like the eyes of a boy of fourteen. Of the two men it was Mark who was the more disconcerted—Mark, who had known her only for a few weeks, while Lawrence was a friend of a year's standing. Lawrence, after the first gleam of irrepressible surprise, became distantly polite, murmured a vague apology, brushed past Mark, and escaped among the dancers. His tact was equal to any strain, but there are situations which are not worth saving. Mark was amazed—and amused; but he felt very awkward. It was not the first time Miss Archdale had gone out of her way to distinguish him, but she had never done it so openly, or at another man's expense. And Lawrence, of all men! He did not know what to say to her, whether to take it seriously or to laugh it off.

Miss Archdale remained standing by Mark in the

recess of the balcony window, a little apart from the
coming and going under the central arch. She was so
tall that her head was on a level with his shoulder, and
so handsome that he could not help feeling gratified as
well as amused. It was a night of mid-July, moonlit
but overcast, and very warm: the day-long sunshine lingered in the balmy air. Framed between high stone
traceries lay the dim verdure of the garden, its infinite
intricacy of beaded turf and bloomy spray all hushed
under the infinite monotone of twilight. Miss Archdale,
slowly fanning herself with a lace-like silver fan, was in
harmony with this nocturne, for over her gray dress she
wore a silver scarf, embroidered in wave-like ripplings
of moonstone and pearl. She wore no other jewels at
all except a moonstone fillet which bound up her lustrous
hair.

"Why aren't you dancing, Mr. Sturt?"

"I was enjoying a little interlude, Miss Archdale."

"Philosophizing?   Criticizing?"

"Merely admiring."

"Ah!" said Maisie, glancing down.

The trivial sensuous delicacy of the barcarolle flowed
out past them into the night like a warm tide.

"Shall we dance this?" Mark asked, shaking himself
out of the dreamy mood which the music or her manner
seemed to be deliberately calling up. "I am no hand at
all these Russian or pseudo-Russian dances, but I think
I could manage a waltz. Why do you look at me with so
much scorn? You should not snub a man when he is
doing his best."

"Because you dance very well and you know it. I
hate affectation from—from people like you."

"My dear child"—the phrase was jerked out of Mark
by surprise—"I danced when I was five-and-twenty—
when I was Harry Forester's age!"

"I watched you with Mrs. Ferrier to-night. No, I won't waltz with you, but you can take me down the garden if you like—do you like?"

"Immensely," said Mark, pulling at his mustache. And he strolled at her side down the steps and over the gray lawn. Plenty of other couples were wandering about near the house, but she led him on away from them all, beyond rosebeds and shrubberies, through a latched gate into the fringes of a beechwood and out again on fields. Like a secondary daylight the moon from behind vague clouds diffused a gray illumination over the undulating countryside—mown hay, belts of covert, the rare lamps of a distant village, the woody bourne of hills; and from the shadow of the beech forest there stretched away the silver levels of a lake. Grey Shotton, the gaunt old Georgian house, was blotted out with all its festal lamps behind trees: faint and far off the violins wailed on muted strings, fitfully audible over the lisp of ripples among reeds at their feet.

At the water's edge the gray roots of an alder, gripping the soil like a wizard's hand, made a natural seat, and Maisie threw herself into it, leaning her shoulders against its clustered stem, while Mark sat down on the bank, keeping a careful distance, pulling at his mustache. He was amused, he was flattered, but in some odd angle of his mind he was sorry. His irretrievable feeling was that Miss Archdale ought to have been kept in order by her mother or her nurse. Failing these, what was Dodo Ferrier doing to let her wear her dresses so low? Before she got her scarf he had seen her and wondered whether she understood the force or nature of the instincts to which she played when she put on those gossamer bodices which seemed constantly to be in danger of slipping off her beautiful shoulders. Other women knew what they were about. But over the lure of her splen-

did dresses Maisie looked out into the world with the
gallant recklessness of a boy.

"Your brother has been telling me you're off moun-
taineering again. When do you go?"

"In a fortnight."

"Really? I read your book about the Andes. I liked
it, but you amused me."

"Did I? How?"

"By your laborious struggle to give all the credit to
your brother and none to yourself."

"Ha, ha!"

"Modesty is so rare nowadays," Maisie pursued, unruf-
fied by Mr. Sturt's hearty laughter, "and family affection
is even rarer, so that I couldn't help being edified by
your display of both. Really you wrote as though Captain Sturt dragged you about on a string!"

"So he did," said Mark, still amused. "He's a much
older hand at it than I am. He was in the Himalayas
five years ago, and New Zealand before that, when I
couldn't get away. You mustn't forget that he's a hunter
by profession, whereas I'm only a tradesman."

"Yes, you look it!"

"I know I do, though it's unkind of you to say so.
We can't all be six feet three of wire and whipcord!"
Mark Sturt was big and heavily built, turning the scale
at fourteen stone, but his weight lay in his bones: a
life of hard work and hard play had left little flesh to
spare on his body, and it never took him long to train
down to the finest point of condition. But he enjoyed
teasing Miss Archdale, a privilege granted to few.
"That's why I didn't get up Aconcagua, as you must
know if you've read my book."

"Your book leaves a great deal to the imagination.
Why didn't you get up Aconcagua? I asked Captain

Sturt and he said, 'That is Mark's usual luck.' What is your usual luck, Mr. Sturt?"

"Haven't an idea," said Mark. He was getting angry but he did not show it. "But I'll tell you with pleasure why I didn't get to the top. I had four shots at it and went sick regularly every time in the high altitudes. One can play that game indefinitely, but it's not fair to the others, so one had to chuck it and return to the base. Hate it? Naturally I hated it, but one accepts one's limitations."

"Does one? Do you? I should have thought you were one of those who go on till they drop."

"Are you satirical?"

"No, it's Pax," said Maisie, smiling. "I really mean it."

"Thank you," said Mark, flushing in spite of himself. "But I must say that is a lady's point of view. When one can't eat and can't sleep and can't stand, the one thing left is to clear out of the way."

"And now you're going to Colorado. How long shall you be away?"

"Five months or so. I must get back before next session. I paired before Easter, but I daren't pair again. Gatton is very good to me, but even Gatton has fitful recollections of my £400 a year."

Gatton was the big industrial constituency which had twice returned Mark Sturt to Parliament.

"Five months is a long time. What shall you do out there—go down the Grand Cañon?"

Mark assented. "And there's always a sporting chance of a row in Mexico."

"What a hopeful tone! Then perhaps you would never come back at all," said Maisie. "Well, I'm going away, too: I wonder if I could manage to get up an adventure.

It would be a jolly change. I'm so sick and tired of everything that it couldn't be a change for the worse."

"Abroad?"

"No, I'm going down to a cottage on the Dorsetshire coast. It used to be a coastguard's cottage, but it has been empty for years, and no laborer will live there because it's so lonely: I bought it out and out for a song and had it put in order, then I got tired of it and I've never been near it since. It's a queer little place, all stone and mortar, at the top of a crack between two chalk downs, and there isn't another building in sight— nothing but the cleft of the hills behind it, and a steep narrow glen running down to an immense waste of sea. No one comes because there's no beach—only a tiny strip of gray sand in between cliffs: and there's nothing whatever to do but listen to the gulls and the waves and the wind in the trees behind you."

"But you don't seriously think of staying in a place like that?—Or perhaps you didn't mean to go alone?"

"I shan't take even a maid. The cottage is all on one floor and I didn't put much furniture in: just a few chairs and pots and pans and a new kitchen range. I shall drive myself over with a hamper from Ushant, the nearest station: and when I've eaten my way through it I shall wire to the Stores for another one. You can get fruit and eggs and vegetables from a farmhouse two miles off."

"What a wonderful plan," said Mark, amused: "and shall you do your own cooking and dusting?"

"I shall: do you think I'm not competent?"

"I'm sure you are if you say so. But I should never have guessed it."

"Ah! You mustn't believe all your brother says about me. I like Lawrence, you know: if I were a man I should want to sit and smoke with him in the small hours." Mark was silent, chiefly from want of interest, partly because he did not care to discuss his brother. "But you can't be friends with him if you're a woman. Lawrence is a *raffiné*." Mark opened his eyes: again he wondered if she understood what she was saying. "However, I didn't bring you down here to discuss Lawrence. I had something exceedingly serious to say to you. Lawrence isn't serious. You are, aren't you, Mr. Sturt?"

"Very," said Mark. He had no idea what was coming. Far off in the woods a melancholy "Hoo! hoo!" proclaimed the hunting vigil of an owl. Some small unknown animal rustled among the rushes near at hand: by the tiny splash that followed it was probably a vole. The stable clock at Shotton was striking two. Chimes at midnight, after all!

"How hot it is!" said Maisie. "It feels as though the moonlight were warm." She leaned forward, letting the scarf drop from her throat as she touched Mark's arm with the tips of her fingers. At that moment the moon came sailing out of a cloud and a great glow of pearl shone over the lake, bleaching the gold of her hair to silver, and painting leaf-shadows in sepia on the ivory of her bare shoulders, so classically strong and pure above the gray mist of her dress. Mark held his breath. He could not read far into those brilliant melancholy eyes, but this he read, that if he took her in his arms she would submit. The fine social mask! He had regarded that phrase as a wayside bloom of Lawrence Sturt's exotic imagination, but it recurred now. In the last fortnight he had seen a great deal of Miss Archdale in the easy intimacy of a country house, and he had watched her with other men: and she was friends with them all—friends with Harry Forester who adored her, and friends with Charles Ferrier who adored his wife. "She is like a boy, and I love her for it," he had heard

Mrs. Ferrier say, in whose judgment he had faith: and which was the mask—that brotherly good humor, or the strange stern passion that looked out of Miss Archdale's eyes to-night? In some obscure way she moved him to pity. She was young after all, not yet four and twenty, and the bloom and perfume of youth still clung to her, intoxicating his senses but invoking his chivalry. And yet what folly! Can there be any bloom left on a beautiful woman whose eyes are as reckless as Maisie's were under their profound and brilliant melancholy? Lawrence Sturt, a very gallant cavalier, would have laughed him to scorn. "Take the good the gods provide thee!" Sturt felt himself stiffening in iron resistance. He turned away his head.

"Hallo! Isn't that an otter splashing about under the island?"

"I can't see. It sounds like one." Her fingers nestled into the palm of his open hand. Sturt wondered what on earth to say next and why he was behaving so churlishly. "Mr. Sturt, I'm not vain as women go, but there isn't another man at Shotton that would have refused to kiss me when I—when I let him. Why—why won't you?"

"May I kiss you?"

"If you—if you like."

His answer was to lay the lightest of kisses on her beautiful wrist.

"Not my hand," said Maisie, careless and bold.

"It would not be fair, my dear, from me to you."

"No—you won't?" She was apparently surprised. "Don't you think me handsome? I don't, I hate red hair, but most people do. You can be quite frank, I don't care much one way or the other, but I should like to know."

"Extremely handsome," said Mark gravely. He had begun to wonder whether he was not asleep and dreaming, but at all events it was a relief to have no difficulty in disposing of that question. "It's profanation to call your hair red. It is gold, real gold, not flax or mahogany. You were far and away the most beautiful lady in the room to-night. I don't pretend to be much of a judge, but I give you my opinion, since you ask for it, for what it's worth."

"I'm glad." She leaned down and fixed her eyes on the clear, dark water under the alder tree. "Altogether I'm what one would call eligible, highly eligible, amn't I? One can't pretend not to know it. So many men have wanted to marry me: I never get through a season without a lot of bother. For one thing, I've really rather a lot of money for a woman: one wouldn't call it a big fortune for a man, but not many women are so rich and so free. It's my own: I could chuck it in the sea if I liked—not that I ever should like. Money's eminently useful. An ambitious man could do a great deal with five or six hundred thousand of his wife's money that was not tied up in any way. If I married I should—I should throw it all into the common stock. Money is never worth wrangling over and I certainly couldn't be bothered with a separate balance-sheet. My husband would have to use mine in and out with his own. Such as it is, it would be useful to an ambitious man—a man who was going in, say, for politics or anything like that. I suppose it isn't precisely true that one can bribe a Whip. Or is it? There is a line somewhere but it's one of those lines that outsiders can't draw."

Mark, from the depths of his confusion, heard himself gravely saying that one could do a good deal by judicious contribution to party funds.

"Anyhow that doesn't signify, that's not the main point." She seemed to brush it impatiently aside. "Ex-

cept that it makes me more independent: too much so, I
suppose. I never have cared a snap of the fingers for
other people's opinion except the two or three that I
liked, Dodo Ferrier's, and Ph—one or two others', and
yours."

"Mine!"

"Yes, I like you. Didn't you know I liked you? I've
always liked you. You're different from most of the
men I know. I liked you best of all just now when you
refused me. It was characteristic of you, that: you're
good at refusing. Oh, I know! that is the sort of thing
that women always want to know, and somehow or other
they generally contrive to get hold of their facts. There
are no women in your life, are there? That—that
is one reason why I've been so bold: I could not have
said all this to most men, because it might not have
been fair to some other woman. But you're like me in
that, you haven't any ties, not even near relations,
except Lawrence, who doesn't count: you and I can
do with our lives what we like. If I've counted the
cost all round and I'm prepared to pay it, there's no
practical reason why I shouldn't do what I'm doing
now."

"But what are you doing?—I beg your pardon, but
honestly I don't understand."

"I should have thought it was clear enough. Too
clear!" Her laugh was only faintly rueful. "But I'm
not afraid of plain English. Mr. Sturt, will you marry
me?"

"Will I—?"

"Wait. I don't want an ordinary marriage, Eaton
Square and the Riviera and all the rest of it. Will you
marry me secretly before you go to America and come
with me to Ushant for a week?"

"Oh, my God!" said Mark under his breath.

Her words could have but one meaning, did she imagine that he would be blind to it? Well, she was young, and the world is hard on women. He subdued his anger before he found an answer, the only possible answer in that impossible position. "My dear, you must tell me all about this. You have no.brother, let me take a brother's place: you're so young, you don't—I'm sure you don't—know what you're doing."

"Oh! I deserve this."

"Do you mean that I'm wrong?"

"Yes, wrong."

"You must speak the truth, Maisie."

"I was brought up to speak the truth." She stood facing him in the moonlight with her direct level eyes. "I am innocent. Oh! I'm not good like some women. I dare say I might, if I were tempted, fall: it's hard to say what one would do if one were tempted, because certain forms of temptation are so—so heavy. But if I came to grief, and if I were in danger of discovery, I'd face discovery. I had that hammered into me when I was a child, that if you do wrong you must stand up to your punishment. I'm doing wrong now." Mark believed it, she looked as haughty as Lucifer. "But, when the reckoning comes, I shall face it. I'm not a coward."

"I can only beg your pardon."

"No, it was my own fault: I've compromised myself so deeply that you think I'm capable of anything. But indeed I'm not."

"My dear, I didn't mean to insult you. I've seen more of life than you have, and I know how hard it can be on a woman. I thought you were a young thing driven into the toils."

"And so I am," said Maisie, trembling and bending down her head. "But not the toils of a farthing scandal."

"Let us talk this over," said Sturt quietly. "Sit down again: and let me put your scarf on, or you'll catch cold." He returned to his place at her side: he showed no sign of emotion except that he was still rather white and that his manner was both more gentle and more formal than it had been. "You asked me to marry you privately and go down with you to Ushant. Why?"

"That I can't explain."

"Girls of your age often have romantic fancies." He turned his head away. "Are you—forgive me, dear, but I can't think of any likelier explanation, and though I'm not a romantic figure, one knows what girls will do in the way of idealizing a fellow. I won't fail you, if you'll trust me. You haven't by any chance been fancying yourself in love with me, have you?"

"I thought you would say that. No, I'm not offended! You can say anything you like. But, Mr. Sturt, think for a moment! I'm not a young girl—I'm not so young as you imagine: at all events, I've seen a good deal of the world. Do you think a woman like me—I am proud and I've always been independent—could be so swept away by a twopenny halfpenny schoolgirl fit of sentiment as to deliver herself up to any man's mercy bound hand and foot—as I'm at yours?"

"I felt an awful fool for asking. But I was bound to say it, Maisie."

"You couldn't have put it more nicely." She looked at him with a fleeting laugh as he had seen her look at Mrs. Ferrier: then with a swift return to seriousness, "Well, here are the facts, so far as I can give you them. I'm absolutely sick of my life, so sick of it that I don't much care what happens to me: I'm in difficulties which I can't describe to you or to any one: and this marriage is my only way out. I came to you because I like and trust you better than any other man I know, and because," her voice faltered but she steadied it, "I had a—an in-tuition that, for the very short and inexacting period I've named, you might be considered available."

"Why?"

"In plain English, I know you don't want to marry any one. Your brother and Mrs. Ferrier say you'll never marry. You're too fond of sport and politics and going off to the ends of the earth. But what I offer would not put a period to your wanderings: there would be the one week at Ushant, which I suppose from all one's ever heard of men you would enjoy, and after that you would be free to forget me."

"Has it occurred to you that marriage for a week may involve one in liabilities which can't be forgotten?"

"How do you mean?—Oh! yes, I've thought of that. But I'd take the risk."

"In that case the marriage would have to be made public."

"Not unless you chose. I take all the risk. If it in-volved my own social smash I shouldn't much care. I'm so tired of it all! My own friends would stick to me whatever happened and I shouldn't care a button for the rest. One ought to value one's good name, I suppose, but it doesn't matter much that I can see. Anyhow that's my own look out. For you there would be no drag, no responsibility after you left me at Ushant: except of course that you wouldn't be able to marry anybody else —I can't help that."

Mark wondered if she imagined that he could remain indifferent to what happened to his wife. But it was not worth while to argue the point. "Suppose when my week was up I didn't want to go to America?"

"Didn't want to leave me, do you mean? Oh! that would be a matter for arrangement. If you wanted to make me your wife publicly and permanently you would have a legal right to enforce your wishes, and I should respect them. I never shuffle out of a bargain. I give you free leave to make the marriage public and to compel me to take your name and to live with you. It's 'Heads I win, tails you lose' for you. I want it to be so. If you do this for me I want you to get all you can out of it.—If you come to that, I might not want to leave you."

"What I cannot conceive is what you yourself get out of it."

"Because you don't know the conditions."

"Tell me them." She shook her head. "I never heard such rubbish in my life!" said Mark angrily. He tried again. "If the ceremony is all you require, why on earth didn't you go to Harry Forester? Eccentric as your offer is, I feel sure he would jump at it."

"Oh! Mr. Sturt——"

"Don't do that." Docile, she let fall her hands. He realized then to what extent she was at his mercy and for his life he could not repress a start. "Maisie, I thought you never felt shy."

"No: well, I don't often blush, but when I do it is an *affaire*. Oh, Mr. Sturt, be merciful!" Maisie murmured. She was still scarlet, forehead and cheek and throat, her modesty was as inexplicable as her boldness, but as her blush ebbed she rallied her courage to reply. "Say, because I wasn't keen on marrying a man who—cared."

"Do you mean——?" Mark began. His voice was hoarse: he stopped, cleared his throat, and resumed rather more deliberately than before, "Do you mean that you addressed yourself to me because I wasn't in love with you?"

"Does that seem strange, to a man?"

"I suppose a young girl never does know anything about anything."

"Thank you. Perhaps you wouldn't mind explaining?"

"I will. Don't you see that whereas, under these very peculiar conditions, Forester, who is a thorough good sort, would marry you for love, I could only be supposed to marry you from a less worthy motive?"

"But I'd rather have your indifference than Harry's love."

"Good heavens!" said Mark under his breath.

Her candor defeated him because he could not tell whether it sprang from the cynicism of her seasons in town or from pure nursery innocence. She jested with the great veiled powers like a child.

He sat with his hands in his pockets looking across the fields to the twinkling lamps of the village and the low bourne of hills. The sough of the dawn-wind shook through the tree-tops and over the short, severed stalks of the hay. It seemed a long while since he had stood watching the dancers and indulging a sentimental regret for youth and its romance. Now adventure had come to him, as it does come sometimes, in middle life, to those who think they are safe over the fence forever: a wild adventure which no sane man could take seriously, yet mixed with practical considerations which no sane man could overlook. For Miss Archdale had great possessions, Lawrence had not overstated her material advantages: richer than himself, many years younger, still in the freshness and fame of her beauty, if he married her there was not a man in his set who would not envy him his luck. Her secret? Some cobweb mystery, to be coaxed out of her at his leisure: at all events he would have staked his life on its being nothing dishonorable. If he married her and declared the marriage he could afford to loosen his grip on Gatton and its trad-

ing ventures and to assure his footing in the political
world.

And was that an argument to be taken seriously?
Mark smiled into his mustache. No: her material advantages inspired in him nothing but a faint recoil of
distaste. Nothing would have induced him to touch
her money. He was too self-reliant, or too fastidious,
to care to accept more than he gave. It would have been
different if he had loved her, but he did not love her,
not at all: like many men who know little of women
he had an ill-defined poetic ideal of female perfection,
and if any woman could have reached his standard
Maisie certainly did not. Remained only to say no politely: to explain to her that a middle-aged politician does
not conduct his private life in the spirit of a French
comedy! She was shrewd enough if she would but open
her eyes: incredibly reckless, but strong, in her detached
take-it-or-leave-it attitude. In five minutes he could be
quit of her without ill-feeling or much embarrassment
on either side. Mark wondered if she would then trans-
fer her offer to another man: he knew not a few who
would have jumped at it, with or without the half-mil-
lion which she was prepared to fling into the scale. How
cruelly she would suffer if she fell into the wrong hands!
But no, she could not be allowed to go on risking her
happiness: she must be brought to book, Dodo Ferrier
must be called in if necessary.

Mark roused himself out of a long silence and turned
with twenty convincing arguments on his lips. He could
not do it. No honest man could do it. She would only
be unhappy if he did. It was midsummer madness, there
could be no earthly reason for it, she must tell him or tell
Dodo Ferrier. "My dear——"

He stopped short.

"Well, what's my fate to be—is it yes or no?"

"It is yes."

"You don't mean it?"

"By heaven I do," said Mark. He took her in his arms and kissed her.

"Oh, but why—why?" Maisie murmured, docile in his clasp. "I didn't think you would. You weren't going to. You were going to say no."

"Was I? In that case I must have changed my mind. But I think you're wrong: I don't believe I ever meant to refuse, no, not for a moment. I always take a sporting offer, and yours, for a gloomy middle-aged business man, has all the charm of the unexpected. You recall the dreams of my vanished youth." He touched with his lips her closed eyelids, ivory blinds drawn down over the brilliance of her eyes. His own, she resigned herself, a city undefended: and the entire current of Mark's being moved towards her in flood. It was not love but it was everything short of love, and prudence and common sense could no more stand against it than a child's barrier of sticks and sand can oppose the incoming tide . . .

The stable clock was striking three: the midnight hours were ended. "Oh, how late it is!" said Maisie, startled. "Let me go now, Mr. Sturt." Mark released her instantly. He had not kissed her again.

She stood up. Mark too pulled himself to his feet, not without an effort: feelings that had let him alone for thirteen busy years were at their narcotic work to-night, sapping his energy. The love of beauty ran in his blood: except by travel, he had scarcely ever indulged it: but it is a tenacious passion, and mountains and stars cannot satisfy it forever. "Time to go back, what?" he said, shaking himself free. "Getting on for dawn, isn't it? You must have cut half a dozen dances by now, and you've had no supper." Over the glimmering windiness of field and forest the flush of dawn was at war with the fading moonlight, and the air was full of the chill scent of grass and budding leaf: from the nearest patch of covert came the faint piping cry of a bird.

He gathered up her fan, her gloves, her handkerchief, and fell into step at her side: betrothed lovers on the eve of marriage, and almost as much a riddle to themselves as to one another. Mark Sturt, who should have known better, was fighting off second thoughts in true gambler's vein: he set his teeth and swore that he would not repent till it was too late to retreat. And Miss Archdale like a frightened child reflected, "I'm riding for a fall," but she had neither power nor will to save herself. She was in the grip of heavy forces, and she did not understand them well enough to cope with them in any way.

She could not read the man at her side. She could imagine what Forester would have done, the handsome passionate young man. She would have had to satisfy a far more exacting claim, but Forester's kisses would not have made her blush. Or Lawrence Sturt, Mark's brother: Lawrence was a dangerous combination of voluptuary and cynic, but she never would have flinched before him, though he was not scrupulous and could be cruel. Mark was slower and colder, and ought to have been easy to read, and yet she could not read him. The rather heavy, impassive face, the shrewd unrevealing eyes and easy manner offered only negative qualities for analysis, and he had an inexhaustible stock of silence: while his sense of humor was an incalculable element, for she could not always tell why he was amused. Lawrence Sturt in his most reckless temper could not have bent her. But Mark could look her down with his laughing eyes.

They came out on the edge of the beechwood, where the gray lawn, deserted now, stretched away to the lighted windows of Shotton. The fleet of cloud overhead was beginning to be shot with pink and mother-o'-pearl, and in its interstices the sky was of a deep indigo blue. "Whew!" Mark whistled softly, glancing at his watch. "Ten past three. Half the people are gone home, you know. Unless you wish to be either cut or congratulated, I suggest sneaking in through the library window and going straight to bed. You must be sleepy though you don't look it."

"I am not tired," said Maisie, smiling. "But I will if you like."

"Oh, Griselda wasn't in it," said Mark. "Very good, I shall send you in by yourself. Slip through the shrubberies and go up the little staircase of the library; no one will see you, and I shall say you had a headache and went off early. I shall stop out here and have a cigarette."

Maisie wondered why he took her left hand, till she found that he was holding it and that he had taken the signet ring from his own finger to slip it on hers. "You can wear it round your neck by daylight," he said in his clear impassive tones. "But I swear you shall wear it on your hand to-night. Good night, my dear."

"Good night, Mr. Sturt."

"Say 'Good night, Mark.'"

"Good night, Mark."

CHAPTER II

"The expense of spirit in a waste of shame . . . ."

MARK STURT did not require much sleep. He smoked his three cigarettes in the beechwood, and then he came indoors ten minutes before sunrise, when the last guests were saying the last farewells. In reply to the reproaches of Mrs. Ferrier he merely regretted that he wasn't a dancing man, but the faint scent of tobacco that clung about his clothes added a shameless footnote to his apology; and when she asked what he had done with Miss Archdale he answered without any hesitation that she had complained of being tired and gone off early to bed. Harry Forester, handsome and haggard after a wretched evening, had placed himself near enough to hear what was said, and Mark's eye sparkled as he saw the young man's face clear; Forester was the right side of thirty, and held a commission in a crack cavalry regiment; the odds were in his favor, and yet he had lost.

Mark went to bed, fell asleep as soon as he laid his head down, and woke again at half-past seven feeling very fresh and cool, and with a hazy impression that something had happened to him the night before. He lay back on his pillows, his tanned features turned towards the splendor of eastern sunlight. There was a ring round Mark Sturt's throat as definite as if it had been drawn with a ruler; the skin was nut-brown above it, and white below. Through the open window he could see tree-tops waving, green against blue, and the song of

birds came in, the lively din of sparrows, the thick
treble "Pretty Dick! Pretty Dick!" of a late thrush.
Mark raised his left hand and fixed his eyes on his little
finger, where a band of bleached flesh marked the re-
moval of a ring worn for many years. Originally his
mother's ring, when she died it had been enlarged for
his father, and from his hand Mark had taken it when
Arthur Sturt lay in his coffin. Mark had offered it to
Lawrence, but Lawrence, always morbid in his shrink-
ing from death, had refused it with a shudder, and
Mark had worn it ever since. It was so small for him
that he could hardly get it off, but it was very loose for
Maisie Archdale's third finger. Mark wondered whether
she would have liked diamonds better than the old worn
ring, with the falcon crest of his mother's family, and
the motto: FORS L'HONNEUR. Would she guess that it
had been the symbol of an older romance? If it had not
been for that band of shrunken flesh on his finger, Mark
would have been inclined to think that he had dreamed
the whole affair.

But, if it was not a dream, what did it all mean?

Seven-thirty a.m. is the time of times for second
thoughts. Mark clasped his arms behind his head and
deliberately challenged them, and they came thick and
fast. He was thirty-five, a sportsman, a politician with
a safe seat in the House, and sole proprietor of the Gatton ironworks, a large business in the northern Midlands
which throve unfailingly even in the slack times after
the war; till within the last year or so Gatton had ab-
sorbed most of his energies, and even now, though he
was getting to leave the details of administration more
and more to his pearl of managers, Sturt kept an extremely firm hand on all the strings. Unofficially he and
Jack Bennet were on brotherly terms, and Jack was free
to slap Mark on the back (they had been at Stonyhurst

together), and call him an unpractical ass, but when
Jack had finished grumbling he did as he was bidden,
and when Mr. Sturt betook himself to the Andes it was
on the distinct understanding that, Socialism or no Socialism, Gatton would continue to be run on his
lines.   Trade, sport, politics, such was the sum of Mark
Sturt's life, and it had aged him; he was the twin
brother of Lawrence Sturt, but he looked five years
older.

Of amorous adventure his course for the last thirteen
years had been remarkably free; in his early manhood
he had had one disastrous passion, the details of which
were not known even to his brother, and no woman had
ever relit the fires which burnt themselves out on a
French battlefield.   Mark thought of Gatton, and then
he thought of Renée; Renée in her young slenderness, a
flower sprung from the French *bourgeoisie,* as he had
first seen her standing in her father's door when his company marched into her village.   He had adored her with
a boy's swift visionary fancy; he had seen her not half
a dozen times in all; the last time he saw her she had
been lying dead four or five days. . . . Mark Sturt at
five and thirty remembered the Mark Sturt of two and
twenty with a strange impersonal pity.   Ardent fancies
pass away in time, and if Renée had lived Mark would
certainly have forgotten all about her long ago, but because of her death and the way of it she had left an
imperishable stamp upon his life and nature.   How hor-
ribly he had suffered!   All Lawrence Sturt knew, then or
later, was that his brother went through the autumn and
the winter fighting like one mad with the blood-lust, till
a heavy wound mercifully laid him low.   For years after
his return to sanity Mark avoided women from cowardice,
as a man avoids whatever may bring on a recurrence of
some dreaded pain.

And now after all these years a woman had come into his life again and challenged him to an adventure which not only was far out of harmony with Gatton and Westminster, with middle age and common sense, but seemed likely to end in some renewal of the old torment. Miss Archdale's intuition had not been at fault; if Mark had kept out of her way, it was for no other reason than because he was pretty strongly attracted by her and afraid of her power. He did not want to marry, still less to fall in love—he wanted to climb another peak or two with Lawrence, to make a good thing out of Gatton, perhaps in the long run (a half-acknowledged ambition) to hold office in a Liberal ministry. Certainly there was no face-reason why a week at Ushant should interfere with these designs, but the small cold voice of common sense warned Mark that he was taking heavy risks, and that passion, like fire, is a good servant but a bad master. With something of a cynical smile at himself, he laid a finger on his own wrist; no, he could not think of Maisie coolly. If she could set his blood dancing now, what would happen at Ushant?

"What will Ushant mean?" Mark said to himself sternly. "Marriage is a sacrament. What sort of sacrament will this marriage be for you—or for her? You know pretty well. Does she? What right have you to take advantage of her? What if you were to hurt her? If after thirteen years' immunity you're driven to make a fool of yourself again, can't you do it on cheaper terms? No? This one woman and no other? The gambler and the sportsman coming uppermost, is it?" He knew his own weakness, watchfully guarded and veiled; there was a vein in his character to which every now and then the high throw or the long shot made an irresistible appeal. "But the thing is folly and worse than folly. Your word of honor? De Trafford would tell you to clear out by the nine o'clock train and break your word from a safe distance."

Good advice is always cheap; but the cheapest and most drastic variety is the advice a man gives to himself when he knows he is not going to take it.

Mark looked at his watch. A quarter-past eight. "Breakfast any time after twelve," Charles Ferrier had said cheerfully. It was not to be supposed that Miss Archdale, after the exhausting emotions of the evening —Mark was happily confident that some of them had been exhausting—would be visible yet awhile, but to be up and active was better than to lie and think of Rénée, or of Ushant; and he rang his bell. Entered decorously, within the minim interval of time, Henham, the ideal valet, his gray hair trimly parted and his whiskers trimly barbered. "Mr. Lawrence down yet?" asked Mark, taking his tea and his letters. Lawrence, like Mark, was an early riser.

"No, sir, not yet."

"Get my bath ready. . . . I am going to be married on Monday, so you can have a week's holiday."

The latter sentence framed itself in Mark's mind, but not on his lips. He would have liked to see what effect it had on the serene Henham, but he really couldn't flatter himself that it would have very much. "Yessir; will your suit-case be enough for you, and shall I pack your golf clubs?" That would probably be Henham's reply. Both speeches, however, were left in the limbo of the unrealized: Mark did not even go so far as to tell Henham that he could have a week's holiday. A vein of Celtic caution which was strongly developed in him suggested that the less time Henham was allowed for practicing the curiosity that all good servants feel about their masters' movements, the better.

He opened his letters, and was amused to find how little interest they now had for him. The gunsmith's specifications, over whose delay he had been chafing yesterday, were thrown down with a yawn. A note from the publishers of *Climbs in the Andes,* enclosing a check and statement of accounts, got even less attention. An illegible scrawl from his cousin, Considine Sturt, in North Russia, held him for a moment, because at first glance he read it: "Dear Mark, I have shot thirteen babies in prams"—but when this genial infanticide resolved itself into "thirteen brace of snipe" he tossed the rest aside and got up. He really did not care what had become of Considine and his erratic pursuits.

Mark dressed rapidly but carefully. Although, like most of his class, he was a vigorous dandy, buying expensive clothes and bullying his tailors if they did not fit him to a hair, he did not usually pay much attention to the smaller details of his toilet, which were left in Henham's care; but this morning Lawrence himself could not have been more imperative or more exacting, and when he had finished tying his tie he looked himself over in the glass, he who did not care as a rule whether there were a glass in the room or no. The hall clock was striking nine as he came downstairs. Floods of golden sunshine everywhere, and not a soul to be seen except the servants: even Lawrence apparently was taking life easy after his late hours. Declining breakfast, Mark strolled out on the lawn—the gray moonlit lawn of last night, striped now in misty sunshine. In the borders which had been so full of mystery, roses and early hollyhocks and sapphire spires of lupin stood up fresh and glittering under a light dew. Mark walked up and down with his hands in his pockets, whistling snatches of Spanish ballads that he had heard the Chilian arrieros sing round their camp fires. Whatever was to come, he was the

gainer by a glorious night and morning; by this dance
of blood in his veins, by the rush of health and energy
and vital force which thrilled him to his finger-tips.

> "Yo no quiero al Conde de Cabra,
>   Conde de Cabra, triste de mi!
> Que a quien quiero solamente,
>   Solamente, es ay! a ti.
> Arroz con leche——"

He had just taken out his pipe when he caught sight
of a feminine figure passing in and out of view between
the rose thickets at the end of the lawn. Surely he could
not be mistaken? There was no other woman in the
house so tall as Maisie Archdale. Mark crossed the
turf with the step of a cat; he had a good deal to say
to Miss Archdale, but he saw no reason why he should
not combine business with pleasure. Here the cluster
roses towered high against the morning blue, great groves
and archways of gold and pink and orange linked by
flaunting horns of honeysuckle or by the mauve and
purple butterflies of the climbing pea; and here he came
on Maisie, in a small clearing where the sunshine, reflected from a million balmy petals, made the very air
burn. She was in a white embroidered dress, her hair
plaited thick and close, and she was kneeling on the stone
verge of a little font, whose musical babble, as it spurted
up and fell back into its own clear pool, drowned Mark's
footfall. Coming up behind her, he passed his arm
round her waist, drew her to her feet, and took a lover's
kiss. Then for one impenitent moment he thought she
was going to faint.

"Oh! Mr. Sturt——"

"Mark."

"Mark."

How exquisitely she pronounced his name! Not the

least of her graces, to Mark Sturt's taste, was her beautiful speaking voice; she dragged a little on her words, now and then, but so slightly that it could not be called a drawl, and when she spoke his name on a half-breath Mark seized her in his arms. She threw up her wrist to defend her lips, and Mark drew it down, smiling. He was not tender; there was nothing in his eyes but passion, the passion that borders on cruelty. "Let me go," said Maisie.

"Rather have Forester, what?" Mark murmured. "Don't be shy, Maisie; has no one ever kissed you before?"

"No one. Oh, let me go, Mark!"

"By Jove, I believe that's true! Virgin soil, eh? I'll initiate you. . . . What a shame, isn't it? Forester wouldn't treat you so." She stood still in his embrace, bending down her head. "Speak to me."

"I can't . . ."

"What can't you?"

"Anything, while . . ."

Mark's arm dropped. He drew two or three deep breaths like a man recovering from a fainting fit. Then he said, "I beg your pardon," and Maisie saw that he was very pale.

"It's I who ought to apologize," she said, smiling as she drew herself free of his clasp.

"Why?"

"For shirking. I didn't really mean to cry off."

"Do you mind my smoking?"

"No, I like it."

Mark filled his pipe and lit it before he spoke again. He tossed the match down and watched it fall and burn itself out on the close turf. "You mustn't mind me," he said. "You reminded me for a moment of a young girl I used to know when—when I was a young man." He stopped, grinding the match into the grass with his heel; he had not meant to speak of Rénée, he had never in his life spoken of her before, but the words were dragged out of him against his will, though under his impassive manner they cost him strange birththroes. "She was rather badly hurt: I do not mean by me. But for one moment your expression reminded me of her. I'd rather die than bring that look into any woman's face." He waited a moment, and added simply, "I suppose you know what getting married means."

"Did she die?" said Maisie.

"She? Who? Oh—yes, she died."

"Did you love her?"

"Yes, I loved her."

"Did you ever tell this to any one before, Mark?"

He raised his head with a jerk. "I'm afraid I can't answer any more questions. Suppose you answer mine instead. I asked whether you realize what marriage means. If you were not happy in my arms just now, do you think you'll be any happier at Ushant?"

"Probably not," said Maisie. "Do I care?"

A gust of south wind, sweet with honeysuckle, went wandering by, ruffling the folds of her white skirt, and scattering the slender pipe of the fountain into silver threads which wet the turf with spray. She turned and began to pace the glade beside Mark. "I'm beginning to understand you, Mark: the little tale you've just told me throws a flood of light on your feelings. You call yourself a business man, but you're as romantic as you were when you were twenty, and as sensitively chivalrous—I've suspected you of it before, only I could hardly believe it of Lawrence Sturt's brother. Now I'm not romantic. A bargain's a bargain, for me. I've Yorkshire blood in me, and I like to pay my debts as I go along. You mustn't be chivalrous with me, because it only makes things harder for me. If you want to relieve my embarrassment, dear boy, you must hold yourself free to take what you like, when you like, and to pursue your own satisfaction irrespective of mine, without regard to any small protests I may be weak enough to make. I'm not like your little girl in the story—I shan't die under it. Is that clear?"

"Perfectly, thanks," said Mark, pulling at his mustache. What was clear to him was that Miss Archdale, after all her London seasons, did not know what she was talking about; clear too that she did not even dimly see what sort of part she was forcing on himself. She was very beautiful; he could not call her stupid; but he did not know which he disliked more, the rôle she assigned to him or the tone in which she spoke of Renée. He was not accustomed to think of himself as a fastidious man, yet at that moment he was near to breaking his word, not because the situation was both difficult and dangerous, but because he was shocked and offended by the woman at his side. "Perfectly," said Mark Sturt; and then Maisie's fingers felt for his hand and nestled into it, as if her heart—the inner spirit which our words often coarsen and belie—were pleading for leniency. Mark's hand clenched itself over hers.

"I did not intend to question you, Maisie, because I feel bound in honor to respect your small secrets, and if you refuse to answer me I shall not make any attempt to find them out, though I'm certain I could compel you to answer me if I liked. I won't do that. But you're young—twenty-three, isn't it? I'm ten years older, and I'm a business man. I don't know what your difficulties are, but it's hard for me, as a practical man, to believe that there's no simpler way out of them than this fantastic marriage. Difficulties that look terrible to inexperienced eyes can usually be settled with a pinch of common sense and a check. If, for instance, any other man is bullying you—I speak in the dark, as you know —give me leave to tackle him for you, and I'll engage to settle his hash in five minutes, not with my fists, dear, but with the prosaic aid of the law. I should be glad to put my judgment and experience at your service. Will you—for God's sake do—tell me why you want to marry me?"

"No."

"I beg of you to do it. I'll keep your confidence."

"I shall not do it, Mark. But I'll give you back your word, if you like."

"And if I take it back, what will you do?"

Maisie did not immediately answer. She stood by the brim of the fountain, dabbling her fingers in its spray.

"Speak to me, Maisie."

"I shall marry Mr. Forester."

"Oh, you will, will you?" said Mark under his breath. "No, I'll be shot if any other man shall wear you. Have your own way, then; I'll not let you go again."

He stopped to relight his pipe, and to move to her other side, so that the smoke should not drift across her face. "Regard that as settled. Right or wrong, I'm not going to give you up to young Forester. And now we'll get to business. You go to Ushant on Monday, do you say? Straight from here? And what then—do I travel down with you?"

"No, that would never do. You'll have to find your own way to the cottage; I might manage to pick you up at the station and drive you over with me in the dogcart, but I think it would be better if you walked. It's not above four miles." Sturt, who was as indolent in travel as he was energetic in sport, looked a trifle resigned. "I know you won't mind that."

"Oh, quite. Is it your idea that no one should know you have a man in the house with you?"

"No, that wouldn't work; some stray passer-by would be sure to see us together, or there would be children hanging round, or those horrid little boy scouts—they crop up in the most unlikely places. No, the less mystery the better. We'll be honeymooners, you and I; legitimate, don't you know, but very daring and unconventional. I'll wear sandals, and you shall go without a collar, which will create a devil-may-care atmosphere of Golder's Green." She laughed, and Mark had again the fleeting vision of a sweeter Maisie, neither cold nor passionate, but natural and friendly as a boy. "I don't think I ever knew any one who looked less like Golder's Green than you do. You're not handsome, Mr. Sturt, but I like the look of you: does that touch your vanity? All men are vain, and most Englishmen are shy. Are you shy, Mark?"

"Very," said Mark.

"I believe you are, though I'm sure you don't mean me to believe you." She looked up at him with her soft, brilliant eyes, derisive, cajoling, penetrating, but Mark had not lived five and thirty years for nothing, and he was steady under fire. "You certainly are impassive. This is a digression. To return to Ushant: all I want is to break the thread between it and London. In a little place like Ushant there won't be a soul, you know, that has ever heard of you or me or any one in our set. Well, I won't say that; the vicar and the doctor may know your name as a promising M.P., and their wives may have seen my photograph in the *Queen*, but that sort of knowledge only widens the gulf. I know: I've lived in that world myself." Mark listened attentively; no mystery hung over Miss Archdale's past, yet he knew nothing very definite about it, and she herself never spoke of it. But she did not break her rule, though for a moment he had fancied she was going to do so. "There is no bridge, believe me, between our small set where every one knows every one, and the great world outside it where no one knows any one. I'm not a bit afraid of 'flying chats' after we get to Ushant; all I do bar is leaving links between Ushant and London which some kind London friend may pick up."

"Quite; we'll be very precautious. But there remains one point to settle."

"Which?"

"Rather an important one. Getting married. Have you thought out your arrangements for that?"

"No, dear boy, I haven't," Maisie acknowledged with an irrepressible faint blush. "I—I left that to you."

"It does seem to fall within my province. Well, I don't want to impress you with a display of learning, so I'll confess that I got up the subject this morning out of a directory. The first point to settle is whether you want to be married in church or at a registry office."

"In church."

"Really? I didn't know—forgive me if I am indiscreet—that you indulged in anything so unfashionable as a dogmatic religion." Maisie looked as if she hadn't known it either. "Dear me! this is very awkward. It raises unforeseen difficulties. I say, I'm afraid it's all off!"

"Because I want to be married in church? Good heavens, why? You're not a militant agnostic, surely?"

"No, I'm afraid I'm something even more uncompromising," said Mark, stopping to knock the ash from his pipe. "Didn't you know I'm a Catholic?"

"Oh! is that all?"

"All!"

"My dear boy, I'd just as soon be married in a Roman Catholic church as a Protestant one! I couldn't stand a registry office—I really am not a heathen, and no amount of registrars would ever succeed in making me feel married at all. But I'm not a bit dogmatic. Very few Protestants are, I think. Oh, I suppose High Church people are," said Miss Archdale hazily, "and they won't eat fish—no, they won't eat anything but fish—by the bye, I don't know how you'll get on at Ushant! One never can get anything but bloaters in a sea-coast village. But perhaps you aren't strict? Anyhow I'm not. I never did really know the difference between the two churches, except that you worship the Virgin and believe in the saints and we don't, and one or two things like that. I'd quite as soon be married by a Roman Catholic priest. Of course they're not like our clergy, but they're just as much priests, aren't they? Apostolical succession and all that. Dissenters are different."

"Ha-ha-ha!"

"Oh, Mark, don't laugh like that! They'll hear you from the house!" Maisie cried out indignantly. But Mark Sturt's shout of laughter was not to be subdued in a moment. "Oh, do be quiet! what is there to laugh at? I dare say I am very ignorant, but no one ever taught me anything, and how am I to know?"

"Ha-ha! Oh, I beg your pardon," Mark said remorsefully. Then he took his pipe out of his mouth to laugh again. "Maisie, you are *impayable!* You ought to have a sash and a bib. Never mind, I won't laugh any more." He struggled back to gravity. "All right, as you're not dogmatic we can go ahead like a house on fire. Only there's one other point which I'm obliged, with apologies, to bring forward. I pointed out to you last night that there were liabilities to be considered. In plain English, which I know you like, I am bound to get

your promise that the children of the marriage, if there
were any, should be educated as Catholics."

"What, all of them? I thought the boys followed the
father's faith and the girls the mother's."

"That is a capital arrangement for those who believe
in two faiths," said the Catholic dryly. "We don't. *Credo
in sanctam ecclesiam catholicam.*" He crossed himself.

"Mark, I didn't know you felt like this about it."

"No?"

"You frighten me."

"Oh, you mustn't be frightened. I'm not a bit a good
Catholic."

"But you are a Catholic—a believer," Maisie murmured. "And I'm a heretic. Mark, I feel as if you had
gone miles away." Instead of replying, Mark turned
again to knock the ash from his pipe, and this time
Maisie drew her own conclusions, though for once in a
way she kept them to herself. She had seen Forester
take equal trouble with his match or his cigarette when
he was nervous, but she had never expected to find the
same trait in Mark Sturt. "I do bother you, don't I?"

"Not a bit; and anyhow you can't help yourself. These
things have to be settled before one can get married in
our Church, that's all. The ceremony once over, you
can safely forget that I'm a Catholic at all, unless——"

"Unless what?"

"Unless, of course, a child were born to us," Sturt
answered impatiently. "Then the subject would come up
again. Otherwise I promise that it shan't worry you.
Indeed, it makes things easier to arrange, for we can
get married in my own parish church by my own priest;
that disposes of the question of residence, and Catholic
priests don't gossip."

"Is he nice?"

"Nice? What do you mean?"

"Is he—don't be cross, Mark, you know they aren't all, and I should hate to be married by a man who dropped his h's—is he a gentleman?"

"I have no idea," said Mark shortly. "He was at school with me."

"Oh! That sort? I'm glad." Miss Archdale's brow cleared, but as Mark's remained clouded she relapsed into deprecation. "Oh, now you are cross! But I can't see why you should be."

Mark looked at her. She was leaning back on a dense thornless thicket of yellow briar against which the gold of her hair glittered like a flame, her arms folded, her knees crossed under her loose-flowing skirts; and her raised eyes were as blindly clear as a child's. No, she really did not see. "What an idiot you are, Maisie!" said Mark very unexpectedly. He was more taken aback by his own incivility than she was.

"Thank you. I don't know why, but perhaps I shall grow up to it in time."

"Don't you mind being called an idiot?"

"No, I love it. You don't know how jolly and familiar it sounds. Besides, you can't go on being cross after that."

"Oh! well, if you like it, I shan't beg your pardon," said Mark, struggling with an impulse to take her in his arms again. But he did better than apologize. "The fact is, I'm very fond of Father de Trafford. He is a saint, Miss Maisie, one of the saints you don't believe in: much better than you or me. Never mind, I forgive you. There only remains to settle the day: will Monday do? I can get things in train by then, I believe, though I shall have my hands full: I must—but I needn't bother you about that." He had been about to speak of the necessity of getting a dispensation.

"Monday would suit me perfectly," said Maisie with

a smile like sunshine. "I could go up by an early train, drop my big box at my own house, and go on by taxi to the church, either before or after lunch, whichever is more convenient. And I could take your luggage down with mine if you put it in the Waterloo cloakroom before I get there; it would have your initials on it, I suppose. Then you would have no bother at Ushant. We had better not lunch together or go anywhere together till we meet at the cottage. You must let me know the time, and of course you must tell me where Father de Trafford's church is—would it be near your rooms?"

"Lane Street—down at the back of Westminster, in the thick of the slums."

"I'll remember. And when shall you leave Shotton?"

"This afternoon. I shall have fifty things to see to between this and Monday."

"So soon? After all I can write to you if anything occurs to me. Shall I address you at your own chambers or at the club?"

"My own flat; but I wouldn't put down anything incriminating in black and white, if I were you. It never pays to trust servants. You, I suppose, will stay on here till Monday. But you might give me your town address and the telephone number, in case of accidents."

"Hadn't we better exchange cards? I don't know yours, either."

"Happy thought!" said Mark with levity. "Here's mine." He gravely gave her one, and she tucked it into her dress. Strange how suddenly they seemed to have slipped into an easier relation, how much more naturally they talked to each other since Mark's small storm had cleared the air! "I'll give you mine when we go indoors," said Maisie. "Oh, and, Mark——"

"Yes, dear?"

"Is there any one you would like to ask to the ceremony?"

"Any one I would like—! I don't follow. Isn't it
to be a secret?"

She looked up at him with a laugh and a fleeting color
and a twist of her level brows. "A dead secret. Still,
after all, Lawrence is your brother."

"Bless me!" Mark exclaimed, "do you mean, should
I like to tell Lawrence?"

"I thought it possible."

He shook his head. "No, dear. Such an idea would
never enter my mind."

"Then that settles that," said Miss Archdale, with the
air of one who brings a laborious negotiation to a satisfactory close. "Oh, Mark, I'm so hungry! I didn't have
any supper last night except some biscuits that Nelly
sneaked up to my room. Do let's go and have our breakfast before all the other people come down!"

CHAPTER III

"O Salutaris Hostia
Qui cœli pandis ostium,
Bella premunt hostilia,
Da robur, fer auxilium."

THE nave of St. Casimir's church was dark, for it was nearly nine o'clock, and only half a dozen lamps had been lit in the aisles for the Friday-night service. But at the altar the Benediction candles shone like a golden galaxy, star above star, honoring with their bright rays the mystery of the Host; and before the throne Father de Trafford knelt with white illuminated face, offering the adoration of incense, which is the prayer of the Church, while the low chant went up from kneeling choir and congregation. Among the latter Mark Sturt knelt with bent head, murmuring the same hymn that men of his faith had sung six hundred years ago:

"Uni trinoque Domino
Sit sempiterna gloria,
Qui vitam sine termino
Nobis donet in patria."

Mark had told Maisie that he was not a good Catholic, and in fact, as practicing Catholics go, he lived carelessly, for the pressure of work, while it staved off passionate adventures, tended also to narrow the scope of prayer and meditation in his spiritual life. But he had always fulfilled the obligatory observances, and when he worshiped he was often painfully conscious of his

44

own deficiencies. To-night, when the bell rang and the priest raised in his veiled hands the sacred mysteries and made the sign of the cross over his people, Mark's head sank lower and lower.

"Adoremus in æternum sanctissimum sacramentum."

It was the world-old challenge of the spirit to the flesh, of the unseen and eternal to the things seen, which are temporal; and it pierced Mark Sturt to the heart because, though he did not know it himself, there was in him a strain of the visionary and the ascetic, which might have ignored any lesser claim, but could deny nothing to what claimed all. In place of lofty nave and lighted choir Mark saw the solitude of Calvary and the Son of God nailed to the cross; and as, with the full keenness of his intellect and the full strength of his will, he bowed himself in adoration of that glorified body which the priest carried in his hands under the form of the Host, there came upon him once again that hunger and thirst after God in which all mortal passions are lost as the river is lost in the sea. And he prayed for purity of life and thought. He forgot Gatton, forgot Westminster, forgot the gold hair of Maisie Archdale: forgot indeed where he was, till his neighbor, a young Irish private of the Leinsters, touched his arm apologetically because the service was over and the way out was barred by Mark's half prostrate attitude. Purity of life and thought for a soldier, a politician, a man of business with a big manufacturing constituency at his back? Strange paradox! Mark Sturt submitted to it. For him no facile creed: but to this hard and heavy bondage, this unremitting tax on will and pride and strength, he could yield without reserve. But he got to his feet rather hurriedly when the Leinsterman touched his arm.

Father de Trafford, coming out as usual by the little

door of the Lady Chapel ten minutes later, was not slow
to recognize the tall figure awaiting him, for Mark stood
bareheaded in the light of a street lamp, hat in hand.
"Is it you, Mark?" the priest exclaimed. "My dear fellow, I haven't seen you for years! How are you, and
what have you been doing? Killing yourself in the
Andes, I hear."

"While you have been killing yourself in Lane Street.
You look tired, Father; you ought to get away. London
in July is too much for you."

"I'm not tired—only worried. You're coming home
with me? That's delightful. You have dined, I hope?
for I couldn't give you much on a Friday night, but I
have some good cigars that you shall try, and we'll talk
about everything in heaven and earth. Now here is a
reward for a poor sinner! I was in a fit of the blues an
hour ago." He slipped his hand through Mark's arm.
"First I want to hear all your own news. Where are
you stopping—at the flat?" Mark assented. "And how's
Gatton?"

"Gatton's very well, I believe. I haven't been there
lately, so Jack Bennet is in command. I'm booked for
the opening of the new town hall in January, which will
be a nuisance. Bennet is angling for the Lord Lieutenant,
but I suppose I shall have to make a speech. Will you
come and back me up? I can't bear facing that sort of
function singlehanded, but I can't get Lawrence to go
near it."

"I never knew any man that had a nicer sense of the
duties of his position than Lawrence," Father de Trafford observed, "or a happier knack of getting out of
them. If one wanted to know what not to do in any
given emergency, Lawrence would be a better guide than
the Holy Father. Still Gatton is your own affair after
all, and I can't imagine why you should want any one

to back you up. After four or five years in the House
you ought to be used to getting on your legs—aren't
you?"

"Constitutional shyness, I suppose. I am shy, you
know; I hate the footlights."

"Oh, rubbish! Where is Lawrence, by the bye? Is he
as meteoric as ever?"

"Quite," said Mark, smiling. "He's staying in Hampshire with the Ferriers. I've been there with him this
fortnight. I only left to-day."

"Pleasant party?" Father de Trafford asked, leading
the way into the presbytery. He was a thin worn-look-
ing man with the gay blue eyes of a boy, and he had a
soft gay manner without a trace of clericalism, so that
in the dark one would not have known him for a priest;
in the light, on the other hand, one could hardly have
mistaken him for anything but what he was, for the
stamp of spiritual authority marked his features, and the
limpid glance, with all its sweetness, was remarkably
piercing and shrewd. "But I know the Ferriers always
get together pleasant people. Now let us make ourselves
comfortable. See my little smiling angle of the country
through this window! *Ille mihi præter omnes*—that's not
Church Latin." The presbytery was within a bowshot of
the church, and between the two lay one of those tiny
and sequestered nooks of garden which survive in the
older quarters of London: a crooked patch of turf enclosed between high walls, a couple of shady plane trees,
a border dense with flowers now paling in the nightfall,
and a wooden bench and table roughly knocked together
by Father de Trafford's own carpentry.

"We might sit out there, shall we?" said the priest,
taking Mark's arm again and propelling him gently towards the open window. Mark smiled, he knew the tiny
garden well; through the dust and smoke of London

there penetrated to his nostrils the sweet night scent of stocks and tobacco-flowers. "I wish it were daylight, then you should see my robin; he always comes and con- verses with me when I'm writing my sermons. Don't laugh, plutocrat! do I own Gatton, or can I go and climb Popo-what's-its-name? Very well then, I won't be put out of conceit with this pocket-handkerchief of a garden of mine. Philosophy lies in liking what you have, and success lies in wanting what you haven't; there is life for you in two nutshells, take your own and leave me mine. Try these cigars: a duke gave them to me, so they ought to be good, but as you know I am no judge. Oh, my dear Mark, I'm very glad to see you again! Were you in church to-night?"

"Yes."

"I did not see you."

"Your Reverence never sees any one," Mark answered, the kindly fun in his voice a thin veil over its deep affec- tion. "I sat near the pulpit in the hope of catching your eye, but in vain. I love your little Friday night talks, they sound as if you were thinking aloud; and I was deeply interested in what you were saying to-night."

"About the sanctity of marriage? I shouldn't have expected you to find that topic keenly interesting, unless it were from a Parliamentary point of view."

"Oh, it's a wide problem," said Mark. Father de Trafford's head went slightly to one side; his vocation had not come on him till he was five and twenty, and his boyhood in a hunting family supplied him with an illustration of Mark's attitude in the swerve of a horse before a stiff fence. It had not taken him long to see that Mark was facing a fence of some sort. "How does the work go on," Mark continued, "and what can I do to help, and why are you worried?"

"Because I have no faith," said the priest with an

immense sigh. "Oh, if people only realized what sort of work it is we churchmen are doing! But few understand; and many don't care, though I know that is not the case with you."

"I'm afraid it is more my case than it ought to be. Tell me some more about it; is there any fresh trouble? The church was pretty full, I thought."

"Yes, one ought to be grateful for that, but it's very difficult not to think more of the streets which are so much fuller. The parable of the pieces of silver was written for us priests, I fancy, but unluckily it is the ninety and nine that are lost, and with all our sweeping we can pick up only two or three. I was talking last night to the parson of St. Sepulchre's, a very nice fellow, and we agreed that all other problems which vex the soul of man put together are not so harassing as this of life's moral handicaps. Pain and death, what are they? You, Mark, you have been as near death as any man, and I know that your experience has left you with more of contempt than of fear in your heart; and yet it came to you in a terrible form. The war taught us that lesson if it taught us nothing else. But the more one sees of evil the more one shrinks from it. What is it H. G. Ward says? 'The world seems on the surface to be a place not of equitable probation but of favoritism.' There are hundreds of Catholics in my own parish who have, so far as I can see, no chance of leading Catholic lives; and as for the folk across the river—it makes me sick to think of them. The men are bad enough, but it's the women that make one's heart ache. They drift into vice as the leaf drifts with the current. They seem born to no other end."

"But they aren't in your parish, are they?"

"They are in God's parish, aren't they?" retorted Father de Trafford. "Now forgive me, I know you didn't de-

serve that. But there's where it is, you see, they are
on debatable ground; and I can do so little. I have my
hands full at St. Casimir's. I am trying to scrape up
money enough to start a mission. Will you give me a
check? Now I didn't mean to say that. You shall not
put your hand in your pocket while you are my guest."

"I can afford it——"

"Don't throw your money in my face," said the priest
severely. "It's very ill-bred of you. No: keep your
hands out of your pockets. I've bled you enough for
this year. If all my children were as generous as you
are, I should never be reduced to mendicancy. There
is Lawrence now, why shouldn't he fork out? I'll ask
him."

"Do," said Mark half-absently, "but I say, Guy, old
chap——"

He broke off with a laugh and a flush. The tired and
preoccupied mind had gone back twenty years to the
days when his spiritual director was merely a little fair-
haired imp of devilry in the Lower Line at Stonyhurst.
De Trafford pressed his arm; to him the old name rang
sweetly with its boyish associations and memories, some
pleasant, some painful, but all mellowed by the after-
light down the vista of years. "Oh, do go on!" he said.
"How that brings back old days! No one calls me Guy
now except you, Mark. I have so few people of my
own, there is hardly any one left who knew me when
I was a boy. I wish you did it oftener."

"Couldn't: I'm far too much in awe of you."

"Oh, I dare say!" de Trafford jeered at him. Shrewd
as he was, the priest was too modest to realize that Mark
had spoken the bare truth. "In awe of the kid whose
head you used to punch. Not that you ever did punch
it as a matter of fact; your line was all the other way.
You shielded me from a lot, Mark. I don't know how I

should ever have got through the rough and tumble of a public school if it hadn't been for you. One realizes these things, looking back. I often wonder if you ever understood the driving force you had among fellows of your own standing, or the responsibilities which were thrown on you. Never mind, you shouldered them as you shouldered Gatton. True Englishman! you never talk, rarely think, and often act."

It was his habit, half artless and half artful, to evoke confidences by pretending to be quite unaware of their coming and indifferent whether they came or not. Mark knew the trick, and smiled; but however well he knew it, he generally fell a victim to it. In the present instance, however, he had come on purpose to confess himself, and the self-betrayal was deliberate.

"Guy, then—Topsy, if you like," he said, smiling: "old fellow, I want you to do me a service. Will you manage it? I want you to marry me."

"What, what—marry you? My dear Mark, are you going to get married?"

"Yes. Wait: don't congratulate me. It isn't altogether a case for congratulation." The inner pain was distinctly audible in his voice as he went on. "I think you must have met her, or if not you'll have heard of her. Miss Archdale."

"The beauty?—Oh, I beg your pardon, but even I can't help hearing as much as that! I've seen her once or twice, and she is very lovely. But I didn't know she was a Catholic."

"She isn't." De Trafford did not speak. "No, you are not going to like it, Father: it is not only a mixed marriage, but it is to be, so far as we can manage it, a private and a very hurried marriage. There I want your help. Will you tell me how to get a license, and will you put the dispensation in train for me? I never was married before, and I don't a bit know how you set about it, except that there are certain necessary stipulations to which of course both she and I are ready to agree. I want you to put me up to the rules of the game."

"Is this all you're going to tell me?"

"Very nearly all. No, not all. I shall come to you to-morrow night, you know." Father de Trafford nodded, but without enthusiasm; he was sure that Mark would not marry without confession, but he knew also that the penitent can, if he likes, rule a line between confession and confidence. "No, I can't explain," Mark said wearily. "Except to say that I really am not asking you to abet a clandestine match; I'm my own master, and Miss Archdale is her own mistress, for she has neither father nor mother nor guardian, so there is no one whom we're under any obligation to consult."

"Does Lawrence know?"

"No."

"Pity, isn't it?"

"Why? We never were on those terms, Topsy."

"Suppose the marriage became known, as no one can guarantee that it won't, I think you would find that Lawrence would be hurt." Mark did not answer, but his expression was both skeptical and stubborn. "Don't you want me to say any more?"

"On the contrary, I want you to say anything you care to say, though I can't pretend that it will have much influence. The marriage will go forward. I won't disguise from you that I'm anxious and unhappy about it."

"You care for her, Mark?"

"Question barred, Father."

"You fill me with anxiety," said the priest very gravely. "What can I say when you leave me in the dark? How can I even take the necessary steps to get your dispensation?" He raised his head, and the shrewd blue eyes flashed into Mark Sturt's as if they would read his very soul, till the blood rose under the tanned skin. "Open your heart to me now, if there's anything in it you're ashamed to let me see."

"I'm always ashamed . . ."

"Ah!" De Trafford drew a long breath. For the analyst of souls there was no misreading that wide candid outlook, or the touch of bewilderment in Mark's tone. "I am a fool, and I see too much of the seamy side of human nature. Keep your secret, and I'll get your dispensation. I don't in the least want to force your confidence in a sphere outside my own."

"No, you only want to worm it out of me!" Sturt turned suddenly and dropped his hand on his friend's knee. "I swear, if I could, I'd tell you everything. I should—I should be glad to have advice—your advice, anyhow." The distress in his face was so very evident that the priest's momentary feeling of estrangement was quite broken down. De Trafford touched with his delicate fingers the strong hand that would have been willing to be led by his guidance. "Why are you troubled," he said gently, "or is that question barred too?"

"It's the answer that I have to bar, not the question. I can't tell you what isn't my secret. I am up against a woman's caprice—yes, caprice," Mark repeated, as the memory of the night by the lake rose before him. "But it's my own fault. I've made an unutterable fool of myself, which is what you would expect of a middle-aged business man who doesn't stick to his office." Father de Trafford, who loved Mark because he was a romantic and a visionary, had to repress a little laugh. "I plunged heavily, shutting my eyes to consequences, and I've been waking up to them by inches ever since. I can't think how I ever came to do it, but it's done now and I can't go back: and the worst of it is that I've let Miss Archdale in as well, a girl of three-and-twenty, all the more at my mercy because she labors under the delusion that she's a finished woman of the world and—that I'm at hers. . . . I know I'm not intelligible. But I'm in the dark myself, and . . . let it go at that. I can't explain."

"Are you troubled because of her heresy?"

Mark smiled involuntarily. "No: not much, I'm afraid. She isn't good enough to be called a heretic. She's quite willing to be married in a Roman Catholic church, and to have the children brought up as Roman Catholics. She thinks the Roman Catholics are quite as respectable as the Anglicans, and much better than the Wesleyans or the Salvation Army."

"Oh, dear me! That's not very hopeful. But perhaps you'll be able—?"

Mark shook his head. "No, I shan't," he said flatly. "I'm willing to promise to try, but I know I can't do it. You can come and stay with us, if the marriage is ever acknowledged, and have a shot at her yourself, but I'm afraid you'll agree with me that her ignorance is most invincible. Bless the dear girl! I'm very fond of her, you know." Father de Trafford, more mystified than ever, murmured pettishly that he didn't know anything about it. "Well, I'm sorry, but the fact is I'm fretted to death. I've been interviewing my lawyers this afternoon; they think I'm mad, which irks me, because I've always had a virgin reputation in the eyes of the law. I could see by Riccardo's expression that he was saying to himself, 'Now if it were Lawrence Sturt who talked this rubbish it would create no surprise, but I did think this fellow had more sense!' It is disgusting to be made to look ridiculous; for heaven's sake don't you laugh at me!"

"I don't feel much like laughing. Tell me, Mark——"

"If I can!"

The moon had gone behind a cloud, and in the shadow of the plane tree it was so dark that the men were no longer visible to each other. All that could be seen of Mark was the vague outline of his shoulders and the red spark of his cigar. Father de Trafford waited a moment, collecting his thoughts, and in the stillness the clock of St. Casimir's began to strike ten. Then other spires took up the tale in many whispering chimes. When the last stroke from the Westminster Tower had died away into infinity like a symbol of the night prayer of London, the priest began again. "All this tirade about your lawyers," the low delicate voice passed deftly behind Mark's guard, "is meant only to throw me off the scent, isn't it? I've never known the day when Mark Sturt, tackling a difficulty in earnest, could be moved by ridicule. Your trouble goes deeper?"

"Yes."

De Trafford heard rather than saw the jerk of Mark's arm as he flung away his cigar. Then he leaned his elbow on the table and covered his eyes with his hands.

"Oh, my dear Mark!"

"Yes . . . It's difficult to express, even if I could tell you all the circumstances, which I can't. Guy . . . you say I shielded you at Stonyhurst. You never needed it. You . . . did more for me than I could ever have done for you. You've always stood to me for something higher than myself. You know I've lived the life of other men of my class; if I've kept fairly straight it was because I hadn't time for things that sap one's energy. But I always meant, some day, to change. . . . I . . . never ceased to be ashamed. Now and again I've had the . . . vision. To-night, when you were kneeling before the altar, I saw the mysteries . . . in Whose presence you live. No, let me go on. I don't pretend that feelings which come and go, and have no appreciable in-

fluence on conduct, are of much value, unless it were
that, having them, I was more deeply bound to do better than I have done. You know that the work at
Gatton has always been to me as much of a religious
as of a commercial problem, but, Gatton apart, I've done
nothing. Not a record to be proud of. Yet I did mean
to do better some day. And now this marriage. . . ."

"You're afraid of yourself, aren't you?"

"Yes."

"Needlessly, I think. You haven't lived the spiritual
life—I grant you ought to have done better; but you have
lived temperately. Action is governed more by habit
than by passion, and you have formed the habits of sobriety and self-control."

Mark threw out his hand with a sound of distress.
"Don't mock me. I don't feel like it."

"What if you were to break off the marriage?"

"I can't. What's more, I won't. But anyhow I can't."

"Your word is given?"

"Yes. More than that. As you doubtless see, I don't
want to break it off; but I couldn't if I did."

"Is it in any sense a question of duty for it to go on,
Mark?"

"Not what one would call duty in the religious sense.
But—in honor——"

"You're engaged?"

"Pretty deeply."

"Then you need not be afraid. Your honor, so long
as I have known you, has always coincided with your
religious duty; it has never been a mere observance of a
social code. The two standards are not nearly so different as they are sometimes said to be. Follow your rule
of honor; you won't lose the vision of God by doing
that."

"Thank you, Father," said Mark after a long silence.

CHAPTER IV

MONDAY, the sixteenth of July, came drenched in fog like a November morning. There were patches of sun on the uplands behind Shotton, but all over the low-lying flats a thick steam went up, drawn over wall and window like a white blind. Here and there in a breathing space the shapes of trees showed faintly dark, and far up and far off a tiny sun hung half dissolved in vapor, which drifted and deadened over it like silver bonfire smoke. The daisy buds on the lawn were smothered in dew, their heads all brushed down as if a roller had gone over them, and minute drops of dew splashed like rain from gutter and leaf.

"Maisie, can I come in?"

"By all means."

Dodo Ferrier entered, but halted on the threshold. It was nine o'clock, and she was on her way down to breakfast, but Maisie was still in bed, her hair scattered on the pillow, her eyes blinking and filmy as if she had only just woke up. Her room, which looked east over the uplands, was full of mist and of the pearly morning light, and a haze of light was in her eyes too, as she smiled at Dodo's hasty "Oh, I *beg* your pardon!"

"Not at all. I know I'm awfully late," said Maisie. "I lay awake all night. Then I fell asleep after Ellen brought my tea."

"Mercy! why did you lie awake all night?"

"Thinking, just thinking. Do you often think? I hardly ever do. Say once a twelvemonth, like a spring

clean. It's going to be a lovely day, isn't it? The fog
is beginning to break. I should like it to be sultry and
blue, like a day in Italy. Hey-ho! I suppose I ought to
get up."

"You had much better go to sleep again," said Dodo,
shutting the door behind her and sitting on the bed. "I
came in to know what time you meant to start, but I
think you had much better not go at all. Stay another
day—what does it signify, if you're only going down to
this horrid little place in Dorsetshire, wherever it is?
You won't like it a bit when you get there, you'll wish
you were back at Shotton." Maisie chuckled like a
schoolboy; she thought that very probable. "Oh, you
may laugh!" said Dodo crossly. "But you won't be a
bit happy. You're a most gregarious person, Maisie.
You'll hate being all alone."

"Now it comes to the point, I don't much want to go,"
Maisie replied. She told no lies, black, white, or gray;
she had never said that she would be alone, and she did
not say so now. The inference was drawn from what
she left unsaid. "But no, thanks—I won't stay. My
plans are all settled and my trunks are packed. Ellen
is in the sulks already because I've just broken it to
her that she's to stop in town, and I don't know what
would happen if I told her to unpack me again. She's
a slave-driver, is Nelly; she likes to maid me up to my
eyelids, and I really rather hate being maided. I succeed
in getting rid of her now and then, but she gives me a
hot time of it when I do."

"If my maid rode over me like that I should get rid of
her permanently."

"Not if she'd been with you ten years, you wouldn't.
Nelly dates from my Cinderella days. She was kitchen-
maid at the John Archdales'. She gives me notice when
she feels that way inclined, but I never give her notice.

I dress her down now and then, but not when she's out of temper, because if I did there would be a row, and I hate rows. Did you want to arrange about my going to the station? Because you needn't worry, I shan't go by train. I have a little car of my own stabled at the inn, and I shall run her over myself."

"Stabled at the inn!"

"Yes. I wouldn't bother you to put her up. I know Mr. Ferrier hates having the garage crowded full of other people's cars. I told them to send her round at ten o'clock. Ellen and the luggage can go behind." She raised herself on her arm and glanced out of the window. "So don't ask me to stay, Dodo. I can't. I should rather like to."

"I can't imagine why you should go to Dorsetshire if you don't want to go."

"I said I would and I will. I expect I'm a bit of a fatalist. It was ordained from the beginning of the world, and what does it matter, after all? My life's my own," said Maisie, looking up at the veiled sun. "In the scheme of creation, I don't see how one woman's life can matter very much to any one except herself. Why shouldn't I do as I like?"

"I don't understand you, Maisie."

"I don't understand myself. Occasionally, in fact, I have a gloomy notion that I don't understand anything at all—that I'm wandering about among natural laws like a civilian in an engine-room. Dodo, did you ever lie still and watch something coming on you that you were afraid of—something you couldn't believe would ever happen, and yet all the while you knew it was going to happen, but you set your teeth and pretended it wouldn't?"

"H'm. Yes, I know what you mean."

"That's what I've been doing these last few days."

"And now it has happened, has it?"

"No: but it was borne in on me last night that it will," said Maisie dryly. "That's why I lay awake."

She folded her arms behind her head and stretched herself indolently at full length. "Do you think I'm nice, Dodo?"

" 'Hope so," said Dodo, smiling. "I like you."

"I know you do. I like you for liking me. I love to be liked." She flung out one hand swiftly and clasped it over her friend's. "Dodo, what little hands you have! Yours will go right inside mine. But then I'm so tall: oh, bother! I think I'm too tall for a woman. I wish I were a man. No, I don't, though."

"You're rather like a man in some ways."

"I? What on earth do you mean?"

"Let me see, what do I mean?" said Dodo doubtfully. "Well, in the first place, you're very independent. I suppose that's partly because of your money; few women can afford to pay their footing anywhere as you can, and even when we're rich we're as a rule more or less accountable to some one or other. Any one but Mr. FitzGerald would have tied you up in leading strings. Still, money apart, it is like a man, you know, the way you come and go in your own car, and settle your own plans independently of anybody else, and hold your tongue about your own affairs. And you have a man's sort of temper."

"Bad temper?" Maisie asked with a twist of her eyebrows.

"You? no! I never knew any one less irritable than you are. You never fuss, and you never turn a hair over small annoyances. You have a large grand good humor, my dear, that shines down like the sun over all sorts of petty people and petty things. Look at the way you bear with that Virgin Vinegar of yours!"

"Oh, I say, Dodo—poor old Nelly! She'd say I trample on her."

"That's just it." Dodo laughed in Miss Archdale's humorously protestant face. "I'm sure you do! Most women would either get rid of her or give in to her, but you walk over the top of her. She would get on my nerves in half no time, but she doesn't get on yours. You haven't any."

"I know I haven't," said Maisie apologetically. "It comes of being so healthy. How can you run to nerves when you never have an ache or a pain? It makes me rather dense, though," she added. "I expect if I had a violent illness I should be much more sympathetic afterwards. Mrs. John Archdale always said I had no tact."

"You haven't much—not that she knows anything about it. You haven't nerves in the tips of all your mental fingers, as most clever women have." Dodo hesitated, but the moment seemed to be ripe for offering a caution which had long halted on her tongue, and she relied upon Miss Archdale to tolerate blunt speech. "Maisie, the other night at dinner, when you were talking to Mark Sturt about his political position, and his chance of office if they reorganize the Ministry, didn't you *know* he hated having that sort of thing dragged out of him before other people?"

"No," said Maisie, blushing slowly and deeply. "I'm sorry."

"I was sure you didn't. Well, never mind," Dodo consoled her. "Your innocence protects you, darling. If any other woman had done it Mark would have got restive, not to say rude, but the men seem to look on you as a chartered libertine."

"Midway between a professional beauty and a jolly good fellow."

"Something of the sort," Dodo agreed, unable to help laughing, though she was sorry to have wounded her friend, on whose fair neck the blush still lingered. "They like you all the better for it, I believe; anyhow I do. You would be too formidable, darling, if you weren't a little stupid now and then."

"Am I formidable?"

"I should not care to have you for an enemy. You hit hard, and you're not afraid of anything."

"Or any one?"

"My dear, what's the matter?"

"Nothing. You can't help," said Maisie. She turned sideways for a moment, hiding her face on the pillow, her right hand still folded over Dodo's small fingers. "I'm terrified. I've been terrified all night. I feel as if I were jumping over a precipice. Do you really like me? You must be jolly stupid if you do. I hate myself. I could—I could whip myself at the cart's tail. That's what I deserve—to be beaten through the town in my shift. I'm not nice. No nice-minded woman ought to like me. I detest myself and I wish I were dead."

"Gracious!" said Dodo feebly.

"I wish I had the pluck to get up and shoot myself," Maisie went on, flinging out the words as if it were a physical relief to be frank. "I haven't, dear, so you needn't be alarmed; besides, I don't want to die just yet —not till I've had my own way. I'm going to take it. Why shouldn't I? I've never had it yet. I will jump over my precipice if I break my neck for it. Who knows? The gods may relent and let me off. I shan't think much of their intelligence if they do. A woman who does what I'm doing deserves to be made to suffer, and I hope I shall suffer. I deserve humiliation and I hope I shall get it. If I am beaten, I'll kiss the rod."

"What does all this mean?" said Dodo. Her manner

had changed; she was grave, simple, and direct. "I thought you were half in fun at first, but now I see you're in earnest. I don't want to misjudge you, but it sounds as though you were going to plunge into a rather bad scrape. Don't you do it, Maisie. Tell me all about it."

"Not one word."

"Is it connected with your going to Dorsetshire?" Maisie smiled, impenetrable.

"Are you—is there—are you giving any man a hold over you, Maisie?"

There was a moment's silence, then, "Not as you fear. *Fors l'honneur,* Dorothea."

"Thanks," said Dodo, drawing a deep breath. She stooped over Maisie and kissed her on the lips. "I know you aren't angry." Maisie flung her arm round her friend's neck and held her down for a moment, Dodo's cheek against her own.

"Dodo, if I come to some sort of panoramic smash— which appears to me to be on the cards—will you stick to me? I'd stick to you. I love you, Dodo. Really I do. And I should like to feel that there was just one woman in the world that wouldn't take her hand out of mine whatever happened. May I believe that of you?"

"Yes."

"And you'll keep my confidence?"

"Of course."

"You married women are dangerous. You tell your husbands," Maisie murmured with a laughing accent. "It must be very queer to be married. Is it agreeable, Dorothea? I can't imagine what it would be like."

"Find out," said Dodo, smiling broadly. "I should love to see you married."

"Well, you never will," said Maisie. Her grip on Dodo's hand had been strong enough to be painful, but it relaxed now, and she shook back her hair and sat up with a merry laugh. "What a shame, isn't it? as Mr. Sturt says. Now you had better run along and let me dress. I've only forty minutes, and I shall probably have to finish packing for myself. I wish Ellen had a temper like you describe mine, but she hasn't. I don't suppose she'll even turn up to strap my boxes."

"But that's outrageous! Why don't you ring her up?"

Miss Archdale shrugged her shoulders as she sprang out of bed. "Too much fag. I'm going to have my bath now, dear. I don't a bit mind your stopping, if you don't."

Upon this vigorous hint Dodo fled in disorder, but her eyes were twinkling: oh, how like Maisie!

Forty-five minutes later Miss Archdale was on her way to town; not a direct route from North Hampshire to the Dorset coast, but the detour, as Maisie carelessly explained, was necessary to keep a business appointment. Careless she was, and merry, for the night-watches were over and the die was cast; one may reflect on the brink of a precipice, but where is the use of reflecting after one has jumped over it?

At half-past twelve she pulled up before the door of her own tiny house in Mayfair, where she had arranged to drop Ellen and the car, with all her luggage except the single trunk that was packed to go to Dorsetshire. Her selection of necessaries for a week in the country puzzled Ellen, who had been told that the White Cottage was a cottage and nothing more, and that its address would not be given to her, because Maisie was going to spend a week in idleness and go nowhere and do nothing and see no one. "But if she don't want to see no one," mused Ellen, "why have she gone and taken them French gowns and all that new lingery?" Maisie's Dorsetshire

trunk contained, besides the tweed suits and shooting
boots which Ellen thought appropriate, two or three embroidered dresses of the airiest French extravagance,
together with piles of chiffon and lawn, richer and more
delicate than Maisie was in the habit of wearing. "If
it had been anybody but Miss Maisie!" said Ellen, shaking her head. But Maisie made a good conspirator, for
she concealed little and explained nothing. Her bold indifference to comment carried her over quicksands which
would have sucked down warier feet.

She was not hungry, but she obliged herself to sit
down quietly to the lunch that was provided for her, and
to drink her cup of soup and eat her bread and butter,
because she had need of fresh bloom and steady nerves.
Afterwards she went to her own room to wash her face
and change her dress; and strange it was to think, as
she entered her chamber, that the maiden Maisie Archdale would never enter it again. It was the only room
in the Mayfair house that bore the print of her own taste,
and it was very spacious, dark, and easy; the woodwork
all of chestnut in its native dusky grain; flowers, pale
in color and rich in scent, overflowing the low window-
sill; some large landscapes on the walls, a couple of
Danish interiors, strange bare studies of light and shade,
and a couple of portraits insolently French. While she
fastened her veil, she lingered for some moments before
the mirror. It showed her a tall girl in a gray suit, her
eyes shaded by a gypsy hat, the long lapels of her habit-
shaped coat opening over a frilled shirt of fine lawn and
a beautiful bare throat, the lawn frills at her wrist falling
back from a beautiful hand which wore no ring except
the signet of Bridget Sturt. A glint of gold was visible
at her breast, and she felt for it and drew it out: a long
chain, and a locket that held a miniature. "Oh! my
own Philip, my darling," Maisie whispered. She

kissed the portrait before slipping it back into its warm nest.

When she came downstairs a taxi was in waiting, and Maisie was driven first to Waterloo, where she put her trunk in the cloakroom, and then on to Lane Street. It wanted ten minutes of two o'clock when she sprang out on the steps of St. Casimir's, and she glanced up and down the street, but Mark was not in sight. A desire to act up to the traditions of a wedding induced her to give the cabman half a sovereign; he drove off blessing his luck, and Maisie was left alone. Some ragged children stared and jeered at her from their sport in the gutter. A truculent woman in a dirty bodice, torn open and flapping back from her generous bosom, came out of a pawnshop over the way and vanished into a public-house. July sunshine streamed down over the mean west front of the church, its red and white brickwork, its stucco tracery, the grimy babies playing on its grimy steps. Minutes passed. A knot of loafers lounged out of the bar and stared at Maisie; one of them made an inaudible joke, and the others laughed. Anger schooled her to wait quietly, but her heart throbbed as if she had been running, and though it was a fiery July day waves of chill went over her. In all her night fears, this one fear that Mark would fail her had never crossed her mind; and isn't it the thing we have never feared that happens to us? At length a thin bell jingled out the hour. Then Maisie forced herself to open the pitch-pine door, studded with imitation nails, much as she would have forced herself to lie down on an operating table. Had Mark failed her?

Without roared the sunlit squalor of a London slum: within, the mystery of the faith of ages brooded over silent aisles. Shut in by high roofs, and paned with stained glass, the church was very dark. It still smelt

of Sunday incense; black rafters and gray pillars loomed
out of a bluish haze. A lamp burned red and dim before the high altar, and at the entrance of the Sanctuary,
beside a low screen of carved marble, a wrought-iron
tripod carried a score or more of burning candles, a gar-
land of fire, whose use and purpose Maisie did not understand. What she did understand—what filled her
full of an immeasurable peace, a child's feeling of secur-
ity, strangely dashed with pain—was the sight of Mark
Sturt, calmly kneeling upright on a tall praying chair,
his face turned towards the mystery of the altar. Used
as she was, in the men of her own church, either to an
excessive and self-conscious reverence or to no reverence
at all, Maisie was strangely touched by the unaffected
austerity and simplicity of the Catholic. He was there,
and in his hands she was safe; and yet between them
rolled the unplumbed seas that estrange the skeptic from
the mystic. He was to be her husband; and in that moment Maisie knew that she was jealous of Mark Sturt's
faith because he would always set the will of God above
her will or his own.

Sturt stood up when she entered, bent his knee to
the Host, and came striding down the aisle. Maisie
had gone through so many emotions in the last ten minutes that she was as much bewildered as relieved when
she discovered him to be his unchanged normal self. He
spoke in his softest undertone, but with no parade of
reverence. "How are you?" he said, shaking hands with
her. "You look very nice. Am I dressed properly?
It is so hot that I let myself off a frock coat. I hope
you don't mind."

"No," said Maisie, smiling faintly.

"Do you like lilies of the valley?" Mark asked. "I
thought you ought to have some flowers. These are wild
ones from Longstone Edge, my old home. May I—?"

Green sheath and ivory bell, he tucked them deftly into the front of her coat.

"They are very late."

"They linger in the high woods. As for this, it is banality itself, but you might wear it to please me. I knew I couldn't beat the Archdale diamonds, Maisie, so I declined on pearls to match your throat."

"You have charming manners, Mark," Maisie murmured. "Oh, what a lovely clasp!"

"It was my mother's. I'm so glad you like them." He smiled in his whimsical way. "It was one for you, dear, and two for myself. I hate diamonds and colored stones, but I love pearls, and I know a bit about them. Manton's a great pal of mine." He saw that she had recovered herself. "Father de Trafford is waiting in the vestry. Oh, let me take your gloves off, shall I? I'll stuff them into my pocket if you like." Drawing off her long gray gauntlets, she felt him start when he recognized his ring on her hand. "You're ready now, aren't you?"

"Yes, I think so."

"Take my arm," said Mark.

Stains of red and blue from the rich foreign glass fell on the pavement as they passed up the aisle. Years later Maisie learned that those moths'-wing panes were a thank-offering of Arthur Sturt for the safe return of his sons from the war; so the generations are linked together, and man's work outlives man. The church was very quiet. There was no one in it but the priest, the bride, the bridegroom, the clerk, and the witnesses provided by Father de Trafford—a fat little sacristan and his own elderly servant. Remembering that Mark had spoken of de Trafford in terms of personal intimacy, Maisie looked at him, and found that he was looking at her. Was he interested in the heretic who was mar-

rying one of his flock? What a refined ascetic face it
was! And young, much younger than she had anticipated
—four or five years younger than Mark Sturt."

"Marce, wilt thou take Marcella here present to thy
wedded wife according to the rite of Holy Mother
Church?"

"I will."

How the priest's voice softened when he spoke Mark's
name! They were friends, then, these two? As the
priest turned to Maisie, she submitted herself to the
flash of his blue eyes: but how stern they were, and
how searching in their authority! A gust of anger shook
her, and all that she had ever heard of Rome's power
rushed into her Protestant mind. How much did he
know, this worn, delicate-featured man to whom Mark
Sturt confessed probably every secret of his inner life?

"Marcella, wilt thou take Marcus here present . . . ?"

"I will."

("Give me your hand, dear," Mark whispered.)

He clasped her right hand in his own. "I, Marcus,
take thee, Marcella, to my wedded wife, to have and
to hold from this day forward, for better for worse,
for richer for poorer, in sickness and in health, till death
us do part, if Holy Church will it permit, and thereto I
plight thee my troth."

"I, Maisie——"

"I, *Marcella*——"

"Oh—I, Marcella, take thee, Mark, to my wedded husband . . ." She stumbled softly through the solemnly
familiar clauses and the unfamiliar reservation, and lost
herself for a moment while the priest's voice ran on,
low and level, "I join you in marriage." It was but a
short ceremony after all, and very little different from
the Anglican. But now Mark Sturt was giving her
money—half a sovereign: what in the world did he

expect her to do with half a sovereign? She held the coin helplessly in the palm of her hand.

"With this ring," said Sturt under his breath, "I thee wed, this gold and silver I thee give, with my body I thee worship, and with all my worldly goods I thee endow. (Other hand, please.)" He drew his mother's signet from her left hand slipped the wedding ring in turn over her thumb, forefinger, middle finger, and ring finger: "In the name of the Father, and of the Son, and of the Holy Ghost. Amen." He replaced the signet, and almost immediately sank on his knees. Years later Maisie learned, by chance, how he had longed for the nuptial mass and the nuptial benediction, privileges denied to those who marry out of the Faith.

Sturt held the door open for her to pass out into the blinding sunshine. The children playing on the steps set up a thin derisive cheer, and he plunged his hand into his pocket and flung them a handful of coppers, which scattered them right and left in a trice, their noses in the gutter.

"Five and twenty past two. What time did you say your train went?"

"Two fifty-four. I get to Ushant before six."

"Mine leaves at half-past three and doesn't get in till seven. Rotten journey, isn't it? Always is, when you have to change. Here comes your cab; I ordered it for you. Can you really manage to take my suit-case with your own trunk? because, if so, here's the cloakroom counterfoil. I suppose I mustn't see you off at Waterloo?"

"Better not, don't you think? One so often meets people one knows."

"Well, good-by for the present," said Mark, opening

the door of the taxi. Maisie slipped in and sank down
on the cushions as though she were tired. She heard
Mark speak to the driver, and then he came back to her
and lingered, folding his arms on the door. "You look
a bit fagged," he said, examining her narrowly. "I
expect you haven't had much to eat. Better get a lunch-
basket at Waterloo, what? I'm going to a club. By the
bye, I've paid your driver, Maisie. I hope you don't
mind."

"Paid my driver!"

"So sorry if it embarrasses you, but the fact is I never
heard of any man letting his wife pay her own fares on
her honeymoon, and I was afraid it might invalidate
the marriage. Here's your ticket. Don't drop it." He
laid it on her knee. "Take care, your lilies are falling
out. Shall I tuck them in for you?"

"Not in Lane Street, dear boy!"

"Oh, why not?" He unfastened the top button of her
coat and deftly knotted the ribbon of her lilies through
the buttonhole; then as he refastened it, under his breath,
in an accent remarkably at odds with the tranquil cold-
ness of his manner and attitude, "Your throat is as white
as your lilies, Maisie, and whiter than your pearls."

"My dear Mark, you'll make me lose my train."

"Oh, by Jove, so I shall. That would never do."

He fell back, lifting his hat, and Maisie was borne
away. When Mark turned to reënter the church he
found that Father de Trafford had come out of it in his
cassock and was standing behind him on the steps.
Mark's face changed. Their eyes met, and after a moment Mark looked down. He touched de Trafford's arm
without speaking.

"I congratulate you, my dear Mark," said the priest
with his gay smile. "Come! why do you look so gloomy?

It is not like you to be nervous or undecided. Your good lady is wonderfully beautiful. Why did you never tell me she was so young?"

"So young? She's twenty-three."

"She is still a child," said the priest.

"Your penetration, Father, is for once at fault. She is a finished woman of the world with I don't know how many thousand a year, and she has refused a dozen men."

"And has accepted you. How very strange! She has the eyes of a child or a very young girl, *Marce mi.* I don't understand her, but I congratulate you with all my heart, and I wish you happiness."

"Happiness," repeated Mark dreamily.

He shook himself out of his abstraction with a vigorous effort and unfastened his pocket-book. "Thanks, no doubt I shall be very happy. What was it your Reverence was telling me the other night about the riverside mission? Here's something for you to play with; make what use of it you like."

De Trafford glanced at the sum named in the check. "But, my dear fellow, this is a mistake! You've written the wrong figures . . . You really mean it? Mark, I don't know how to thank you——"

Sturt's own brougham had drawn up by the curb, the versatile Henham at the wheel. Sturt halted with one foot on the step, turning an inexpressive face to his friend. "Pray for me," he said. "I can do with it."

CHAPTER V

M ARK'S train was late: it was ten minutes past
seven when he got out at Ushant station. He
had no luggage to see after, and was soon swinging along
a level country road which ran at first through a straggling village street. Low-browed Dorsetshire cottages
stood sunning themselves in the light of a pleasant, almost
cloudless evening. Small children, of healthier aspect
than Father de Trafford's black lambs, were playing
about in and out of open doorways, and they looked up
open-mouthed at the strange gentleman as he went by.
Mark, in homespun tweeds and a Panama hat, cut an
altogether unfamiliar figure in Ushant street with his
great height and drilled shoulders and easy, swinging
stride from the hips. If they were interested in him,
however, the feeling was reciprocated, for Mark from
the outset liked the look of the little place, its unsophisti-
cated quiet and its pleasant country smells. The sur-
vival of the thatcher's craft appeared in strips and patches
of honey-colored straw, combed smooth and trimmed off
razor-clean, amid the dim and ragged brown of the un-
repaired roofs. Each little garden had its plot of late
pinks or early phlox, or summer-long mignonette and
roses, and their ordered sweetness brought an indescrib-
able feeling of refreshment to the heart of a man who
loved rural England far better than Mayfair. He was
soothed also by—what never fails to impress a towns-
man—the intense quiet which brooded over everything,
a quiet as intimate and profound as the quiet of the
solemn blue sky, and which seemed only to be accen-

tuated by the small sounds that broke it: the cling-clang
of a bicycle bell, the barking of a dog in a yard, the
clink of hammer on anvil in the smoking furnace of a
forge. As he was leaving the village behind him, the
church bells began to ring; Ushant possessed a peal of
six, mellowed by age to a plaintive harmony, and from
time immemorial the ringers, whose office was hereditary
in half a dozen families, had been accustomed to practice
on a Monday evening. Other lands, other manners: this
peal ringing out of the stone brooch-spire had for Mark
Sturt the sacred sweetness of the Angelus.

But now the last houses had strung themselves out
behind him, and he swung on into the empty country
east and south towards the sea. For a long time there
was nothing remarkable in his surroundings; the broad
road, raised slightly and dyked on either side beyond
broad ribbons of grass, rolled on out of sight between
broad fields of barley, or sainfoin, or mustard, varied
only by an occasional patch of trees or the shade of an
occasional avenue. A chain of low blue hills lay along
the landward horizon. Then gradually, as he went on,
the country began to rise all about him in slow undula-
tions; the crops grew poor, were striped with scanty
pasture; insensibly the arable land was melting into
down-land and the wide view across the plain was ex-
changed for a broken prospect, sometimes opening far
out over the fertile distance, but embraced at every turn
by the soft breasts of the hills.

And the air, which had all along smelt of seaweed
and spray, began to freshen; the tang of salt in it sharp-
ened; Mark breathed it in with expanded chest—he was
nearing the sea. Strange it was that he had not yet
caught a glimpse of it since leaving the train, but he remembered that in this part of Dorsetshire the inland
country slopes up to the coastline of cliffs. At last, the

road rising over a small eminence, the Channel came into view, but still only as a distant field of silver rounding off the gaps between the hills. At the same time the road, apparently thinking that it had gone as near the coast as it cared to go, took a decided bend to the left, with the sweet irresponsibility of roads built by the muddle-headed English race and not by the trenchant Roman. Mark halted and pulled out his map, on which Maisie had traced out a course for him in red ink. Yes! here the road bent to the left, "and a little farther on," Maisie had written, her bold "park-paling" hand cramped into the margin, "you come to a gibbet at a X-roads. There you see rough track like farm by-way turning off towards the sea. That brings y. t. White Cottage."

A few paces farther and Mark came upon the straggling cross-roads, over which a weather-beaten gibbet and a newly painted sign-post combined to preside. And there facing him was the farm-track—rough enough in all conscience; Mark wondered how Miss Archdale would manage with her French heels among its antiquated ruts, stiffened in the mold of the previous winter. Grass grew thickly over it, and poppies and corn cockles mingled with the grass, and on either side the swelling of the downs locked it from all observation but that of the birds and the sky. It wound among those low contours for some time, the air freshening at every step; at last it turned a corner and brought him out within a stone's throw of the White Cottage.

Mark halted. Here was one of those unforeseen revelations which take the most hardened traveler's breath with surprise. Landward all round him the downs reared their great chalk shoulders, sparsely covered with turf where a few sheep grazed; steeply the track wound down between them, tumbling through a strait and shady glen full of smallish trees; a brook appeared out of nowhere and went prattling along by the way; the White Cottage itself crouched within a stone's throw, sending up a thread of smoke from its one chimney, and catching a scarlet glare on its narrow panes; but what one saw first and last and beyond everything else was the changeful-changeless splendor of the sea. Flat as the floor of a room it lay spread out below him, woven all over in a silkwork of shining wrinkles, and every foamless ripple danced in gold and silver under the triumph of the sunset, which was burning itself away in strange fires along the water's edge. The few clouds there were only made the flame more ardent, the abyss more profound; the eye lost itself in that illimitable glory. *Et lucem perpetuam.* . . . Was that a stairway of burnished gold going up out of the sea into infinity? and were those doves' wings folded in airy pallor, unlit, over the fires of sunset?

Mark came up to the White Cottage where it crouched against a shoulder of the downs; it had no garden, nothing but the purple thyme and blue scabious which sprang wild in the virgin turf, and the track he was on led directly to the door and then no farther, except as a mere thread of footpath which plunged down through the glen to the sea. He thought it the loneliest spot that he had ever seen. But the smoke signified habitation, the windows were all open, and there was a mark of fresh wheel tracks which had turned on the level patch before the glen. She was there, then. Mark knocked at the door.

"Is it you, Mark? Come in."

Mark came in, bending his head to avoid the lintel. The White Cottage was still, as Maisie had warned him, a cottage and nothing more, and he incontinently found himself in the kitchen. He took his hat off and looked about him. The first impression which the place made on him at his entry was the same, *mutatis mutandis,* as it made on Maisie—"Oh, my dear boy," she exclaimed, "how big you are!" Mark felt as though, if he stood upright, his head would touch the ceiling. But it was a pleasant place and of a good size, built with Government money in the days before the cheap contractor. It was put together of stone, covered with plaster, and washed over with a coat of chrome-color; the roof was peaked and raftered like the roof of a garret, and the lattice windows were small and set low. The principal articles of furniture were a dresser, set out with blue crockery; a deal table; a couple of heavy wooden chairs; a shining modern stove; and rows of aluminium saucepans, frying-pans, and other unknown utensils, which glittered on the shelves above a little stone sink. Maisie herself was poking the fire when he came in, and after her cursory greeting instantly returned to it. "You're late," she said, "but I was really rather glad because I've only just got the kettle to boil. It's always tiresome work struggling with a new stove, and I couldn't manage the dampers at first. Did you find your way easily by the map?"

"Quite, thanks," said Mark, laying down his hat and stick on a wooden locker under the window. "What can I do to be useful? I'm a nailer at cooking."

"Do you want to?" said Maisie doubtfully. "That's such a nice suit, it seems a pity to spoil it. How much did you give for it?"

"Twelve guineas. It's new for the occasion."

"I thought it was. Didn't you bring some old clothes with you—flannels, or anything like that?"

"I did; they're in my suit-case. How did you manage about the luggage, by the bye? It never entered my head till after you had driven off that when you got here you would apparently have to drag it out of the trap by yourself."

"No, I brought a youth over with me from the inn where I hired the dog-cart. We carried the boxes in together, and afterwards he drove the cart home. Your suit-case is in the other room, if you would like to go straight in. I'm afraid I can't offer you a bath; I did think of having one put in, but the time was so short, and then there's no water laid on, only a well at the back of the house, and it really is rather a fag if you have to pump every drop and carry it about in a kettle."

" 'Couldn't think of it. Besides, you don't want to have a bath in a bath when you can have a bath in the sea. Which is the room?"

Maisie left the poker in the fire and came to do the honors of the house. She was wearing a serge dress, very short in the skirt and open at the neck; her sleeves came to her elbows, and she wore a muslin collar and cuffs, and a white linen apron with a bib and pockets. "Allow me to show you over the domain," she said. "Please take particular notice so as not to lose your way another time." She opened a door on the right. "The parlor. I haven't had time to get it tidy yet—I felt that the kitchen was a more vital matter." Mark looked over her shoulder into a dim interior of strawberry-colored walls, oak furniture, rose branches in a Sèvres pot, and a case of books half-unpacked. "Charming," he said politely. Maisie shut the door again—"To keep it cool," she explained: "the kitchen gets hot when you're cook-ing, though the air is so fresh here towards evening that I don't think we shall mind that much"—and opened the door on the opposite side of the kitchen. "Our room," she said. "That's all; there isn't any more to see."

Mark passed in while Maisie held the door open. It was the largest of the three rooms, and the airiest, for it had two windows facing south and west, and the south window, which overlooked the Channel, was so much

bigger than any other in the place that Mark guessed
it to have been recently put in. An old-fashioned four-
post bedstead was flanked by a tall Ferraran mirror, and
on a table in the window stood a Chinese bowl full of
sweet peas. His own suit-case, unstrapped, stood beside
Maisie's trunk.

"I've left you half the cupboard," said Maisie cheerfully. "I unpacked one of my boxes to get it out of
the way. There is a sort of shanty at the back where I
keep coal and wood and other oddments, so I shoved it
into that, and I shall put the other out there too as soon
as I've had time to clear it. I'm afraid there isn't much
room to spare, but it won't be so bad when we've got
the boxes out of the way."

She stood on one leg with the other foot drawn up
and kicking her ankle, her hands in her apron pockets
and her shoulders propped against the door, in the happy-
go-lucky attitude of a girl of sixteen; the Greek curves
of her hair under their gold fillets were roughened by
the wind, her face was faintly red from stooping over
the fire, and her bright eyes were entirely friendly and
entirely unembarrassed. Her husband was speechless.

"I'd have unpacked for you if I'd had your keys," she
continued. "In the middle classes the women always
unpack for the men. Well now, I must get back to my
stove. Don't you think you'll be more comfortable if
you change out of that noble thing in suits?"

"I think I will, thanks," said Mark. He stood very
still, leaning his hand on the window-sill, and one who
knew him well might have noticed that his voice had
gone flat. Under the drilled manner he was disabled by
such a fit of shyness as had not seized on him since he
was twenty. He concealed it; but he could not have
done even that if he had said any more.

"Right. Don't be long," said Maisie.

She went out, shutting the door behind her, and Mark recovered himself and straightened his bent shoulders. In the reaction he was hot with anger; it chafed his manhood that it should have been he and not Maisie who was shy, and the more so because he could not believe that Maisie had not read him like a book. He had always regarded Lawrence Sturt's gallantries with a mixture of amusement and dislike, but he did find himself, for one moment, envying the dash with which that practiced swordsman would have beaten down Maisie's guard. Lawrence would not have let her go without a kiss. . . . Mark had reached this stage in his reflections when Maisie knocked at the door again. "It really is chilly to night. Wouldn't you like some hot water?"

"Have you any handy?"

"Lots!" Maisie sang out.

"Thanks most awfully. I'll come and get it in a minute."

There was no reply, but shortly after the door was opened and a white arm came round it with a kettle. Mark splashed some water into his basin—"Don't take too much," said Maisie, "I want about half"—and returned the kettle to the hand; after which he was left to complete his toilet without further interruption and in a more sober frame of mind.

When Mark came out, dressed in an old suit of flannels, the kitchen had undergone a change. A white cloth was thrown over the table, and the oak chairs were drawn up to it. Silver and glass were set out, and in a branched silver candlestick candles were lighted, which flickered in the draught from the window and threw giant and distorted shadows on the walls. Maisie raised a flushed face from the fire. "The plates are hotting on the rack here," she said. "Do you mind putting them on the table while I dish up? I do hope you can resign yourself to having only ham and eggs for to-night, we'll do ourselves better to-morrow, but I haven't had time to unpack the Stores hamper yet."

"Couldn't have anything better. Oh! *sac à papier!*"

"What's the matter—did you burn your fingers? Dear boy, I knew you would. Never mind, tell me if you like fried bread and how many eggs you can eat. I've done four for you and two for me, but I can put some more on while we're eating these."

"Oh, we'll eat these first, anyhow. Is that beer on the window-sill?"

"Yes: there is some claret in the locker, but I know you always drink beer when you can get it and I rather like it myself. It goes with the furniture, don't you think?"

"It goes very fast," remarked her husband, raising his face from an empty tankard. "Sea air makes people thirsty. Maisie, you are a genius! When did you learn to cook?"

"When I was a girl. Yes, mustard, please."

"Brown bread or white?"

"Brown—let's each have half the crust."

There was an interval of silence.

"Aren't we pigs?" said Maisie. "It's like a German table d'hôte. You know the awful hush that falls when they bring in a fresh course."

"I've never been to Germany."

"Never—been—to Germany!"

"Not I. Had enough of them in France. Surely you knew I was through the war, didn't you?" Maisie shook her head; she knew nothing whatever about Mark Sturt's early career, and had never heard of him except as a business man and politician, though when the idea was once offered to her she could only say "of course," and

wonder that she had not recognized before the military
stamp on his broad shoulders. Mark was smiling as if
at some private joke, but there was a flush on his cheek.
"Really? Well, how should you know it after all! I
never got my captaincy. No, I didn't volunteer; I was
in the army before war broke out. I was only a linesman—1st Derbyshires."

"Did you see much fighting?"

"Had my whack. Not so much as Lawrence; he was
out from start to finish and never got a scratch, which
is a bit of a record, considering that he was in some of
the hottest corners. Incidentally I may add that he
saved my life at the very imminent risk of his own.
Lawrence shines, you know, when he gets out of civilized
life; he enjoyed the show, I believe, which is more than
I can say."

"Why did you go into a line regiment when your
brother was in the Guards?"

"Possibly because I wasn't keen on being a gay Guardsman."

"Don't snub me, Mark, please. You might have liked
the gunners or the cavalry."

"Too heavy for the cavalry." He shrugged his shoulders. "Really I don't know. I think my father settled
it for us, but I don't remember raising any objection.
Why should I? The opulent and ornamental were never
in my line. It was a good regiment, too. Yarrow was
our colonel, the men worshiped him; he was killed at
Loos." Mark checked himself with a sigh.—"Anyhow
it made no great odds, for I was invalided out of the
Service at three and twenty, so that was an end of that."
An end of the subject too, Maisie thought, judging by
his tone, and she was too cautious to press her point,
though she longed to speak her mind on Lawrence Sturt's
charmingly mannered selfishness. She knew, even she,

that a man's old regiment is one of the topics that are ruled out of criticism. One other question she risked. "Oh! yes, I got a nasty cut over the hip," Mark answered impatiently. "Are there any more eggs going? Don't get up, please—I'll bet I've fried more eggs than you have. Very good they are, too. Did you get them at the farm?"

"No, I fetched them with me from Ushant, and the milk and the bread as well. I knew I shouldn't get over to the farm to-night, it's every step of two miles."

"Something of a walk for Miss Archdale—I beg your pardon, Mrs. Mark Sturt. I was wondering as I came up the lane how you would get on in your pretty little slippers." Maisie replied by sticking out her foot, shod in a thick square-toed boot. "Come, that's better!" said Mark. "I hate those silly shoes women generally wear. Why do you wear them? Senseless little things."

"To match the women," said Maisie.

The caustic contempt of her tone made Mark raise his eyebrows. "Have some more beer and think better of it."

"I will have half a glass more beer—I hope it won't make me drunk—but I won't think better of it. We can't help it: we were educated to be senseless. Were you ever drunk, Mark?"

"Often," said Mark cheerfully.

"Rubbish! Tell me—I want to know."

"Are you reflecting that you're alone in the house with me?" Mark asked. He leaned back in his chair laughing at her. "Ha, ha! what a hopeless kid you are at times, Maisie! I have been drunk once or twice in my life, but I'm not an habitual drunkard, dear. Would you like a list? Once when I was at Sandhurst, after a boatrace night—a very mild affair, terminating in a gentle reprimand; once when I was in the army, on an occasion

which I won't specify, when the drinks were mixed and
we were all rather glorious; and once I believe in China,
but there was opium in that and I don't remember much
about it, bar the headache I had afterwards. I'm afraid
that's the limit." He leaned across the table and captured the hand that wore his rings. "Did you flatter
yourself that I'd been a devil of a fellow? Ha, ha! what
a disappointment, isn't it?" His shyness had left him,
and in its place there came again the strange heavy beat
of excitement along his pulses. "Your turn now to confess. Why do you sneer at women? I hate to hear a
woman do that. Women ought to stick together as men
do. Esprit de corps, what?"

"Oh! Mark! Not with my rings on, please—you
hurt."

"So sorry. But why do you say you were educated to be senseless? You seem to me distinctly
competent."

"Ah! but I wasn't brought up in my present atmosphere," Maisie retorted. "I had plenty of sense hammered into me when I was a girl."

"When you were a girl?" Mark repeated, amused.
"Where did you live in those dim and distant days when
you were a girl?"

"In the country. We'll take it in turns to clear the
plates away, shall we? If you get up, too, we shall only
fall over each other. To expedite matters I'll put them
straight into the sink. I'm afraid there's not much for
a second course—only bread and cheese and fruit and
cream."

Mark registered a vow to get the tale of her early life
out of her by and by, but it would evidently take a good
deal of getting, and the present was not a fitting oppor-
tunity. They finished their supper, while out of doors
the splendor faded into twilight, the mist and chill of

night settled over the sea, and the ceaseless dash of waves sounded ever louder and louder in the withdrawal of those small unnoticeable noises which are woven into the fabric of the serenest daylight quiet. When neither of them could eat any more, Maisie turned Mark out of doors while she washed up and set the kitchen tidy. His offers of help were refused. "Not to-night: I can do it quicker by myself till we get used to finding our way about, thanks all the same—I'd really rather you went and had a smoke." Mark suspected that it was done chiefly in order not to throw too great a strain upon his patience, whose durability—tried by many vicissitudes of camp life—was not yet understood by his companion; but he gave way, and walked up and down outside on the patch of level sward between the sea glen and the downs, watching the light from St. Catherine's lighthouse wink and wheel in taper beams across the gray floor of the Channel. How still it was, and how fresh! There was not a sound to be heard but the recurrent murmur of a wave against the cliffs and its long surge and suck over the hidden beach below.

In the open kitchen doorway Maisie appeared, silhouetted black against fire and candle light, carrying in either hand a cup of coffee. "No milk, no sugar," she said, giving him his portion. "Pure Turkish, no chicory. Is that right?"

"Pure chickish, no turcory. Exceedingly right."

"You have a baby sense of humor, Mark," said Maisie. "Just like a man. Ouf! I'm almost tired."

She sat down on a hummock of grass and thoughtfully stirred her coffee. She had taken off her apron and smoothed her hair, which shone like gold in the twilight, and the schoolgirl neatness of the blue serge rose and fell with her even breathing. Mark stood a little behind her watching that soft rise and fall. So Renée had looked as she sat in her father's garden and listened to the young English officer's lame attempts at French, the shuttles flying under her downcast eyes; but Maisie Sturt was no Renée, and with some years of London in her memory, and Mark a captive at her side, what title had she to wear Renée's aspect of untouched maiden calm? Passion flamed again in Mark, the response of his senses to the goad of his vanity; if she had thrown herself into young Forester's timid hands she could not have appeared more secure. Youth has a right to a man's infinite gentleness, and womanhood to respect, but experience masking as innocence has forfeited either claim. . . . Or was it, after all, Maya, illusion? A dream, prolonged and vivid, but rushing on to its inevitable end?

The wind, what there was of it, was setting towards the sea. A faint breath went by them like a sigh over the thin grass of the downs and through the sea-dwarfed oak-trees. It carried with it, plaintive and remote, the chiming of the tower clock in Ushant far away.

"It's striking eleven," said Maisie. "I shall set my watch, because Ushant church is five minutes faster than London time. When in Ushant, do as Ushant does. I can't afford to get up late to-morrow."

She gave her little unembarrassed laugh. "Let me take your cup," said Mark, conscious as he said it that the common courtesy sounded quaintly formal in that natural setting. But Maisie gave him her cup smilingly, and Mark took them both indoors and washed them under the tap. "Where do you keep the cloths?" he asked through the kitchen window. "You'll find one on the clothes prop, drying," Maisie answered. Mark wiped the little cups, set them on the dresser, and came out again. Maisie was on her feet, shielding her eyes with her hand, gazing out far-sighted over the gray tides of the Channel. Mark came softly up behind her, put his arm round her waist, and bent his head so that his lips touched her ear.

"Past eleven o'clock, Maisie, and you've had a long day. You'll never be up in time to-morrow if you don't go to bed soon."

"I should so awfully like to run down and have a dip in the sea."

"Now? It's too cold; you would get a chill."

"Not I, I never get chills. I'm as strong as a horse."

"Well, it's too late," said Mark peremptorily. "Wait till the morning."

"I am rather tired," Maisie confessed.

She went indoors, leaving the door open, and a moment later he saw the light of a lamp spring out in her room. Mark glanced at his watch. Ten minutes past eleven. Maisie appeared at the window and drew the blind down. But it was a thin blind, and the discovery that he could still see her, defined in shadow against the lighted canvas, her arms lifted to take the pins out of her hair, drove Mark Sturt away from that vicinity. He lit a cigarette and strolled slowly down the glen, thinking of nothing, noticing nothing except the stony roughness of the track underfoot. The sea was hidden now, the trees rose up between it and him; only the voice of its deep breathing still encompassed him like a benediction or a serenade, and the wheeling stare of the lighthouse flashed periodically behind the leafy gloom. He followed the track till he came out upon the silvered and deserted beach, and saw dark waters lapping at his feet, a bath of stars. They invited him with their crystal freshness, and lazily he threw off his clothes and plunged in. Cold it was, cold and shallow, soon deepening towards the entry of the cove; a few strokes carried him out of his depth. He turned over on his back and floated, lying between shadow and shadow. Bright

over the Channel glittered Altair and Sagittarius, and
Cassiopeia sphered up in her diamond chair, and Alde-
baran far in the west; further inland the Northern wag-
oner hung inverted over the downs, while the cove caught
the sparkle of the Tyrian mariner's guide—

> the stedfast starre
> That was in Ocean waves yet never wet,
> But firm is fixt, and sendeth light from farre
> To all that in the wide deep wandering arre.

Mark splashed about lazily; a powerful swimmer and
indifferent to temperature, he loved to feel the light slap
and curl of the water over his chest, and to-night more
than any other night every nerve in his body seemed to
sparkle with the pleasure of energy. He lost all definite
thought as he breasted the water's yielding caress. At
last an insane fear fastened on him that he had been
away too long, and he swam ashore and huddled on his
clothes again, wet as he was, and took the precipitous
footpath at a run. But when he regained the cliff-top
the light was still burning in Maisie's room. Mark
looked at his watch. Twenty minutes to twelve. He
moved towards the open door.

And all at once he knew that he could not enter it.

There was no struggle in his mind, the decision seemed
to have been made for him; he turned sharp round and
walked away, not towards the glen, but inland, towards
the downs. He took out his cigarette case and lit another cigarette, not because he wanted to smoke, but as
a man dazed after an accident will perform some small
action to test his own faintness; for the world had again
grown fearfully unreal. He put his hand up to his forehead and found that it was streaming with perspiration.
He walked on till he came to the bend in the track, but
there he turned back, remembering that he could not

leave Maisie by herself and out of earshot in that solitary spot. He felt as tired as though he had just undergone a severe operation, but there was still no struggle, no rebellion; the fiat had gone forth from laws deeper than the passions of his own being, and he obeyed it.

He threw himself down on the grass by the wayside. Some time passed: how long he did not know. Presently the light behind the blind moved and the blind itself was lifted. Maisie looked out. She could not see him, and she stood for some minutes at the window, waiting. At last she called him softly by name. "Mark."

He did not answer.

"Mark"—she raised her voice—"are you there?"

"I'm here, dear," said Mark, standing up.

"Oh, there you are!"

By the relief in her voice he understood that she had been frightened.

"I'm—ready now."

"I'm not coming."

"You—?"

"I'm not coming."

"Not coming at all?"

"No. I shall sleep out here. Go to bed, dear. Don't worry about me."

She stood for a long time silent, holding up the blind. "Is it—Don't you want to come?"

"Yes," said Mark, stamping his foot. "Go and lie down. Drop the blind and go away from the window."

"But, Mark——"

"Drop the blind and go away from the window."

She let fall the blind and he saw her cross the room with a steady step. The light in its turn was extinguished. Now shadows and soft starshine enveloped everything in heaven and earth. It was some time before Mark dared to move from the spot where she had left him, but at last he went with a swift light tread to the open casement of the kitchen, caught up a coat that he had left lying on the locker, and passed on into the fringe of the wood.   There he made himself a hole for his hip after the fashion of an old campaigner, doubled up the coat under his head, and lay down to sleep under the shelter of the trees and the stars.   But no sleep came. With the first accent of his wife's voice, immunity was over, and fatigue.   He looked up at the stars, the sign manual of God, but he could not pray; and then he thought of his friend, who preached the beauty of purity and the transience of human pleasure and pain, and he wondered whether Father de Trafford had ever stretched his own limbs on that rack.   Pleasure may cheat our wish, but in pain there is no illusion.   His will held firm, however.   Mark Sturt's wedding night was passed under the stars.

CHAPTER VI

"**M**ARK." Mr. Sturt, who was stretched at full length on the turf before the cottage with his pipe and a book, looked up lazily. "I have to go over to the farm for some more eggs. Will you stay where you are and look after the house, or come too?"

"I wonder if I've finished digesting my breakfast," said Mark. "I ate a good deal." He rolled over on his back and cocked one knee over the other.

"Make up your mind," Maisie admonished him, "because if you don't I needn't lock up the house."

"Oh, I expect I'd better come," said Mark, getting to his feet. "Let me just shy this book in at the window. Is that the kit you're going in? Pity it's thrown away on old Biddle. He doesn't know a good thing when he sees it."

Mark was in flannels—the same flannels that he had worn on the night of his arrival, but dirtier by a week's hard wear; and Maisie was in a harebell-colored cotton frock, bare-armed and bare-throated. The skin that had been white a week ago was now a warm pale brown, and in place of her Greek waves she wore her hair down in two thick plaits which swung below her waist. She looked younger than ever, and had a boy's indifference to the sun. "You'll get sunstroke if you go out like that without a hat," said Mark. He said it every day.

"I'll take my new sunshade," replied the biddable Maisie, catching up a flowered cotton parasol which she had bought in Ushant for two and elevenpence, three

91

farthings. Mark had not yet got over the surprise of finding that she generally did as she was told to do. "Here's the latchkey, don't drop it." Mark put it in his pocket; it was one of the incorrigibly feminine idiosyncrasies which fascinated him in his wife, that in spite of her thick boots and indifference to wind and weather she never had a pocket in any of her dresses. She carried her handkerchiefs up her sleeve or in her belt, and when she dropped them she borrowed Mark's.

They swung off over the downs in step together, Mark shortening his stride to keep pace with Maisie's long level tread; comrades thoroughly at ease with each other, in spite of the precarious delicacy of their relations. Perhaps it was strange that it should have been so, and certainly a small defect of sensibility on either side would have made the position intolerable; but Sturt and his wife came of a stock that has, among many less useful qualities, the knack of taking things for granted. There had been ten difficult minutes the first morning, but when each realized that the other had accepted the situation, and that there would be neither discussion nor reproach, the gap was soon bridged, and in the small familiarities forced on them by life at the cottage they were soon able to ignore the fact that there had ever been a gap at all.

"Our last day," said Maisie, as they breasted the downs to the south-east. "What shall we do this afternoon— take the car out, or go for a row?" Mark had discovered in the village a dilapidated car for hire, and after a hot and happy morning spent chiefly on his back in a farrier's yard he had managed, as he said, to "whack her up" to fifteen miles an hour, at which breakneck pace he and Maisie had taken turns to drive her through stony lanes, across the downs, and even over the beach. "We might dine somewhere at an inn and save washing up."

" 'Shouldn't wonder if we had a storm," said Mark,

scanning the weather. "Hallo! things look a bit queer ahead. What's all the smoke?"

It was one of those sultry days when the country seems to be worn out with the burden of holding up the fleecy stillness of the clouds. An overcast night had prevented any dew from falling, and the sky was still packed with faint shapes, which never seemed to move, and which dissolved into a mere smudge of vapor over the bronze sixpence of the sun. There was no wind. Far as the eye could see, the gray-blue floor of the Channel stretched without a speck of foam, till it shaded off through infinite gradations of silvery shade into the silver dazzle of the horizon. A tramp steamer plowing along left behind her a wake that lay for miles like a stain, while overhead the smoke of her single funnel rolled itself out from a pennon to a string of beads, and those again into mere puffs and curls of whiteness, which dispersed themselves imperceptibly into the surrounding haze.

But Mark was not looking at the sea. As they came over the rise, they saw before them a patch of downland, covered with a low scrub of heather and gorse-bushes, which was burning furiously. Some tramp had thrown away a lighted match, or some spark had flown from a traction-engine along the road, and the grass and shrubs, parched by a long drought—for no rain had fallen since Mark's coming to Ushant—had caught like tinder. Before the line of fire, smoke rolled in low clouds; it had gone over their heads while they were in the glen, but now the smell of it was bitter in their nostrils. Mark halted, leaning on his stick, and looked round him with a practiced eye.

"No harm done. Eastwards they've beaten it out already; north you get the high road, southward the cliffs, and in our own direction it will stop at the dyke. Pity

to leave that black scar on the downs, but at least it
won't touch crops or farm buildings. Ever seen a heath
fire before? Come along over the dyke, it's worth watching; not quite like a forest fire I once saw in Canada,
though."

The dyke, a tolerably broad ditch of ill-defined Roman antecedents, now used as a watering-place for sheep,
was spanned only by a couple of planks, and Mark turned
to give his hand to his companion. "My dear girl,
what's the matter?" he said hastily. "There's nothing
to be afraid of!"

"I'm not afraid. Go on: I don't want a hand, thanks."
Mark opened his eyes, but said no more, and led the way
across the footbridge, his wife following. "Yes, we'll
wait and watch it," said Maisie. She sat down on a
cushion of heather and Mark threw himself on the turf
at her feet; he had to choose his couch warily, for the
gorse grew thick all about them. Maisie pulled a long
feathery shaft of grass, and drew it lightly, like a proxy
caress, across his upturned face.

"You are sunburnt, Mark: tanned like a gypsy. Your
neck was white under your collar when you came, but
it's as brown now as a coffee berry. I should have
thought China and the Andes and all the other places
would have tanned you from head to foot, but I suppose
it wears off after a few weeks of civilization. You are
thin, too—thinner than you were when you came, I believe."

He put up his hand and drew hers down and took
the grass-blade away. "I don't like being tickled, thanks.
Maisie, why are you afraid of fire?"

"I'm not afraid of fire," Maisie averred, gazing with
steady eyes at the distant surge of smoke. "What's the
time? We mustn't leave the eggs too late, because of
getting home to see to lunch."

"Tell me, Maisie."

"There's nothing to tell. I thought you knew. Oh, I think I'd like to tell you if you really care to hear, but do you? Long tales about other people's pasts are so very, very dull."

"Still you might take the chance of boring your husband."

"Ah! if you were."

Mark's hand closed over hers with a force of which he was unconscious. "Don't, dear—don't. You don't know what you're talking about."

"And do you?" said Maisie sadly.

"Tell me about the fire," Mark answered after a moment. He could not, in fact, explain himself to Maisie, because he had not yet succeeded in explaining himself to himself. "Were you ever in one?"

"Yes. Did you really never hear that? How little we know about each other, even now!" She named a famous ocean tragedy. "We were all in it. I lost every one."

"You lost—?"

"My father and mother, two brothers older than myself, and a young sister. We were all on our way home from the Cape. She had a dangerous cargo, and they could not get the blaze under. You remember, don't you? It was only ten years ago. I was a girl of thirteen. There was no panic, and all the passengers were got into the boats, but there was a heavy gale blowing, and one boat was swamped as they lowered it. My mother and Philip and Jim and Lucy were in that one, and my father and I were going in the next. They were drowned before our eyes."

Mark took her hand again and held it.

"Hardly any one was lost except that boatfull," Maisie went on. "The rest of us were picked up in the course

of the day, but my father died before we got to England.
He was a delicate man and he couldn't stand the shock.
They put it down to the exposure and the wetting—he
jumped in after my mother and was all but drowned
himself—but he could have pulled through if he had
cared to live. He worshiped my mother. I couldn't
do anything to help him, and I was glad for his sake
when he died. He had nerves, my father. Every one
was very good to me, particularly the people off the
Redruth Castle, but I couldn't answer them at all. I
remember Lady Dene—Viola Dene, the Governor's wife
—taking me in her arms and telling me not to ride myself on the curb, but of course I couldn't tell her anything. I never have really told any one before."

"Clever woman, Viola Dene. Go on, dear."

"Philip was my special pal," said Maisie. Her eyelids
fell, and her teeth fastened for a moment on her lower
lip.

"Your young brother?"

"He was seventeen; four years older than I was. He
was coming home to go into the army. He was an ugly
boy with beautiful eyes like my mother's, and he was
always in hot water. He taught me to ride and swim
and row; he could ride anything on four legs himself.
Jim was unimaginative, and Lucy was only a plaything,
but Philip and I were always about together. He said
I had more sense than Jim, and he treated me exactly
like another boy—he used to cuff my head if I didn't
do things properly. I loved Philip. I love him still,
and I still want him. Oh! my dear, dear Philip."

"Don't cry, dear," said Mark. He sat up and put his
arm round her.

"I'm not crying," said Maisie, leaning her cheek against
his. "Feel! not one tear. That's because Philip invariably
cuffed me when I cried. He said if I cried I was a silly

idiot of a girl, but if I didn't I was very nearly as good
as a boy. I—I think, looking back, Philip must have
been awfully fond of me, but one didn't analyze it at the
time. I did so wish afterwards that I had made him
say good-by to me before he got into the boat. I know
exactly what he would have done. He would have kissed
me perfunctorily over one eyebrow and said, 'Good-by,
old girl, I wish you were coming too,' which would have
been something to live on afterwards. But the last words
he actually said to me were, 'You confounded little
messer, you've been messing about with my gun again
with your wet paws,' and I defy any one to get any satisfaction out of that."

"What happened when you reached England?"

"Death and damnation," said Maisie. She shook herself free of Mark's arm. "I died on board, and I was
damned in the suburbs. I went to live with my uncle
John and his wife and family in a big house on Chislehurst Common. My father had never saved a farthing,
so there was nothing for me except a small Civil Service
pension, and there was no one else who could have taken
me except my mother's brother, who was Irish, and eccentric, and a bachelor, and flatly refused to have anything to do with me. The John Archdales were the obvious people. Uncle John was not of the same type as
my father, and he hadn't any nerves. He had married
a tub merchant's daughter, and they had six children—
George, Muriel, Hilda, Rosie, Tom, and Gladys. We
wore camisoles and underskirts, and wiped our mouths
on serviettes, and sent soiled clothes to the laundry, and
Uncle John asked a blessing. I went to school with my
cousins. Uncle John always used to say that he never
made any difference between us, and he didn't—I had
just the same clothes as his own girls, and the same
'extras,' and the same tips and treats. They were all

very kind to me, and Aunt Gladys said I was to look upon
her as a mother, and the boys and girls would be like
brothers and sisters to me now I hadn't any of my own.
One day when I had been there four or five months she
came into my bedroom—I shared it with Hilda—and
said she wanted me to have some new frocks because she
couldn't bear to see a young girl like me all in black;
and while I was being turned round to be measured she
told the dressmaker all about it. She kept appealing to
me for details. I thought of what Viola Dene said about
the curb. I was polite and diffuse. . . . But, indeed,
Mark, it is not healthy for any girl to suffer like that."

Mark nodded.

"Remember that when you're judging me," said Maisie
softly, "I'm not good; I'm not half as good as you are,
Mark of mine. But if some day you come to know why
I married you, and find it hard to forgive me, don't
leave out of the reckoning those five years at Chislehurst.
Thirteen to eighteen is an impressionable age."

"How did you escape?"

"Easily enough, after I left school. I said I wanted
to earn my own living, and I fancy Uncle John wasn't
altogether sorry to get me out of the way. Tom and
George were a good deal at home just then."

"Oh!" said Mark, smiling.

"Exactly," Maisie returned with composure. "So I
got away and turned in to work. I wanted to be a nurse,
but they won't take you as probationer till you're twenty-
three, so I took a post as mother's help and nursery
governess (I haven't any brains, you know). But I only
had a couple of years of it, for when I was twenty my
mother's brother died and left me every farthing of his
money. He didn't even appoint Uncle John trustee. He
detested Uncle John, and they say he was very fond of
my mother; but I firmly believe that his ruling motive

was to play a last posthumous prank in the character
of Cinderella's fairy godmother. I'd only seen him once
in my life, when he turned up at Chislehurst in an immense Rolls-Royce, and insisted on carrying me off, a
pig-tailed schoolgirl in a sailor hat, to lunch at the Ritz.
He refused to get out of the car or wait while I changed
my dress. He gave me champagne and ice-pudding and
a £10 note, and told me I was an unlicked young devil
and that he should like to see what I should do if I had
a free hand."

Mark reserved his opinion of Mr. FitzGerald. "And
what did Cinderella do when the glass coach came for
her?"

"Went to the ball," said Maisie, smiling. "I wrote
straight off to Lady Dene, recalling the old South African
days and telling her what had happened. Her reply
was a telephone message asking me to come and see her
in Berkeley Square. I went for a week-end and stayed
for the rest of the season, and after that my life is
public property. I go to see the John Archdales now
and then, but they don't like me very much; they say
I'm worldly, and they won't let the girls come and stay
with me because it isn't proper for a young lady to live
alone as I do. They are just what they always were, my
money hasn't made a pin's difference to them; I respect
them for that, but I don't think about them unless I'm
obliged. And so now you know why I winced when I
saw the fire." She unfastened a gold chain from her
neck and put an open locket into Mark's hand: the ivory
miniature of a spirited boy of fourteen or fifteen, with
curly brown hair and large, speaking eyes.

"I shouldn't have guessed it," said Sturt, studying
Philip's features.

"That he was my brother?"

"I didn't mean that. You're like him; you have his

eyes. I should never have guessed that you had led a life like that." He laid the locket on her knee.

"No: well, I didn't propose that any one should guess it," said Maisie carelessly. "Oh, Mark, look at that silly rabbit!" White scut and hunched quarters, a little doe loped past them with the sneaking gait of a housewife bound for her own front door though frightened to her toe-tips. But the front door, alas, was behind that screen of flickering flame, now not many yards away, and the little rabbit, after a prolonged stare, scampered off again with bolting eyes. Maisie sprang up. "I don't like that. Poor little wretch! Come along and get the eggs."

Mark dragged himself to his feet. The lassitude of his movement attracted Maisie's attention, and she turned her bright, veiled eyes on him. "You look fagged. Sleeping out of doors can't be very restful."

"Oh, I like it. I've done it often enough, you know, under less pleasant conditions; rugs and cushions are a luxury. But I've got a devil of a head to-day," Mark confessed, "which means either liver or thunder. The latter, I fancy. Whew! Time to get a move on, what?" In a momentary flicker of wind the smoke reached out a long arm after them, and Mark fanned it away from Maisie with his straw hat. "The fire will be up to where we were sitting in ten minutes' time."

Quickening their pace, they recrossed the dyke, to make their way down to the farm by a track on the other side. By now the fire had licked its way in patches almost to the water's edge, and the heat was becoming oppressive. Mark inobtrusively shielded his companion as much as he could, for Maisie was still very pale, and Lady Dene's pregnant comment, taken together with the story of the *Redruth Castle,* had set her for him in a new light. She was so cool and hardy that he had always supposed her to be emotionally immature, unversed in sorrow and probably incapable of any strong feeling, but Philip's sister was not cold. "Poor wretched little rabbit!" said Maisie presently, her mind reverting to its previous train of thought. "Mark, do Catholics believe in a heaven for animals?"

"It isn't an article of faith, but some of the Fathers upheld it. Why?"

"Sometimes I wish I were a Catholic. No, I don't. I might surrender my will, but I could never surrender my reason. How can you do it?"

"Do what, dear?"

"Believe what you don't believe because the priests tell you to. It's more than weak—it's immoral." Mark's eyes danced. "Ah, you laugh—you think you can get behind whatever I say. Yours is an arrogant creed."

"Maybe," said Mark. "It's an old one."

"You look like an adept listening to the irresponsible prattle of a neophyte."

"There goes your rabbit across the road, I know her by the white patch on her quarters. I wouldn't worry about her; the fire will have burned itself out in an hour, and she'll be able to get back to her bunny-hole. Hallo!"

"What, then?"

"Where's your locket?"

Maisie put her hand up to her throat. "Gone; I dropped it where we were sitting. I know I did. It was on my knee, and I forgot it when the rabbit went by."

"Wait for me," said Mark, and ran off. In spite of his heavy build, he was fleet of foot, and had need to be, for even the brushwood blaze of an English down is hot enough to melt the soft gold of an ornament, and under the puffs of a rising wind the flames were traveling

fast. "Oh, don't, Mark—don't go!" Maisie cried out,
but he naturally took no notice. She watched him dash
straight across the heather and leap the fifteen-foot dyke
in his stride, and then he was lost to sight behind a swell
of the downs.

It was a race between Mark and the advancing fires.
They caught from bush to bush, the papery unreality
of daylight flame dancing over an intense glow of scorch-
ing heat; they stretched out capriciously in gulf and in-
let, leaving bays and promontories behind the general
tide. Mark tore off his flannel blazer and dashed forward with his arm over his head to keep the smoke out
of his eyes. So long as his retreat lay open the danger
was of the slightest, but the discomfort was considerable,
and if he had had to cast about for his direction he would
have been driven back for want of time. Luckily he had
taken his bearings after the inveterate habit of the trained
woodsman, and was able to pick up the landmarks as he
ran. There on the right was the thornbush, now spit-
ting and crackling in a whirl of ardent tongues; there
was Maisie's deep heather tussock still uncaught; within
a yard's radius the locket must have dropped when she
sprang to her feet. But the heat was intense, and the
smoke was rolling up in clouds. Mark staggered as it
surged round him, and for the first time a distinct idea
of peril darted into his mind; if he stayed long enough
to let that suffocating vapor get him by the throat he
would go down under it, and this trumpery heath fire
would burn the flesh from his bones as surely as any
league-long Canadian furnace. But to go back to Maisie
without the miniature was impossible. Mark scanned
the grass: it was not there. Then with his heavy stick
he beat open the thorn bush. "Oh, damn!" he said
peevishly. For there lay the locket within arm's length,
but the slender chain was wound in and out low down

among the branches, and to get it he had to plunge his hand straight through the surface blaze.

Maisie was about to recross the footbridge when Mark came up to it, a figure-out of a Mayday sweep's revels, his white clothes grimed with smoke and soot from head to foot. But he had slipped on his blazer again, he was smiling, and he held the locket dangling by its fragile chain. "Saw it directly," he said. "Awfully sorry I broke the chain, though. Most clumsy of me."

"But, Mark, aren't you hurt? You had only those low shoes on."

"Pricked a bit," said Mark philosophically. "Scorched my arm, too. Let's leave the eggs, what? I might create surprise. Unless you would like to go on to the farm by yourself, in which case, if you'll excuse my escort, I'll wait for you."

"No, thanks, we'll do without the eggs. Come home and let me see to your arm."

She hurried him back along the downs to the White Cottage, or tried to do so, for Mark refused to hurry; he was honestly amused by her solicitude, but the mishap and the prevision of awkwardness to come had jarred his temper, and amusement would soon have turned to annoyance if Maisie had not let him alone. Luckily Maisie was bred in the same tradition. Till she had him indoors she ignored Mark's *malaise* as stoically as she would have ignored her own, and when she spoke it was with a laconic trenchancy which disposed of opposition.

"Come in here," she said, leading the way into the parlor, "it's too dark in the kitchen. Sit by the window and let me have a look at you. Oh, Mark, don't be stupid! If your arm is burned it must be dressed, and whether you like it or not you'll have to let me help you." Then as she drew off the loose blazer she saw that there was not much sleeve under it to cut. "Hallo!

Oh, I see. Because of the smoke? H'm: that smarts, I should say. Your shoulder too? You might have warned me before you got your jacket off. Luckily we've some olive oil in the place." With the aid of the oil she was carefully removing the charred linen, and Mark admired her deftness. "So I ought to be," said Maisie carelessly. "I hold every certificate you can get under the Red Cross. Can you get your arm into warm water if I stand the basin on the window-sill? Quite like old days, this." She was tearing up a linen sheet into strips, and Mark sat still, fretted but amused; his arm was scorched from elbow to shoulder where he had plunged it into the blazing sprigs, and, little as he liked the situation, his body appreciated her unflinching delicacy of touch. "Now I'm going to bandage you." She stood back, regarding her handiwork. "Look here, Mark, you mustn't move that arm or you'll make it really bad. You'll have to let me help you into a fresh shirt. Where are they—in your suit-case? Don't get up."

"Thanks very much. I'm fearfully sorry to bother you."

"I wonder what uncivilized man does when he feels embarrassed and hasn't a civilized mask to wear," the say-all Maisie observed with her irresponsible irony. Mark twisted his mustache to hide a laugh, but he did not like it, and he was beginning to get angry. She drew his shirt down from the bandaged arm. "Good heavens! where did you get that scar?"

"St. Éloi," Mark answered laconically.

"It must have been touch and go."

"It was, I believe. That dark-blue tie—do you mind? Can't tie a knot with one hand. Thanks ever so much. You might fix me up a sling while you're about it."

"No fear!" said Maisie scornfully. "Can I take a couple of these handkerchiefs? Dear, dear, what a dandy we are! Irish linen, and finer than mine. Never mind, I like you for being a dandy. Philip was too." She came behind him to secure the sling, and swiftly, when it was done, she leaned down over his shoulder and kissed him lightly on the cheek. Mark started and flushed. "Just one kiss, because you saved my locket for me," Maisie whispered. "I haven't thanked you—what? Oh, Mark, you didn't mind?"

Sturt had risen to his feet. "You are far too kind," he said, and the courtesy out like a whip. "But don't let me give you any more trouble, I can manage now by myself."

By the time Mark came in to lunch, the beauty of the morning was over. Clouds had gathered with the swiftness of storm, the wind was moaning in the glen, and thunder was rolling all round the horizon, while big drops of rain, the first they had seen at Ushant, had begun to splash down on the hot stones, which smoked under them like a furnace. Mark had changed into a serge suit, and in putting it on seemed to have put off the gypsy; he looked as he had looked on his first arrival, rather out of place and too big for his surroundings, and he was very polite to Maisie and very constrained.

The conditions of life at the White Cottage were in fact so difficult that they could be ignored only so long as the fiction of unconsciousness could be kept up, and constraint was sure to follow the trying relations into which Mark's slight accident had thrown the husband and wife; but it would have been nothing if Mark had not lost his temper. Modern intercourse is so nicely adjusted that it is probably harder to get back to friendly terms after a hot speech, than it was in Tudor times after a blow. Mark would have liked to apologize. He was exceedingly ashamed of himself. But how could he

reopen the subject? He felt himself obliged to step delicately; and meanwhile, though he did not know it, Maisie
was suffering torment under his impassive gentleness.
Ever since the night in the garden at Shotton, Sturt had
looked on Maisie as female mystery incarnate; but what
had never once occurred to him was that, if he did not
understand her, still less could she understand him. His
mental processes were a complete blank to her, and, while
Mark was casting about for a form of apology which
should not double his offense, Maisie was a prey to blind
panic. As soon as lunch was over she fled. She said
she was going to get the eggs. She refused to let Mark
go with her, and swung off bareheaded and without an
umbrella through a gathering storm which threatened
every minute to become a downpour.

Mark settled himself with his pipe and a book, but
The Origins of the Twentieth Century failed to hold his
attention. The wind rose steadily, the thunder became
almost unintermittent, rain began to fall in sheets. An
hour and a half went by; ample time for Maisie to get
to the farm and back. Mark went into the bedroom and
looked out seaward. Spray was mixed with rain on
the glass, he heard the drumming of great breakers on
the cliffs, and far as the eye could see the Channel was
an angry waste of black and white under a louring sky.
A big ship went by far out, keeping wide of that tormented shore. Lightning fell in steep flashes, sometimes
in two places at the same moment. By force of will
Mark obliged himself to go back to his book, but when
six o'clock struck and Maisie had been gone between
two and three hours he gave up all pretense of reading.
He would have gone to meet her if he had known in
what direction to go, but he had no idea what had become
of her. He tried to persuade himself that she was shel-
tering at the farm, but he could not believe it. Maisie

disliked the Biddle family, who were Strict Baptists and looked down their noses at the strange tenants of the White Cottage. Half-past six struck, then seven; Mark in sheer desperation was just groping among his wife's dresses to find her waterproof before he went to look for her, when the latch lifted and Maisie came in.

Mark came out of the bedroom—and stopped short. "Good heavens! where have you been?"

"Out," said Maisie baldly.

"You don't say so! My dear girl, what have you been doing?"

"The Biddles hadn't any eggs, or anyhow they wouldn't let me have any. I walked into Ushant and got them at the shop."

"Two miles to the farm, five by road from the farm to Ushant, four back to the cottage. Is this your idea of a joke?"

She put the basket of eggs on the table and passed slowly into her own room. A small river marked her track on the floor. "Dear Mark, don't scold me! I got sick of it long before I turned back, but I said I was going to get those eggs and I got them. The sky was magnificent—well worth a wetting. It won't hurt me, you know. Nothing like that ever does. It was too bad of me to leave you to get your own tea, though. How's the arm?"

"Are you getting out of your wet things?"

"Oh, yes—stockings and all. Why, Mark, you sound quite anxious! Have you been wondering what had become of me? I thought you would be sure to guess."

"Naturally I was anxious. I should have come to fetch you back if I had had any idea where you were. If I go into the parlor will you come and dry yourself by the fire?"

"Bless you, I'm not cold!" Maisie sang out, laughing.

"I was walking too fast to get chilly. Eleven miles in
three hours and a quarter isn't bad going for a woman
in a wind like this. I'd much rather you would take the
top off the stove and put the soup on, if you can manage
it with one hand; it's all ready in the big saucepan. What
a storm, isn't it? Let's have the curtains drawn and
light up. It's like a winter's night, as wild as December."

Mark set on the soup and drew the curtains, shutting
out the early-fallen dusk; he could not shut out the wind,
which crept in between the joists of the floor and the
crannied masonry of the walls, or rushed down the chimney and drove puffs of smoke and sparks out into the
room, making the starry candle flames flicker and pine.
He spread the cloth for Maisie, laying the china and
silver as she liked them to be laid, and a bowl of branching scabious and sea-poppies between the candelabra.
"Aren't you nearly ready?" he called out. "You ought
to be hungry, Maisie."

"Ye-es. I feel a little shy."

"Why?"

"I can't get it up anyhow, it's as wet as if I'd just
washed it," said Maisie apologetically. She came out
into the doorway of her room, the flicker of shade and
shine playing over her from head to foot; and Mark
stood up and raised his hand. She had changed her wet
serge for a French dinner dress of silver tissue, her high
boots for silver sandals; and over all she wore, like a
fairy mantle, the damp glittering tresses of her long
hair.

"I salute the Princess Cinderella, Maisie."

She slipped into her chair without meeting his eyes.
"Oh, Mark, you shouldn't have done all this. How
good of you! I wish you would tell me how your arm
is."

"All right, thanks, I'd forgotten about it. May it please your Highness——"

"What? Oh, Mark, don't! oh, how can you?"

He had passed from a military salute to one of a purely civilian nature. Maisie turned away from him, leaning her cheek on her palm, but her other hand lay passive in his grasp, and Mark, bending his head, touched it with his lips. "Am I forgiven? I know it was my bearishness that drove you out of the house this afternoon, and I can't sit down to dinner with you till I've received absolution. I'm very sorry, and I never will do so any more."

"Yes, Mark, you are forgiven. It wasn't your fault, it was mine; it is all my fault, all."

"Glad to hear it," said Mark cheerfully. "I quite thought some of it was mine, that time. So now we'll have our soup."

Outside the wind shrieked, threatening wrecks, the lightning was so bright that it shone through the curtains and dimmed the candles, and hard on the heels of every flash a roar of thunder seemed to shake the house; but inside deep peace had fallen, that peace of heart which no storms can break. Neither Mark nor Maisie said anything more than the small remarks proper to the occasion, as when Maisie offered to butter Mark's bread for him, and Mark asked if she would very much mind unscrewing the bottled beer; but after all it is of these homely threads that the stuff of intimacy is woven, and Maisie felt herself nearer to Mark while she cut up his cold chicken than she had ever been before. When the meal was over, Mark essayed to help her clear the table, but his aid was refused. "No: you had all the bother of laying it, and anyhow you couldn't wash up with one hand. Go and sit in the big chair by the fire and be comfy, it's as cold as cold to-night." She slipped on a big apron and caught up a ribbon to tie back her hair.

"I never in my life saw a woman with hair like yours, Maisie."

"It's too long and too heavy," said Maisie with un-affected impatience. "I should like to cut it off."

"I enter a caveat."

"Then I won't," said Maisie sweetly.

Mark sat down sideways in the big oaken arm-chair, crossed his knees, lit his pipe, and lounged at ease, watch-ing his wife. Maisie washed up the dinner things rather slowly; perhaps she was more tired than she was willing to confess. She went into the parlor, and he heard her closing the heavy storm shutters and barring them; then she returned to the kitchen and shot the bolt of the door. Their small preparations for the night were complete. Maisie slipped her apron off again and came back to the fireside, blowing out the candles on her way. She dropped half a dozen cushions on the floor and sat down at Mark's feet, her flounced skirts flowing out all round her like a silver lakelet: she leaned her head against his knee. Mark sat very still.

"Our last night at the White Cottage. I'm sorry you should have had such a rotten time to-day. Is your arm smarting badly?"

"Hardly at all, thanks."

"Will you let me change the dressings for you before you go to sleep?"

"I shall be most awfully grateful to you if you will. That stuff you put on—salad oil or whatever it was—did me ever so much good. I expect I should have had quite a bad arm if you weren't so exceedingly skillful."

"Thank you, sir. Mark."

"Yes?" said Mark cheerfully. He held a match to the fire—he could not strike it with one hand—leaned back at full length in his chair and relit the nearer candles.

"Why do you do that?"

" 'Hate sitting in the dark. Dismal show to-night anyhow; sure to be wrecks along this coast before morning —By Jove, that was a near thing!"

The wind came roaring up the glen, shook the cottage, and traveled on over the downs in a high continuous shriek like the note of a siren. As it passed, came flash and crash together, and then the smash of splintered wood, a loud tearing creak, and the splash of leaves and twigs dragging down through other foliage to the ground. "Tree struck," said Mark. "In the glen."

"I should think even you won't want to sleep out of doors to-night, will you?"

"I've been out in worse weather, but not from choice. No: I shall turn in on the sofa in the parlor."

"What a wretched state of things!" said Maisie slowly. "Mark, I know you're fagged, I know you don't want to talk to me: I know you're trying to put me off. But this is my last chance, and I must speak to you. After all, I am your wife."

"Yes," said Mark lightly. "And no other man's."

"Why—why won't you, Mark? Is it because you don't like me?"

"On the contrary, I like you exceedingly."

"You mean—don't you?—like me for what I am, not only for my looks?" Mark assented. "I know," Maisie went on. "We're good companions, aren't we? There must be thousands of contented husbands and wives who aren't so companionable as we are. That is what I don't understand. If—if you really didn't like me, I could understand your refusing: but feeling as you do it seems so overstrained." She looked up at him with her fearless brilliant eyes, the eyes of a child, as Mark

had come to believe. "After all, I am your wife. We're
bound to each other for life, and neither of us can ever
marry any one else. We couldn't even get a divorce,
because no judge would believe such a story. You're
putting us both into a false position. When I struck
this insane bargain—for I see now that it was insane—
I had no right to do it for anything on earth—but at all
events it never crossed my mind that you would repu-
diate your share of it; that you meant to give me the
protection of your name without accepting any return
for it."

"I did not mean it."

"You didn't mean it when you came down here? Oh,
I'm glad! You changed your mind—at the eleventh hour,
wasn't it? Literally? Somehow I thought that was the
way of it, only it seemed so queer. Why did you change
your mind?" He was silent. "Mark, I'm very stupid
and ignorant, but I'm not absolutely blind. You look
tired to death, tired and downright ill. No man's nerves
will stand this sort of thing without wear and tear, they
aren't made that way. Any man of the world would
tell you that you had far better, both for your own sake
and mine, make the best of the position." Still he held
his peace. "Speak to me, Mark. To-morrow you'll go
away from me and I don't know when I shall see you
again. Why—why won't you marry me?"

"Do you want me to marry you, Maisie?"

"Yes."

"Oh, my dear!" said Mark under his breath.

He drew her down against his knee again, stroking
her hair with his hand.

"I'm afraid I can only tell you that I don't think it
right. You know that to a Catholic marriage is a sacrament. I suppose—it sounds a rotten thing to say—what
I feel is that I don't love you."

"Oh."

"And you don't love me. Apparently you think that doesn't matter, but I can tell you that it does matter to many women, and I think the odds are you would find you were one of them. But you say you are my wife. Well: I never ought to have married you. I'm sure this must seem overstrained to you: I know most men would not feel about it as I do. I dare say I'm all wrong. But, having taken one false step, I won't go on and take another. You might hate me, Maisie, if I did."

"But if I don't mind——"

"You think you don't mind, dear, because you are only a child and don't know anything about it. That's why I was so much more in the wrong all through than you were. I ought to have guarded you. You had your small reason, I suppose—I don't know what it was and it doesn't much matter. You didn't know that there was any particular reason for not doing it. You see, dear, you don't understand."

"And you do, I suppose."

"Yes," said Mark sadly. "I do."

"And where did you get your experience?" said Maisie. "From the girl who died?"

"Good God!" said her husband.

He walked over to the door, threw it open, and stood leaning against the woodwork, wind and rain beating in on him. Maisie rose languidly to her feet: she glanced at Mark once or twice, but she did not speak to him. She went about one or two small duties which were generally left to the end of the evening, throwing on more coal and laying a bundle of sticks on the rack to dry before they were needed to light the fire next day. At length she touched Mark's sleeve. "Shall I dress your arm now?"

He turned and stood looking down at her. "About

the girl I told you about. I ought to tell you that I only saw her half a dozen times. She died at sixteen. She was—she died at the hands of drunken Prussian soldiery."

"I know, Mark."

"You—know?"

"I know she died innocent. I only struck at her to hurt you. Poor child! I can't hurt her."

"I don't understand you, Maisie."

"I'm sure you don't. Will you let me see to your arm?"

"No. Go to your room."

"Mark——"

"I'm not angry, but you must leave me alone. I don't blame you for wanting to hurt me, because I don't doubt that I myself have hurt you, though most unwillingly. But I really can't stand any more of it at present, my dear."

He opened the door of her room and stood aside for Maisie to pass in.

"What are you doing with my key, Mark?"

He had taken the key from the inside of the lock. "What are you doing?" Maisie repeated—"*Mark!* Really, that isn't necessary. Don't be afraid, I shan't renew my —my solicitations."

Mark stepped back into the kitchen, shut the door between them, slipped the key into the lock on his own side, and turned it. Then he went back to his chair by the fire and sat for hours without movement, leaning his head on his hand.

CHAPTER VII

"From of old, virtue in man is by men praised with a sneer."

L AWRENCE STURT, Mark's elder brother by twenty minutes, had rooms in Chelsea, where he stayed
when he was not hunting, or shooting, or fishing, or
otherwise making life uncomfortable for the animal
world.

He was an inch or so taller than Mark, half a stone
or so lighter, and much better looking, though they
were alike; the strong regular features, which in Mark
had been left blunt, were refined in Lawrence to an
almost effeminate delicacy, and the general coloring was
more pronounced. In character the difference, in spite
of a large common stock of experience, tradition, and
impulse, was even more marked, though here again it
followed apparently the same line of cleavage, for Lawrence got credit for much more originality of action
than Mark. Lawrence, though happy to trade on his
seniority, had consistently declined to perform any of
the duties of his position, while Mark had gone first into
business and then into Parliament without expressing
any pronounced views or tastes of his own. Mark was
a Liberal Unionist as his father had been before him.
Lawrence—when he thought about it—proclaimed the
doctrine of Feudalism, as evolved after the war by a
small reactionary clique of *intransigeants* who held that
Labor had proved itself unfit to govern. Mark remained
a docile member of his mother Church, Lawrence distinguished himself in his salad days by writing violently
atheistical articles in a clandestine College review, and

115

later settled down into what is sometimes called "the
religion of all wise men." Lastly, Mark kept clear of
women, while Lawrence shot by an eccentric orbit from
one bright and dangerous luminary to another—but never,
to vary the metaphor a little, burned his wings on the
way.

Lawrence was at the present time not best pleased
with his brother, who had vanished in a most irregular
and uncharacteristic manner at the moment when he
ought to have been getting together his outfit for the
Colorado journey. Lawrence, who had come up to town
in the heat of late July to expedite his own arrangements,
was annoyed when he learned from Henham, at Mark's
flat, that Mark had been away for a week and had left
no address. Repairing to a club, he found it in the hands
of the paperhangers, and was obliged to dine at a restau-
rant and go on by himself to a dreary and belated play.
After three acts he gave it up and went home. He came
into his drawing-room in a thoroughly bad temper, tried
to grope his way across in the dark (the service was com-
munal, and in one of his fits of medievalism he had cut
off the electric light), knocked over a chair, swore, and
struck a match. When he had lit the immense hanging
lamp of wrought Moroccan brass, which stained the
room from end to end in ember red, he turned round and
saw that he was not alone. Mark Sturt had been sitting
waiting for him in the dark. Lawrence, a sensitive medium, experienced a slight disagreeable shock. He tilted
up the lamp and looked sharply at his brother, who sat
far back in a deep chair in a favorite attitude, more quiet
even than usual because he was not smoking.

"Hullo, Mark! I've just been round to look you up.
What possessed you to go off and not leave any address?
I cursed you high and low."

"Did you?"

"Good God! what have you been doing with yourself?"

"Nothing: what should I?"

"I suppose it's this red light that makes you look so queer," said Lawrence: "hanged if I think it is, though. I say, Mark, have you been ill?"

"Not I."

Lawrence opened his lips—and shut them again. "Either that, or you've been on the spree, my friend," was his unspoken comment. But since Mark did not seem to be at all inclined to receive sympathy he judged it wiser to quit the subject.

"I went round this afternoon to row Bannatyne about the guns," he said, dropping into a chair and crossing one knee over the other. "Have a drink—no? Well, you are in a bad way.—I asked him if yours were ready and he said they weren't. So then I asked him why he was so infernally slow, and he said he'd written to you about them and got no answer. Didn't you get his letter?"

"I believe I did, but I forgot to write back."

"My good chap, perhaps it has slipped your memory that we start on the second?"

"That's what I came to see you about. I'm not going."

"Not going to Colorado?"

"No."

"Why not?" Mark shrugged his shoulders. "But what are you going to do, then? You don't mean to stop on here in town by yourself?"

"No: but I can't get as far as Colorado. I simply haven't the energy. Besides, I want to go to Gatton. Bennet has been having trouble with a section of the men, and wants a free hand, which I don't propose to give him. Then there's the session coming on in January. It wouldn't give us much time."

"You knew all that a week ago," said Lawrence, staring at him. "You were keen enough then. What's put you off? What do you mean by saying you haven't enough energy?"

"Simply that, Lawrence. I've been out of sorts these last few days; nothing wrong, only fagged and out of sorts. I really don't feel up to the American trip. I'm sorry to throw you over, but if you don't want to go alone why not try to get hold of Considine? Last time I heard from him he seemed to be at a loose end."

"Because I swore I'd never take Considine on a shooting trip again. He always wipes my eye if he gets the chance, and he has a trick of firing down the line when he gets agitated which inspires me with deadly alarm. I like sport, but Considine is the limit."

"Hugo Wilson would jump at the chance."

" 'I—ah—never shoot with the same guns two seasons running. Bannatyne has a standing order to build me a pair a year.' " Lawrence, a born mimic, dropped swiftly into the classic Cambridge drawl. "Thank you."

"Sorry: I didn't mean to let you down." Mark was genuinely apologetic: he knew that Lawrence hated his own company, and he knew too, from long experience, that no finicking sportsman stood any chance of toleration. Had there been no second side to Lawrence Sturt's life the brothers would have drifted apart because they would have had nothing whatever in common, but the Mirabell of purple and fine linen whom fair ladies knew in town was a different man from the bearded ruffian, dirty and cheerful, for whom no days were too long and no conditions too severe. "Surely you can beat up another fellow between this and the second?"

"The time's so short. Besides"—Lawrence Sturt turned his black eyes again on his brother, and the cameo delicacy of his profile was drawn a trifle sharper—"the whole thing's so silly. You may be out of sorts now, but that's all the more reason for getting away. By the time you've crossed the Atlantic you'll be as fit as you were ten days ago, whereas if you knock about here doing nothing you'll only get more hipped every day of your life. Change is what you want. If you had been through it all as often as I have, you'd know what prescription to take."

"Through what all?"

Lawrence shrugged his shoulders. "How do I know your precise turn of vanity? You've been away with some woman, of course."

"Oh, have I?"

"And she's let you down, or you've had a fit of conscience, some rotten nonsense or other; and you think none of it ever happened to any one before. Go to Colorado, you ass! That's the worst of men like you; when the things that happen to everybody happen to them, they labor under the delusion that it's all quite novel and exciting. You come to Colorado and let her rip."

Mark laughed. He was amused, not so much by what Lawrence said, as by a snapshot imagination of what Lawrence would have said if the truth had been related to him. There was no man on earth to whom Mark would less willingly have confessed it. Lawrence Sturt was a natural cynic; he affected nothing and concealed nothing. He was very fond of his brother—more fond perhaps of Mark than Mark was of him—and he admired what he called the solidity of Mark's position and character, but Mark's attitude towards women inspired in him nothing but amusement. In his own attitude Lawrence was more French than English, for he was profoundly interested in women, and in the leisured intervals of roving their society was a necessity to him, but he never

lost the sense of sex, and though he had many women
friends they were not immune from pursuit. Several
such intimacies had come to an abrupt end—one way
or the other—by his unforeseen transition from friendship to passion; and this from pure neglect of the moral
issue, for to him passion was merely a coming to terms.
Preference of one man to another he could respect,
though he was inclined to share Donne's view of a con-
stant lover, but virtue in the abstract as a motive for
refusal moved him merely to derision in a man, and in
a woman to pity. Useless to resent his mocking coun-
sels; he did honestly think Mark a fool to let himself be
moved one step out of his way by any woman, whatever
the link might have been. However, nothing could have
thrown Lawrence out more effectively than Mark's short,
unwilling laugh, which made him doubt his own diagnosis;
the patient is not as a rule amused by the surgeon. He
shifted in his chair and reached for his pipe.

"I saw a friend of yours to-day—two, in fact; both
clamoring for your address. One was Father de Trafford. Met him in New Bond Street. Is it you that are
financing this new mission scheme of his?"

"Did he tell you so?"

Lawrence grinned. "Not precisely! I don't know
why the idea came into my head. But he was so overflowing with gladness that he kept me standing ten minutes in the sun and got a tenner out of me in the end.
I hate chucking my money away on charity, but one
can't help admiring de Trafford though he is a priest.
After all it's better form to keep oneself in order. Some
o' these days I shall chuck up everything and turn Carthusian monk. You see if I don't."

"Oh, I think not."

"You may be right. So then I went a bit farther on
and ran up against Jenny Essenden, in half mourning—

Field died at Nice, you know—and looking prettier than ever. She really is what I call a pretty woman. Well, she was asking after you too. I didn't know you knew her."

"I don't, except that I was stopping in the same hotel when Field had his first attack of hemorrhage. Naturally one had to see something of her in the circumstances. Field wanted a lot of looking after, and the hotel people tried to kick up a row, and Jenny behaved as one would expect her to behave. Then his mother came out to look after him, and Jenny moved on. She went back to him when he got better, though. She was a pretty woman, as you say."

"*Is* a pretty woman," Lawrence corrected him. "Black and white suits her; lovely brunette skin she has. She's at a loose end now, I fancy. She was annoyed when I couldn't tell her where you were. I don't think she believed me."

He made Mark Sturt throw back his head and laugh like a schoolboy. "Lawrence, you are impossible! Take her on yourself—these adventures don't happen to me."

"H'm. What about Miss Archdale?"

"Miss Archdale?" Mark repeated. He had rarely been so taken by surprise, but he was not gun-shy, and his face expressed nothing but surprise and some faint annoyance. "What on earth do you mean?"

"I suppose you never look at a woman with your eyes open." Lawrence stooped to strike a match on the heel of his boot. "But I think I pointed out to you before that it's precisely you fellows who never look at a woman—well, of all the touchy beggars! 'Ten rounds rapid,' hey? My good Mark, if you don't want to know what I mean, why ask?"

"How on earth was I to know you meant anything so idiotic?" Mark retorted; but, irritation overborne by curiosity, he was weak enough to add, "Besides, you saw ten times more of her than I did. It was not I who sculled her up the river!"

Lawrence regarded him fixedly. "No: and shall I tell you what she talked about? You, my young friend, you. I tried to head her off, because I could have found a more amusing topic of conversation than the feats which you didn't perform in the Andes, but it was no go, though I pointed out to her that my own achievements were really rather creditable. So I gave her, two-pence colored, that famous spill on the Horcones corniche, as the first and last time on that expedition when you kept your head and your footing: and, I give you my word, when you cut the rope between yourself and Mathias the lady was as white as my shirt."

"Oh, rot," said Mark, feigning a yawn.

He swung himself to his feet. "Good night. I'm sorry to have had to throw you over, but it's unavoidable. Gatton is good enough for me just now. If you bar going alone you might take Mrs. Essenden—what?"

"What's the matter with your arm?"

"Scorched it," said Mark, letting himself out of the door. He paused to add, with ribald indifference to truth or even probability, "So now you know why I can't go to Colorado, don't you?"

CHAPTER VIII

L AWRENCE and Mark Sturt were the twin sons of
a North of England ironmaster and his beautiful
Cornish wife. Bridget Sturt—she was Bridget Saltau
before she married—died when her sons were three years
old; Mark retained a faint memory of her, from Lawrence's mind her image had vanished as a reflection van-
ishes out of a mirror. Mrs. Sturt had not loved her
husband, and she died partly of heart failure after in-
fluenza and partly because she found the business of
life too fatiguing to be carried on any longer. Even her
beautiful boys could not reconcile her to the necessity
of satisfying Arthur Sturt's demands.

It was from her that Lawrence derived both his looks
and his temperament. Mark was more like his father,
though in him too a strain of Celtic softness crossed the
hard uncompromising stock of the Sturt family. Arthur
Sturt liked to call himself a tradesman, and a tradesman
he was, but on a grand scale. Born of an old North of
England family, but younger son to a younger brother, he
had settled in a Derbyshire dale where land was cheap
and waterpower plentiful and had built up for himself
a business which made his name known far and wide.
"Sturt's Patent Reaper and Binder" was now gathering
sheaves across half Canada, while "Sturt's Patent Plow"
eared the fertile acres of the Cape. A town had sprung
up round the foundry, a small kingdom in which Arthur
Sturt was king; he had the knack of handling men, and
it was his one secret vanity that among his employees

123

there had never been a strike. Trouble had come near
more than once, but had been averted by prompt and
personal action. Gatton loved Arthur Sturt, whom it
called "The Squire"—a queer nickname for the autocrat
of a manufacturing center, but justified by his tall figure,
fresh color, and blue eyes, as well as by his love of long
tramps, gun on shoulder, and his easy seat in the saddle,
and the endless anecdotes told about his genial ways.
That these anecdotes were deceptive—that the man who
traded on the Squire's reputed geniality would speedily
regret his little error—were the facts on which the
Squire's popularity was solidly based. He would have
been called "soft" for his Tudor friendliness and ac-
cessibility if Gatton had not early felt the Tudor grip
of steel. The stern resolute man, hard as the rock of
his own fells, would have made a slave-driver whose
slaves never mutinied. In command of English labor
he used different methods, certainly, but much the same
spirit; absolute fearlessness, absolute inflexibility, absolute impartiality between their claims and his own.

Perhaps it was in this last quality that his strength lay.
It is said that there is no such thing as commercial
honesty in England to-day, but Arthur Sturt was cynically
honest, for he never lied, never broke his word, never
took a secret or unfair advantage,. never abused the
power of his capital, never overlooked or forgot a cheat,
and was so entirely devoid of the Christian grace of forgiveness that he liked no sport better than the hounding
down of the man who tried to cheat him. It may be
added that he was an indefatigable worker. He did not
marry till he was fifty, and up to the time of his marriage he lived in a red brick villa within half a mile of
the works; when it was represented to him that Bridget
Saltau could not be transplanted from Saltau Avery to
a red brick villa, he bought up Longstone Edge, hill and

dale, lock, stock, and barrel, and settled the estate and the sixteenth century manor house which bears its name upon her and her eldest son after her, but he continued to motor in to Gatton every day.

After Mrs. Sturt's death he became even more devoted to his business than before. He had certainly loved his wife; whether he realized that she had never loved him and that his marriage had been a failure it was impossible to say, for he never spoke of her. His energies were all concentrated on the expansion of Gatton, on the development of new enterprises, and on the acquisition of land, which he bought up right and left, chiefly for building purposes, while politics of the Chamberlain school provided distraction for his leisure hours. Lawrence and Mark were looked after by nurses and governesses in their tender years; at the age of ten they were packed off to a preparatory school; Stonyhurst followed. For their first sixteen years of life their intercourse with their father was confined to state meals on Sundays, state attendance in the Catholic chapel, and an occasional state interview in the study—for Mr. Sturt was a believer in the educational value of a sound thrashing, and the ferulas they got at Stonyhurst were mild in comparison of the paternal riding whip. Looking back on his youth, when he was old enough to contrast it with that of other boys, Mark supposed that it had been in some ways a Spartan discipline; but he was too healthy and happy to be conscious of any want at the time, for he loved the tradition of the old Catholic school, the daily Mass, the yearly Retreat, the sodalities, the rich setting of hill and woodland, and the immense playing fields, and the unusual clash of rank and type and age which under the segregating atmosphere of the older Faith made of the place a microcosm a little apart from non-Catholic England; while in the vacations, if there was no petting at Longstone Edge, there were guns and horses and an extraordinary range of freedom.

Throughout these early years the brothers were closely and tenderly linked; they did everything together, and were never happy out of each other's society. Gradually, however, they began unconsciously to develop individual tendencies and to drift apart, and by the time they passed into the Higher Line each had his own set, and interests which diverged ever more widely. Mark's bosom friend was little Guy de Trafford, a born saint under all his devilry; Lawrence, a born rebel, led a movement which dignified itself by the name of Free Thought, though its more obvious badges of union were smuggled cigarettes. Mark was more bookish than Lawrence, and Lawrence was a keener sportsman and more adventurous than Mark; more popular also than Mark, who masked, in his later teens, a paralyzing shyness under a front of indifferent calm. The Sturts were a military family, and Mr. Sturt had meant to put both his sons in the army, but, to the astonishment of his father, Lawrence at seventeen, politely insubordinate as usual, struck for Cambridge and the diplomatic service.

It was at this time that Arthur Sturt began to realize how little he knew of his children, but for the shrewd merchant prince it was not too late to repair the error, though the gulf is wide between a man of seventy and a boy of seventeen. It did not take him five minutes to decide that Mark was docile and that Lawrence was neither to hold nor to bind, and that Mark was a Catholic by temperament while Lawrence was not and probably never would be one even in name. Then Arthur Sturt went to Stonyhurst and had long talks with prefects and form-masters; what he heard interested him very much, perplexed him a good deal, and caused him to slap Lawrence on the back when they next met, and to eye Mark with imperfectly concealed mistrust. Lawrence was annoyed by the one demonstration, and Mark was hurt by the other. Decidedly the belated fatherhood of Arthur Sturt was working out on odd lines.

Mr. Sturt was a Catholic, but a Catholic of a lax type. He shrugged his shoulders over Lawrence, but, if Lawrence wished to go to Cambridge, to Cambridge he should go, though the air of a mixed university was not likely to foster a pining faith. But Mr. Sturt would have been more surprised than he was if he had known that the choice was dictated largely by a desire to get away from Mark. Twins! there was a hint of compulsion in the tie which annoyed the adolescent Lawrence. Were they to be expected eternally to do the same things in the same way? With his own serene candor, he put the case to Mark on the eve of their eighteenth birthday. "I am sick to death of you, Mark. Aren't you sick to death of me? Let us, for heaven's sake, get away from each other for a bit. It isn't our fault that we're twins, but it'll be our fault if we continue to be Siamese twins, and I propose to put a stop to it. What say you?"

"Don't know that I much care one way or the other," said Mark after pondering for a moment. "I don't particularly mind seeing you about, if that's what you mean." He paused, blew out a whiff of smoke, and looked up at his brother through the cloudy rings with a spark of laughter in his eye. "I don't particularly enjoy it either, if you come to that. Rather like a piece of furniture—what? A handsome wardrobe."

"Oh, that's how I affect you, is it?" said Lawrence. "Well, you affect me like an ugly wardrobe which gets in my way. Why do you say 'what' like that at the end of a sentence? Silly trick."

"You do it yourself. I didn't know I did."

"There you are again! We are alike: too much alike.

I could murder you, Mark, when you do the same things I do. I should like to punch your head."

"Try."

Lawrence looked longingly at his brother. "Will you really? Nothing would please me more, but I didn't think you were sportsman enough. With or without the gloves?"

"Without."

They had forgotten that the schoolroom was over their father's study. Mr. Sturt, after listening for some minutes to the sounds overhead, came upstairs and found his sons engaged in a scientific and violent fight. He dragged Lawrence off—Mark desisted as soon as the door opened—and then standing between them illustrated a family idiosyncrasy by giving way to a gust of laughter. It was characteristic of the Sturts that they laughed when other people would not as a rule have been amused, and Arthur Sturt, iron founder, aged sixty-eight, made the room ring as he stood between the disordered twins. Mark had lost a front tooth, Lawrence had a black eye, both were streaming with blood.

"You idiotic young puppies!" said Mr. Sturt as soon as he could speak, "shake hands, will you? or I'll knock both your heads together. You won't? Yes, you will, my lads. Come! Enough nonsense. Mark, you have more sense than t'other one." Mark, after a brief struggle with himself, held out his hand. "Now, Lawrence, will you have the goodness? No hanging back when the other fellow leads the way. Gentlemen don't do it." Lawrence obeyed sulkily. "Now, no more of this: d'ye hear?"

"Why didn't you let us fight it out, sir?" said Lawrence, with his handkerchief at his nose. "We'd hardly begun. And there were lots of arrears."

"Why did you choose the room over my study for

your battle-ground, young ass?" said his father, strolling
to the door. "Might have gone down to the stables—
what?"

His conclusion was that on the whole it was as well for
the lads to be separated for a year or two.

Lawrence shone at Cambridge. That is to say, he became President of the Union, and got his rowing blue.
In the intervals of these pursuits he read for the Modern
Language Tripos, and, more to his own than to his tutor's
surprise, was "allowed a pass." Mr. Sturt did not seem
to mind much, nor did he grumble when Lawrence's bills
began to come in; tailors' bills, wine merchants' bills,
livery-stable bills, hotel bills, garage bills—it really seemed
as though Lawrence in the three years of his University
career had taken an oath not to waste a farthing of his
large allowance on any account which could be left or
induced to run on. The total was startling—it mildly
surprised even Lawrence; but Mr. Sturt paid it without
turning a hair. Indeed he had small right to complain,
for he had turned a deaf ear to the tutorial warnings
which began to rain on him while Lawrence was still a
freshman. Mr. Sturt had come up each year for the
Mays, and had satisfied himself that Lawrence was
playing through his University days *en prince,* handsome,
brilliant, merry, and beset by friends. Mark meanwhile,
being put down for an infantry commission, had a much
less shining and expensive career at Sandhurst, and came
out of it with superfluous honors and a tinge of melancholy in his eyes.

It was about this time that it became plain that Mr.
Sturt, in his old age, was growing very fond of his elder
son. He kept a tight hand over Mark, even in the matter
of an allowance, and since Mark paid his debts the dis-
parity between the twins was still wider than it was

meant to be. At this time indeed the brothers were
farther apart than ever before or after, for the difference
of position accentuated the difference in temperament;
Mark, modest by nature, malleable by training, depressed
by want of encouragement, and painfully conscious of
being the poorest subaltern in his regiment, was forced
back more and more on his own stoic pride, while in
Lawrence on the contrary Mr. Sturt's wayward favors,
acting on a headstrong will and ardent passions, pro-
duced sheer license of speech and act. Mark went shabby
to pay his mess bills and sold his hunter to meet the
subscriptions which drain a young officer's purse; while
Lawrence was off to Paris and Vienna, nominally to
study languages, in reality to have as gay a time as
Europe can offer to gilded youth. The severities of
training, coupled with a nice dislike of cheap fruit, had
kept him moderately straight at Cambridge, but in France,
behind the smart Ministerial gateways and within the
gray old doors of the Faubourg Saint-Germain, which
were unlocked for him by the letters of his relatives,
the young man's *éducation sentimentale* went forward
apace. Meantime the brothers continued to see nothing
of each other till the cataclysm of the war tore up the
order of their lives and threw them again across each
other's path.

Long before the crisis, Lawrence was back in England
clamoring for a commission. He had got a hint of what
was coming, and he cursed himself—in fluent German—
for having risen from the table where so great a game
was to be played. Luckily it was not too late to pick up
the cards—as a University graduate and ex-lieutenant of
the Officers' Training Corps he was still eligible for
Sandhurst, and Arthur Sturt, hot-blooded as any boy,
wrote off post-haste to claim the nomination which his
old friend Lord Vere had promised him long ago, and

which, alas! he had not cared to claim for Mark. Nevertheless, do what Lawrence would, Mark had the start of
him. Mark was sent immediately to the front, landing
at le Hâvre in the early days of August, when nine-
tenths of England did not know that a man had left her
shores; a subaltern in a line regiment, he went through
all the horrors of the great retreat, dreamed his dream
at Vitry-le-François when the tide turned, and left his
youth between Meaux and Soissons, when stubborn flight
collected itself into grim advance, and the Germans were
hammered back at ten miles a day over bridgeless rivers
and treeless fields and roads aflash with discarded shells
and accouterments and smelling of dead horses and men.
Early in October Lawrence came out with a draft of
reënforcements, and chance threw him straight across
Mark's path. They met in a village street after a nameless action, linesman and guardsman, both mud from
head to heel, both deaf with the roar of the guns, both
reeling with exhaustion.

"Hullo, Lawrence!"

"Hullo, Mark!"

"You're lucky to get out here so soon."

"Lucky for you fellows too, ain't it?"

"Oh, we're all right now. How's father?"

"So-so. You look a bit pallid—anything wrong?"

"No, only a raving headache from those infernal guns.
You haven't a cigar to spare, have you?"

"Masses. Here, you can have all these."

"Oh, I say, can you really? Oh, thanks most awfully!
My kit has gone astray. You couldn't let me have a
clean shirt, could you, and a tin of Keating's, while you
are about it? Oh, good! Bring 'em round to-night, I'm
in the *pâtisserie* shop over there with half a chimney.
'By."

There were many such meetings.

During the death-wrestle of October and November Lawrence saw a good deal of Mark, for it so fell out that their regiments held adjacent strips of line by Ypres, and in the disintegration and confusion of the British forces there came one desperate day when the brothers found themselves firing side by side with a miscellaneous collection of cooks and servants behind them. Then the line was shortened, and they were thrown apart, to meet again on the eve of La Neuve Chapelle. But Mark's military career was cut short at St. Éloi, and it was when the roll was called and Mark was missing that Lawrence for the first time realized that after all, in spite of that trick of saying "what?" he loved his brother. He refused to believe that Mark was dead, he hoped that Mark had been taken prisoner. Two days later he learned from a captured Saxon that an English officer was lying wounded but still alive, half-buried in a shell pit between the lines—a very tall man, a lieutenant of the Derbyshires. The Saxons had tried to get him in, but the place was cross-swept by a tempest of artillery fire and raked by snipers, and after losing two men in the attempt they had given it up. Lawrence got his prisoner to point out the exact spot; it was close to the German lines. He had to wait till dark—such dark as was left by star-shells and pistol-flares; and he refused to take a stretcher-bearer with him; he would risk his own iron nerve and iron sinews, but no other man's. Luck befriended him, and he came reeling back with the wreck of a human form on his shoulders five minutes before a false alarm of the German gunners pounded that particular spot of ground where Mark and two dead comrades had been lying into empurpled mire.

It was Mark's luck that he should be out of the rest of the fighting; he was insensible when Lawrence brought him in, insensible (happily for him) in the horse ambu-

lance which covered the rutty roads behind the front,
insensible in the train to the base except for red intervals when he listened to his own moans and pitied the
poor beggar who was having such a devil of a time.
Two months he lay at Boulogne, and Lawrence, chafing
in the trenches while the spring flowers came out in
war-scarred cottage gardens, thought every day to hear
that his brother had gone west. But Mark was very
strong, and the youth in him locked fast hold on life; and
when he went west at length, late in May, it was in the
blue swinging cot of a hospital ship.

Mark never forgot his home-coming. Longstone Edge,
like many another manor house of less and greater pre-
tensions, flew the Red Cross flag from the beginning of
the war; it was transformed into a convalescent home
for wounded officers, and by the aid of a little wire-pull-
ing Mr. Sturt managed to get his own son sent to him as
soon as the military hospital relaxed its grip. It was
two o'clock in the morning when the Red Cross ambu-
lance drew up before the lighted entry, and Mark—
still a stretcher case, after all those racking weeks—
was lifted out by the orderlies. He looked up and saw
his father's tall spare figure standing in the porch, the
dark hair much grayer than it had been a twelvemonth
before, the shrewd eyes surrounded by a network of
wrinkles. Shrewd as those eyes were, they traveled over
Mark's face without a gleam of recognition. It was not
till Mr. Sturt had watched the last case out of the van—
not till he had felt the shock of disappointment and
anxiety—not till he had turned back into the hall for a
despairing second survey, that he recognized Mark's quiz-
zical smile. And then Arthur Sturt could not find words
for a moment. Essentially a fair-minded man, he had
always meant to hold the scales level between his two
sons, and yet when the news came of Mark's almost

mortal wound his instant, mute, irrepressible cry had been, "Thank God it isn't Lawrence." He would not have let Lawrence lie at Boulogne two months, nor yet two weeks, without going over to see him. And now he stood by Mark's side—he a man of seventy, still full of health and vigor—and there lay Mark, prostrate, helpless as a child. The young man was very much moved by the sight of his father's emotion. He held out his hand, the large, long-fingered hand of a powerful man, bloodless now, and so weak that he could hardly lift it. "Well, my boy," said Mr. Sturt in his coolest tones, "glad to have you home again. We'll soon get you on your legs now, what?"

"Oh, yes," said Mark; and added, unaware of the turn his father's thoughts had taken, "I saw Lawrence last week, sir. He's put in for five days' leave, and he thinks he'll get it." Then he wondered why Mr. Sturt's reply came so sharply:

"Lawrence isn't the point. It's you we have to think about now, my son."

Later, when Mark was in bed in his own room, Mr. Sturt came in with the surgeon and stood by with his hands in his pockets while the dressings were changed. Poor Mark, for whom dressing-time was still a dark hour, could have dispensed with the paternal observation, but he had early learned to regard his father as the incalculable element in an otherwise stable world, and he held his tongue. "You've had a grueling," was Mr. Sturt's comment after the surgeon went. "Feel bad, eh?" He wiped Mark's wet forehead with his handkerchief. He had, and Lawrence inherited, the last talent that one would have expected to find in either of them—the wary, patient, and delicate fingers of the born nurse; but he was intolerant of the sick-room tact that conceals or evades.

Mark smiled with wry lips. "Rather sore, you know. Did Trent say if there's any chance of my being fit to go back?"

"Do you want to go back?"

"Yes. 'Hate leaving my men: Lawrence too."

"No chance of it, I'm afraid."

"Not before the show's over?"

"Not at all." The nurse was signaling to Mr. Sturt to be silent, but he ignored her. "Trent swears you'll never sit a horse again." Mark set his teeth on a cry: the shock was very great. The nurse, scarlet, fairly ordered Mr. Sturt out of the room. But he stooped over Mark and touched the young man's cheek with his lips —the incalculable element again. "Better know the truth —eh?"

"Trent's a damned fool," Mark gasped out.

"Think so? Better prove it, then," said Arthur Sturt with his dry smile. "You're a Sturt: you come of tough stock. But, go or stay, you've won your spurs, Mark. Run away for two minutes, my good girl. I've had a letter from your Colonel. God bless you, my boy. You've made me very proud of you."

It was Mark's natural luck to be invalided out of the Service which he loved; he proved Captain Trent a fool in the end, but it took him two years to do it, and when Lawrence came home in August on leave Mark was barely able to crawl about on crutches. It was Lawrence's luck that he went through the whole campaign without a scratch. What did seem strange to those who knew them both, and most strange to those who knew how much luck has to do with such rewards, was that it was Mark, not Lawrence, who won the cross for valor. What had he done? Till Lawrence told the tale, Mr. Sturt knew little more than was conveyed by the bald

official narrative of the War Office; indeed he hardly
knew as much as that, for the incident dated from
crowded days, and Mark had not taken much notice of
it at the time and had incontinently forgotten all about
it. But Lawrence Sturt told the story one summer evening on the lawn at Longstone Edge. Gallantry went
cheap in the autumn days from Mons to Ypres, when
more crosses were earned, perhaps, than were given in
the whole length of the war; but there was a bizarre
coolness about Mark's act which tickled his father's fancy.
Mark vainly swore that he had a revolver. "No, you
hadn't, old chap," said Lawrence, grinning down at him
in an immense fraternal amity. "Till you got past the
wood you had nothing but a cane. Tom Wentworth and
I were watching from the hill with field-glasses, and Tom
yelled to me, 'Who's the feller with the walking-stick?'
Then you slued the gun round and I saw the bandage
on your wrist and a large patch of red clay on your
trousers, and I yelled back, 'It's Mark,' and just then
we were ordered forward in support and poor old Tommy
only went about three yards before he toppled over. I
saw him going down on a stretcher when the fun was
over, so I went up to ask him how he felt, and the first
thing he said was, 'You ought to tell Mark to keep that
cane and cut his initials on it.' 'His initials?' I said.
'Yes,' said Tom, with a pallid grin, 'M.S.V.C.'"

Mark smiled. In all humility and sincerity he recognized, as most men do, that he had done no more to deserve the distinction than nine out of ten of his acquaintance who had not won it; and yet he did not undervalue
it or blind himself to its significance. Few men—very
few educated men—came out of the war the same as
when they entered it. Of these few Lawrence was one,
but not Mark; and perhaps even Lawrence would not
have escaped scot free but for the charmed life he bore,

immune amid the hottest fighting, though it must be owned that in point of good impressions Lawrence sick or well was a non-conducting medium. "Sir," said Arthur Sturt to his darling son on one unfortunate occasion when Lawrence was distinctly less dear than usual, "sir, you have not enough moral sense to cover a threepenny bit." But Mark, whose character, naturally reflective, had taken longer to set and harden, owed a great deal to that stern school, for it killed the diffidence in him and made him sure of himself. Gallantries in the heat of action win the conspicuous honors of war; Mark knew, Lawrence guessed, that a much more difficult courage had dictated Mark's conduct during those two days when he lay wounded between the lines.

"Did you know where you were?" Lawrence asked one night when they were alone."

"Pretty well," said Mark.

"Did you realize that you were within earshot of our trenches?" pursued Lawrence.

Mark did not answer, and Lawrence dropped the subject. For all his levity, it still turned him sick to think of that night—the glazed eyes, the death-mask features, the untended body ripped open by the slash of a bayonet from breast to flank . . . Difficult to associate that dying wreck with Mark! Yet it was Mark; and for the first twenty-four hours Mark must have had long periods of consciousness, when the temptation to call out for help, the help of his own side, must have been hard to subdue. He had subdued it; believing himself done for, he had lain without a cry, waiting for the death which came by inches, by a slow and foul agony, sooner than risk a comrade's life to save the fag-end of his own. For that, certainly, far more than for his bizarre adventure with the machine-gun, Mark deserved his cross.

Slowly, very slowly, Mark came back to health and

strength; it was a miracle that he lived at all, and he would not have done so had he not possessed not only an iron constitution but also iron nerves. Pain alone kept him awake, and when that eased off he slept like a child, long healing slumbers in which life seemed to be visibly flowing back into his broken frame; life mental as well as physical, for the Mark Sturt who lay on the lawn at Longstone Edge was saner and clearer-visioned than the madman who stormed the barricades of St. Éloi. He never consciously spoke of Renée. That he spoke of her in delirium he knew because one day Mr. Sturt asked abruptly, "Who is Renée, my boy?" but, though in most ways Mark was frank with his father, to that question he answered with gray unwavering eyes, "I don't know, sir." There are wounds of the spirit which can bear no human touch, and within this category fell Mark's fantastic, pure, and fleeting romance, sealed immortal by its bloody end. Yet the lacerated mind recovered with the lacerated body, for Mark, disciplined by the exhaustion of pain when he was too weak to feel anger, learned to see Renée's death in perspective as part of the general suffering caused by the war; and there came a day when he confessed to his director, "Father, I accuse myself of wishing to take revenge into my own hands."

When Lawrence took his second week's leave Mark was fairly on his legs, allowed a little mild golf and an occasional day's shooting, but his military career was at an end, for the army surgeons had certified that he would never cross a horse again. By the time Lawrence came home for good, Mark had ridden fifteen miles in a morning. But he was still leading an invalid life at Longstone Edge, dragooned by Mr. Sturt, whose blunt humorous tyranny stood on guard over Mark's chafing imprudence. "Good heavens, Mark," cried Lawrence, when Mark was

ordered to a sofa the first evening, "I wouldn't be kept
in leading strings if I were you!" "Aye, that's the line
to take," said the sardonic Arthur Sturt. "You always
were a sensible fellow, Lawrence." And Lawrence shut
up under that cold blue stare. He was immensely amused
and pleased to find himself snubbed in Mark's favor.

A month later Mr. Sturt sickened and died, after a
ten days' illness; died, holding the hands of his tall sons,
and smiling with easy reassurance into Lawrence's eyes.
The strings thus broken, it could be seen how well they
had done their work, for Mark, whom the medical world
had sentenced to a life of dependence, at once came
forward and took command of all business arrangements.
Lawrence, the brilliant and the hardy, shut himself up in
his room and wept. He was, in fact, perfectly useless;
he sobbed like a child at the funeral, and left Mark to
do the honors to a concourse of distinguished mourning
guests. "Just like Lawrence!" said Mark to himself by
the graveside; and as he drew his brother's hand through
his own arm he realized, as Lawrence had realized after
St. Éloi, that in spite of mutual irritation and impatience
the link of birth held fast. To the end of the chapter
Lawrence would go on thinking Mark slow and occasionally dense, while Mark was aware of a vein of emo-
tional weakness in Lawrence, but their qualities were
rather complementary than hostile, and the relation between them was rooted in mutual respect.

Mr. Sturt's will came as a surprise to both his children. That Longstone Edge would go to Lawrence they
had always known, and they had taken for granted that
the business and the bulk of the money would go with
it. But Mr. Sturt had other views. He explained in a
prefatory note that the English law of primogeniture had
always seemed to him less satisfactory than the French
system of equal division; and he left Gatton and all its

revenues unconditionally to his younger son, "because he may possibly develop business aptitudes, whereas my son Lawrence never will." Mark's impulse was again to protest; but when they came to look into matters he grew resigned. There was a great deal of money going; Mr. Sturt had made large gains, and his investments had turned out well. He was one of the first men to back the fortunes of the aeroplane, and the big sums put into a popular Flying School had proved a gold-mine. Gatton and all its future profits apart, there was enough left to make Lawrence a very rich man, richer than Mark; and besides Lawrence did not want Gatton, and frankly owned that if it had come into his hands he would have sold it to a syndicate. Mark did not precisely want Gatton either—he had had no business training, and he liked an active life. But facts spoke with a loud voice to Mark's ear, and there was no doubt about it that Gatton was a big fact. He took up the work where Arthur Sturt had dropped it, and for the next four or five years he had little leisure to repine.

When peace was signed, Lawrence resigned his commission, out of sheer boredom. He had enjoyed the war; there were few who could say as much. It had left him with a thirst for adventure which life in barracks could not satisfy. He had a passion for sport and exploration, and he was rich enough to indulge it. At first Mark was too busy at Gatton to see more of his brother than before the war, but when things got into train he formed the habit of accompanying Lawrence on his long trips to shoot strange beasts and climb strange peaks in the less habitable districts of the globe. When the wanderers returned their paths diverged—Lawrence took up his quarters in town, while Mark went back to keep an eye on Gatton. Years passed on, youth ripened into full manhood; presently the House of Commons beckoned, and Mark, almost before he knew what was happening, found himself member for his own division of the county. Gatton had brought him in, to his own surprise, with acclamation. It was all hard work, collar work, and Mark gloried in it. He liked labor for its own sake, and he forgot that he had ever been a soldier. He liked London too, and the society which swiftly opened to the young Northern member, a society which was ready to like him for the sake of his beautiful mother and his brilliant brother, not to speak of Sturt and Saltau relatives in all the Services. Was he ambitious? He had hardly time for it. His hands were always full of work, or full of play. When Parliament was up, there were markhor to be shot above Kashmir; and behind all else there was always Gatton with its swarming operatives, its complexities of procedure, its pressure of conflicting claims.

Mark did not run Gatton precisely on his father's lines. He kept it going for a year or two on the old footing, till he had mastered the working of the machine, and then having called together his lieutenants he told them that he was going to make a change. He had faith in an experiment which he was rich enough to carry out. He meant to run Gatton on a profit-sharing basis. There was opposition of course, but Mark had not fought through the Retreat for nothing; he knew his own mind and carried it through, paying no more attention to old Holmes, who prophesied the Bankruptcy Court, than to Lawrence, who jeered at him for a Socialist. He was vindicated by the issue, for, in the first place, Gatton on the new lines continued to pay as well as Gatton on the old, and in the second he focused the attention of his political neighbors on his doings; ambitious or not, this had formed no part of his plan, and he disliked it at first, but resigned himself to it because it was a fact, and ended by growing interested in his own position. He rarely thought about himself, but it was plain that a man of five and thirty, in control of a business as big as Gatton, and possessed of a competent fortune and a safe seat in the House, was a force to be reckoned with.

On his entry into public life Mark spoke little and modestly, but when problems came up for discussion in which he was directly interested—problems academic to three-fourths of the House, but to him the staple food of his most anxious thought—he began to make his voice heard, and it was a telling voice. Mark had by nature the "Parliamentary manner," so hard to acquire. He was clear, easy, humorous, pleasantly respectful to the chiefs on either side, but pleasantly tenacious of his own views. He was not visibly nervous, or not more nervous than the House likes a new hand to be. As he gained a firmer foothold, he developed an unexpected facility in debate. Lawrence, who did not admire his brother's usual oratorical style, changed his mind one night when he strolled into the Gallery by chance in time for a breeze. It was a peculiarity of Mark's position that the Conservatives called him a Fabian and the Socialists called him a Tory; it was the Labor men who were at him that night, and the skill and power of Mark's defense gave Lawrence great delight. As they drank their coffee together on the Terrace, and Mark accepted congratulations from authoritative quarters, the conviction came on Lawrence that his brother was on his way to a position in the great world—the world which acts and governs, as distinct from the world which watches and talks.

Even a Lawrence Sturt has his periods of reflection, and for ten minutes, while Mark stood apart talking to the Senior Whip, Lawrence lay back in his chair overlooking the dark, full-flowing river and reviewed the two lives, linked in the mystery of birth, passing on side by side from infancy to manhood. Or should one say to middle age? There was a touch of its gravity in Mark, bending his courteous head to catch the low tones of Hubert Grayson-Drew. Already custom lay on him

> with a weight
> Heavy as frost, and deep almost as life.

Behind him Mons and Ypres and St. Éloi, his wrecked soldier's career, long months on the brink of death, then Gatton, now Westminster . . . But Lawrence had escaped untouched; at thirty-five he was as handsome and as irresponsible as he had been at five and twenty . . . His was a generous nature, incapable of jealousy, but he had no illusions.

Grayson-Drew passed on, and Mark sat down again. His features expressed no elation, but some quiet confidence. He glanced at his brother, whose interests were notoriously non-political, with an apologetic smile. "Bored?" he inquired.

"Not I," said Lawrence. *"Je me dis mes vérités, mon bon."*

This was in the spring session before Mark met in with Maisie Archdale.

CHAPTER IX

"In her strong toil of grace."

MARK did not go to Colorado. He went to Gatton; not to Longstone Edge, though it was always at his service, but to Jack Bennet's bachelor villa within a stone's throw of the works; and for the next ten days an accumulation of business drove Maisie out of his head, for except when he snatched an hour off to share Bennet's bread and cheese lunch, or to run to earth an evasive grumbler, he was in his office from nine a. m. to eleven p. m., sifting papers, checking accounts, and interviewing an endless stream of callers. Mark hated officials. He could not now say, as Arthur Sturt had said once, that he knew every "hand" in the works by name, but he was not far off it, and it was still his rule that every man and boy had the right of personal appeal; and here his training as a company officer stood him in good stead, for he could get on terms with any type. Gatton was no industrial paradise—grievances were always cropping up; but it was indisputable that every grievance taken before Mark's tribunal would be investigated to the bottom, and despite the enormous power of class prejudice, and the sleepless grudge which the English proletariat bear against their capitalist employers, Gatton had a queer faith in "young Sturt's" justice. This the men had learned, that if two points came up for settlement Mark was as likely as not to give the lesser for and the greater against himself.

But when the pressure of work relaxed Mark found

144

himself very tired. Bennet, coming in late one evening from a dinner which Mark had declined, discovered his chief asleep on the sofa, and was struck, as Lawrence had been, by the change in him. Mark woke up heavy-eyed, and Bennet, whose relations with him out of office hours were unaltered from Stonyhurst days, opened fire from the hearth-rug. "I say, aren't you well? You look fagged to death."

"Headache," said Mark briefly.

"It strikes me you have too many headaches. You're getting as gray as a badger, Mark."

"Gray, am I?" said Mark, rather startled. He got up to look at himself in the glass overmantel (Bennet's furniture, like Bennet's clothes, was in shop taste, not his own). "So I am. And look at you with not a hair turned in your brown wig! I shall be going bald next, I suppose. I must look out for a hair restorer. I do get the most infernal heads, certainly." He leaned his forehead on his hand.

"Why not wire Captain Sturt that you'll join him after all?"

Mark involuntarily shook his head, and then took it between his hands with a groan. "Oh, you little devils! I bar croquet balls trundling to and fro between one's eyes, there isn't room for them. No, I can't go to America; I can't go so far out of the way. Besides, what do I want of a holiday? I've done no work since Easter. I was fit enough three weeks ago. I am fit now, if you come to that."

" 'Expect you ought to have lain up a few days with that arm of yours."

"Gone to bed! I think I see myself."

"Well, you might do worse, old man," said Bennet. "You look thoroughly run down. Shan't you go North for the twelfth? I would if I were you. Off your sleep, aren't you? I heard you walking up and down last night." He laid his hand affectionately on Mark's shoulder. To his astonishment it was impatiently shaken off.

"My health isn't on the books of the firm, thanks."

"I beg your pardon."

"I beg yours, Jack."

"Not at all," said Bennet stiffly. "Sorry I forgot myself. I won't again." He walked out of the room.

Bennet was a short-tempered man of dour Northern pride, and he had taken Mark's little fit of irritation for an official snub. Twenty years earlier Mark would have dashed after him and abased himself, but he could not do it now; the generous boyish impulse was as strong as ever, but stronger were the frost of custom and the shyness of middle age. Bennet was still stiff when they met at breakfast, and ten times it was on the tip of Mark's tongue to say, "Jack, after all these years, don't you know me better?" and yet he could not say it. How many of us are there who carry to our life's end the smart of some such trivial misunderstanding? But it was after this incident that Mark settled to go abroad. Irritable nerves are a dangerous luxury for men who keep the warm heart of twenty under the inelastic manners of thirty-five; moreover Mark, whom Lawrence called a sentimental Englishman, saw a chance of softening Bennet by an indirect apology—"I'm going to follow your advice and take a holiday. I was feeling rotten last night."

It was neither Gatton nor his own health that made Mark refuse to go to Colorado, but the feeling that he ought not to be out of reach of his wife. Mark had not seen Maisie since they parted on the Ushant platform. Their last night of storm remained fixed in his mind as having set a seal of tragedy on the checkered experiences of the week. How slowly the hours had passed as he sat by the dying fire and listened to the periodical chime of Maisie's clock and the ceaseless droning shriek of the wind! Why he did not yield was and remained to him a mystery; it was not from generosity, for every generous instinct urged him to yield. Mark had simply obeyed one of those edicts of the moral law which enforce themselves, with a sterner stringency than that of reason, on man's trembling heart and brain.

Towards morning, when dawn came late and sullen, the wind lulled, and the inner conflict wore itself out about the same time, and Mark dropped to sleep in his chair. But then came the dreary waking, when he was roused by her "Let me out, Mark": and he had to go and unlock the door like a jailer for her to pass out. How worn she had looked, she too, how white and fagged, as she went about her morning duties! She had not slept, perhaps, any more than he. She was too proud, and Mark too nervous, to reopen the night's broken explanations, and they talked lightly like strangers, at breakfast, in the dogcart, on the platform, till Maisie's train came in.

"Good-by, Mark."

"Good-by, my dear. You know where to find me if you want me."

"In Colorado? That is rather a long way off."

"I am not going to Colorado. My London address will always get me in twenty-four hours."

Mark fancied she was glad, but there was no time to say any more, and the train carried her away out of his life, it might have been forever. What a parting! She did not understand, and Mark was incapable of further explanation; it was one of his venomed torments that he had left her after all in the dark. What did she think of him? What does a woman in her heart of hearts think of a man's virtue? Mark winced when he tried to

estimate his wife's opinion of him. A saint may turn
his back on temptation; but Mark Sturt did not enjoy
the prerogatives of a saint. Mere men of the world have
no title to pretend to the insolences of virtue. It was
nothing short of an insult for a man of his class to refuse what a woman of the same class offered. And he
was dumb: he could not say, "I would give ten years of
my life to take you, but there is a fiery sword between
us which I dare not pass." The worst of it was that
Maisie was no believer in fiery swords.

Mark went to Normandy. He left Henham in charge
of the flat; he was tired of the routine of expensive European travel, and he meant to go to inns where the ideal
valet could not be expected to put up. He had a kindly
memory of certain small villages on the Seine which he
had visited once with Lawrence as a schoolboy on a
holiday, and he thought he would try whether by going
back to them he could recapture something of the schoolboy's happy inexacting mood. He fetched up at last ten
miles below Rouen in the little old-fashioned town of
Duclair, found a room for himself at a tavern on the
river, and strolled through the market—it was a Monday morning—to fetch his letters from the *bureau de
poste* and to buy six sous' worth of Reines-Claude, their
melting greenness scorched to gold and purple where the
sun had scarred them through the leaves. Then he came
back to the *terrasse* beside the shining Seine and settled
down to a pipe and a *consommation* with something
nearer to enjoyment than a sheaf of correspondence commonly inspires in a busy man. There was the usual drift
of business letters, charitable appeals, and cards of in-
vitation; out of them he weeded three or four envelopes
of a more private and promising aspect.

The first was from Lawrence, dated from "s.s. *Tran-
sylvania*, Liverpool Docks"; Lawrence wrote on the point

of starting, and with the usual grievance; rarely had
Mark received a letter from his brother which did not
air a grievance. This time Lawrence was annoyed because after ten days' delay he had not found any one to
take Mark's place: "you silly ass," he wrote, "but I am
avenged, because long before you get this you will be
sick to death of French cookery and wishing you had
not been a silly ass." Crowded into a postscript at the
bottom of the sheet, Mark read news which did, it must
be confessed, interest him faintly: "I ran up against
Mrs. Essenden again before I left and she had another
shot at your address. I foiled her. Effectively. But
she's a pretty woman." Mark whistled a pensive little
Spanish tune and thought, with a momentary touch of
sentiment, what a pretty woman Jenny Essenden had
been in Freddy Field's days, and at that moment the
idea crossed his mind, coming out of nowhere, that in
Jenny Essenden's case there would have been no flaming
sword. He could not have said why, unless it were that
Jenny was not worth any such heavenly attentions.

The next letter was from Father de Trafford, and ran
in a very different strain. The priest wrote, with a gay
confidence that disarmed indifference, freely about the
work that was being done with Mark's check; he spoke
of his meeting with Lawrence, "whose character fasci-
nates me. I sometimes wonder what is going to become
of him. It seems to me that he is as likely as not to end
in a monk's cell, but do not, my dear Mark, tell him I
said so. The likeness between you two is as perplexing
to a poor student of human nature as the unlikeness."
Mark thought of what Lawrence himself had said, but
did not, as most men would have done, conclude that
Lawrence had said it also to de Trafford; on the contrary, he had so rarely found the priest's penetration at
fault that he sat for five minutes trying to adapt his

own knowledge of his brother to this novel point of view. But he could not see Lawrence in the habit of a Carthusian.

The next letter he took up was a long intimate screed from Mrs. Ferrier, full of political news. Charles Ferrier represented his county with credit and indeed with intermittent distinction, but scandal said that his wife got up his speeches for him. At all events she was a keen little politician, and her letter was in some ways the most interesting of the three, because it brought Mark into touch with London life again. An important bill was coming on in the spring session, and Dodo wrote with acid humor of the intrigues behind the Front Benches. "I am glad you are not gone to Colorado," she said. "That is all very well for Lawrence, who is not and never will be an *homme sérieux*"—how about Father de Trafford and the cell?—"but for a man like you nowadays it really does *not* pay. Will you come to us for Christmas? We have Mr. Mallinson coming, whom you said once you would like to get to know personally, and I am sure it would be a good thing if you did. He and you are much of the same stamp and the same tradition. And they want new blood; and they want—want in both senses—some one trustworthy. Freville is their ablest among the younger men, and he has no money, and I don't think he's true to his salt; anyhow he drops so much on the turf that Mr. Mallinson is afraid of him. My own dear boy will never of course run steady in harness; his latest freak was to vote with the labor men on a snatched amendment one night when there were not fifty people in the house, and the faddists all but upset the applecart. When they reviled him he said he was very sorry but it happened to be a point of principle. Principle! As Mr. Grayson-Drew said to me afterwards, 'What can you do with a man who is capable of upsetting

the Government on a point of principle?" I told Mr.
G.-D. that I washed my hands of him, and he said
Charles was turning his hair gray. But you, old Mark,
would never turn a Whip's hair gray."

"No, my own instead," Mark thought ruefully. He
laid the letter on his knee and sat looking far out over
the Seine, whose dark glossy tide washed softly among
the reeds and loosestrife along the cobbled shore. South-
wards lay the town, eastwards upstream stretched a great
bend of river, going away into the distance round a
headland of rock and woody chalk bluffs white over the
dark leaves of August. Beating up against the current,
a trading vessel from the Piræus went by to Rouen, her
funnel banded with the black and white key-pattern ornament of old Greece, the waves of her wake slapping
lazily along stone pier or grassy bank. It was all fresh
and peaceful in the pale sunlight; and from the *Place*
came the human stir of the market and the barking of
dogs and the tolling of church bells, levity and piety
tempered together into the pleasantly skeptical bonhomie
of rural France. Mark's wedding night under the stars
seemed very far away.

He returned to Dodo's letter. "It is dull here till the
shooting begins. So far no one else has turned up except
Harry Forester and Miss Archdale, who came on together from the Beningfields. I wonder whether they
will make it up after all? I half hope they will, for I
like her very much, and she seems to me to be very unhappy. Perhaps that is partly why I like her. I used
to think one would never get far with her because she
was too prosperous to want a friend, but now I think
she is not a bit happy, and after all there are not many
men as lovable as Harry Forester. Every one says . . ."

"Oh, the devil they do!" said Mark. He crushed the
unfinished sheet into his pocket; he could not stand any

more of Dodo's gossip just then. But the peace of the morning was scattered, and he caught up his hat and stick and prepared to go for a walk—and the first person he saw when he stepped out into the cobbled street was Jenny Essenden.

She was lying back at ease in a big gray car, her silk-coated toy Yorkshire terrier perched on her knee, her small French hat and flying veil tipped at a rakish angle over her small head. Jenny Essenden was a very pretty woman. She was definitely out of the world; but she held a record of her own. She was not poor, and had never been poor as far back as her history was common knowledge. She was not to be had for the asking— still less for a price. Poor Field, who died at Nice, was not a rich man, but Jenny had stayed by him faithfully to the bitter end, and since his death rumor connected her name with no other. It would be going too far perhaps to say that she had principles, but at all events she had tastes, which served to some extent the same purpose. She had a graceful manner too, a manner which easily passed the searching observation of servants and hotel proprietors. The host of Mark's inn was standing bareheaded by the door of the car, evidently unaware of any peculiarity in Mrs. Essenden's position, and she was speaking to him with her pretty infantine graciousness—but she broke off when she caught sight of Mark. "Mr. Sturt! How nice to see somebody one knows! Are you staying here?"

"Yes, for a day or two. Are you?"

"No, indeed, I'm in my own château. What can you be doing in a tiny place like this—penance for your sins?" Mark smiled, but did not answer; he had early decided that there is far less necessity for answering questions than people commonly suppose. "I heard you were going to Colorado."

"So I was; but I didn't go. I think my brother Lawrence must have poured out that grievance to you when you met him in town."

Mrs. Essenden never opened a book and could not write a note without a slip in spelling, but beyond these educational limits she was as little of a fool as it is possible to be. She met Mark's eyes and laughed out merrily. "He did tell me that, and another friend of yours told me that you were going to Normandy. Does it seem shameless of me to run you down like this when you want to get away by yourself? But it really is an accident. I can't help it if Duclair is only a few miles from my dear château, can I?"

"Who told you I was going to Duclair?"

"That very delightful person, Father de Trafford."

Mark involuntarily opened his eyes. "I didn't know you knew him."

"Saints and sinners always meet," said Jenny. "Well, now, tell me what you were going to do before you met me. Tweeds and a straw hat, let me see: had you any excitement on? I can't guess."

"I was going for a walk."

Her face of unaffected dismay made Mark laugh again. "A walk? You like walking? *Mon Dieu!* Drive with me instead. I don't hesitate, now, to press you, because no one could possibly like walking better."

"You are very kind," said Mark with a touch of formality. "But won't you lunch with me to-day? I had hoped you would give me that pleasure."

"At that little tavern? No, my friend; I would do much to give you pleasure, but there are limits to my benevolence. Come, get in; see, Fifi is making a pretty face at you—you can't refuse a lady."

Mark got in, feeling and indeed looking a little resigned; but his resignation was cheerful compared with

that of Monsieur Védie, who had followed a good deal
of the conversation, and had certainly not missed the
significance of the wave of the hand with which Jenny
flicked his tavern from her horizon. Such were Jenny's
courtesies all too often, sweet in the mouth but leaving
an after-taste of bitterness. The car shot away, and
Monsieur Védie retired to console himself with a *petit
verre;* Jenny lay back on her cushions, and Mark, taking
an easy attitude by her side, allowed himself to be
amused. After all, Lawrence was right—Mrs. Essenden
was a very pretty woman. With the ingratitude of men,
Mark was the more ready to pick holes in her prettiness
because she had followed him to France; but how few
there were to pick! How like a roseleaf was the texture
of her rounded cheek! and how bright her eyes were,
under the shadow of that rakish little hat!

The car raced on through the warm and sunny countryside, and Mark unbent more and more. After all it
would have been mere folly to play the saint with Jenny,
who, poor dear, would have languished under moral
criticism like a flower bewildered in an east wind. They
lunched together on a shining balcony in Caudebec,
fetched a wide circle, and returned a little before sunset
to Jenny's château, which Mark saw for the first time
dark against the golden evening light. A long valley
winding between forested heights; a stream, the clear
Clérettes, flowing down to the Seine through meadows
gray after hay-harvest, where high-arched elms, grouped
as Claude le Lorrain would have grouped them, extended
their long shadows with the penciled effectiveness of art;
gates of lace-like ironwork under a covert of beechwood;
and then the strange broken façade of Clères itself, me-
dieval manor raised on wreck of Norman fortress, glowing like a jewel in rose-red plaster and black timber and
stone bastion, among rose-gardens and firwoods, under

the sunset gold. Mark fell silent as the car turned in
under the poplar avenue. In him as in Lawrence, though
neglected and repressed, there ran a pretty strong vein of
the passion for beauty, and this old French château, dim
with ghosts and perfumed of rose-leaves, appealed to
him with a heady melancholy, a refined and sensuous
charm. Subtle Jenny saw it and sank her voice. "Isn't
it," she whispered, "an unhappy place, my château? All,
all dead! The race are extinct, after six hundred years.
—Come, I give you thirty-five minutes before the soup."

She sprang out: and Mark was led away to his room
by an English servant of such distinguished mien that
Mark wondered if he could be aware of the irregularity
of Mrs. Essenden's position. The chamber itself was a
pleasant novelty after Ushant, and Gatton, and the Trois
Piliers. Mark bathed at leisure under the rosy fire of
sunset, and wished he had brought his evening clothes
with him, though Jenny had assured him that she liked
him best in tweeds. When he was ready to go down, the
man-servant reappeared bearing a tiny cup on a tray.
Mark took it mechanically; but a liking for a thimble-
ful of black coffee by way of *apéritif* is not common
enough to be gratified by chance, and Mark as he drank
it looked curiously down into the sober honest face.
"How do you know I like coffee before dinner?" he
asked.

"I have waited on you before, sir, when you didn't
bring a valet of your own. I was in service with Mrs.
Desmond for two years."

"You know me, then?"

"Yes, sir."

"Wonderful head you must have. Well, do you think
you could find me a clean handkerchief?"

"There are some in your drawer, sir."

"Oh, ah—thanks," said Mark, taking the loose fol'·

of fine linen from Carter's speckless hand: and he strolled
downstairs feeling very fresh and comfortable, and saying to himself that Mrs. Essenden's valet was all a valet
should be.

So, he soon discovered, was Jenny's dinner: and so
(within her limits) was Jenny herself. Good as the
wine was he did not linger over it, but came out to join
his hostess on the terrace in the twilight, while the bats
"on leathern wing" flitted and wheeled over the dewy
lawn, and the firwoods on the hillside opposite were
relieved like a frieze of black fern-leaves against the
honey-colored west. Jenny was half sitting, half lying
among green cushions on a gilt couch, and Mark pulled
up a chair and sat down near by. But she was disinclined for talk, it seemed; she signed to him to help
himself to a cigarette, and then she lay very still, her
long eyelashes tangling over her bright eyes, her bosom
scarcely rising and falling with her quiet breath. She
was in a black dress, graceful and flowing; and it flashed
across Mark's mind by a freak of memory that she was
more modestly dressed than Maisie would have been of
an evening. Mark smiled to himself and Jenny looked
up and caught him.

"What are you thinking of? No—*whom* are you thinking of?" she amended swiftly.

"Do you imagine," Mark answered, lazily and not
too respectfully courteous, "that when one is in Mrs.
Essenden's company one ever thinks of anything but
Mrs. Essenden?"

She colored vividly. "Ah, you think that sort of
answer is good enough for me! No, don't apologize,"
for Mark, startled, was trying to do so. "One can never
unsay oneself, can one? And I deserved it for asking
you questions, which I know you hate."

"How do you know I hate it?"

"Because you're so intensely reserved, of course. I never knew any one so reserved as you are; I don't believe you could give yourself away if you tried."

With many men this would have been a useful opening. Mark spoiled the effect by listening in a contented silence. The content was due to the excellence of Jenny's cigarettes.

"Besides," said Jenny, trying another tack, but rather at random, "it's a family trait. Your brother hates it too. He's a very interesting man, your brother Lawrence"—strange how Jenny's view agreed with Father de Trafford's!—"though infinitely less interesting than you are, Mr. Mark; but it's difficult to get anything out of him if he doesn't want one to." She added with a funny little grin, "Addresses, for instance."

"Mine, for instance," Mark assented. "By the bye, I didn't grasp how you came to hear of it from Father de Trafford. Who told you I knew him?"

"Captain Sturt."

"Did he? ('I foiled her.' Oh, Lawrence!) When was that?"

"Oh, ten days ago; before he went to Colorado. He dined with me one night," Mrs. Essenden's eyes were dancing, "and I—I'm afraid I pumped him. But I don't think he found it out. You haven't heard from him yet, I suppose? Men never write to each other, do they?"

"Oh, my brother's a great correspondent; in fact I heard from him this morning, and he mentioned having met you, but he didn't say anything about Father de Trafford."

"I'm sure he never thought of it," said Jenny merrily, "and yet it was very easy. Oh, I didn't say anything to compromise you, Mr. Mark! I know what dangerous people priests are to meddle with. I went to Father de Trafford on my own affairs, and then I just spoke of

you as having been very kind to me, and I said I should
have liked to write and thank you if you hadn't gone to
America . . . are you shocked?"

"Not a bit," said Mark. In point of fact he was gratified, as was Jenny's desire; but he was also—and this
was by no means Jenny's desire—faintly startled and
restless. Lawrence—Father de Trafford—Carter, who
knew his ways—even the coffee and the handkerchiefs—
why, what a web it was that had been spun about him!
More than half accident? For a moment, till he thought
of the château itself, which could hardly have been rented
and staffed in ten days, he wondered if accident had had
any hand at all in bringing Mrs. Essenden to Duclair.
But it was a lovely evening, Jenny's chef knew his trade,
and . . . Jenny's tokay was so delicate, after the *vin
ordinaire* of the Trois Piliers, that Mark had taken perhaps a little more than his usual temperate allowance.
His nerve was cool and his hand steady; it took more
than an extra glass or so of tokay to throw Mark off his
balance; but he was disposed to look with a lenient eye
on the slips of a pretty woman who flattered his vanity.
"Not a bit," said Mark. "But, I say, Mrs. Essenden, why
did you want my address?"

She looked up, clear-eyed. "I don't know. I just
sort of thought I should like to see you again, that was
all. You were so very kind to me when poor Freddy
was ill. I never have had anything to do with illness,
and I hate it and I'm afraid of it; but I was fearfully
sorry for my poor Freddy, and I did so want to help
him, and you—somehow—showed me the way."

"*I* showed you the way to help Field?"

"Yes. You were so gentle with him, and you·seemed
to know just how best to manage him. I thought then
that if ever I were very tired of everything I should like
you to be gentle to me in the same way, Mr. Mark. You

never seem to be afraid of anything yourself, and I'm afraid of—oh, ever such a lot of things. Death, for instance."

Mark rose, tossing away his cigarette, and folded his arms along the high carved balustrade. He had first to clear away the trails of red Chambéry roses that had twined their thorny sprays in and out among the carving, and the scent of crushed petals mixed its incense with the damp breath of the woods. And now that he was no longer watching her there came a subtle change of expression into Mrs. Essenden's face. Dark against the clear night sky, either artist or sportsman would have admired Mark Sturt's heavy frame, broad of shoulder, lean of flank, essentially a male type, destructive and creative; and so Jenny admired him; her eyes fastened on him with a peculiarly hungry look.

"Listen to the Angelus in the valley," she said. There was no harmony between her musical voice and her eyes. "You are a good Catholic, aren't you, Mr. Mark? And I'm a very bad one. Some day I shall repent, and confess my sins, and be good ever after, but I don't want to do it just yet. I want to sin a little more first."

"But you are not a Catholic, are you?"

"Oh, yes, I am," Jenny answered. "One of my other lovers converted me."

"How old are you, child?" asked Mark roughly.

"Twenty-five."

Two years older than Maisie. Mark was silent.

"It is the only faith to die in," Jenny ran on softly. "And I'm fearfully afraid of death. Not now, you know —not while you're here; but when I'm alone. I stuck to Freddy till the end, he died in my arms, but I hated it all the time. Of course that was horrid of me; still I did stick to him. But afterwards I was tired—oh, so tired! So then I thought I'd come away by myself and be quiet, but that didn't pay either. Women like me can't afford the luxury of their own company, there are too many ghosts. Am I boring you?"

"No," said Mark. She was in fact sending him to sleep; but he was not bored. Under the low, lulling voice a hint of dead passions glimmered like wreckage in shoal water, and Mark was not one of those men for whom sea peril has no lure. He liked his company. It did not strike him that he stood in any real danger; after fourteen years' immunity, after the fight at Ushant, he was not afraid of such a thing as Jenny Essenden.

Jenny knit her brows: he was difficult—she liked him for it. She had been almost as much attracted by Lawrence Sturt as by Mark, but she had fixed on Mark because Lawrence was to be had for the asking.

"Not that I want to pretend I'm sorry about anything," she said with a light laugh. "I'm sorry Freddy died, but I'm not a bit sorry for the rest of the incident. I'm not one of those dreary ladies who lose their money on both sides of the bet. Virtue may be a pretty person—I haven't the least desire to make her acquaintance: mine also is *le beau rôle,* and I'm sure it's much more amusing. Oh, here comes Riché. Now I want you to tell me what you think of this chartreuse. I took over the cellar with the château, and they told me great things of it; and Riché and I would like your opinion."

"First-rate, if it's like your tokay," said Mark. He held it up to the light; the bubble-fine Venetian glass was as precious as the green dew within it. "First-rate it is! No, no more, thanks."

"But you can leave the tray," said Jenny; and then as the servant withdrew, "Riché is pleased. He said he was sure you were a connoisseur. He is such a nice man—so trustworthy: you might say just a word to him about it if you get the chance. I always seem to be so lucky with my servants," she added merrily. "I wonder why."

Mark did not answer, but by his kindly eyes Jenny knew that another subtle stroke had gone home. Fifi bundling down the terrace, an animated mat of curls, to subside with snufflings of deep affection in the crook of Jenny's arm, was an undesigned but effective ally. Mark was not fond of little dogs, but Fifi was all right for Jenny, and, if he liked to see a woman fond of animals, he liked even better a woman of whom animals were fond.

The western light faded, and the stars came out. Lamps flashed like jewels in the windows of Jenny's château. Mark lingered on the darkening terrace, indolent with the indolence that comes of a good dinner and a good digestion, perfume of flowers, perfume of a summer sunset, perfume of wine; his senses were all rosed over with a pleasurable warmth. Jenny had fallen silent for some time, when the distant chiming from a church tower roused Mark Sturt to glance at his watch. "Eleven o'clock!" he said. "I must be getting back. They go to bed early at Duclair. Thank you, Mrs. Essenden, for a delightful evening——"

"You are not going back to-night?"

"But of course! Didn't you very kindly say I could have the car?"

"Yes, but I thought you had given up the idea. Why, it's miles and miles, and all through dark country lanes! I'm sure that little estaminet of yours will have shut up ages ago."

"But I have nothing with me."

"But the man will see to that! I told him you might be staying the night, and you don't know how clever he is. I'm sure you'll find everything in your room. Oh,

Mr. Mark, I can't let you turn out at this time of night.
I never heard of anything so inhospitable!"

She slipped to her feet, and Mark felt her little hand
settle on his arm. He stood rigid under her touch. The
furtive expression had vanished from her eyes; they
were bright, there was a haze over them, and her bosom
fluttered.

"Why—why won't you stay?" she murmured. "Is—
is it because I am what I am?"

He was speechless.

"You wouldn't feel safe with me?" Jenny breathed.
"The—the woman who knows how to make the running?
The woman whom a man needn't respect? That tempts
you, does it?" It did: with such a potent shock of
temptation that Mark's will seemed to turn to water.
Oh! after the racking strain of Ushant, what if he were
to resign himself, for the briefest interlude, to the practiced, the exquisite facility of Jenny's unholy charm?
What, after all, does a Jenny Essenden more or less count
for in a man's life?

"Oh, I didn't think you would say this to me!" Jenny
murmured. She sank her face in her hands, and her
very neck was rosy; then lifting her head, with an infernal sparkle in her wet eyes, "Well, and—and if it
were so? If I were to own that I'm a little in love with
you? Why—why not?"

"Why not? Faith, why not?" Mark repeated.

He threw back his head and laughed. After all, why
not? For his wife's sake? She had left him. For
Guy de Trafford's sake? That bond snapped like thread
in a candle flame. For love of the vision of God? Mark's
eyes were bloodshot and his brain was whirling; he
could still laugh, but he could not pray.

Mark laughed at himself, but Mrs. Essenden naturally
thought he was laughing at her. The rose-red turned

scarlet; she snatched her hand from his sleeve and
leaned her forehead on the balustrade with a little wail
of sobbing.

"Good heavens! what a brute I am!" Mark exclaimed.
It was the second time within a month that he had made
a woman cry. "Jenny, Jenny, don't!" he said, slipping
his arm round her waist. Jenny made a brief pretense
of rebellion; she knew in that moment, and hated him
for knowing it, that her victory was won. He would not
escape her after having made her weep. "Jenny, sweet-
est, dry your pretty eyes!" said Mark. "I can't tell you
why I laughed, but it had nothing to do with you, I
swear."

"I hate you!" said Mrs. Essenden passionately.

"Do you?" said Mark, taking her in his arms. "I understood you to say you were a little in love with me."

"I don't. Oh, I hate—hate you!"

"That's very unkind. And mayn't I stay, then?"

"No, no; you don't want to stay. What am I to you?
Freddy Field's mistress. You like innocent women.
Leave poor little Jenny alone—you and your moralities
—what do you want of me? an *ancienne*, a——"

"Kiss me," said Mark in a sudden flame of passion.
She was a small and slender woman, and he lifted her
like a child and set her on the balustrade, and pressed
his lips against the coolness of her white throat. It
was dark; but if it had been noonday Mark would not
have cared.

"Oh! how strong you are!" Jenny murmured. She
nestled down, clinging to him with her arms about his
neck. "Oh! but, Mark, not here . . . indoors . . ."

No, Mrs. Essenden was not worth the flaming sword

CHAPTER X

MARK did not go back to Duclair that or any subsequent night. He stayed on at the château, amusing himself in a fit of thorough-paced indolence with Jenny and Jenny's cuisine and her car and her gardens and—delightful unforeseen accessory—her mile of trout stream. It may be confessed that he did not take himself, or Jenny, very seriously. When he did reflect at all upon his own doings, the one definite scruple that came up was dislike of his position as Jenny's guest, but after all she was a rich woman and the money was her own. He heard a good deal of her history from time to time in those warm August days: a history perhaps a little edited, a little glossed, but true enough in its main outlines.

Mrs. Essenden was the second daughter of a country clergyman, and had been brought up after the straitest sect of Evangelical doctrine: long family prayers night and morning, droned out through Mr. Simpson's long hooked nose; dresses cast off by a rich cousin; roast mutton and suet pudding, muddy roads and starved hearths. Catherine, the elder sister, was placid and fond of good works; Maggie, the youngest, had wits that carried her to Newnham. Jenny had nothing but her prettiness and her baffled social aptitudes. When she was seventeen her father found her out in a fiery flirtation with the curate, and after a still more fiery lecture Jenny was packed off to a situation to act as governess to an elderly widower's little girl. What never entered Mr. Simpson's head was that Jenny would marry the widower;

but she did within six months, and brought him home
in triumph, unenvied of her family.

She made him a good wife. She had a keen sense of
what was due to others, and would have felt it wrong
to defraud her husband of his bargain. Timothy Essenden, brewer, was a little bald kindly man with a thin
neck like that of a hen, reddish and covered with goose-
flesh: very fond of his young wife, very anxious to
make her happy, very little able to do so by any other
means than the course which he ultimately followed—
that of dying within a year or two of his marriage and
leaving her half his money.

Jenny was not a greedy woman, and she did not complain because the other half went to little Laura. But
she had no quarrel with Providence when Laura, whose
small frame had not derived its full share of vitality
from Mr. Essenden's exhausted middle age, sickened of
scarlet fever and died at her boarding school. Mrs.
Essenden was now left alone in the world, a rich woman
of twenty without encumbrance. Her father offered her
a home at the parsonage, but when Jenny spoke of travel
he agreed, not without relief, that she might as well see
the world while she was young. It never crossed his
fancy that one of his girls could go astray. Jenny therefore set out for France without even a chaperon. With
what plans she went it would be hard to say, for the influence of a decent upbringing was still strong on her,
and though her eyes courted insult her acquired instinct
was to resent it. But, if blame falls to the man who
broke Jenny in, at least he found an apt and merry
pupil.

A friend of the family met Jenny in Venice. Scandal
was already flying about, and Mrs. Morgan, in the rôle
of a woman of the world, spoke to the lovely unguarded
young widow. Mrs. Morgan used to say afterwards that

she had never been so shocked in her life. Jenny had had enough of sermons, and was not fond of other women at the best of times; she told the truth roundly, and drove the elder lady from the field. Letters from home followed, incredulous, touching, stern: Jenny tore them up. At last Mr. Simpson came out in person to Venice, and was met, not by Jenny, but by Jenny's deputy. The scene was brief, and the expression controlled on both sides, for Mr. Simpson was a University man, and he did not fall into the blunder of sermonizing Jenny's deputy, though he would certainly have sermonized Jenny. He stayed only long enough to make certain that Jenny knew what she was about, and went home a harsher and a sadder man.

An unexpected issue of the interview was that Jenny's deputy, who had not liked his rôle, departed at the same time, leaving the little sinner to her own devices. Jenny wept—for twenty-four hours: then shrugged her shoulders and looked out for a successor. That was four years ago, when she was barely of age; she was twenty-five now, and there had been plenty of adventures, with intervals of repose, between the Venetian calamity and the capture of Mark Sturt.

Why had she planned to capture Mark Sturt? Because she liked him, but not for that reason only. She was fascinated by his physical attributes, by the tanned skin, brilliant eye, and powerful frame which set him as far apart from her little bald husband as from Frederick Field's pitiful surrender: the last months of her connection with Field had been a sore trial to Jenny, and she took no small credit to herself for sticking to him to the end. Now she could not associate Mark Sturt with any idea of sickness or death, still less of delicacy. Then again he was known to be difficult; his notoriously cold temper—notorious because he was Lawrence Sturt's

brother—was a challenge to her notion of her sex's do-
minion. Men ought not to live without women, Jenny
thought: if any man indulged the delusion of his being
able to do so it was high time that he should be brought to
book. Last, but not least, Mark was a big fish for Jenny
to land. She had many correspondents, and it tickled
the very marrow of her vanity to be able to write with
artful-artless vagueness, "What a dear fellow Mark Sturt
is when you get to know him! Pots of money, and as
simple as a boy. I am learning all the ins and outs of
political life from him—I forget if I told you he is here
in Normandy."

This was not true, for Mark never talked politics with
Mrs. Essenden; but it was as good as true, for by dint
of talking a good deal herself and watching his expression Jenny did manage to pick up some ideas about the
lighter side of political life. That she could not get any
further annoyed her, but to her probings Mark remained
impervious. Nor would he talk about Arthur Sturt, or
Lawrence, or Gatton, or the war, or any other personal
topic. Maisie often jarred his taste, Jenny rarely; and
yet he did not much mind what Maisie knew about him,
while for Jenny all doors were barred.

Once, after some weeks at the château, he borrowed
one of Jenny's horses to ride into Rouen. Jenny would
have liked an explanation, but she got none, and Mr.
Sturt was away several hours. Jenny waited for him in
the garden, sitting on the lawn in the shadow of an aspen;
bowers of roses made a screen for her, while near by a
fountain dispensed innumerable jets of water, which fell
in a soft splashing and rippling over the chipped limbs
of a struggling nymph and faun. Peering between the
flowery branches, Jenny saw Mark stroll down the terrace and vault across the balustrade. She called to him,
and he came to her over the grass, still breeched and

booted, and threw himself down on one arm beside her cushions. "Pretty thing, kiss me," he said with sparkling eyes. Jenny's heart began to throb; it was in this temper that she loved him, or nearly loved him. Mark threw his free arm round her and dragged her down, crumpling all her rosy muslins. "What a shame, isn't it?" he whispered. "My dusty head against a roseleaf throat like yours. How cool you are, Jenny, and how sweet you smell! It was hot in Rouen and the stinks were pretty bad . . . See us? They can't, and what the devil does it matter if they do? Don't be bourgeoise, Sapho."

"Mark! If you call me that atrocious name, you—you shan't have what I've got for you."

"What might that be? Chocolates, with any luck." Then he saw what it was and his manner changed. "Oh, a letter for me? Thanks. Fifi, you shut up."

"I've half a mind not to let you have it."

"Please do." He took it out of her hand, glanced at the writing, and put it in his pocket.

"Who's it from?" demanded Jenny.

"Another lady, of course," Mark grinned.

"It's from Lawrence, isn't it?"

"My brother—yes."

"Why does he address it to Duclair?"

"All my letters go to Duclair except those that Henham forwards from the flat. I was obliged to let him have my direction because he gets a lot of official stuff which ought not to be delayed, but he is trustworthy."

"You haven't told any one but 'Henham where you are?"

"You seem annoyed!"

"Not even Lawrence?"

"Does that surprise you?"

"Rather," Jenny admitted. "I thought men always

kissed and told." She took his temples between the tips of her fingers, and a caress, light as a moth's wing, brushed his lips. "I rather like you for not telling." In reality, she reflected, it was one for her and two for himself; he was ashamed of her. "Well, aren't you going to read your letter? I haven't read it; you see it was sealed."

"Yes, my brother often seals his letters," said Mark, breaking the envelope. "Silly trick, because there's never anything in them." He glanced down the sheet and put it in his pocket.

"Do 'you and Lawrence often write to each other?"

"He writes pretty often. I hardly ever do."

"You and he are twins, aren't you? I suppose you're very fond of each other."

"Oh, very."

"Whom do you love best in the world, Mark?"

"You, of course."

"Oh! pass for that," Jenny said with her little grimace. She had no illusions. "Whom after me?"

"Er—Fifi," Mark answered, pulling the little dog's ears. Fifi showed her teeth; jealous like her mistress, she hated Mark, and would go into convulsions of miniature rage if endearments passed in her presence. "Love me love my dog. Fifi doesn't love me, though, do you, Fifi? Bite then." He put his finger in her mouth.

"And after Fifi—whom? Lawrence? Or the other lady?"

"The other lady, I expect." Mark yawned without apology. "Ouf! I must go and change. I want a bath, Jenny, the Rouen road is inches deep in dust. Oh, I forgot to say the other lady lives in Rouen. That's why I went over. I've been buying her a cracker brooch. Do you think she'll like it? The cracker shops aren't very good in Rouen, but it's too far to go to Gamage's."

Jenny bit her lip. A judge of stones, she knew that the price of the spray of ruby rosebuds Mark tossed into her lap had run into three figures. Was she grateful? Jenny Essenden loved jewels; but one reason why she hated Mark Sturt was that he had power to remind her of Jenny Simpson.

"Mr. Sturt settles his hotel bill," she said scornfully.

"Jenny!" Impassive as he was, she made him start; she had hit the nail on the head. "Good heavens, child! I only meant to please you."

"With rubies; and you won't tell me one little single thing about yourself. No man ever before made me feel as you do that I was nothing to him but a toy."

He took her in his arms, whispering reckless ardors, and after a brief struggle Jenny lay still. She let him pin the ruby spray at the curve of her breast, she let him brush away the dew from her lashes; she was more exquisite in her pale surrender than in her rosy triumph, and when she murmured, "Be nice to Jenny," Mark very nearly forgot his predecessors. Nearly—not quite: in the very hour of passion the ghost of poor young Field warned him with its monitory eyes, "Such the look and such the smile" she "used to love with, then as now." It was not Jenny's sins that came between her and Mark, it was this ill-defined yet haunting sense of the unreal, the factitious, in Jenny herself. He would as soon have taken Fifi seriously.

And he was not always nice to Jenny; now and then, unintentionally, he gave her a glimpse of this profound indifference which underlay his fiercest desire. She knew that she held him only by a frail thread, and the knowledge made her ten times more resolute to hold him. She matched her wits to his, and when he was tepid she turned cynically cold, and would absent herself or very nearly ignore him for days at a time. Then there would follow the flare-up of a tiny quarrel, and then the nerve-sapping sweetness of reconciliation. She had the whip-hand of Mark because she was in earnest, while he did not care enough about her to analyze her conduct or his own. If he had realized that she was straining every nerve to keep him, he would soon have shaken himself free, but she never let him find it out; indeed, between her quarrels and her sweetness, and the fishing, and the car, and the cellar, and the soul-destroying apathy of satiation to which she condemned him at will, Mark had small chance to think at all. After fourteen years, riot ran pretty strong in Mark's veins: Jenny provoked it: she knew her trade as well as any street drab, and reveled in it. It charmed her to fire him to brutality by twenty-four hours' neglect. A gambler born, Jenny played high; and for this reason the break in their relation came from her and not from him.

Jenny retired to her room one day to think about the future. It was nearing the end of September, and in a week or two the golden season was sure to break, for Norman autumns close early; the château was fairyland in the misty sunshine, but the first blast of cold rain would turn it to a desolation, and then—Jenny was sure of it—Mark would find out that he must get back to work. She knew that there is always work to be done by a man in Mark's position. She knew all about Gatton. How did she know? Jack Bennet did not seal his correspondence. There were loose political threads to be knit up before the coming session. Mark's friends too were getting impatient; Jenny seized her earliest chance to pick his pocket of one of Mrs. Ferrier's letters, the feminine writing having stabbed her into jealousy, and its gay intimate tone and frequent political allusions filled her with rage and dismay. Sad to tell, she set down Charles Ferrier as an injured husband, and Mark went

up in her esteem; but her wrath against Dodo would
have surprised that lady.

Jenny reckoned Dodo as a dangerous rival, one indeed
for whom on her own ground Jenny was no match. Dodo
touched Mark's life through his work, Jenny only
through her sex. Once riveted on Mark's neck, Jenny
believed that her fetters would stand any strain; but
he was not half hers yet, and Dodo's light lure was not
the only peril Jenny saw ahead. Of whom was she
afraid? A man of Mark Sturt's antecedents must be
sunk drowning deep in inertia before he will bear, without revulsion, certain forms of moral shock.

Therefore, playing high, Jenny struck first. She chose
a veiled September evening, blowy and mild; the evening
of one of those days that ripen the pears and apples,
and set the sap stirring in late blooming roses. Mark
had been out with a gun all day, and came in quite happy
with a brace of rabbits; it was not precisely sport, but it
was a harmless method of whiling away the silken, sunny
hours. He looked, to a superficial glance, much the better for his time at the château, and he had put on weight;
Father de Trafford's glance would have darkened, and a
trainer might have questioned his staying power, but he
was still in pretty fair condition, hand and eye in happy
accord. Dinner over, Jenny strolled into the salon and
sat down to the piano. Her playing was her one accom-
plishment, and she had early found out that it was one
which appealed to Mark Sturt; no pianist himself,
he was passionately fond of music, and would sit
for hours listening while her small fingers danced over
the keys. So now: she had scarcely got through a dozen
bars when Mark lounged into the room.

It was a room that made a rare setting for Jenny's
bizarre charm. Gilt moldings divided the walls into
panels, which were filled, some with water colors, some

with valuable antique tapestry: faint tints of vermeil and azure and straw-color telling the tale of Perseus and Andromeda in a sequence of dim pictures. The house being old was draughty, and when the wind blew, as to-night, it worked its way in underfoot and overhead, puffing up the Aubusson carpet into little swells, and swaying the framed arras, till a trembling like life passed over Andromeda's discolored limbs, and the tail of the dragon waved under the high gilded cornice. The furniture was light and graceful, and so arranged as to increase the effect of space; there was a profusion of pale wood and ormolu, of marquetry and vague brocades. This room had distinction, and it was to Jenny's credit that she shone in it; its effect even on Mark was to make him pull down his white waistcoat and give a little twist to his mustache.

"Come and sing," said Jenny. He had a baritone voice, untrained but naturally easy, and a good ear, and it had amused him many a night to stand behind Jenny's chair with his hands in his pockets and run through the score of an opera with her. But to-night he shook his head and sat down in a big chair, leaning his elbow on the arm of it and his forehead on his hand. "No, you play to me. Something with a nice tune in it—what?"

"Gay or melancholy?" asked Jenny, preluding in brilliant runs and trills.

"Don't care."

"Tell you a little story, then," said Jenny. "This château was the dower house of the Comtesse de Clères. She was a widow with two sons, Philippe and Rohan. When the war broke out they naturally went to fight. One autumn evening in 1915—it was late in September; perhaps for all I know this very night—the Countess was standing in the window, there by the bookcase, waiting for the *facteur*. She saw him a long way off in the avenue, and she beckoned him across the grass. He came up and put into her hand two official envelopes, just alike, printed forms from the French War Office. Philippe had been killed in Champagne on the twenty-sixth, and Rohan in Artois among the orchards of La Folie one day later. Philippe was twenty-five and Rohan nineteen; they were the last male descendants of the line. Madame de Clères took the veil, and she is a nun in the convent of the Sacred Heart in Rouen to this day. Now this was her own piano, and these that I'm going to play to you are some of her tunes."

And she began to play light French operatic airs of the Second Empire, trivialities of Offenbach and Auber, La Vie Parisienne, Les Diamants de la Couronne, sweet and *folichon,* not the music of a nun. Mark, tired after his long tramp in the open air, listened and dreamed of the war; of the cruel tragedy which had extinguished an ancient line, that September evening fourteen years ago; of his own ghastly experience between the lines at St. Éloi; of Maisie, and her comment on his scar; and so on from one random memory to another, till thought grew vague in the immense lassitude which came upon him, and through which Jenny's music grew as indistinct as the rippling of a brook. . . . He woke with a start, and with words on his lips: "No, dear, no: not that." Jenny had left playing; she had spun round on the piano stool to face him, her hands on her hips, her small ankles crossed below her opalescent skirts.

"You were asleep, Mark."

"Was I?"

"And talking in your sleep. If you do that I shall learn all your secrets. How will you like that?"

"You terrify me." Mark yawned. "What was that last thing you were playing?"

"The barcarolle out of the Contes d'Hoffmann." Sway-

ing across the polished floor like a dancer, her Pompadour
curls and long slender waist emergent out of a mist of
gauze, she came to him and leaned down over him till
her long lashes brushed his cheek. "Did you know that
you talk in your sleep, Mark?"

"Do I?"

"You woke me up, last night."

"So sorry: I'll take a dose of quinine. I had malarial
fever years ago in China, the sort of thing that hangs
about you forever, and now and then in autumn, when
the nights are damp, I get a bit of a temperature. Er—
no: not infectious, Jenny. Wasn't that what you were
going to ask?"

"Am I such a coward, Mr. Sturt?"

"Pretty fair." Mark grinned. "Who was late for
Mass last Sunday because there was a cow in the short
cut? I watched you from the terrace, Jenny: wasn't
that a shame? She was such a dear old moo-moo."
Jenny went to Mass every Sunday; but she went alone.

"You might be nice to Jenny to-night," Mrs. Essenden
murmured, enlacing him for a moment in her arms, "because it's our last night. I'm going to London to-morrow."

"To London!"

"Yes; did you think I was going to stay here forever?
No, no, my dear Mark: I am a town bird, as you know,
and much as I love this pretty French country there
comes a time when I pine for my native streets. Confess now—won't you rather like to smell a London fog
again?"

"Bless her, she's turning me out!" said Mark, amazed.
"Are you tired of me, Jenny?"

"Not tired of you. Perhaps a little tired of—of being
in love with you."

"Well, I'm hanged!" said Mark, getting up and stretching himself. "This is rather sudden. You might have given me longer warning! But that's the way with your fair but inconstant sex: to use a novel metaphor, when they tire of a man they fling him aside like a worn-out glove. Amn't I poetical to-night? Kiss me, Jenny, and let's let London rip."

He advanced towards her. But Jenny, slipping through his hands, ran away into the embrasure of the window. "No—you can't touch me here—not where the Countess stood."

Mark stopped dead, arrested—not for the first time in his experience of Jenny—by the striking of a deep fantastic note which jarred among her pretty French harmonies. "Jenny, you have a *macabre* fancy. Come away from the window."

"Non . . . Enfin, c'est fini . . . je suis à bout . . . tu m'embêtes . . . laisse-moi, m'ami . . ."

Jenny played high.

"Je le veux bien!" said Mark with his unexpected laugh. In one swift spring he caught her round the waist and snatched her out of the window. "As a defensive weapon, Jenny, ghosts are overrated. How about London now?"

"Put me down!" said Jenny, passive but with flashing eyes. Mark's answer was to shift his clasp, so that she lay at full length across his arms, the slippers falling from her feet. "Don't force me to be angry; you are my guest."

"Ah! and if I cared two straws whether you were angry or not, no doubt I should set you down. But you lie, Jenny, you lie: you're not a bit angry—you like it."

She hid her face on his shoulder. "You make me ashamed."

"I think not, Jenny."

Mrs. Essenden's small white teeth fastened on her lip;

if he could have seen her he would have known his own danger. But only her curls were visible, and a moment later her arm crept round his neck. "Mark, my beloved . . . how strong you are! Oh, have your own way with me—what do I care? I am only a woman, and you are a man. . . ." She turned in his arms and clung to him as the nymph of the fountain clung to the faun, enlacing him in the perfume of her disordered curls and flying gauze. "I adore you. . . . But I shall go to London to-morrow all the same."

"And leave me? No, Jenny!"

"Have I the courage? You could come to me whenever you like."

"Whew!" said Mark, whistling softly. He set her down.

"Come and see you in London, Jenny? Of course I could. But where will you be? I'm a public man, Jenny: I have to think of my reputation. Shall you stop at an hotel?"

"Stop at an hotel? Of course not! I shall be in my own house. Did you really never go there before—before we ran away together? Why, I thought you must have seen it in poor Freddy's time." She knew he had not, but it was her cue to seem to have forgotten. "It's a quaint little spot in Green Street, near the Green Park, quite close to Westminster."

Mark did not answer. He had made no definite plans for the winter, but he had always meant to break with Jenny when he left the château; the escapade had helped him over a bad time, and he was grateful, but after all it was Jenny's *shikar*, and by the strictest code of honor such a liaison can be broken at will. He had never dreamed of carrying it on in England. But then he had not thought of going back to England for another month or six weeks, by when he expected to have had enough of Jenny. He was not ready to give her up yet awhile. And yet there was, as he had said, his reputation to be thought of : people wink at a holiday indiscretion, but an *homme sérieux* ought not to let himself be entangled in any permanent folly. Jenny read his indecision and struck with practiced hand.

"Oh, no, that would never, never do," she said, hopping on one foot like a little stork to put her slippers on. "I forgot you were a public man, *mon ami*. It would be a great to-do if it came to the ears of your chiefs—Mr. Mallinson, too, so Puritanical! No," she swayed before him on the tips of her toes, holding by the lapels of his coat, "we will have this one evening more and then we will say good-by like sober people. You are quite *rangé*, are you not? and even I, sinner as I am, like to keep my *toquades* away from English soil. Perhaps later on we will arrange a second little honeymoon, but for the present, Monsieur, we shall have to say good-by."

"Shall we?" said Mark slowly. There was a libertine glow in his eyes that she had never seen there before, and the line was drawn deep from nostril to jaw. "Sure you'll find it so easy to throw me over, Jenny? You pursued me to France, didn't you?"

"Cad!" said Jenny tersely.

"Oh, quite. But—are you sure you can do without me, Jenny?"

"Why *will* you call me Jenny every time you speak to me?"

"Because it's a pretty name, and you're a pretty girl, Jenny. Answer my question."

"I didn't listen to it."

"Is Jenny sure she can live without me?"

"Quite, quite sure!" Jenny sang out with a little peal of laughter. Mark, who had expected blushes, turned rather white; however little he cared for Jenny, he had always flattered himself that Jenny, after her fashion, cared for him. And while he was digesting a new idea, Jenny suddenly ran away. Mark cursed his own carelessness, but he was too late, she had escaped into the hall where a footman was waiting. But while he was angrily reviewing this unexpected turn of his affairs, Jenny stuck her head round the door again—her little curly head, her slender shoulders gleaming through the disorder of her torn laces. "You see the truth is," she said, "men are so monotonous. I adore you forever—but I'm tired to death of you!"

She flew off. Sturt followed, abandoning the circumspection which he had habitually practiced: at that moment he desired nothing on earth but to bring Jenny to her knees. Did she take him for a second Freddy Field? . . . Entrance was barred: Mark fell back defeated after an interval of indiscretion, to which Jenny vouchsafed no heed beyond the derision of a distant laugh. In his own room, after a cup of coffee, he got some sort of shaken hold on himself and fell asleep vowing vengeance on Jenny in the morning.

In the morning Jenny was gone.

CHAPTER XI

"WELL, Henham, how are you? Everything going on as usual, I suppose?"

"Yes, sir, thank you," said Henham. He added after a moment, "I'm glad to see you back, sir, if I may say so. Keeping pretty well, I hope?"

"Hey? Oh, quite, thanks," said Mark carelessly. He stood by the hall table turning over a tray of cards. "Yes. Any letters?"

"I forwarded them up to Saturday, sir. The others that came since your telegram are in the smoking-room. Mr. Considine called last Friday to get your address. I don't know whether you would have wished me to give it him, but as you said no one was to have it I didn't. He lef' this note for you." Mark took it. "And Father de Trafford came round the day before, and he wanted your address too. So I gave it him."

"You gave it him!" Mark swung round on his heel to face the little gray man. "Confound you, Henham! why did you do that?"

"I beg your pardon, sir, but you told me once I was to always let Father de Trafford have your address, wherever you was, whenever he wanted it."

"So I did. Quite right."

Mark passed on into the smoking-room, and Henham gave a little jerk of the head as he watched the tall figure disappear. "Now what have *you* been up to?" he seemed to be saying to himself. Henham knew, it is hardly necessary to say, all about Mrs. Essenden, and could have given his master details of her career—in

186

fact, Henham and Frank Carter were members of the same club; he did not disapprove of the connection, or at least he had not done so up to the time of Mark's return. Now, as he went away to warm Mark's claret, the shadow of perplexity rested on his face; he could not quite make out Mark's manner. "I do hope," he said to himself as he got Mark's coffee ready, a task never deputed to the cook's hand, "we shan't have any nonsense about marryin' her. We're a bit soft where there's a lady in the case—yes, we are. But I don't think we're soft enough to marry one of her sort. I fancy we should draw the line at takin' her into the family."

Mark warmed himself at the fire, and looked round the room with the freshened observation of the traveler who has been away a long time. He was struck by the change of weather, late summer to early winter; three nights ago he had sat with Jenny among roses by moonlight, but here in London there was frost in the air and the trees in the Park were stripped. He had been in France only six weeks, but the time seemed longer because of this turn of the seasons. He was struck no less by the change in the character of his surroundings. Loving light and space, and disdainful of ornament, Jenny had left the château untouched in its age-old beauty and severity, the Classic setting of a Classic race; and the transition to the dark shabby comfort of Park Court was not altogether agreeable.

Mark's dwelling was in a nook off Victoria Street, high up, overlooking a medley of roofs and chimneys; very unlike those lovely rooms near the river which Lawrence had filled with the spoil of his wanderings. Mark, always hard-worked and in a hurry, had taken over a furnished flat which he left pretty much as it stood. A Turkey carpet, a flowered paper of his pre-

decessor's choice, and a Victorian "suite" in leather and
mahogany were good enough for him, and there was
little to represent his own tastes except a stand of
weapons which occupied the greater part of one wall,
and a bookcase that ran the length of the other. Item, a
"Sargent" portrait of Mr. Sturt in riding dress, startlingly
life-like in its vigorous pose, ruddy color, and jeering
smile; but this by the way. Many a time Mark had returned to the flat after longer wanderings with all the
satisfaction with which a man gets into an old coat or
old slippers. To-night, for the first time, he did not like
it. Why? There was no dust or disorder; the fire was
burning merrily, his big chair was drawn up in his own
corner, a couple of evening papers lay within arm's length,
there were chrysanthemums on the table, and Sobranies
in their cool china box. Yet—was the room ugly, after
all, or was it lonely? Mark tried in fancy to seat Mrs.
Essenden in one of those leather chairs. He smiled;
this was no frame for Jenny. Mark leaned his arm
along the chimney-piece and looked down into the fire.
Was it possible that he missed Jenny?

Jenny was in Green Street, no doubt, settling in. He
had not seen or heard of her since the scene of the night
before last, except for a note which Carter brought in
with his breakfast; a strange note, Jenny all over, a piece
of formal courtesy begging him to stay on at the château
as long as he liked, followed by a Gallicism which made
the blood burn in his cheek and haunted him across the
Channel. He had not stayed on at the château; he had
waited one night at Duclair to collect his letters; then
home by Dieppe and Newhaven in a blinding gale of
rain. As he tramped the deck of the *Rouen* Mark's mind
was as chaotic as the tumbling wintry sea. Uppermost
in it then and now was a desire to score off Jenny. The
wind wailed round the high flat, a gust of rain lashed

the windows. He could be with her in twenty minutes. "She won't want me to-night," Mark said to himself. "It will take her more than twenty-four hours to unpack herself. But little Jennies can't have all they want. Suppose I go round for an hour and make her give me some dinner? Compromising! After all, what's the odds? Who cares? My wife?" He laughed. "If my wife tears about the country with young Forester, what's the odds if I dine with Jenny Essenden?" he reflected savagely.

But as he raised his head he caught sight of his own reflection in the glass. "Hallo!" he said aloud. He had seen those lines about other men's mouths, and he knew well enough what they meant. He looked into his own eyes as if they had been those of a stranger. "No," he said. "Curse you, no. Not that. Oh, good heavens! what am I doing? I'll go and see the Ferriers; no, they're not up yet. Considine, then." He opened his cousin's note, but Considine Sturt had no permanent footing in town, and with characteristic carelessness had forgotten to put an address. "De Trafford? Can't, after Henham's giving me away. Bridge at a club?" He shrugged his shoulders. "I wish Lawrence were in London." As the wish framed itself he read in it the measure of his own weakness. "Well, upon my word, what am I coming to? Jenny, you little jade, I swear I won't go near you to-night. I'll turn in and do some work. There's Mallinson's latest White Paper, that ought to keep me going for a bit." He dropped into a chair and began to read closely.

Twenty minutes later he was on his way to Green Street.

To be conscious of mortal weakness, to be resolved to break loose from it, and to fail over and over again is a

frame of mind and life of which many men, at one time
or another, gain experience. Some fail from pure want
of stamina, from pure inability to govern their actions
by their will; others—and in this class every child of
man is liable to find himself—because in the given case
the will is divided. This was Mark's position that autumn. He had always meant to renounce Jenny, but it
was to be at his own choice of time, and Jenny by fore-
stalling him had called into play all the uncivilized instincts of the hunter after his quarry. To put it baldly,
he had meant to drop Jenny when he grew tired of her,
and it was the flick of a whip across his fighting temper
that the little jade should presume to grow tired of him.
More somber and more dangerous still, he was jealous.
He did not love Mrs. Essenden, he did not respect her—
not at all, not so much as she deserved; it was the purely
physical jealousy of the dominant male; but it ate into
his nerves. At Clères he had been safe, but in London
Jenny had many friends. There was a harmless man
about town named Horton, a tall, fair, decadent fellow,
a frequenter of Green Street and similar purlieus, to
whom Mark was always rigidly civil, but "Hanged if I
think your cousin likes me!" said Horton with his noiseless laugh to Considine Sturt.

Shortly after this incident Considine dropped in one
evening at Park Court, where he found Mark dressed
and on the point of going out. Considine, a small, dark,
slender Irishman, nearly as handsome as Lawrence but
in miniature, threw himself into a chair by the fire.
"You're in a hurry—it's early yet. Do you dine at the
Verneys? Because I am going there myself and I can
take you on."

"I am dining out, but not at the Verneys."

"In Green Street?" Considine cocked a deliberate eyebrow. "Felicitations. The lady is charming."

"You think so?"

"You're not alone in thinking so," Considine retorted. "Well, well, I hope she gives you a good dinner. Horton swears she has the same chef she had in Freddy Field's day—or was it Lessingham he said? I forget what happened to Lessingham. Went under, didn't he? Drink or drugs."

"Can't say," said Mark, unmoved. "I'm afraid I'm not a Who's Who like Horton."

"Horton isn't a bad chap," said Considine, rearranging his buttonhole. "He's fearfully nervous of you. Says you look at him like an injured husband. I beg your pardon." Mark had consigned Considine to that region whose streets are paved by the well-intentioned. "Come, come," said Considine, "that's putting the saddle on the wrong leg. After you, my boy."

"You confounded little Irishman," said Mark, laughing against his will, "what do you want?"

"Sure I thought you were out for congratulations. No, now, hit a man your own size!" as Mark stood over him. "If you're so shy about it why do you put it in the papers?"

"Put what in the papers?"

"Why, your marriage, of course," said Considine, arching his perfectly formed eyebrows. "Don't tell me it's off, when I've just spent my last tenner on a teapot?"

"My—what?"

Considine pulled a paper out of his pocket and pointed to a marked paragraph. "Do you mean to say you didn't put that in yourself?"

Mark read the paragraph; it was one of a series headed "A Little Bird Tells Me That"—and the report of the particular little bird was that a certain well-known M.P., tired of his wanderings in cold climates, was going to settle down to domestic bliss "in a snug little house not

far from Green Street, where visitors always get a *warm*
welcome, and we wish him joy, but oh, dear, what will
Mrs. Grundy say?"

"Do you know, I thought it wasn't quite your style,"
observed Considine placidly, as Mark thrust the horrible
little sheet into the fire.

"Did you come here to show me this, Considine?"

"Thought you might like to see it."

"Thanks. I'm sorry I wasn't more genial at the outset. What infernal cheek! Of course I can't take any
step. Can't even flog the editor. Shouldn't I like to,
though!" Mark added rather boyishly.

"H'm-m-m."

"What now?"

"Well, I admit," said Considine, contemplating his
now perfect buttonhole, "that the style of the commu-
niqué isn't in faultless taste. But if you were to flog all
the fellows who are saying it you would have your hands
full."

"On my word, one's friends are very obliging!"

"That they are! Trust them for that."

"But you didn't believe it?" Considine was silent.
"Good heavens! you surely know me better—?"

"Well, you see, Mark, you've been uncommonly indiscreet. I don't want to pry into your affairs, but if it's
true that you pay the fair Jenny's bills, which is what
I never heard of her letting any other man do——"

"Fair and softly," Mark said. "This is poisonous
gossip. I never dreamed of marrying Mrs. Essenden. I
should never marry a woman who let me pay her bills."

"Nor should I. That's why I remain a melancholy
bachelor." Considine winked at him. "All the same,
I can't, in that case, understand your feeling for the lady.
You don't, by any chance, think it your mission to re-
habilitate the victim of a harsh social system?"

Mark grinned. "Not precisely."

"Far be it from me to ask if you don't think you're playing the fool?"

Mark did not answer. He shrugged his shoulders in a tacit assent which struck a spark of gravity out of Considine's whimsical impertinence.

"Sick of being alone, is that it? You ought to marry. Why didn't you cut in at Shotton and spoil Forester's game?" Mark started under the familiar pinprick. "Lawrence swears you had a sporting chance. However, that's off now, by what I hear; Harry's the happy man." Mark leaned his elbow on the mantelpiece and kicked the brands together; it was all he could do to keep an unmoved face. His pride was cruelly wounded. "But there are lots of other nice women going," Considine pursued. "Really I should cut Green Street if I were you. It isn't respectable. One Lawrence is enough in a family. Besides, to speak seriously, you're not Lawrence; you've a big part to play." A jerk of the head indicated the mocking portrait of Arthur Sturt. "*He* believed in you."

"He? he cared more for Lawrence's little finger than for all my fourteen stone."

"Not latterly. Oh, I don't say he didn't like Lawrence better! but he had more faith in you. Last time I was at Longstone Edge, the summer he died, he said to me, 'Lawrence will do nothing. The women will suck him dry. But Mark will make his name.'"

"What about Watson, and Carden, and Delany?" Mark named some well-known members of the Liberal party who had not escaped scandal. "Or Sheddon, a married man; his constituents haven't shot him out yet."

"They are not in office."

"Nor am I."

"You could be, if you liked."

"You mean well, Considine."

Considine Sturt had a peculiar grimace. "I do, I mean extremely well, but I've done pretty badly. Eh, old Mark? I wish Lawrence were at home. Well, you're fretting to be off, so I won't keep you." He rose. "Give my love to your enchantress, she's an old flame of mine." He was thunderstruck by the uncontrollable alteration in Mark's features. "Powers above, I didn't mean that!" Mark was speechless. "Ah, now, if that's the way you feel about it, you're harder hit than I thought."

"Good night."

Considine, shocked into earnestness, laid his hand on Mark's arm. "I say, I've known you all your life—will you let me take a liberty? If you don't jolly well mind what you're doing, old man, you'll go under like Lessingham did. He was mad on Jenny, mortgaged every stick and stone; and the night he left England I saw her at the opera in Freddy Field's box. You fellows that idealize women, you never know where you are with the Essenden type. I'd lay any odds she sent that par. to *Adderley's* herself. I'm not qualified to talk morality, and I'm not clever like you are, but I've forgotten more about women than you ever knew, and I do beg of you, Mark, to steer clear of that little —— in Green Street."

Mark did not quarrel with the term applied to Mrs. Essenden, though its coarse vigor rang strange from Considine's fastidious lips. He gathered up his hat and coat and drew on his gloves as he strolled to the door. "Good man," he said gently. "Well, I must be off now, but Henham will look after you. Have a Sobranie, won't you? I remember you like them."

Considine sat on by the fire. He felt like a snubbed schoolboy, but he bore no grudge. In the Sturt family, as among many Catholic families in England, there was a good deal of clan feeling, and Considine, sagacious and affectionate, grieved for his cousin's plight. Mark's look haunted him—the look of a man drowning in deep water. "And I can't pull him out. I don't carry big enough guns," Considine reflected, lucidly Irish. "But I wonder——"

Mark was in deep water. He was dimly aware of it—aware that he was living too fast in more ways than one—but, though he sickened in the night watches, there was no will left in him to resist Jenny. To resist Jenny? Jenny never appealed to him—except to keep away. An onlooker would have thought that he held her by right of conquest. He came and went in Green Street like the master of the house, and like a master who had small respect for its mistress; and when Jenny stormed he took his own way to quiet her. It was significant of a change in their relations that he was no longer her guest; after his first visit to Green Street he told her that for the present, so long as their connection lasted, he should pay the rent of the house and the salaries of the servants. "No one has ever done that for me," panted Jenny, and strange to say this was the truth. "I shall do it, however," Mark replied, "or I shan't come here any more. And I've every intention of coming here, Jenny, and I'm sure you wouldn't like it if I didn't—what?"

Jenny raged, and trembled, and was torn by twenty passions, in which the lust of revenge predominated. She acted the woman beaten down and humbled, and gave him all the illegitimate sweets of a forced surrender; and when he went away she laughed at him—yes, and let her maid laugh at him. "Mon Dieu comme il est drôle ce gros monsieur!" Louise would say, holding up her hands: "et ça ne dérange pas madame? si j'étais madame je l'enverrais promener, moi—mais quand on aime à distraction—hein? pas moyen de s'en tirer." "Je l'enverrai promener, moi," said Jenny, fastening her teeth on her lip with the sudden little snarl of a teased cat, "Ah, oui! mais pas encore . . . non, non, ma fille. Attends que je lui aie plongé mon poignard dans le cœur!"

Meanwhile London was filling up again, and externally Mark's life resumed more or less its usual form. Not altogether, however. Lawrence of course was still away; an occasional scribble from a township off the line of march told of his doings, and never failed to rouse in Mark vain regrets that he had not taken his brother's advice and gone to Colorado. Once in a fit of frankness he owned as much in writing back. "I could wish I'd taken your advice. You were in every way right. But if a man elects to be a silly ass he must pay for it." He could see Lawrence reading those words perhaps by matchlight, and raising his eyebrows over them with a twist of his cynical delicate lips. A second friend of Mark's might as well have been in Colorado for all he saw of him; this was Father de Trafford, who had never come to the flat since the night when Henham gave him Mark's address at the château. Miss Archdale—it was still as Maisie Archdale that Mark thought of her— was staying in Norfolk. Other houses, where in previous years Mark had been admitted as an intimate, gave him this winter a less cordial welcome; others again, where manners were easy, dispatched more frequent invitations, and in a more confident style.

"Let's see, who's coming to us for Christmas besides our own people?" asked Charles Ferrier, leaning over his wife at her writing-table and ruffling up her curly fair hair.

Dodo ran over a few names. "And Mr. Mallinson— he is due to-morrow; and I think Mark Sturt. He hasn't

definitely accepted, but I asked him months ago. I was
going to write to him to-day."

"I don't suppose he will accept."

"Why?" Dodo asked, wheeling round on her chair
like a flash.

"Been going the pace a bit. Generally supposed to
be making rather a fool of himself."

"I knew it!" said Dodo. "I met him in the Row the
other day and reviled him for not coming to see me, and
I knew by his eyes that there was something wrong.
Tell me about it, Charles. Who is she?" Ferrier pre-
served a discreet silence. "Oh, dear boy, don't be silly!"
said his wife. "In the first place, if it's all over London
to-day it will be all over Hampshire to-morrow, and I'd
rather know the rights of the case than the wrongs. Sec-
ondly, I'm very, very fond of Mark, and if he is in a
mess I vote we get him out of it."

" 'Fraid we can't do that, darling. It'll have to run
its course."

"Men always say that. Who is she?"

"A Mrs. Essenden."

"In or out?"

"Out and out. Surely you've heard her name—Jenny
Essenden?"

"Oh-h." Dodo primmed her lips to a whistle. *"That*
woman. I remember. The Fields were furious, they
routed her once, but she came back, and she was alone
with Freddy when he died. Well, I dare say poor Freddy
would rather have had her than anybody else. I hate
Mrs. Field, I wouldn't a bit like to have her near me when
I was dying, she looks like a jet mausoleum in a bonnet.
Freddy hadn't any money of his own either, so if that
were all it would be rather to Mrs. Essenden's credit.
But if I remember rightly Freddy wasn't the first?"

"Not by long chalks," said Ferrier dryly. "And un-

luckily you see he wasn't the last either. I only hope
Sturt won't be green enough to marry her."

"Oh, I *hope* not," said Dodo. "Idiot, why do you
laugh? If—if the mischief weren't done it would be
different, but I hate whitewash. And what would become of his career, if he did? Poor Mark! it's bad
enough already, because people nowadays mind that sort
of thing so much more than they used to; if it gets wind
in his constituency one never knows what may happen.
I suppose there is no doubt it's true?"

"Not the remotest. In fact Horton says he's running
the establishment, so that it must be fairly serious. She
has, or had, a house of her own in Green Street, but
Horton swears Mark pays."

"Did Mark tell him so?" Dodo's tone was skeptical.

"No, I rather gather that the woman told him herself."

"Would she tell Mr. Horton a thing like that? Why
should she? It sounds just a made-up bit of scandal,
that last. Somehow I can't see Mark mixed up in this
sort of thing—not seriously; I should have thought he
was too—too fastidious to fall in love with a woman of
that class." Her husband smiled. "Ah! you mean that
that isn't a man's point of view. Dear child, I know it;
but look at the risk! One can't see Mark taking that
risk unless he were more or less in love. He's a Roman
Catholic, too."

Ferrier shrugged his shoulders. "She's a very pretty
woman. I told you Sturt was making an idiot of himself."

"Have you spoken to him about it?"

"I? Good Lord, no!"

"No, no—I mean, does he *afficher* himself with her?
Does he talk of it, or take her about in public?"

"Oh, I see your point—no, really, the information

comes, as I understand, all from the female; she gives the show away with both hands. But it's true enough; Horton dined with her one night when Sturt was there, and—well, really, darling, I can't give you chapter and verse, but Horton said he was obviously the master of the house."

"What's she like? I suppose you know her by sight: oh, perhaps you've dined with her too, like Mr. Horton?"

"Er—no," said Ferrier, winding one of his wife's curls round his finger. "I've never spoken to her, that I remember. Yes, I have, by Jove! I met her once at Goodwood with Morris Frere. She was very pretty then, and quite young; quiet clothes, quiet manners. She was a country parson's daughter, I believe."

"Like me. I wish I knew her."

"Why the devil—?"

"Oh, I don't know," said Dodo, rising impatiently. "Sixpence, please. Yes, you did, you said devil." She shook the missionary box under Ferrier's nose. "I've always wanted to know a woman who had got right over the fence: not a Maggie Frere, who only put one leg over and got back again, but one of the real wrong set— the Jenny Essendens of London. It's a handicap for us, you see, that we never know what we're fighting."

"I wouldn't try to fight Jenny Essenden, darling, if I were you. Leave her alone; and leave Sturt alone, too. He'll drop it before long—sure to; he'll get tired of her, or she'll get tired of him. It's probably only a casual aberration, an outcrop of the same sort of streak Lawrence Sturt has in him. But don't you meddle. You won't do any good."

"N-no," said Dodo reluctantly: "but all the same, if you don't mind, I think I'll try to get hold of him for Christmas."

"No, don't, dear."

"Why not?" Ferrier was silent. "Charles, is there anything more?"

"Er—yes: if you will have it. I don't care to have to watch a man at table in my own house, Dodo."

"Mark Sturt? You mean—? I don't believe it. They say that of every one!"

"I've seen it."

"Where?"

"At the Savoy, the night I dined with Haynes. As we left he was coming out of a private room with two or three other men: not drunk, I don't say that, whatever Haynes may swear, but far enough gone to be rowdy. They were expostulating with a waiter. Haynes and I fled."

"Oh!" said Dodo. Tears of grief and indignation brimmed her eyes, but she dashed them away and slipped from her husband's arm. "Oh, my poor old Mark! Oh, and you want me to let him go!—Charles, I shall write to him to-night."

CHAPTER XII

M Y DEAR MARK,
Have you any hazy recollection of the fact that
I asked you to come to us for Christmas? You never
said yes or no, and I have seen so little of you lately
that I haven't had a chance of settling with you, but if
you will come—*do* come!—Charles and I and Terry will
do our best to make you happy. It will be the most awful
infliction you can possibly imagine, a real old-fashioned
country Christmas, turkey and plum pudding and Dumb
Crambo in the nursery. You are so tall, you will be
most helpful in the decorations. Mr. Mallinson is coming, also some of our own people, and one or two others.
I should love you to see Mr. Mallinson playing Dumb
Crambo. Dearest Mark, you aren't going to forget old
friends, are you? They never forget you.

Yours always,
DODO FERRIER.

Mark was breakfasting by himself in Green Street
when this letter reached him—Jenny was never down
before eleven—and when he had read it he leaned his
arm on the table and dropped his forehead on his hand.
He looked exhausted, and worse than exhausted; his
features were beginning to wear the stamp of deteriora-
tion. He used to think back now and then over the
events of the past month or two, and wonder how they
had all come about, and what Jenny had done to him.
A long way off seemed the nights when he had slept under the trees at Ushant. He had begun to wonder why

he had taken so much pains to refuse what the gods offered him; and there was enough left in him of his old
self to recognize Jenny's destructive influence in that
changed point of view.

His Christmas plans were still vague, for a simple
reason; Jenny had maneuvered to get him to spend Christmas with her in Paris, and in doing so had inadvertently
struck against a force with which she had not reckoned
—the strong, secret force of religious feeling. Some
element in Mark's very bones rebelled against a Christmas spent with Jenny. Unacknowedged instincts sprang
up in him demanding a season, however brief, of clean-
ness and peace of mind. Once and again he thought of
going to de Trafford—as a man to his friend, not as
penitent to confessor—but by now he knew his own
weakness, and with bitter self-disgust he owned that he
was capable, if Jenny stayed in town—and she would not
go to Paris by herself—of coming straight back from
de Trafford to Green Street. Better keep clear of the
priest altogether than so profane his own soul. But he
longed—how he longed!—to get away from Jenny for
a season.

Dodo's letter came to him in his distress and weakness like the clasp of a friendly hand. He rose straight
from the breakfast table and went to Jenny's desk; there
he hesitated. What could it seem but a deliberate insult
if he wrote to Mrs. Ferrier on Jenny's note-paper? But
he had no other at hand, and bitter experience warned
him that he had better commit himself before his impulse failed; and what did it signify after all? Did not
every line of Dodo's letter prove that she knew what
was in fact common knowledge? Mark, whose eyes
were keen even when slightly *grisés* with fatigue and
champagne, had recognized Ferrier in the vestibule of
the Savoy. He took a sheet of Jenny's paper stamped

with Jenny's address, and wrote his reply standing at Jenny's little rosewood desk.

19, Green Street,
Westminster, S. W. 1.
Tuesday.
Thank you, I will come to-morrow.
O. M. Sturt.

"Wire me off, if you like, after that," he said to himself with a smile which softened his heavy eyes; and he went straight out into the street and posted the letter. He did not return to the house, and next day Jenny got a curt note telling her that he was gone to spend Christmas in the country. By way of consolation, and because he knew that he was treating her badly, he sent her also a ruby pendant, and a check, with a line of writing: "Make what use you like of the enclosed." He smiled into his mustache as he set his name to this broad absolution. What if Jenny's liking covered Christmas at the Bristol with Horton?

He reached Shotton by four o'clock on Christmas Eve; and walked up from the station, the better part of two miles along a quiet country road. No sooner had he stepped out on the platform than there came on him the same sense of refreshment as had come on him at Ushant; though there was an immense difference between the illumination of that golden sunset and the stealing twilight of December. Unlit save for a streak or two of sand-color and argent in the west, a fell of cloud, gray overshot with brown, lay in bank after bank immovable from pole to pole, and under it a north wind blew cold and pure through the stripped brown woods and over the matted and faded fields. Mark never wore an overcoat, and when he first left the train he shivered, but

swift walking soon warmed his blood, and when he
reached the heavy woods of Shotton, and the gaunt house,
pale against the empurpled twilight, he was looking and
feeling more like his old self than he had done for many
a day.

Tea was in the library, so Davis said, the white-haired
butler; and his "Mr. Sturt, ma'am," was an old servant's
welcome to a friend of the house. There was no light
in the room except the rich glow of the hearth, stacked
with faggots and peat half-way up the chimney, but as
Mark entered with his easy stride, carrying his head
rather high, various figures detached themselves in bas
relief, rosed over by the fireshine or dim against
the linen-folded panels. In the great bay with Charles
Ferrier were gathered a group of riders, the men in
breeches and boots, the women in habits; two of Mrs.
Ferrier's brothers, young army men, and some friends
of the family of many years' standing whom Mark had
met before at Shotton. Near the fire in a big chair he
recognized the gray head and plain, dignified features of
George Mallinson, and at his feet Dodo, slender as a
young girl in her cream color and ermine, was sitting
on the hearth with her arms about her knees. So much
Mark saw before Dodo uncurled herself and almost ran
to meet him. "I'm so glad you're come," she said, giving
him both her hands. "Charles, here's Mark! You do
know every one, don't you?—ah! Terry, you little fiend!
don't let him bother you!"

When Mark had shaken hands all round and dropped
into a chair near his hostess, he began to feel that he
was going to enjoy himself. Mrs. Essenden had taught
him that he was lonely, but she could not satisfy the
want she had created, no, not for a moment; no more
indeed could Dodo, but her warm uncritical kindness
soothed it for a time. Nor was it only Dodo who went

out of her way to make him welcome. A woman's welcome can do no more for a man, if his own sex give him
the cold shoulder, than men can do for a woman in the
parallel case, and Mark had come down slightly on the
defensive, for he had not forgotten the Savoy night, and
he was pretty sure that Ferrier, a Londoner to his finger-
tips and with all the Londoner's dread of a scene, would
remember it too; but there was no trace of criticism in
Ferrier's steady eyes, and Mark's stiffness melted when
he found himself adopted on the spot into the charmed
intimacy of family life. Terry alone was enough to keep
Mark happy; an imp of four, he took to Mark as children always did in spite of the fact that he never knew
what to say to them, and precipitated himself upon
Mark's legs as soon as he sat down. "I've got some new
knickers," he said, fixing Mark with a gimlet stare.
"Would you like to see them, Mr. Shirt?"

"Mr. Sturt, darling, not Mr. Shirt," interpolated Dodo
hastily.

"Shirt," said Terry with a riotous giggle. "Shirt. Mr.
Nightshirt." From dancing up and down on Mark's
knee he fell into Mark's arms, planting one foot on his
friend's stomach after the inconsiderate manner of small
children in big chairs. "Ow, I've hurt my foot. Mr.
Nightshirt, can you play bears?"

"Rather!"

"Ow. I shall come an' play bears to-morrow morning before you get up."

"Well, don't forget," said Mark with his hearty laugh.
"I shall lie awake all night thinking about it."

"Will you?" Terry said. He had been trying to tie the
tips of Mark's mustache into a bow, but he desisted suddenly and flung his arms round Mark's neck. "Yen I
like you better yan Mr. Potiphar."

Mark, like many, perhaps the majority of men, was

fond of children, but he had never connected them with
himself; his life had been too full to be handicapped with
the ties of a family, and he had none of that feudal feeling towards his Northern property which makes a man
crave for an heir. He had never desired a child. But
now he thought to himself, without tracing the fancy to
its origin or its conclusion, "And I might have a kid like
this—but not by Jenny Essenden."

Mrs. Ferrier fancied he was tired, and rose. "Terry,
fly to your father," she said. Terry, declining to fly anywhere, was carried writhing to the window seat, where
Ferrier was telling an apparently scandalous tale to his
brothers-in-law and Miss Travis. Mark watched him
scoop up the elf in one arm as he continued to make his
point, amid the ribaldry of his audience; what the point
was Mark did not hear, for Dodo had taken him out of
the room. She stopped beside the fire in the hall, arching one small foot to the flames, her blue eyes, blue as
steel, lifted to Mark's face. "I do, do hope you won't
be bored!" she said frankly. "We're terribly *intime*, I
know, and the Earles always behave like infants of
twenty when they get together. But you look so fagged,
Mark; I believe, if you only don't mind, it'll do you
good to be just one of us and put up with Terry's plati-
tudes."

"Oh, I like it," said Mark, smiling.

"Provided you don't get tired of it," said Dodo with
her inexpressive keenness of glance. Mark felt himself
flushing; surely she could not be going to cross-examine
him? But no; Dodo did not number want of common
sense among her irregularities of character.

"A person of simple tastes, aren't you? like Mr. Mallinson. I think men who work hard often are," she ran on,
apparently at random. "It is the Mr. Potiphars who
always have to be amused. Oh, that's Terry's joke, he

is great on nicknames, but really he did think it was Potiphar; I'd been telling him the story of Joseph just before Mr. Forester came."

"Is Mr. Forester here?"

"Yes, you haven't seen us all yet——" Dodo began, and then she broke off, as the outer door was thrown open. "There she is!" she said with a touch of vexation; and Mark saw framed in the entry against a somber sky the figure of a very tall woman in sable coat, cap, and muff, followed by Forester himself. Dodo's swift glance went from Mark to the new-comer, and then came back to him. Vague misgivings, so vague that she had felt thoroughly justified in disregarding them, rushed back upon her as she realized how badly she had blundered. But what was it—what was wrong between those two, that each looked at the other as if at a ghost, Mark Sturt reddening slowly to the roots of his hair and Maisie white as paper?

There could be no pause, and there was none. "Well, my darling," said Maisie, coming forward and giving her hand to Dodo, "how are you and how is Terence? Oh, yes, thanks, I came in the car, but I saw Mr. Forester at the gate, so I walked up through the park with him. No, we're not cold—are we, Harry?" Then she turned to Mark. "How d'ye do, Mr. Sturt? I'd no idea you were going to be here. Unexpected pleasure."

"Who is it?"

"I—Dodo."

"Oh! come in."

Dodo entered. She was wearing another of the soft ivory-colored dresses that Ferrier liked her in, and with her curly fair hair and slender shoulders she seemed younger and less a woman of the world than her friend, who, in black velvet and Mechlin lace, resembled one

of Vandyck's gallant ladies. Maisie's splendid hair was
dressed elaborately as usual, and she was in the act of
fixing a pearl-set Spanish comb among its soft puffs and
coils. "How smart we are!" Dodo said, kneeling down
by the fire. "But why do you never wear your wonderful diamonds, Maisie? Are you afraid of their being
stolen?"

"I shouldn't care a pin if an enterprising burglar made
a clean sweep of them," said Maisie. She patted a second comb softly into place, and then she put out the lamps
and threw herself into an easy chair on the other side
of the hearth. "Diamonds are vanity. Dodo, you look
pale and conscience-stricken. What is it? Pass me my
cigarettes and tell me all about it."

Dodo prepared to comply, but seemed to find a difficulty. "I do wish you wouldn't sit with your knees
crossed," she said irrelevantly. "You have very nice
ankles, but——"

"But you are not looking pale because I show too much
of my legs," said Miss Archdale in the high classic drawl
which enabled her to speak her mind with so much point
and fluency. "If you have any questions to ask, ask
them. I know I gave myself away this afternoon, thanks
to your talent for arranging surprises. On the whole
I think I'll get the first shot in myself: why didn't you
tell me Mr. Sturt was going to be here?"

"Why should I?"

"Poor," said Maisie, "very poor. Have another go."

"But upon my honor I don't know!" Dodo answered.
She sat curled round on a cushion, one hand clasping her
foot, while in her eyes danced golden specks reflected
from the flames: leaping flames, yellow ribbons veined
with sapphire and vermilion, and branching upwards into
weedy fringes of brown and hyacinth blue and chryso-
prase green. "Twice or three times I was going to tell

you, and then I thought I wouldn't, but I didn't, and don't, know why. You didn't seem to see much of him when you were with us in July."

"I saw more of him than you knew."

Dodo was silent, and after a moment Maisie went on. "This much I will tell you, Dodo, because I want you to play up. You didn't tell me he was going to be here, or tell him I was, because you had an inkling that if you did one of us would stay away. You were quite right. He is connected for me with the most painful, the most humiliating experience of my life. It was no fault of his, and you need not think you can guess what it was, because you can't—the conditions were too unlikely, too bizarre. But there it is, if you had warned me I couldn't have forced myself on him."

"I'm very sorry."

"I'm not. It had to come. I shan't run away. Only, be content with what you've done, dear child. Leave me to make the running. Don't, in your affectionate zeal, send me in to dinner with him, or arrange accidental tête-à-tête."

"Is it likely? Do you think I ever would have asked you if I had known there was any feeling of this kind between you?"

"Do I? Don't I?" Maisie stuck out her slender foot, shod in the Louis-Quinze slipper that matched her velvet dress and the pearls in her hair. "No, I don't think these·shoes were dear at fifteen guineas; it's always satisfactory to be unique. Really I can't see why you did it at all. You must have had some motive—you were matchmaking as far back as July. Why have you set your heart on marrying me to Mark Sturt?"

"I like you both so much. And"—Dodo hesitated—"I always did think Mr. Sturt was a little in love with you."

"Mr. Sturt in love with me!" Maisie repeated in an accent of profound surprise. "Good heavens! why, he never spoke to me if he could help it!"

"Ah, you don't know him as well as I do." Maisie smiled ruefully, feeling that Dodo's words were true, though not as Dodo meant them; Maisie's judgment was entangled in personal relations, and she could not step far enough back to gain the detached standpoint of the critic. "He was caught, fascinated, but he wouldn't yield to the fascination. He didn't much want to marry any one. And then he's proud—men of his age always are; he knew you had refused twenty people, and he wouldn't a bit have liked to be the twenty-first."

"He never would have been."

"*Maisie!*"

But Miss Archdale passed on so carelessly that Dodo could not decide if the words were a confession or no. "You're wrong: quite wrong. I'm not the sort of woman he likes. He doesn't want a woman of his own height, he wants a little clinging person with brown eyes and an affectionate disposition. He's very domesticated, is Mark. His ideal lady would exist to warm his slippers and bring his babies into the world."

"Cynic!" said Mrs. Ferrier gently. Lifting her keen blue eyes, she searched her friend for a sign of relenting, but the handsome mask was impenetrable in its good-humored scorn. Dodo sighed, and suddenly her impatience overflowed in blunt speech. "Don't pose, Maisie. If you married, you wouldn't shirk motherhood."

Maisie took her cigarette out of her mouth to laugh. She stretched out her long limbs with a touch of the old vanity, the flame-light flickering over her sculptured shoulders and the deep curves of bosom and waist. "Faith, shouldn't I? Think of my figure."

"Thanks for that."

"Why?"

"Because now I know you are romancing by the yard," said Dodo placidly. "You forget, my love: I've seen you with Terry."

"With Terry? Well: ah, well . . ."

The broken murmur ended in a long sigh, and she tossed her cigarette into the fire. "Would you like me to come and kiss you, Dorothea? I'd rather not, but it's the orthodox prelude to a girlish confidence, and I have a very great desire to confide in you. Also I have a very great desire to weep. I don't know why one should always ride oneself on the curb. I jest at holy things because I don't want to cry, but after all why shouldn't one cry now and then? Oh! my heart . . . I shall if you bother me about Terry. Happy woman! you have everything. But you weren't happy always. Did you want children, before you married?"

"No: do you?"

"Yes, very much: I should love to have one of my own. It makes me ache to feel Terry in my arms. He isn't mine, though. I want something right out of me, made of me. Dodo, didn't Terry take to Mark? I'm so glad he likes him better than Mr. Potiphar. Poor Harry! he is full of good intentions, but he hasn't a way with children. Mark has. He loves them, and he is sweet with them: he doesn't a bit know what to do with them, but he lets them do anything on earth they like with him. I watched him with Terry this evening when they didn't know I was there; Terry was a little demon, but Mark was a willing victim. He was a German, and Terry shot him. I should love to see him with a child of his own."

"I suppose you know what you're telling me."

"Perfectly, thanks."

"And you don't mind my knowing?"

"Rather. No, I don't care; I don't care much about anything, if I could only stop the—the pain for a little while. It is a silly position, isn't it? I can still see it's silly, but I don't feel it as a humiliation, I only feel it as a pain. Usedn't I to be rather a proud, independent sort of woman? I haven't any pride left; if Mark held up his little finger I would go to him, and I wouldn't ask much either—only the crumbs from his table. I wouldn't stipulate for ardor, I would be content with a little affection. Just to warm his slippers and bear his babies."

"Oh! Maisie! Maisie!"

"And that is love," said Maisie. She leaned forward, stretching out her hands to the fire as if she felt cold; her eyes were steady and brilliant, but Mrs. Ferrier saw that she was trembling. "Love that the poets write songs about. I don't think it's any fun at all. Do you suppose other women do the trick as completely, Dodo? Did you?"

"Yes."

"And you were very unhappy. But it's over now. Or do the scars never fade?"

"Never," said Dodo, her face darkening for a moment. "But that doesn't matter. Never to be happy is the price one pays for loving another person better than oneself."

"And you think it's worth while?"

"Yes."

"So do I," said Maisie simply. "But oh! it hurts."

Now and then in dark hours the need of human companionship is very great. Maisie covered her eyes with one hand and laid the other on Dodo's knee; a maiden hand, for she had taken off Mark's rings in the train that carried her away from Ushant, and had slipped them on the chain that bore Philip's portrait. Dodo, who knew nothing of either rings or locket—she was vaguely acquainted with the tragedy of the *Redruth Castle,* but not from Maisie, and she had never heard Philip's name —Dodo drew courage from her own experience to throw her arm, for a moment, lightly and shyly round Maisie's neck. There was much that she did not understand; but that Maisie had suffered, and suffered deeply, was evident from the indefinable change, the saddened maturity that had come on her since July. Six months ago and Maisie was still a girl, high-spirited and impatient; she had been in the thick of the fight since then, and had come out of it scarred and sobered. Youth takes wing when we begin to realize that we have no particular right to be happy, and that the universe will not, on our account, go one step out of its way; this lesson Maisie had learned, apparently—the old nursery lesson, "You must not snatch." But in what school had she endured discipline?

What perplexed Dodo most of all was the way in which Maisie spoke of Mark. She loved him; he did not love her; surely there was an end of the matter? The rest could only be a question of bearing pain with fortitude. But Maisie seemed to look on the game as only half played, and the candor with which she spoke of possible further developments would have shocked Dodo if it had not been vindicated by its own simplicity. Mrs. Ferrier was no prude, and she was not, as some women are, afraid to face the mysteries of life and passion, but she was a wife, and it seemed strange to her that Maisie should disregard the conventional delicacies which veil them from the unmarried. How came Maisie by this intimacy of the imagination? And what right had she to assume, as she did implicitly in every word, that there was to be any future relation between her life and Mark's? Dodo was baffled.

Later she was to realize that what baffled her was precisely this nameless, pervasive difference between the married and the unmarried point of view. Even such a marriage as Maisie's must confer rights and constitute a bond. Loved or unloved, the wife has a lien on a man's private life, on the disposition of his future, on the very substance of his nature. This is fact, not fancy—law, not whim; Mark himself, having done little cool thinking since he went to Normandy, was scarcely awake to it, but it was the foundation on which Maisie based her few remaining hopes.

"And, Dodo——"

"What is it, dear?"

"Is he—do you—have you——"

"Oh, Maisie! Maisie!"

"What is this rotten tale that is going about? You know what I mean; I suppose Charles doesn't turn a deaf ear to the gossip of the clubs. Louis Haynes' wife tried to tell me, but I shut her up. But to-night, when I watched him— He has changed."

Dodo winced, she had dreaded this question.

"Dear, forgive me: are you wise—indeed, have you any right to examine into Mr. Sturt's private life?"

"Yes, I have the right."

"Oh, I don't understand you. Yes, it is true." Maisie was mute. "True so far as it goes. Such things don't go very far, do they? Anyhow, women have to bear them. But, if it's any comfort to you, my own impression is that he'd be thankful to be rid of her."

"Her?"

"Mrs. Essenden—you meant that? Oh, goodness!" Dodo murmured in an accent of dismay. "Oh, you only meant that time at the Savoy?"

"Who the devil is Mrs. Essenden? His mistress?"

"Maisie! Maisie!"

"Come, it only wanted that!" said Maisie with the wreck of a laugh. "Is it the lovely Jenny Essenden that Freddy Field went off with? How very nice for Mark! Has it gone on long?"

"Since August, Charles said."

"August? you don't say so. My high-minded Mark! August . . . and I who loved him because he was a Catholic and a mystic . . . oh, and he was, he was! oh, my darling, oh, my darling . . ."

The tears had their way at last. Dodo sat still, not daring to touch her friend now. Not many drops fell, however. Maisie was not one of the women who find relief in tears. She dashed the bright dew from her eyelashes and lay back in her chair, pressing her handkerchief to her lips to still their trembling.

"Don't take it so to heart," Dodo pleaded. "You know these things don't count in a man's life as they do in ours; not an unmarried man, anyhow. It's all wrong, of course, but it's the world we live in."

"And all men are alike: and you wouldn't care, would you, if Charles—?"

"He is my husband."

"True: and I am not Mark's wife," said Maisie with an indefinable accent of irony.

She pulled herself languidly to her feet. "I must wash my face; it's ten to eight. Oh, yes, I shall come down to dinner; a little *blanc de perle* will hide the ravages of grief. Oh, dear me, where's my rose-water? Tell me everything you know about this affair with Mrs. Essenden—is it casual or settled? Does she live with him?"

"She has a house of her own in Westminster, which Mark is supposed to be paying for; that may or may not be true."

"But it is certain that he goes to her? It's no mere club gossip?" Dodo reluctantly shook her head. "But why should you think he wants to be quit of her?"

"Because he did such an extraordinary thing when I asked him here. I wrote to him at his flat in Park Court, but I suppose he was——" Dodo stumbled—"it was forwarded to him in Green Street, for he wrote his reply to me from that woman's house and on her paper. I tore it up, because I knew how Charles would storm if he got hold of it, but I'm pretty certain Mark didn't do it out of carelessness, and still more that he didn't mean it for an insult. For thirty seconds I was cross, and I thought of wiring to him not to come, but directly I thought it over I saw what he meant."

"And what did he mean?"

"A confession and a fair warning; if it didn't sound so absurd, I should say just a little bit of an appeal. I am convinced that he wouldn't have done it if he weren't feeling rather sick about it all."

"Yes, I dare say he is sick about it," Maisie assented in level tones. She crossed to the window and stood looking out into the dark night; her thoughts were as somber as the wintry landscape, over which a rigor of frost was settling down under a heaven of tropical stars. ". . . Oh, my beloved: oh, Mark, my darling, I'd have died for you, and I've thrown you straight into this woman's hands. For it's all my doing, I tried you too high, and so in the reaction my knight without reproach has fallen as other men fall. And I who could have kissed the ground under your feet at Ushant because you weren't like other men! You're in the dust now; you're not much better than I am. I shall have something to forgive, as well as to be forgiven. That is bitter. I suppose it's always the way, the envenomed torment of sinning is that one makes others sin whom one would have died to keep superior to oneself. But it will bring you back to me. Some day when you're sick

of her you'll remember that you have a wife and you'll
turn to me for deliverance. Beloved, for your sake I'd
rather you never came to me than that you were brought
to me by sin and weakness, but for my own? . . . Thank
God she can't give you legitimate children."

The last words were half audible. *"What* did you say,
Maisie?" asked Mrs. Ferrier, startled.

"I say," answered Maisie, strolling back to the fire,
"that it's lucky Charles doesn't open your letters, or
there would have been a row. He would not have followed your subtleties, he would have said it was an un-
gentlemanly thing to do."

"But Mark is a gentleman."

"You stick up for your friends, don't you, Dodo?"

"You like to hear me stick up for Mark, don't you,
Marcella?"

"Rather," Maisie admitted. "Not that I care much,
after all. I have the makings of a good wife in me,
Dodo, a humble, faithful, unassuming Griselda of a wife;
if he swore at me, if he beat me, if he went away to
Green Street now and then I wouldn't care, if he would
let me stay with him between times. Come, let's go
down; I promised to try over Harry Forester's new
song with him before dinner, and I forgot all about it.
One's so apt to forget Harry Forester."

CHAPTER XIII

Dire que j'ai vécu avec ça . . .

SOME hours later, on that same Christmas Eve of his arrival at Shotton, Mark Sturt, for the first time since he went to Normandy, settled down to think out his affairs.

Long after the rest of the household were in bed and asleep, he sat back in a big chair by the fire in his room, pulling hard at his pipe, and staring from under shaded eyes into the chase of flames. Political work trains the faculty of concentration, and Mark, who was not weak —though he had acted weakly—tackled the problem of his own conduct systematically point by point. "Quelques découvertes que l'on ait faites dans le pays de l'amour-propre, il y reste encore bien des terres inconnues." Mark had not liked it when from Considine he heard his wife's name linked with Harry Forester's; but when hearsay turned to eye-witness—when Forester led Maisie in out of the snowy night—Mark was shocked out of five months of drifting by the recoil of jarred pride. He sat down to think: and his conclusion was that since July he had played the fool, actively or passively, in every branch of life.

What brought home his own folly to him as nothing else would have done was having to fight off an in-clination to stimulate thought by resort to his hunting flask. He stood aghast at himself. The impulse was brief but strong—so strong that he was tempted to end it by emptying good brandy out of the window. Tempted?

Yes, tempted to fly temptation. "Well, I'm damned!" he said aloud, standing flask in hand beside the windy night. "No, I'm not, but I'm within arm's length of it." He screwed the cap on again and pitched the flask, still full, back into his drawer: then, returning to his chair by the fire, "No, my friend," he said with a jerk of his shoulders, "no more of that rot. Understand once for all, Mark Sturt, that little bottles of brandy don't rank as temptation."

Indeed the imp of the spirit flask had never gained any hold over Mark, and in five minutes' time he had forgotten it in a struggle with fiends more robust. He was astonished to find how little grip he had of the forces with which he was contending. Five months of drifting —five months of Jenny's tutelage—had disorganized his brain. "What have I been doing since July?" he asked himself, forcing his fogged mind to classify and concentrate. "Take Gatton first." What of Gatton, the preoccupation of thirteen arduous years? Locked in his dispatch case lay half a dozen letters from Jack Bennet, all of them unanswered, the last even unread. Mark fairly shrugged his shoulders over his own folly. "I'll tackle those letters and write to Jack before I sleep," he said. Luckily Bennet, though unutterably bewildered and sore, was a loyal and able lieutenant, and Gatton was not likely to have suffered by its master's aberration. Mark wished all other debts could have been written off as swiftly.

What of his Parliamentary ambitions? "Five months to the bad," was Mark's net verdict, and he grew rather white about the mouth as he framed it. The favor of a less conspicuous lady might have passed virtually unnoticed, but Jenny was a torch to scandal. Mark had talked to George Mallinson that night, and it had not taken him ten minutes to gauge the attitude of the white-

haired Chancellor. Those kind gray eyes, accustomed
to the reading of men, would have been more friendly
and less reserved if Mark had met him before it became
necessary to make allowances for the Savoy night, and
the house in Green Street, and all the poisonous exag-
gerated rumor that Jenny had set flying about Mark's
name. "By Jove, I'll sit in Mallinson's pocket for the
next ten days!" Mark said to himself with a savage laugh.
"My hand is steady anyhow." As for the liaison with
Jenny, he could but hope that when it was broken the
rumors that had sprung out of it would die away of
themselves.

"When it was broken." It had to be broken, then?
Yes, if Mark hoped for office; he knew that no official
post could be held concurrently with that of Jenny's
lover. "She is too *panache,*" he reflected with a hard
smile; "I must break that link"; and then it seemed to
him that his very being dissolved in weakness. He shifted
in his chair and the sweat came out on his face. What!
break it once for all? break it from to-night? Never
again? Never. . . ? "Never," repeated the tiny warder
of his will. But his hand shook as he wiped his streaming temples, and his nerve gave way before the image of
Jenny which rose up out of the dark, in the firelit room,
like a ghost—and what a ghost! Her long curls fell
across his eyes, her sweetness, warmth, and perfume
came into his arms: but, though the lure of this ghost
of passion was as strong as life, it could not quench the
fires it lit. Only Jenny's self could do that. Oh! once
more, for the last time! "Once more?" said the warder
of his will. "No, my friend, never again. 'Once more'
has broken lives innumerable of better men than you.
Your solitary chance lies in 'never again.' Make your
mind up—if she has left you a mind to make up—and
stick to it."

An hour later Mark was back in his chair beside the sinking fire. He looked ravaged, but a measure of peace had come to him after the fight. Mrs. Essenden had not had time enough to do her work thoroughly; she had sapped his will but not broken it. "I'll settle with Jenny before I go to Gatton. A check-book and a waiting taxi. I wonder what she'll stand me in to get quit of her? A pretty stiff figure, I fancy." Such was the sum of Sturt's reflections, in which it will be seen that he did not flatter Mrs. Essenden; but men's thoughts rarely flatter ladies of her craft.

So much for Gatton, and Mr. Mallinson, and Jenny: and now to home affairs. But on this topic Mark could by no means reduce himself to method. He could think only by flashes. "She is my wife," he said. "She holds the place my mother held." His wife! Aye: though the fascination of Jenny was still on him, he felt the difference between the durable and the impermanent tie. "She is the only woman who can give me legitimate children." Though by a different path, he had come to the same landmark that Maisie had reached months ago. "I ought to have a son. It is ten to one Lawrence will never marry. When I die, who will take my place at Gatton? Besides . . . that's a jolly little beggar, that kid of Ferrier's." In the ellipse lay a world of dim feeling, the slow, shy instinct of paternity that rarely stirs in men till after marriage, the sense of duty to the State, and to his own manhood, and to the linked generations of the dead.

"Then there's Forester." All the evening Mark had stood aside; he was not going to exchange shots with Harry Forester—he, the husband, with that luckless innocent lover! but his pride bled inwardly. "They all think she'll marry him." Maisie gave Forester no encouragement, Mark acquitted her of that meanness; but it did not strike her, apparently, that there was a third point of view to be considered. "The position has become insufferable." The position had not changed at all; it was Mark himself who had changed, imperceptibly shifting his point of view from day to day. "I must put a stop to it." He had only to pronounce certain words, and at Ushant it would have been easy to say them. But Ushant had gone as far away as another man's life, and the Maisie who had poured his tea and buttered his bread had turned into a friendly stranger. Mark groped in darkness.

"Time enough to settle that when I'm quit of Jenny." This was as near as Mark had got to a decision when he rose at last and began to undress, after scrawling his unbusinesslike Stonyhurst signature—"Yours ever, Mark"—at the foot of a long letter to Jack Bennet. "Till then my hands are tied. Meanwhile I mark time and take my chance to disabuse Mallinson of his crotchets." He stood by the open window in his shirt and trousers, and the north wind, bitter with frost, blew in on his chest. Mark rather liked the bracing cold. He threw up his arms with a yawn and stretched his great body, into which, sleepy as he was, the hot blood of power and determination came flowing back as he realized that from that night onward he was committed to a fight. He stared out into the dark, and his heavy eyes softened. "Ah! Guy, old fellow . . ." He had not prayed since he left Duclair with Jenny; why pray, when one is living in mortal sin? But now, with his inveterate simplicity, he bent his knee.

Salve regina, mater misericordiae, vita, dulcedo, et spes nostra, salve.
Ad te clamamus exsules filii Evae,
Ad te suspiramus.

Jenny's lover had need of that prayer. " 'Must go round to Green Street now," was Sturt's final reflection as he flung himself into bed.

"Dear me, what a pretty scene!" said Mr. Mallinson. "This is the sort of day that makes even old stagers like you and me feel young again—hey, Sturt?"

"Oh, quite," said Mark cheerfully. "Let me buckle that strap for you, sir, shall I?"

"No, no, please don't," said Mr. Mallinson, fumbling with his gloved fingers: "—oh, thank you, my dear boy, but you really shouldn't!"

It was New Year's Eve, and "seasonable weather." The snow that fell on the night of Maisie's arrival continued to fall thick and soft for four and twenty hours; then the clouds blew over and the sun came out in a pale blue sky—but the temperature held. The lake froze in one night, and the ice hardened in the very noonday under the breath of a north wind. The scene that had taken Mr. Mallinson's fancy might have been a Russian landscape, so clear was the western lighting and so pure the mask that sparkled under it over the undulating valley. The beechwood was plumed with snow, the pastures glittered, oak and ash and elm threw long blue shadows across them, not the skeleton shadows proper to December, but dense and blurred as in summer leaf. The lake itself, in its frame of forest and field, resembled a drawing in water color, so animated yet so delicately clear appeared the knots and couples that dissolved and reformed on its gray and polished floor.

Mark helped the Finance Minister on with his skates. Mallinson was a plain, blunt-featured, blue-eyed man of sixty, with a broad forehead queerly modeled by the calculating brain within, and till ten days ago Mark had never understood why Mallinson was so well loved in the House. Ten days ago Mark had seen in him only a useful man to cultivate. But this ambition, never very keen—Mark was not made of supple stuff—had not survived an hour's experience of the great statesman's transparent honesty and goodness. Mallinson was one of the most powerful factors in the Liberal government of the day, because in no matter what ministerial combination he was secure of his own post, but in private life he was as simple as a child, with a courteous modesty of manner that seemed to deprecate a snub. He was no orator; he had no backing of wealth or landed influence; but he had budgeted for England in the first stricken years of peace, when deficits were piling up and every man urged economy on every class but his own; and Gatton had trained Mark to appreciate the vast work that those lean gentle hands had done. Comparing record and manner, Mark conceived for the elder man a deep admiring affection, while Mallinson in his turn was grateful and touched. By what law does amity spring up? Politics were merged in the unexpected pleasure of a friendship that bridged the gap between thirty-five and sixty, between the untried private member and the high command.

Mallinson safe on the ice, Mark returned to put his own skates on. It was the first time that he had been down to the lake; throughout the genial festivities of Christmas he had stood a little apart, friendly but preoccupied; but as he pulled down his white sweater and stamped the snow from his boots his spirits began to rise. He was out of practice, but he had learned his form in Petrograd, and he had not gone twenty yards before the old ease came back. He looked about him. A military band from Hillingdon was playing merry French airs from a pavilion on the island, and far down the lake Maisie was waltzing with Harry Forester. Harry was rather conscientious than graceful, and his reversing was a trial to his partner. Mark's glance sparkled. What of Amyas Saltau's wife, the Dresden China Frenchwoman with the forget-me-not eyes? Mark had watched her at Prince's. She was, by her marriage, some connection of his mother's family.

"Madame," said Mark, "will you waltz this with me?"

"I did not know you waltzed," said Claude Saltau. "I have been waltzing with Mr. Forester. I am a little tired." She stuck her head on one side. "Are you—are you a bay horse?"

"Er—a bay horse? Oh, I beg your pardon, do you mean a dark horse?" returned Mark, who was accustomed to Mrs. Saltau's lapses into imperfectly mastered slang. "Come and try."

"A bay horse is a dark horse," said Claude, affronted. "These distinctions are very stupid. But, since you are so confident, come then, my pippin."

Light faded, shadows lengthened; a windless cold settled down over the white fields, dispersing the elder company and thinning the younger. The far end of the lake, where the beechwood stood on guard against the brilliant pallor of sunset, was now comparatively clear. In the east the moon hung broad and bright like a gold coin over a peak or two of snowcloud scarlet in the afterglow. Skilled ice-dancing is the poetry of motion; and Mark and his cousin, flying over the glassy floor in the long sweeping curves of the waltz, swayed to the merry music as the reed sways to the wind.

"How well you skate!" said Dodo, poising in front of Mark like a gray bird in her soft chinchillas, after Claude had left him. "I had no idea you were such a dandy."

"Thank you." Mark accepted the compliment gravely. He was enjoying himself. "Not so well as my brother."

"But then you don't do anything so well as your

brother," Dodo was impertinent enough to retort. "I
don't remember ever to have had so many figure skaters
on the ice before. Let's do something to astonish the
natives!"

"Might get up a Lancers, what?" suggested Mark
lazily. "Bags I you for my partner if we do. There
would be plenty of light, with a clear sky and a full
moon."

"Oh, yes, let's!" Dodo cried. "Fly and tell the men
what to play while I get the set together."

There was no difficulty in arranging a set of sixteen.
They were forming on the ice when Mark came back:
Roderick Earle and Grace Travis, Claude Saltau and
Charles Ferrier, Harry Forester and a daughter of the
vicarage, and so on. There was a hitch over the last
couple: Dodo wanted Mr. Mallinson to come in, and
Mr. Mallinson, laughing like a schoolboy, protested that
he had not been on the ice for fifteen years, and also
that he had forgotten how to dance the Lancers. "So
have all of us," said Dodo cheerfully. "It's as old as
the hills. But what does it matter on the ice? Of course
we shall get into a dreadful muddle, but anyhow it will
be great fun."

"But I'm not steady on my legs!" said the statesman
ruefully. "I shall tumble down and upset you all, you
mark my words. You young things will get on far better without me, and I shall be quite happy sitting on the
bank."

"Come and dance with me, Mr. Mallinson," said
Maisie, appearing from the island where Ferrier had
been tightening a strap for her. "I haven't any partner,
and I should love to say I had skated the Lancers with a
Finance Minister. I saw you doing the most wonderful loops this afternoon."

Maisie was in her sable cap and coat, the latter thrown

open and revealing her beautiful throat, bare under its veil of tulle as if the day had been midsummer. She had a cluster of purple violets pinned at her breast, and her eyes were sparkling as she tossed away her muff and stretched out her warm bare hand to the statesman. George Mallinson shrugged his shoulders, laughed, and surrendered at discretion. The band were already striking up the prelude as they glided to their places, filling the last gap; and not till then did Maisie realize that she was standing next to Mark Sturt. It was too late to escape.

Perhaps it was due to Mr. Mallinson's gray hairs or perhaps to the influence of the scene and hour that the dancers found themselves going through the old-fashioned, intricate, and graceful evolutions with unexpected decorum. Riot would have been out of harmony with that gray arena, the solemn guardianship of snowy woodland, the mingling light and shadow of afterglow and moonshine, the sweet, plaintive music a little dimmed by distance and dispersal through the open air. Advancing and retiring, crossing hands and exchanging courtesies, they all fell under the same spell. The other skaters had stopped to watch them, and there was scarcely a sound except the dry grinding clash of steel on ice.

Disaster, however, came with the Third Figure. It was a graceful group, Mark thought, as the men stood waiting with hands locked together, the women on the edge of the circle poising easily for flight; but as soon as they glided off he realized that the chain would not hold. The ice was too smooth, the pace too hot, and the centrifugal force too violent for undrilled resistance. A woman's nervous laugh, then Roderick Earle's "Look out, Gracie!" and "Oh, Lord!" from Ferrier, a gasped "So sorry!" from another man—and then the link of hands broke and the dancers scattered. Mark himself and Charles Ferrier stood fast. But Mallinson, out of practice and hampered by the stiffness of his sixty years, was the first to let go, and as he staggered back, reeling to a heavy fall, he dragged Maisie with him. Instantly Mark released Dodo, whose balance had never been imperiled, and struck forward to throw his arm round Maisie, drawing her round with him and away from Mallinson till she came naturally to a level footing. For that moment she was in his arms, and as he bent over her he saw the glitter of a gold chain under her tulle vest. Ushant—the smart of flame on his arm—harebells dancing in the grass before the White Cottage—the sting of salt wind in the open doorway—it all came back like yesterday as Mark watched the scarlet blood burn under the fine skin, and the intervening time dwindled to a shadow in retrospect. A stranger? No, Jenny was the stranger: this was his wife.

A moment later they were standing erect and disengaged, and Maisie, as her blush ebbed, raised her brilliant eyes and murmured an easy "Thank you." Mark bowed silently. A voice from the bank said "Bravo!"

Mark turned round, unable to believe his ears. But there was no mistaking that very tall, slight figure, or the delicately cut colorless features, or indeed the costume—Lawrence all over: a Russian jacket to the hips, fur-lined and fur-bordered, high boots laced from point to knee, and arrowy Russian skates; Lawrence back from Colorado, and appearing with his habit of dramatic abruptness at a moment when his brother would have preferred to be unobserved. "Is it you?" said Mark, quitting his companions without apology, and skating over to the bank. "Lawrence? I hadn't a notion you were coming back. Or did a letter miscarry?"

"Not to my knowledge. But let me apologize first to Mrs. Ferrier," said Lawrence, stepping on the ice. He was bareheaded, with an indifference to cold which was as characteristic in its way as the hardy male coquetry of his outlandish furs, and he came up to Dodo with one of his deep foreign bows. "Will you forgive me? I'm only just home from Colorado, and I've done a fearful thing. You never will forgive me, I know."

"Yes, I shall forgive you anything if you look at me like that," said Dodo helplessly. She was far from approving of Lawrence, whose affectations filled her with rage, but he had his own way with her when he liked, as indeed he had with many women. "What have you done? Eloped with some one, I suppose—I do hope it isn't my cook!"

"Taken possession of a bedroom and unpacked and changed my clothes," said Lawrence, showing his white teeth in a hearty laugh. "Do you mind—awfully? I only got in last night, and they told me Mark was down here, and there didn't seem to be a soul in town, and I was bored to tears, so I thought the best plan all round would be for you and Ferrier to take me in too?"

"Oh! is that all?"

Dodo's tone of unaffected relief made the culprit laugh again. "All, on my honor! What do you take me for? Any one would think I came to steal the spoons!"

"Go: I want to look after Mr. Mallinson," said Dodo, waving him away. "Go and talk to Mark, if that's what you came down for; you might at least have the decency to *pretend* you came to see me. Have you had anything to eat, poor wanderer?"

"Oh, yes, thanks—they gave me some lunch as soon as I got here."

"I might have known it!" was Dodo's perfectly audible comment, as she flitted away to look after the statesman, who was sitting on a chair on the bank, nursing his shoulder and apologizing to his anxious friends for having been the first to break the chain. Lawrence, who hated amiable people, stared at the group for a moment from under dropped eyelids, and then turned to his brother.

"Get away down there where the ice is clear and we'll show the aborigines a trick or two, Mark."

Mark, who was indifferent to comment but not fond of it, hung back, but Lawrence laid a hand on his arm.

"Come along, you ass—I've traveled over five thousand miles to talk to you, and I'm going to do it now." He dragged his brother down the lake, a long stone's throw away from the group on the bank, and began solemnly to perform the intricate evolutions which he and Mark had learned together one winter on the Neva. "How it all comes back! Remember that time we skated up together from Petrograd to the Gulf of Finland, and the queer white nights at the winter gardens on the way? What was that figure they called the trepaka? We'll do that. I'm out of form, but I doubt if the connoisseurs on the bank will discover it. Do 'em good to see what real figure-skating's like, silly fools. Well, how are you?"

"Much as usual," said Mark, wondering what possible motive could lie at the back of his brother's proceedings, which appeared to him to be even odder than usual. However, it was less trouble to give in than to argue, and he followed Lawrence with stoic gravity in the half-forgotten maze of figures; many a time they had wheeled through it together amid the medly of students and nobles and bagmen at the Usúpov Club.

"You don't look it. Curious tangle you seem to have wound yourself up in while I've been away! The crowning indiscretion didn't burst upon me till I saw you with Miss Archdale just now. No accounting for tastes, old man; she's excessively handsome, I admit, but I doubt if you can drive her tandem. However, you seem to have her very well in hand."

"Look here," said Mark, stopping short, "if you came home from Colorado to say this kind of thing, I'm sorry you took the trouble. That subject is barred."

"Temper!" said Lawrence: "wait a bit. I haven't begun on my subject yet. When I do you really will want to kick me, but you see you can't do it out here." He performed a maneuver which brought the whole supple length of his figure to an angle of sixty degrees with the ice, came erect again with a swinging pirouette, and paused to light a cigar. Some of the spectators on the shore had begun to drift towards the western end of the lake to watch the curious, foreign-looking performance. Lawrence shifted the cigar between his teeth and spoke softly. "Though I only got back last night, I've snatched time to call on Mrs. Essenden."

"Who said anything to you about Mrs. Essenden?"

"You yourself, when you regretted not having taken my advice."

"Brilliant as you are, Lawrence—!"

"Considine, then, if you will have it."

"Ah? Very amiable of Considine."

"Yes, he said he felt sure you would thank him for his damned officiousness."

"No, I don't thank him, and I don't thank you," said Mark, out of patience. "I wish to goodness you would all mind your own business. Do I ever preach to you or Considine? I can't see why every jack-sprat in town should think he has a right to shove his nose into my affairs. Lord Vere collared me the other day, and I couldn't tell him to go to the deuce, but I can you and Considine, and by Jove I do! As for the woman I don't know anything about her, and I thought she was in Paris."

The anticlimax of the last remark made Lawrence shout with laughter; but he soon grew grave again. "Oh, you thought she was in Paris, did you? She is not, then. She's in Green Street. You owe me one that she hasn't turned up to-day down here."

"Turned up at Shotton!"

"Yes. You don't understand the fair Jenny. It seems you've annoyed her, my friend; you ran away, didn't you? without leaving your address. Jenny's particularly good at getting addresses. Few things annoy her more than for a man to try to break away."

He flashed off down the ice with his own erratic grace, reverting to a solo performance of the trepaka. Mark knew him well enough to be sure by now that affectation so whimsical could only cover news of weight. He waited: in a few moments Lawrence was at his side again.

"You're right, Mark, I really have something to say to you and I don't know how to begin. I thought it would say itself more easily if we were not alone, but I can't stand all these people staring. Let us get off the ice and walk up through the wood, it will be quiet there."

Mark was startled. He said no more till they were in the wood together, threading its frozen aisles. The last splendor of sunset had faded out by now, and they walked by the illumination of moonlight and starlight and snowlight; buried deep in crystal silence, they heard nothing but the crunch of dry snow underfoot, they saw nothing but the silvershafted beech trees gleaming away in dim reiteration under their hoods of snow. Far in the north the heavenly husbandman drove his glittering Plow, and in the east the Hunter knelt with arm thrown up, his sword belted to his thigh. Suddenly the air was full of a hollow moaning, and the plumed branches trembled; a gust of wind shook through the wood like a great sigh, and was gone again.

"What is at the bottom of all this, Lawrence?"

"Pretty the blue shadows are on the snow, aren't they? Bah! I'm cold." He turned up the wolf collar under his chin. "There is a breeze getting up. I thought the weather meant mischief. Aren't you going to thank me for calling on Jenny? A warm quarter of an hour you would have had if she had come down here and made a scene before all your little friends."

"Who told her where I was?"

"Some fellow she knew—Horton, I fancy. I doubt if he knew he told her."

"I must talk to Jenny."

"Aye: but the point is, what are you going to say?" Mark smiled, and his mouth hardened. "Think you can bully her, do you? My poor Mark! that shows how much you know about it. There's only one way to manage women of Jenny's type."

"That being—?"

"Beating them," said Lawrence grimly. "She wants the cat. Civilized countries don't allow it, more's the pity. I was much inclined to take the job on myself. What possessed you to let her fix her claws in you? I warned you. But I thought you were safe in Normandy. I had no idea Jenny had left town. I had a letter from her in October, postmarked Westminster. But I might have known it was a blind. I might have known she would not let a man go when she had once marked him down. She's a pest, is Jenny. A social pest. She wants killing. I've more than half a mind to do it myself."

"I don't," said Mark slowly, "dispute the general force of your observations, but in Mrs. Essenden's case they

aren't deserved. She was anxious to break the connection. I refused to let her go."

Lawrence stopped and faced his brother in a moonlit
clearing. His right hand opened and shut once or twice,
much as though he wished it were clenched on Jenny's
throat. Deep affection mingled with the deep impatience
in his tone.

"You silly ass!" he said again: "oh, Mark—you silly
ass!"

"Look here," Mark spoke wearily, "you mean well, I
dare say, but you're neither lucid nor civil. The whole
affair seems to me commonplace enough. What on earth
is there to make a fuss about?"

"She wanted to break the connection, did she? My
good chap, she marked you down six months ago—the
more fool I, to flatter myself I'd fooled her. She break
off? I'll be sworn! If she hadn't, you would have.
Reculer pour mieux sauter is a wile as old as Eve."

"You may be right," said Mark after a silence during
which his memory took a flying survey of the past and
found the charge unpleasantly confirmed. "I'm not an
expert. Haven't had your varied experience. But every
case hangs by its own rope. In the case of Jenny Essenden—how do you know?"

Lawrence paused to relight his cigar, which had gone
out. By matchlight Mark saw the fine-drawn sharpness
of his features, and the flicker of his momentary smile.

"She was my mistress before she was yours."

"You lie."

"Better have stayed by the lake, what?" said Lawrence. "Drop it, Mark." He knocked the stick out of
his brother's hand.

After a minute they walked on together in silence.

"Now you see why I returned from Colorado," resumed Lawrence. "Indiscriminate connections of that

sort aren't in your line, are they? Nor, to say truth, in mine. Not that it signifies a pin's point of course: if there were question of legality, one couldn't even call it illegal. Still I thought you would like to know about it."

"She knew."

"Naturally! You don't fondly imagine she'd care?"

"Thanks for telling me," said Mark. They had come out on the edge of the wood, and he stopped, holding out his hand. He made no other apology for his momentary flare of violence: had not Lawrence foreseen it? One could trust Lawrence to see in the dark. "Go back to the lake if you don't mind, we don't want them to think there's anything up. We'll talk this out later on. You'll have to give me place and date. But I'll take an hour to get used to it first." He was holding his brother's hand in a grip like that of a drowning man; Lawrence could not draw it away.

"Feel sick?" said Lawrence simply. "I did, the first ten minutes. Seems so—so perverse, doesn't it? I'm not precisely fastidious, and the connection, I may add, didn't last long; but all the same it filled me with disgust to think I'd lived with that."

"Quite," said Mark, letting him go. "Will you tell Ferrier I've gone on?"

CHAPTER XIV

THE skating party was already breaking up when Lawrence returned to it. After excusing Mark to Mrs. Ferrier, he had only time to take Maisie Archdale for one long flight over the darkling ice, their arms interlaced, the bright plaits under the sable cap lying close against his dark shoulder, before the music was brought to an end and the lake left deserted to the frost and the moon. But when they all walked up together through the snowy fields Lawrence kept fast at Maisie's side, and his attitude was sufficiently exclusive to provoke indiscretions. "So that was what fetched Lawrence Sturt back from Colorado!" was Roderick Earle's candid comment to Grace Travis, with whom he was on semibrotherly terms. Grace, however, answered with a sigh, "Oh, I hope not!" and refused to explain herself even under charge of being unduly taken with Lawrence's furs. Maisie herself, recalling the July passage-at-arms, began to wonder if she was to be the victim of another fit of adoration. She need not have been afraid. The truth was that Lawrence, with his hawk's eyes, had seen in that brief moment of his arrival more than any one else had ever seen, and, in the deep clannish affection for his brother which was the toughest though not the ruling force in his life, he was trying to find out how the land lay.

"Gloomy old place, Shotton," he remarked, as the gaunt Georgian façade loomed up twinkling through the dusk. "If I were Charles Ferrier I should let it. But I have no landed sentiment. It is a thousand pities Longstone Edge didn't go to Mark. That's our own feudal mansion at Gatton, you know; the feudality so far as we are concerned is not forty years old, but I believe Mark loves every stick and stone of it. Has he ever talked to you about it?"

"Never," said Maisie briefly: then giving way to a natural yearning, "Would Mr. Sturt ever talk of anything he really cared about?"

"Possibly not," said Lawrence, laughing. "I remember when I lunched with him at the Ritz the day when he was given his V.C.——"

"When he—*what?*"

"Didn't you know he was a V.C.?"

"No, I never knew it."

She was not a keen reader of the papers: she had never seen a letter addressed to Mark Sturt; and in conversation she avoided his name.

"It was earned," said Lawrence soberly, standing aside to let Maisie pass in. He had amused himself in the war, but even for him, even after thirteen years, some of its incidents were a sobering memory.

"I'm sure it was," said Maisie. "But I must go and dress now. You see we dine at seven to-night." And then she left him with a little smiling bow and ran away upstairs. There are tales that one would rather never hear at all than hear from an outsider. Lawrence Sturt, as he joined the knot of men who lounged round the hall fire, drew his own conclusions, and kept them to himself.

"Come in here for ten minutes, will you, Lawrence?"

Lawrence's eyes said, "Now I am going to be bored." But he turned into his brother's room without protest, though he hated to be hurried over dressing, and it was already after six o'clock. Shotton was an old house and solidly built, but the wind had risen in the last half hour, and Mark's room in the bachelor wing faced north. Lawrence looked vexed and ruffled. He dragged a sofa closer to the side of the fire and threw himself on it. "Do for heaven's sake shut those windows, Mark! What a beggar you are for draughts! One can have too much of the best fresh at six o'clock on a January night." He shot out a long arm and poked the fire to a blaze. "That's better. Are you going to dress up to-night?" Mark signified assent. "Thank heaven I can't." One would not have guessed from his expression that he was grateful to the fate that doomed him to appear in ordinary black and white at a New Year's masquerade. "Give me a cigar." Mark obeyed. "And a match—Mallinson took my last. Yes, and I'll have that other cushion." Mark threw it at his head. "Silly ass!" said Lawrence placidly, tucking it behind his neck. For an M.P. of thirty-five, I must say—!"

Mark, his hands buried in his pockets and his shoulders propped against the mantelpiece, spoke rather indistinctly across the stem of his pipe. "Do you happen to have seen a paper lately?"

"I occasionally glance at *The Times*." Lawrence grinned. "Don't be witty, it's not your form. Yes, I know you're a coming man. Time enough too. What does Mallinson say?"

"He doesn't say much. He can't very well, off his own bat. But if Morrison dies—which appears to be only a matter of days—it is admitted that there will be a shake-up all round. Ancaster will go to some Colonial outpost, they won't have him at the Home Office any longer. His last feat is the limit. He was sent down, you know, to settle the Western railway strike, but when he was driving from the station there was a row of sorts in the street, and Ancaster ran away. Wouldn't face the music. He was booked to speak at the Corn Exchange, but when he found he couldn't persuade the Chief Constable to telephone to the barracks he scratched. I mean to say, he had a heart attack."

"Good Lord!"

"Mr. Mallinson of course will stay where he is, and I believe Lauderdale sticks to the War Office. They hate him, but he's able." Mark paused, exhaling a cloud of smoke through his nostrils. "And strong. Awful rows in the Cabinet, I gather, when Lauderdale attends. Even Mallinson admits that he's difficult to work with. By that same token, Vesey will probably take on Home affairs, because he's one of the few men with whom Lauderdale is still on speaking terms. You remember, Miss Vesey married young Lauderdale."

"I remember—he was a Trinity man of my year. So Vesey goes to the Home Office? H'm. That leaves Vesey's Under-Secretaryship vacant."

Mark nodded. "Of course it's all in the clouds at present."

"You would like it?" said Lawrence, half-incredulous. It was difficult for him to believe that any man could find pleasure in the dusty ways of politics, or indeed in taking on any sort of hard work unless he were driven to it. Mark smiled.

"I should like it very much indeed," he said emphatically. "Of course I don't count on it for a moment. I can only give you the broad outlines that everybody knows; there are all sorts of ins and outs which I mustn't repeat, because they were told me in confidence. But I know Mallinson means business. He was good enough to say I had done some useful work on Committee."

"Your debating power would tell. Mallinson is no speaker, nor is Vesey; as for Lauderdale, his oratorical style reminds one of those immortal guns we used to call the Neutral Battery. Half his shells drop in his own lines."

"I'd rather work with Lauderdale than with Ancaster any day. His hands are clean, and when his mind is made up he rides straight across country. Imagine Lauderdale funking the railway men! I said that to Mr. Mallinson, and he agreed with me."

"Ah? You seem to hit it off rather well with the great man." Lawrence's eyes traveled furtively over his brother's face; he knew Mark to be intractably disinterested, and he feared to start a scruple. "He likes you personally, I think. I've just been talking to him in the billiard room, and I was amused at the paternal tone. He referred warmly to your speeches at the International Congress of something-or-other, and your striking monograph on Coöperation. I didn't know what it was all about, so I said 'Oh' and 'Really' at proper intervals. Is it a fact that you write the middles for the *Liberal Review?*"

"Not regularly. Litchfield has asked me for an article once or twice."

"Once or twice, eh? All this year, Mallinson said."

"How does he know? I don't sign them."

Lawrence laid his head back and laughed softly. "He said nobody could mistake your sledge-hammer prose. Don't blush, Mark, my boy! Not but what you ought to blush for writing anything at all in that pestiferous rag. Socialism, rank Socialism! Let us hope there isn't any chink in the world above; if there is, I think I see father with his eye glued to it, cursing himself for leaving you Gatton. How is Gatton, by the bye?"

"Oh, Gatton goes on swimmingly. I'm due for the

opening of the Town Hall this day week. It pays, you know; we have a bigger turnover every year." Mark mentioned a sum which made Lawrence raise his eyebrows. "But I don't take much out of it," Mark added. "Reckoning one year with another, I doubt if my personal expenses average more than a couple of thousand. I may have to take more in future." He smiled to himself.

"That sounds like matrimony."

"Yes, doesn't it?" Mark's smile broadened; he had not the faintest intention of admitting Lawrence further into his confidence. Then his features darkened and his manner changed. "It is late, and I shall take half an hour to get into my clothes. Let us come to the point. About this sickening Essenden affair. Will you give me chapter and verse?"

"Oh, with pleasure," said Lawrence. He laid down his cigar and sat up, leaning on his arm. He was perhaps not free from nervousness, for he spoke quietly and with unusual precision and restraint. Mark listened; the tale was brief.

"So that was what you meant when you said you had foiled her."

"If you like to call me a fool I shan't quarrel with you. Actually it never occurred to me that she would hold on her way as soon as I was out of England."

"Am I in a position to call any one a fool? I've been a fool myself. What did Considine say?"

"Very little. You know his epistolary style. It took me three-quarters of an hour to gather the drift, because for some time I labored under the impression that he was breaking the news of your death. When at last I made out that the word was Essenden and not erysipelas, I dried my tears and packed my traps. One thing struck me. Mark, who set the talk on foot?"

"What talk?"

"Considine said the whole affair was public property —that it was common club gossip that you had been away with her in Normandy, and that you were financing the establishment in Green Street. Some other rubbish too, which Considine apparently believed. I did not." Mark had picked up a Dresden toy and was looking at it attentively; he felt hot and uncomfortable, but he did not speak, though Lawrence waited for a moment. "But we don't want to go into that," Lawrence said gently. He was not even watching his brother. "My point is that these things must have originated with somebody. You did not, I suppose, give yourself away. Who did?"

"What do you mean? Fellows always talk."

"More or less. Why more?"

"How on earth do I know? Probably because it was out of my line."

"You don't think Jenny fanned the flame?" Mark did not answer, but his eyes flickered. "She has her knife into you, Mark. Revenge is sweet."

"But what has she to revenge?"

"That, of course," said Lawrence lightly, "is known only to yourself. I can but transmit the impression that I got of her this morning, when I let her know that I was on my way to you. I should say," he weighed his words, "that she hates you rather more violently than she hates me. Sorry if I wound your feelings." He paused again. Mark gave a short laugh. "Being unfortunately enslaved to an effeminate social system, you and I are equally powerless to tackle Jenny as she deserves to be tackled. But I fancy Jenny is well aware that whereas I, if I weren't unfortunately civilized, should like to beat her, you wouldn't touch her with a forty-foot pole. Now the Jennies rather like being beaten, but no woman on God's earth will stand being snubbed."

"But—snubbed! Good heavens, Lawrence, it is she who has done the snubbing!"

"You think? I doubt it. You are occasionally a little inhuman, Mark. What is it?—the religious strain in you, perhaps. You despise the Jenny type. Amen to that! I am not going to sentimentalize over Jenny as a fallen woman. Jenny never fell. But if you use the woman you despise—! *Vaya.* I have spoken. Rather, I have preached! I have got my own back." He laid himself flat on his cushions and shut his eyes.

A rake's sermon is apt to be impressive, and Lawrence Sturt's point of view was novel enough to keep Mark silent for a minute. He felt that there was some rough justice in it. Yes, he had despised Jenny from the very first. "She ran me down," Mark said frankly to himself, though he would not have said as much to Lawrence; and on the strength of it he had bullied her, consciously or unconsciously—or tried to bully her. Was it true, as Considine and now Lawrence suggested, that she had given him away? It was odd, now he came to think about it, that the details of his liaison with Mrs. Essenden should be known so fully and in such precision. Watson and Carden and Delany had escaped with a casual laugh or two, a vague contradictory whisper which their party could affect to disbelieve, but London had laughed openly over every point of Mark Sturt's indiscretion. How came London so well-informed?

"Of course a lot of men go to Green Street," was the issue of his meditations. "Horton, for instance. He is good for any amount of chatter. He wasn't there to-day, by any chance?"

"I did not see him, Mark."

"Well, well!" Mark yawned and stretched himself. "I'm sick of the subject. Thank heaven the whole epi-

sode will be over in twenty-four hours! I shall run up
to town to-morrow." He did not think it necessary to
tell Lawrence that the breach would in any case have
come about within a few days—the rake's sermon rankled
slightly.

"You're going to see her?" Lawrence asked. "Far
better go than write. I say: if she has any letters of
yours, better make her give them up."

"She has no letters of mine. She may have a note
or two; nothing that might not be published in *The Times*
for all I care."

"H'm. Wise man! So you didn't trust the fair
Jenny all the way, after all?"

"If you want to know the truth, Lawrence, I don't
think I ever thought about her."

"H'm. As I expected. And then you wonder that
she hates you! Well, take a bit of advice from me, will
you? you didn't last time and you were sorry for it afterwards. Think about her now."

"You mean—?"

Lawrence swung himself erect and faced his brother
in the dim firelight, thrusting his hands into his breeches'
pockets and swaying slightly on his feet. "Think hard,
Mark; think like the devil."

"You take her seriously?"

"I take her damn-seriously."

"But she can't do anything."

"Can't she!"

He was smiling down into Mark's eyes. "I tell you,
Mark, that lady would not stick at much, to get her
knife into you. She knows her game is up. She won't
get any more out of you: and she's not a bit afraid of
you—don't you flatter yourself. You've lived with her
—what is it?—five months. Now you, if I know you,
were off your guard; and Jenny, if I know her, was all

eyes and ears. She probably knows you inside out, better than you know yourself. Can't she do anything?"

"She might turn up and make a scene somewhere, I suppose, but she'd be sorry for herself if she did. She would not come to my flat twice. I should have her warned off the premises."

Lawrence laughed. "Good; stick to that frame of mind, and you'll have the range of her. But don't under-rate the forces of the enemy, and for God's sake don't take any notice of the white flag." He ground the heel of his boot with sudden violence into the ashes scattered on the hearth. "Would you call a truce with poison or fire? Then call a truce with Jenny."

CHAPTER XV

IN the meantime, after leaving Lawrence at the foot of the staircase, Maisie had gone to her own room to dress for the early dinner that was to precede the New Year's Eve masquerade. When she was out of sight of Lawrence her step grew languid and the brightness faded out of her eyes. There are times when the inner world is more real than the outer; those who are drilled to the social mask will play out their part in it without self-betrayal, but in every interlude the mind reverts automatically to a more exciting dialogue and a richer-colored scene. One moment laughing down into Lawrence Sturt's eyes, the next Maisie was reliving, with a doubled keenness of sensation, her own feelings on the lake when Mallinson's stumble flung her into Sturt's arms.

In her own room there was a leaping fire on the hearth, and when she had thrown off her sables she knelt down before it, warming her chilled hands, and wondering, not for the first time, whether if anything precious to her had fallen into it she would have had the courage to snatch it out. Brushwood fires in the open air are not so hot as a sea-coal hearth, yet flame is flame; and one of the Ushant memories that Maisie liked was that of Mark Sturt's calm face as he came back to her over the downs, holding up her miniature with his unaffected English indifference to pain. "I wonder if you still carry that scar, Mark," said Maisie softly. "You had your share of scars already. You're hardy enough, my friend. And so you hold the cross, Mark of mine? Ah! now I know why you colored up when you said, 'Surely you knew I was in the army?'" She covered her sparkling eyes with her hand; she was so deeply one with Mark that she felt, not her own woman's triumph, but his soldier's shame.

"Please, miss," said Ellen, coming into the room in her decent and disapproving black dress, "there's a lady wants to see you. I told her it was a very inconvenient time to come, but she said it was on business and she wouldn't keep you many minutes. What shall I say to her, miss? You won't have time to see her now, will you?"

"What's her name?"

"She didn't give it; said she was only business and you wouldn't know her."

"Some begging letter imposition, I suppose," said Maisie impatiently. "What do you mean when you say she is a lady—is she a lady?"

"Oh, yes, miss; quite the lady. Quite nice in her manners, too, and quietly dressed; and said she was very sorry to be so late, but she couldn't catch an earlier train. I thought p'r'aps you'd see her when you was dressed. She didn't look poor, an' she drove from the station in a fly, an' said it was to wait for her."

"It's past six now, and dinner is at seven. Ask her if she would mind coming up to my room and talking to me while you do my hair; if it's really a matter of business I dare say she'll be glad to get it over and get back again."

Ellen went out, and Maisie continued to kneel by the fire. But her chain of thought was broken, and among dreams and memories a faint prick of curiosity made itself felt. Six o'clock on New Year's Eve was a strange time to choose for a business interview! Probably the woman would turn out to be a beggar—Maisie had been

pestered by many beggars since she came into Philip Fitz-
Gerald's money; and yet even for a beggar the time was
tactlessly chosen.

Ellen stood aside respectfully holding open the door,
and there came into the room a little elegant figure in a
little serge suit of Puritan sobriety, topped by an astra-
chan cap and a flying black veil. A beggar? Hardly;
those clothes were of the plainest, but they smacked of
the Rue de la Paix a mile off, and even the mendicant
who only begs for charity is not apt to lift up her skirt
in a hand as small as a child's, over a Lucile petticoat
and a Viennese shoe. A lady? Apparently; and yet the
scent of roses which clouded her was heavier than Maisie
was accustomed to breathe.

"Leave us, Ellen," said Maisie on the instant. "I'll
arrange my own hair to-night. But don't be out of the
way, I may ring if I want you."

She turned to her visitor. "I'm afraid you've had a
cold drive. Will you sit here by the fire, and will you
excuse me if I go on dressing? We dine early to-night,
as I think my maid told you, because there is a dance
on."

Her visitor smiled. "Please do not let me be in the
way more than I can help. I know it's the most unpardonable time to arrive, but I had something I really
wanted very much to say to you, and it was only after
lunch I made up my mind quite definitely that it had
better get said to-day. So I took the first train down
to Shotton, but it's a tiresome, changing journey, and
when I got here I could not find a cab at once. It is
very kind indeed of you to receive an utter stranger in
this unceremonious way. For I expect I am an utter
stranger to you."

Maisie had fetched an ivory brush and was taking off
her dress. She threw a lawn coat round her shoulders

and began to unfasten her hair, which was roughened into curls by the frosty wind; as she took the pins out it rolled down below her waist in two thick plaits of gold, which scattered into an iridescent mantel when she unbraided them.

"At present," she said, smiling, "you must remember that I don't even know your name."

"No, you don't, do you? I wouldn't give it to your maid in case she might have heard of me; these women know everything. I'm Jenny Essenden."

Maisie's comb ran into a tangle. She waited a moment to ravel it out, laid the comb down, and moved with her slow easy stride towards the bell. Jenny got up and threw herself in front of it.

"What are you going to do?"

"Ring for a servant."

"To get rid of me? Oh! you virtuous women! Ring then: get the footman to throw me out—who cares what happens to a courtesan?"

Maisie looked down at her steadily. "Mrs. Essenden, if I don't behave to you with civility it is your own doing. If you had sent up your name to me in a straightforward way I should probably have decided to see you. But when you worm yourself in by a trick what am I to think you come for, if it isn't some more or less improper motive?"

"Well, you're wrong then," said Jenny defiantly. "Put yourself in my place: ah! you think you could never be in my place. Now I wonder if you're right there? I'm not so simple as to think all women are no better than myself, like the wise man who said, 'Il y a peu d'honnêtes femmes qui ne soient lasses de leur métier'—I'm sure there are plenty of proper ladies, even pretty ones, who couldn't be naughty if they tried; but I'm not a bit sure about you, Miss Archdale. Turn me out—turn me out

if you're positive that you haven't a spice of my own
little familiar devil lurking under that grand calm blond
temperament of yours."

She moved away from the bell. Maisie stretched out
her hand to it, hesitated, and finally drew back. "Women
ought to stick together," was her entirely unforeseen reply. "I'm not sure that I'm doing right, but I might
equally do wrong if I sent you away. Go on, then:
I'll listen."

She went on brushing out her thick tresses. Jenny
with a soft sigh of relief returned to her chair and leaned
back at ease, pulling off her loose gloves and stretching
out her shoes to the warmth: small shoes, high-heeled,
and trimly buckled over the fine silk stocking and the
fine arched instep. At this moment, in the bachelor's
wing, Lawrence Sturt was warning Mark that Jenny
was dangerous. She had thrown back her veil, and her
delicate little face was bright and full of life, as if she
were enjoying herself.

"I want," she said, "to talk to you about a man in
whom we are both deeply interested—if you'll confess
it to be possible that you and I could be interested in
the same man and in the same way."

"Who?"

"Mark Sturt."

"I knew it," said Maisie inaudibly. She had finished
brushing out her hair; she began to gather it up, Spanish
fashion, into high smooth coils, and loose ringlets that
shaded her fair neck.

"I want you," said Jenny, curling sideways in her
chair and watching wide-eyed over her clasped hands,
"to give him up to me."

"Assuming, which I don't admit, that there is this dis-
tressing rivalry between us"—Maisie was steady under
fire, her tone was admirable in its good-humored scorn—

"I should like to know why you want me to give him up —to you."

"Because," said Jenny softly, "I have the better right to him."

"Do you mean—forgive my putting it bluntly—that you're fond of him?"

"I'm very fond of him, but I'm afraid I've traveled past those considerations. I'm his mistress."

"Since when?"

The expert Jenny told the truth, though she would have liked to risk a lie. "Since the middle of August."

"I heard some scandal of the sort, but I didn't pay much heed to it. You must remember, Mrs. Essenden, that Mr. Sturt's friends, of whom I am one, take a strictly practical view of the situation. I don't for a moment profess to judge either him or you, but there is one judge before whom every man in his position is permanently on trial—I mean the British public. Perhaps you aren't much interested in politics? I dare say you don't know that at the present time there is a great deal of activity going on in the political world. It is almost certain that there will be a shuffling of places after Parliament meets on the fifth, and Mr. Sturt's friends hope very much that he will get something in the re-arranged Ministry. Now just at this time it would not do him any good to have his name mixed up with any woman's in the way in which it would be mixed up with yours."

"Why not?" said Jenny—"if he married me?"

"He won't marry you."

Mrs. Essenden gasped under the insult; and an insult it was, for Maisie would have said the same words in the same tone even if she had not known that Mark could not marry Jenny if he would. Mark Sturt marry a Jenny Essenden? No: like Henham, Maisie felt pretty

certain that he would draw the line at taking her into
the family. She had not designed to wound—she had
forborne to point out a fallacy in Jenny's argument—
but she felt no compunction when she saw Jenny quiver
under the lash; it was good for Mrs. Essenden, probably,
to hear the truth now and then; Jenny in tears would
have appealed to Miss Archdale's stern chivalry, but
she was not saint enough to pity Jenny triumphant.

"You devil!" said Jenny passionately, "why shouldn't
he marry me? He couldn't take me any closer to him
if I were twenty times his wife."

Maisie ignored that remark. She had taken up a hand
mirror to examine her hair, and the profile that she pre-
sented to Jenny was as inexpressive in its serene good
humor as if there had been no Jenny in the room.

"Don't you want," said Jenny, "me to tell you how I
found out that you and I were in the same boat?"

"Yes, I'm frankly very curious. I can't think how
you came to connect my name with Mr. Sturt's."

"How could I but in the one way? He told me himself."

"Oh, no, he didn't." Maisie paused in the act of putting on her gown. "Now, Mrs. Essenden, this ceases to
be amusing. When I promised to listen to you I did
not mean that I would listen to anything you liked to
invent."

"He told me himself," Jenny answered with her cruel
smile. "In his sleep."

Maisie's memory flashed back over the still nights at
Ushant. "He does not talk in his sleep."

"Good gracious, Miss Archdale," Jenny cried, round-
eyed, "how do you know that?"

"Sorry," said Maisie with her imperturbable irony.
"Perhaps you have never heard him chaffing his brother
over their tent experiences in the Andes."

"Oh, I see!" Jenny gave way to a ripple of laughter. "Well, it did sound very—very odd, you know. But, since you know Captain Sturt so well, perhaps you've heard him say that Mark gets a touch of fever now and then. He was light-headed one night, and he talked of you and to you in quite a touching way. He appeared to be declining invitations."

Maisie crossed to the window and threw it wider open. Clouds had come up, quenching the moonlight; the snow had begun to fall again, thick, soft, and pure, and a whirl of it was borne in, on the breath of a north wind, over Maisie's splendid dress, her glittering wreath of hair, her shoulders and breast. She stood up unmoved under the blast, looking out over the gloomy woods of Shotton, slowly lacing her dress; she was in the flame-color and black and silver of an old Spanish painting, and on the rich brocade the scattered flakes thawed in dim patches of tarnish. Jenny had struck home. It needed the ice-blade of the wind on her forehead to keep Miss Archdale composed. And still there was no respite from the little voice, soft and sweet with its childish overtones, which ran on behind her in ribald Rabelaisian variations on the same theme. Jenny's game was up. But the retreating enemy has always one resource. He can poison the wells.

"You see, Miss Archdale, that is what you virtuous women never will understand. You think it is good for us others to be shown now and then what you think of us, and how completely we are beneath your attention and the attention of your men; but what you don't realize, and what we think it's good for you to realize now and then, is that your men are more ours than yours. Now I hadn't found out, when I came into this room, how helplessly you were in love with Mark, but I did know for certain that Mark was in some way or other

mixed up with you and that it was a case of pull-devil
pull-baker between you and me. We get very clever at
reading things like that. It's our trade, don't you see, to
understand? All this time you've been talking with so
much intelligence and so much self-control (more, I will
say, than one in a thousand of your class) about dear
Mark's political position and the upset I should be to him,
it's been child's play for me to see that you haven't known
how to keep your voice steady or conceal the palpitations
that are going on under that pretty little coat. I'm sorry
to wound your pride, but why did you let yourself get
into such an undignified position? Men never like it.
It flatters them, but it annoys them, because in this sort
of sport three-quarters of a man's pleasure lies in walking up his birds. I was quite as keen on dear Mark as
you are, but I wasn't silly enough to let him see it."

The wind shrieked and rattled in the chimney; the
heavy-headed elms in the avenue groaned, rubbing their
great branches together and straining under their weight
of snow. Small avalanches were rolling down from the
roof like minute-guns. Jenny cowered over the fire,
she was cold, but very happy.

"And if in these few minutes I've been able to read
your heart like a book—if for all your money and your
class pride I've told you things about yourself that will
sting you to your dying day—do you think it was any
harder for me to read what was in Mark's mind when
I had him with me morning, noon and night, when he
was off his guard? Why, to take only the most obvious
aspects of the situation, do you suppose I didn't read
his letters? He used to come to me with all sorts of
things in his pockets, political letters, letters from his
brother, bits of private scandal, silly scribbles from Mrs.
Ferrier in which she was always throwing you at his
head; and when his back was turned I used to read

them all. Used to? why, it's only a week ago that he was
with me! This is Wednesday night, isn't it?—New
Year's Eve? Well, he spent the twenty-second in Green
Street."

The whirl of flakes had lightened, and between great,
vague stormfields appeared Orion, the eternal hunter,
girt with his diamond belt. Incredibly steep precipices
of cloud were seen silvered by the flying moon. Below
them stretched the dark, dense laboring woods, the frozen
lawns. A night of tempest, and of purity: how cold,
and how remote from the hushed room where Jenny's
pretty little voice continued to dribble poison in her
enemy's ear! Maisie leaned her forehead on the window-
pane. An ache of cruel anguish shook her so that she
was near to weeping—not for her own shame, but for
Mark. How weak they are, these strong men! He had
earned the cross, the highest military honor; and he had
laid his head on the breast of a Jenny Essenden.

"That is what I mean," Jenny had not done with her
yet, "when I say that whatever you virtuous ladies may
like to think a man really does belong more to his mistress
than he ever does to you. A very charming man married to a very charming woman once said to me, 'Damn
it all, Jenny, I can't swear at my wife.' I often think
of that and smile, when I see my old lovers driving with
their wives. For, after all, when a man respects a woman
he can't be altogether at his ease with her; or not, at
least, till he's been married to her for a year or so, and
the gloss has worn off, and he begins to swear before her
if he doesn't swear at her. Think what an advantage it
gives a woman to be on those sort of terms with a man
that he doesn't mind swearing at her from the very first!
Then again, in the case of a man like dear Mark, in the
most devoted marriage there are all sorts of reticences
and reserves; he will want his wife's love, of course,

but he'll want her to keep her illusions as well. So that
if you, say, had been married to him for a twelvemonth,
I should still know more of the real Mark than you would,
because you would always have seen him on his good
behavior, whereas I——"

"Whereas you . . ."

"Ah!" Jenny laughed. "I've seen him at his worst."

Maisie strolled over to the mirror by the fire to pin a
Spanish posy of carnations behind her gold ringlets. She
seemed to be thoroughly indifferent to Jenny's presence
in the room.

"You *are* plucky," said Jenny, smiling up at her.
"Really I do admire you most awfully, Miss Archdale,
and I'm very sorry for you too. I declare I shouldn't
mind going shares in Mark with you. I dare say you're
right and that it wouldn't do for him to marry me. I
think I shall tell him so next time I see him; he is sure
to be back in Green Street within the next few days. Of
course I shan't give you away; I never give away another woman; I shall only tell him that if he likes to
marry you I won't make any fuss so long as he doesn't
throw his little Jenny overboard. But perhaps you
wouldn't like that arrangement? It's quite a common
one, only the wives don't as a rule know anything about
it. They're proud, you see, the proper ladies are; but
you're so dreadfully in love that I don't suppose you
would be very proud." She glanced at her watch. "However, I can't settle that till I get Mark to myself again.
You haven't heard him speak of running up to town,
have you? On business? Well, when you do, you'll
know what it means." She began drawing on her gloves.
"Ten days ago—yes, I think he'll turn up pretty soon."

There was the impudence of a street Arab in her deft
little wink. It broke the spell. The tears that ached behind Maisie's eyeballs dried up in flame. She took a step

towards Jenny, and her hand clenched itself much like Lawrence Sturt's. Decidedly there was that in Mrs. Essenden which appealed to primitive instincts. Jenny started up, she had no mind to be beaten.

"Don't be afraid," said Maisie good-humoredly. "I was only going to ring the bell. I really don't think you can have any more to say?"

"No, I don't think so. It's nearly seven' o'clock, isn't it?" said Jenny. She glanced into the mirror as she drew down her veil. "Thank you very much for your courtesy to a poor little outcast. Now I mustn't keep the cab waiting any longer," she was making for the door. "To be sure, it's Mark who pays."

She gave Maisie her little smiling bow, and vanished. Almost in the doorway Ellen passed her; Ellen who had had misgivings after all, and had waited in the corridor just out of earshot, in case her mistress were to ring for her. As Ellen drew up and curtsied, Jenny gave another little laugh and a little wriggle of her shoulders. She had a sudden conviction that, if Ellen had known one word in twenty that Jenny had been saying, Jenny would have been slapped.

When Ellen came into the room Maisie was bending over her jewel case.

"Miss Maisie! whatever's the matter?"

"Find my keys."

"They're in the pocket of your blue serge," said Ellen shortly. She was not used to the imperative mood, and she flounced over to the wardrobe.

"Thanks. Is my hair smooth?"

"Yes, miss. Why, it's all damp! Miss Maisie dear, whatever's the matter?"

Maisie stood erect, looking herself over from head to foot in the tall mirror. "Really I'm looking very handsome. Flora made a success of this dress, faith, she did!

Rather daring, a Spanish dress for a woman as fair as I am; but I believe the Gothic strain is often blonde like me."

"Miss, do you know you've got the window open and the snow have come in all over her ladyship's carpet?"

"Shut it, then, and don't look so startled; I'm not a ghost! Pin up this fold of brocade—there, that goes better; I hate folds that fall crookedly. Now give me my diamonds."

"Miss, you won't never wear your diamonds for a little dance like this?"

"The circlet in my hair, the collar and chain, the bracelets, and the star in my dress. Don't worry, Nelly; I've had a—a facer, and the diamonds are a prop to my self-respect. You knew the foreign woman wasn't up to any good? Wrong both times, Nelly; she happened to be cockney, and it wasn't she who administered the facer; I don't care two straws for her one way or the other. You're not to sit up for me, do you hear? It is an order, so good night."

She caught up her long white gloves and left Ellen to her own reflections.

There was no one in the hall when Maisie came down the great staircase. An immense Yule log blazed between silver andirons on the hearth, and the candles set high in silver sconces flickered lightly in the draught. As she neared the foot of the stair, Mark Sturt came out of the gun-room. He wore the court dress of a Tudor ancestor, and its rich strangeness set off his heavy distinction. He stopped dead at sight of Maisie in her Spanish draperies and constellation of diamonds; five minutes earlier, and it would have been Jenny that he met.

"Salutations!" he said, coming forward. "We shall not need any lamps to-night, Maisie. You blaze."

His wife remained standing on the last step but one,

her bare right hand clenched over the balustrade. "If he went away to Green Street now and then I wouldn't care . . ." It had been easy to feel that when she had never seen Mrs. Essenden. Perhaps the facile forgiveness of women springs, more often than their husbands understand, from ignorance.

Mark glanced round the deserted hall. He had meant to settle with Jenny before approaching his wife, but Jenny was on the eve of settlement, and after all a New Year's Night revel counts for little either way.

"I want a dance, Maisie. Don't say you've given them all to my brother or to Mr. Forester?"

"A dance?"

"One of the old waltzes," Mark explained. " 'El Dorado,' or 'Toreador,' or the barcarolle out of the *Contes d'Hoffman*. I'm going to bribe the orchestra. It will cheer me up before I go."

"Before you go?"

"Didn't you know I was going away to-morrow?"

"Oh! Are you? Running up to town, I suppose?"

"Yes," said Mark, faintly startled. "But only for a single night——"

"On business?"

"Business of a sort, yes——"

"And you want your dance with me first?" said Maisie, smiling down at him. "Oh, Mark! I'm afraid your tastes are as Catholic as your faith."

He drew back, and his manner was to the full as haughty as her own. "I beg your pardon? I don't follow."

"Shall I translate?" said Maisie. She flicked him across the eyes with the gloves that she carried in her hand. "Is that clear?"

"Perfectly, thanks," said Mark, his color changing gradually from his bronzed fairness to a dusky shade of gray. "Don't do that again, Maisie." He took the gloves out of her hand. "Silly trick. You tempt me to remind you that you're my wife."

A door slammed on a landing and Lawrence Sturt appeared on the stairs. It seemed to be his fate that evening to play eavesdropper on his brother, for as he stepped over the threshold his keen ear caught Maisie's reply—

"Thanks, I remember everything. This time the door is locked on the inside."

Lawrence passed his hand across his lips to brush away a smile. He was sorry for Mark, who seemed to be in hot water all round, but he was also faintly amused. These moralities and these emotions!

CHAPTER XVI

"On a bien de la peine à rompre quand on ne s'aime plus."

MARK yawned himself downstairs before eight o'clock on the morning of New Year's Day, and read the paper over a solitary breakfast to the tune of flames crackling on the hearth and a bleak wind howling round the snow-jammed windows. To his surprise, when he came out into the hall, he found Lawrence pulling on his gloves by the fire. "You're not coming, are you?" said Mark in no very cordial tone.

"Drive you to the station," said Lawrence briefly. "My coat, Basil." His servant, a Levantine Greek named Basil Copanaris, put him into a huge fur coat and buttoned it under his chin like a baby, and Lawrence moved to the door, where his own powerful car was standing tire-deep in snow. "Bah! I hate these English winds," grumbled the Sybarite, settling himself at the wheel. Since it was too much trouble to protest, Mark dropped into the seat beside him, though he would rather have been alone. At the last moment a man-servant came hurrying up, a sealed letter in his hand.

"For you, sir." Mark took it, puzzled. It was from Mr. Mallinson, Brown explained: he had hoped to have the pleasure of seeing Mr. Sturt that morning, but his neuritis had been that bad all night that he wasn't able to get up. "It's his shoulder, you see, sir, fallin' on the ice."

"Oh? I'm very sorry," said Mark, absently fingering the envelope. He lay back staring out over the wintry

255

landscape. "All in?" said Lawrence curtly, and the great car shot away.

They covered the run to the station in silence—the silence, it must be owned, of extreme ill-humor on one side and suppressed amusement on the other—which was not broken even when a violent double sideslip, the natural result of taking ill-swept turns at forty miles an hour, hurled them from the brink of a viaduct to the brink of a coal cart. It was not till Mark was dumbly extricating himself and his suit-case from under Captain Sturt's counterpane of rugs that Lawrence said what he had come to say. He leaned far back over the side of the car and slapped Mark gently between the shoulder blades. Mark shook him off impatiently. "Lord love you," said Lawrence, laughing, "what an amiable beggar it is! Is this because I shot over your coverts last night?"

"My train's due and I'm on the wrong platform, Lawrence."

"It shall be due, and you shall sprint across the line in front of it, and the guard shall curse you. Was I shooting over your coverts last night?"

Mark raised his gray eyes, clear and angry. "Confound you! yes, you were."

"Oho!" said Lawrence. Under his penetrating stare Mark felt as though he were made of glass. Deep beneath the drift of circumstance and temper the link of birth held fast, that blood-link which through all the changes and chances of the world binds parent to child and brother to brother and still more closely twin to twin, as the cables hold unseen under the deep seas. Mark's train ran into the station; "Beg pardon, sir—" an anxious porter touched his cap, and Mark swung off unhurried. It was a retreat in good order, for he pretended not to hear Lawrence Sturt's loud laughter ringing after him through the booking office.

Except to wonder fleetingly whether any man had ever knocked Lawrence down, and if not why not, Mark did not give much further thought to his brother or to his wife. Mark had not enjoyed the New Year's Eve dance. Between the splendor of her dress and diamonds, and the flare of her own white beauty, Maisie's apparent design had been to make herself the most conspicuous woman in the room, and she was ably seconded by Lawrence, who had never been known to hang back from any sort of mischief; the pair had danced together half the evening, while the husband and brother looked on with what philosophy he might. But Mark was not seriously angry with Lawrence, because he had recognized from his boyhood the futility of getting angry with Lawrence; while his feeling for Maisie was of that durable sort which a man is content to postpone.

Nor did he give to Mallinson's letter all the attention it deserved, though swift study showed him that for his own ambition it was vitally important. Mallinson had scribbled it in bed, after reading his own mail; a rough sheet, oddly intimate in tone, or paternal, as Lawrence said: "because this shoulder of mine is an old enemy, and if it gets troublesome I may have to go home and nurse it before you get back. And, my dear boy, I have just heard from the Chief, and I should like you to know how things stand." For shrewd Dodo Ferrier was right; Mallinson had taken an immediate fancy to Mark Sturt, and liking had ripened into confidence when the two men compared notes, finding themselves in agreement on points where Mallinson had expected difficulty. "An able man," Mallinson had said to Dodo, "able and thoroughly honest. No, my dear, the quality of political honesty is not so common as you seem to think, and the men who can convince the public and their own colleagues that they possess it are sure to get on—if, that

is, they have the necessary backing in the way of position and brains. Your friend Sturt has all that, and
his business training will come in very useful. We want
new blood." So Mallinson wrote in the double character of personal friend and Minister of State. Mark,
however, put the letter by, placing it carefully in his
pocket-book and the pocket-book in the breast pocket of
his coat, for George Mallinson in confidential vein was
occasionally more witty than discreet. Mark was dropping with sleep after a white night, and he lay back
and shut his eyes, but no sleep came. "Think hard,
Mark; think like the devil." He had an ugly interview
before him, and Lawrence Sturt's warning haunted him
more than he cared to own.

It haunted him in the train, in a hasty lunch at his
flat, and in the motor-brougham which whirled him to
Jenny's door; it haunted him because he could not for
his life see where danger lurked for him in or after his
break with Jenny. Another man, mindful of his own
earlier degradation, might have feared the worse disaster
of a relapse; but for Mark, reared in Catholic traditions
and with a distinct natural bent towards asceticism, that
risk was barred. Prudence hinted that to go to Green
Street was to expose himself to the hottest fire of temptation, but Mark, though he had read *Sapho*, felt safe
on that score. It was necessary to visit Jenny because
he agreed with Lawrence that it would be dangerous to
write to her, but so far as personal feeling was concerned Mark would never willingly have gone near her
again.

In a fit of newborn caution, he dismissed the brougham
before he got to Green Street, and walked to the door.
Jenny was certainly at home; the aspect of the little
house, the glitter of its brass dragon knocker, the gay
window-boxes blooming extravagantly with cut flowers

in January, proclaimed her dainty presence. But when Mark rang the tall parlormaid's face fell as she opened the door. Yes, Mrs. Essenden was at home, but she was not in, and would not be in for some time, perhaps not before night; she had gone to a matinée and was going on to tea somewhere afterwards. The maid stood with the door in her hand, and Mark hesitated; it might be better to write a line and ask Jenny to be at home at a given hour next day. But on second thoughts Mark did not care to defer the operation. Better go through with it and cut the ropes that bound him before lying down for another night's rest. Rest! it seemed to Mark that he had had no rest since before he went to Ushant.

If he had felt any further indecision, Polly Whibley's demeanor would have settled it. She did not want him to come in; she urged the uncertainty of Jenny's return, the tedium of the long hours of waiting. Struck by a sudden suspicion, Mark put a query point-blank; had Mrs. Essenden gone out alone? He got, as he had half expected, a confused and shuffling stammer. Yes, she was alone; oh, yes, certainly, she was alone—no, she was not bringing any one back with her. Mark was disgusted with himself for having stooped to question a servant. He put the girl aside and strode past her into the house; the first object on which his eye fell was a man's walking stick thrown across the hall table. Mark shrugged his shoulders and registered the fact for use against Jenny if, as he phrased it to himself, she turned nasty; not that there was any reason why Mrs. Essenden should not receive visits from her men friends, or go with them to a play! but, taking that stick in conjunction with Polly Whibley's manner, he was sure enough of his ground to risk a stray shot.

He looked round the little hall and cast his mind back to the last visit he had paid in Green Street. True to

the streak of caution which sometimes influenced his actions more than it became definite in his thoughts, he had
on every occasion been on his guard against leaving any
of his own property behind him; he could not call to
mind that Jenny had any possessions of his or any letters,
unless it were the most trivial of notes. He went into
the morning-room and looked round. Nothing: not a
trace of masculine occupation except a book on political
economy, which had no name in it, though an observer
might have safely argued that it was not Jenny's own
choice in literature. In the drawing-room there was not
even a book. Polly the maid had followed him and stood
fingering her apron—perhaps she thought he was looking
for a different sort of evidence. But Mark sent her
sharply about her business, and she obeyed him; probably all the servants knew, though none of them could
have proved, that in that house Mr. Sturt was pay-
master.

When the door had shut which banished Polly to the
kitchen quarters, Mark went upstairs to Jenny's room.
It was as it had always been, white, fresh, and dainty;
he had no fault to find with it except that it was kept
at too warm a temperature, and that it was too full of
roses—branched and budding roses, white and pink, La
France and Châtenay, Jenny's favorite flower. On a table
by her pillow lay a *Garden of the Soul,* hand-bound in
white vellum, an *Imitation of Christ,* a *Key of Heaven,* a
Rosary of the Blessed Virgin, manuals of Catholic devotion—Jenny's devotion! Mark turned over the little
books with the shadow of a smile, remembering how
Jenny had stormed one day when he threatened to put
them in the fire. Decidedly that was one of the occa-
sions when he had not been nice to Jenny! Near the
door hung a little Holy-Water stoup, and in a shrine,
so placed that Jenny's eye lit on it when she woke of a

morning, blessed candles were burning before a tall crucifix in ebony and silver. A pair of long white gloves,
exquisitely fresh—Mark had never seen Mrs. Essenden
in any garment that was not spotless—lay on the sofa
beside a pair of French *mules,* little rosy slippers that
recalled a little rosy foot. Pretty gloves! pretty shoes!
Of any other tenancy there was again not a trace.

Mark passed on into the dressing-room. Here if
anywhere he might have left something behind. But he
had not done so. He glanced through the drawers and
found them empty, he turned over the leaves of a writing
portfolio, he even examined the blotting paper, but it
was an illegible blur in which not a line of his own writing was discernible. It was an ironic commentary on
Mark's own folly that he should have risked so much
for a relation which had meant so little to him. As he
stood in the dressing-room he could not get up any sentiment at all. Even the fury which Lawrence's tale had
inspired in him was cooling as he passed back through
Jenny's chamber. It had been an ugly episode, but it
was over now, so completely relegated to the past that
it was hardly worth a man's while even to feel disgust;
what did it signify, after all? what signify the Jenny
Essendens of this world, and what they do or are done
by? Mark shut the door behind him and came downstairs breathing more freely now that he had got away
from that eternal scent of roses.

The house remained perfectly quiet. He went into
the drawing-room and dropped into a chair before the
fire. Almost immediately Polly Whibley reappeared to
know if he would like some tea. Mark packed her off
again, the more sharply that he saw she wanted to speak
to him; if he could, he would have said, "My good girl,
you are sorry for me because your mistress is deceiving
me, and you would like either to get me out of the way

or to break the news to me and soften the shock of her
return; you may save yourself the trouble, for your mistress can go to the devil for all I care, and as you seem
to be a decent sort of girl I strongly advice you to take
example by me and clear out of the house." In the mani-
fest impossibility of saying any such thing, he dismissed
Polly to the kitchen and disposed himself to wait. He
was tired—dead tired; he had had little sleep the last
few nights, and little peace of mind by day. It was
not unpleasant to sit by Jenny's fire for an hour or two
and immerse oneself in vague dreams of the future,
even though there was still a stiff bridge to cross before those dreams could be realized. . . . He fell asleep.

"Wake up, Mark!" said Jenny's voice, playful and
soft. "You've had a nice little nap. Do come in, Mr.
Horton, he's wakened up now."

Mark came to himself with a start and a glance at the
clock. It was close on night; he had slept for hours,
the drugged exhausted sleep which comes after long
vigils. The room was full of light, and Jenny was
standing by his chair in her theater dress of black silk
and gauze, an ermine scarf slipping from her transparent shoulders. In the opening doorway appeared the tall
thin figure of George Horton, his lined features pinched
into a nervous grin.

"Mrs. Essenden! I apologize for my behavior," said
Mark, getting to his feet. "Your maid said you would
be in to dinner, so I took leave to wait for you, and I
suppose the hot room after the cold outside made me
drowsy. How are you, Horton? You look rather blue.
Take my place, won't you?"

"We've been to a theater," said Jenny, drawing off
her gloves. "Mr. Horton took pity on my loneliness.
It wasn't a very good play, though. Rather a melan-

choly piece, about a poor girl that was deserted by her lover. You'll both stay and dine, won't you?"

"Thanks very much, I'm afraid I can't do that," Mark replied. "If Mr. Horton will excuse us, I should like just ten minutes of your time on a small matter of business; you don't mind, do you, Horton? I shan't keep Mrs. Essenden long."

Surprise, relief, amusement were legibly inscribed one after the other on Horton's features. Though he was no coward, Horton would not have gone to Green Street that night if he had known Mark Sturt would be there, and while Jenny went to reconnoiter in the drawing-room he had shivered by the hall fire, mentally measuring his own attenuated muscles against Sturt's superior inches and powerful frame; when Jenny called to him, Horton had gone in to back her up in rueful anticipation of a shindy; but apparently there was to be no shindy! The master of the house had accepted his situation without a murmur. Horton was amused, and pigeon-holed the affair in a retentive memory as worth telling for its flatness, but he was happy to be let off the risk of broken bones. And Jenny? Jenny was merry and placid; she turned to Horton with a little wave of her baby hands. They were covered with rings and bracelets that Sturt and other men had given her.

"Do you mind—you don't?—smoking a cigarette in the morning-room for just ten minutes? It will be as long as that before dinner is ready, so you won't lose anything by waiting."

Inimitable Jenny! She made no apologies or explanations on either side; she waited till Horton had gone out, and then when she had shut the door behind him she returned with her funny little reflective smile and sat down opposite Mark in a high-backed Chippendale chair. Clearly Mark had learned the truth from Lawrence: in Jenny's opinion it was on the cards that Miss Archdale also had been telling tales. But Mrs. Essenden had burned her boats when she went to Shotton, and in George Horton she had provided an overland retreat. "Well," she said, "and what has my lord and master to say to his handmaiden?"

"Little enough. I won't keep Horton waiting long, Jenny."

"Oh," said Jenny with an ambiguous laugh, "he won't mind."

"He can take his own time, you mean?" said Mark.

He stopped. Horton had been nearer than he knew to broken bones; after all, whatever Mrs. Essenden was now, she had been Mark's ten days ago, and something in him older than morality, older than love, very much older than prudence, revolted against this tame acquiescence in another man's poaching. But he was on his guard; he saw the latent spark in Jenny's eye, recognized his own danger, and shifted his ground.

"I didn't come here to indulge in recriminations. Your movements are entirely at your own disposal from this time onward. The connection between us ceases from to-night. If you have any further communications to make to me, you'll make them through my lawyers."

"Oh?" said Jenny softly. "Yes?"

"I'm giving them instructions to pay the rent of the house and the servants' wages up to next Lady Day."

"Riccardo will be amused," Jenny murmured.

"In ordinary circumstances I should have given you fair warning before I broke with you, and so far as the financial aspect is concerned I propose to do the same now: if, that is, you keep the few conditions I make."

"Yes?"

"Not to try to see me: not to write to me: not to do

what I hear you were insane. enough to threaten doing
—make a scene at any house where I may happen to be
staying."

Jenny nestled her head back against a cushion and
her teeth closed. softly on her lower lip. She had won
that trick, then; her tongue had done its work with Miss
Archdale. Jenny hugged herself for joy. She could
hardly think of her excursion to Shotton without laughing in Sturt's face.

"That's all I have to say," said Mark, reaching for
his gloves. All things considered, it was not much. Five
months he had lived with Jenny, and he was prepared
to break with her in as many sentences. He had not
loved her nor she him, and, though he knew that she
laced her stays from the middle and pattered her prayers
in French, she was essentially a stranger to him. Temptation? It was dead; Lawrence Sturt's tale had killed it,
apparently. Mark rarely analyzed his own motives, and
he saw no incongruity in the terms of his farewell to
Jenny, nor. could he have explained why he was no longer
allured by her exquisite facility and grace. He had but
one thing more to say, and he said it as he rose. "I
ought to warn you that if you try your hand at any dangerous game I shall set the police in motion. A prosecu-
tion for libel, Mrs. Essenden, is a thing some men are
disinclined to face; I shouldn't have the slightest scruple
in handling it, and it generally results in a swingeing
bill for damages."

"You are not very nice to me, are you?" said Jenny,
smiling up at him. "Not very nice to me, Mark, after
all these months, to talk of prosecuting me for libel! Me!
poor little me! What have I ever done to you that you
should scold me like this? What makes you think I
would do anything dreadful? I'm sure I'm a very peace-
able little person. I only want people to be nice to me."

"Yes, it's a shame, isn't it?" Sturt answered with his unexpected laugh. "Poor, ill-used Jenny!"

"Well, I do think it is a shame!" Jenny cried. "You may go away if you like—I'm sure I don't want to keep you if you don't want to stay—but why need you be so horrid over it? I never did you any harm. I admit I did make love to you a little just at first, but only a very little—you didn't need much tempting, did you? Men never do. And after that, all through the time at Clères, it was you, and always you, who—— And when I came back to town I wanted you to keep away, you know I did, but you would come to see me here, though I said I didn't like it. But you were so impetuous." She stopped; she could have stabbed his pride very deeply if she had told him what she knew, that he had used her as an anodyne. It has been said that Jenny possessed tastes, though she lacked principles, and her taste precluded that particular taunt as hitting below the belt. "And now as soon as you are tired of me you think I shall want to blackmail you. Men are all brutes when they get tired of women, but I did think, Mark, you would always be a gentleman."

He looked down at her, faintly amused, quite impassive. "Yes, it's very sad. Cheer up: tell Horton all about it."

"Oh!" said Jenny under her breath. She snatched a handkerchief from her bosom and pressed it to her lips: she bit into the cambric: Mark shuddered, the soundless writhing spasm was so like that of a trapped beast. For the first time in all his experience of Jenny he felt afraid of her. But nothing happened; she wiped her lips, and slipped the handkerchief back among her soft laces.

"Good night," said Mark.

"Good-by, Mark," said Jenny.

He moved towards the door. Before he gained it, in

one spring she had flung herself on his breast, her arms
clasping his neck, her lips pressed to his throat, every
curve of her slight shape abandoned to his support.
"Don't—don't leave me, Mark," she murmured, and he
felt the heavy throbbing of her heart under her thin
laces. "My God, I love you. Stay with me once more.
I'll send Horton away. Oh, I love you better than all
the world."

"Better than my brother?"

Shaking from head to foot, Sturt wrenched open the
clasped arms with small regard for Jenny Essenden's
womanhood. He threw her from him across a chair—
it was mere chance that she did not fall on the floor.
Horton heard the noise, and dashed in; he would have
stopped Mark, but Mark pushed him out of the way
with a touch and escaped into the street. He was still
unpleasantly shaken as he shut the house door behind
him, but he was sufficiently master of his nerves to have
caught up his hat and stick as he crossed the hall, and
before he turned out of Green Street he had regained his
composure. It had been an ugly scene—a very ugly
scene: but there had been no danger in it after all, and
it was over now: he had set foot in the little house for
the last time: he had done with Jenny Essenden forever.

CHAPTER XVII

MARK went home and went to bed. It seemed to him that he had never been so tired in his life, and he went straight to his own room, refusing even Henham's offer of dinner. He could not eat; Jenny had taken away his appetite. All he wanted was to sleep—sleep and forget the existence of Mrs. Essenden; and he flung off his clothes and flung himself into bed as a man does who feels a heavy sickness coming on him. But it was health, not sickness, that was coming to Mark Sturt—health and the prospect of sweet calm slumber after so many fevered hours.

He slept without turning till eight o'clock next morning, and woke feeling as he had not felt since the early days at Ushant; full of life and vigor, keenly looking forward to the day before him. He rang, and Henham brought him tea and letters, among which he was amused to find a note from Lawrence. "How have you sped? For heaven's sake let me know. I have had devastating premonitions of evil all day. Do not murder the lady, at all events—the prettiest of pretty women is not worth getting hanged for." Mark laughed, and tossed the characteristically indiscreet little missive into the fire: yes, Lawrence should hear without delay. He scribbled a telegram to let the Ferriers know that he would be back in the course of the day, and dispatched Henham with it on the spot. Mark's irritation had evaporated. After all, why blame a man for shooting over lands unfenced and unguarded? He forgave Lawrence, he forgave George Horton—had not Horton served his turn with

Jenny?—he forgave Jenny herself because that little defeated enemy was not worth hating, and, though Maisie
was not yet included in the general amnesty, he had
every intention of forgiving her too, in set form, before
the day was out. His eyes sparkled as he rehearsed the
scene. "What a jolly morning!" he said as the little
gray man laid out his clothes. It was a brilliant frost,
and Henham smiled in decorous sympathy; he was sin-
cerely glad to see Mark looking so fit and cheerful again,
so much better than was to be expected of a man who had
had no dinner. Henham did not like unsettled ways.

Mark bathed and dressed himself, and came down
about nine o'clock very hungry. For some time his attention was concentrated on his eggs and bacon, but at
length he found himself at liberty to unfold the morning
paper and glance through the headlines. He skimmed
his own Liberal sheet first, found nothing in it of conse-
quence, and turned to the leading Tory organ, the *Journal*. "Railway Disaster at Sutton," he read: "American
Labor Storm": "British Naval Rights"—how that
smacked of old days! "Ministerial Changes"—on the
last he fastened. Tentative lists are more often wrong
than right, but the man who expects to see his own name
will skim every one of them. This, however, was not
on ordinary lines. "By the courtesy of a correspondent,
whose name we hold but are not at present at liberty to
reveal, we are enabled to publish the following communication, which throws some curious light on the system
by which a modern Cabinet is formed." Mark passed
on to the "communication," and found himself reading
his own name: "My dear Sturt."

He stopped and went back to the beginning. "By the
courtesy of a correspondent . . ." Yes. But what was
it all about? "My dear Sturt, I very much regret not
being able to get down to breakfast, as there are vari-

ous points which I should have liked to clear up before you go. You will of course treat this letter as most strictly confidential. . . . I have just heard from the P.M. . . . It is proposed to redistribute certain of the vacated offices as follows. . . ."

It was his own letter from George Mallinson that he was reading.

In the first terrible revulsion of feeling, Mark sat still at the breakfast table leaning his head on his hands, and staring blankly at the paper which was propped against the coffee-pot. He could not, for a minute, grasp what had happened. But there was Mallinson's letter, printed *in extenso,* staring him in the face: a letter "most strictly confidential," dispatched indeed, though only from bedchamber to hall, under Mallinson's private seal—and the seal had not been tampered with, Mark had instinctively made sure of that before he broke it open. "By the courtesy of a correspondent . . ." After reading the letter in the train, Mark had put it in his pocket-book and the pocket-book in his breast pocket, and, tired as he was at night, he had not forgotten to slip the case under his pillow, ready to return to his pocket in the morning. He felt for it, and found it. But when he opened it there was no letter in it. He had dropped it, or it had been taken from him.

In the first recoil, most men, confronted by a disaster, cry out, "I do not believe it," but the measure of the trained mind is its rapid acceptance of facts. Mark's spasm of skepticism was over when he opened the empty pocket-book. The thing was done, and he was responsible; his guilt or innocence was a side-issue. He had, however, a partner in his official crime. That the editor of a respectable paper should have dared to print a private letter which fell irregularly into his hands!

Mark sprang up, taking the paper with him, jumped into a taxi, and was driven to the offices of the *Journal*. It was still early, but he sent up his card, and was at once shown into the large shabby room where the editor-in-chief was at work. He rose as Mark came in—a small, spare man with a pointed beard and piercing dark eyes; it occurred to Mark that Wynne was not surprised to see him.

"Good morning, sir," said Mark, curtly civil. "You publish a letter of mine this morning."

"A letter addressed to you, sir—yes, we do."

"A private and confidential letter addressed to me not as a politician but as a personal friend of the writer. You had absolutely no right to print that."

Wynne swung round on his revolving chair and touched a bell. A messenger lad entered the room. "Send Mr. Ashton to me," said Wynne. Ashton, a secretary, entered within a few seconds. "Mr. Sturt's letter and the covering letter, please, Ashton."

"Here, sir."

"That'll do." Ashton went away. Wynne held out to Mark the lost letter from George Mallinson. "That is, as you see, the letter we publish."

"And had no right to publish."

"Excuse me. This is the covering letter, which we did not publish because we were not authorized to do so. But you see that it authorizes us to publish the enclosure."

Mark took from Wynne's hand a sheet of his own paper, stamped with the address of his own flat.

13, Park Court, Westminster. S.W.1.
Thursday.
Make what use you like of the enclosed.
O. M. Sturt.

Mark gave a short, hard laugh. Was that his sentence of political death?

"I beg your pardon," he said, raising his head after a brief silence. "That is perfectly clear and correct. You were justified in publishing Mr. Mallinson's letter."

"I suppose you are going to say that that note is a forgery. Believe me or not as you like, Mr. Sturt, but if I had dreamed that it was not authentic no power on earth would have induced me to take advantage of it. But it so happened that I myself had been reading your Andes book, which has, you may remember, a facsimile of your signature under the frontispiece; and on careful comparison the handwritings appeared to me to be identical. Yet I should have got you to confirm it if I had known you were in town."

"It is not a forgery," said Mark. "Except that the date has been altered from Tuesday to Thursday. You would not examine that, of course, and it has been very carefully done; but if you hold it sloping to the light you will see that it is so."

Wynne turned the paper slantwise. "Yes, I do see, and I wish with all my heart I had held it over till I had consulted you."

"Oh, not at all," said Mark.

He stood up.

"Sorry to have made a fuss. You were, of course, entirely correct in your action. I shall not take any steps in the matter. Let it stand as it is."

"No withdrawal?"

"Ah! that is not in my hands. I dare say I am not your first caller, am I?" Wynne hesitated. "Don't answer: I'm not asking any questions. I have heard nothing myself so far, but then no one except Mr. Mallinson knows I am in town." Mark smiled; he could imagine that the telephone bell at Shotton had been kept going.

"If they come to you, show them these letters and say
what you said to me. Don't point out the alteration in
the date, please. I shall be, as a personal favor, grateful if you will forget my coming here. My hands are
tied." He did not know how haughtily he spoke, nor
how unwaveringly certain Wynne had grown, in their
brief interview, that this man with the clear stern eyes
and indifferent manner had never been for sale. "Because you're in it with me, I have said more to you than
I shall say to any one else. But you are clear. You
understand, Mr. Wynne, I take all responsibility and refuse all explanation."

"That shall be as you wish," said Wynne.

The rest of that morning passed like a nightmare.
By the time Mark got back to his flat, the official world
had found out that he was in town, and the only occupation left him was to sit in his chair and refuse to
answer questions. Theoretically it should be easy to say,
"I have no explanation to give you," but in practice, in
the teeth of indignant authority, Mark found his position very nearly untenable. He stuck to it, because he
had nothing whatever to gain by telling the ridiculous
truth: but he was reminded of the tortures of Sing-Sing.
Henham kept the journalists at bay. But Henham could
not bar out the sardonic humor of Lord Vere, Arthur
Sturt's friend and Lawrence Sturt's godfather; or Considine Sturt, who had motored up from Buckingham-
shire to get his cousin's denial; or the gray-haired, hot-
tempered Premier, striding in to know "what the devil
this means, sir?" or Lauderdale's private secretary, silk-
enly hinting that in the long run it pays a man better
to be true to his salt. . . .

Mallinson himself appeared shortly after twelve, and
then Mark's cup of gall was full. Mallinson was an
old man, and the fracas had shaken him. He was not

suspicious, he was not even angry; he murmured, "Thank you, my dear boy," when Mark, dropping his guard of indifference, put him into a screened chair by the fire and asked after his neuritis; but he was extremely hard to face. He took for granted that the letter had been stolen. "And I don't like to say much, Mark, because I recognize that it is worse for you than for me; but I feel—I do feel that you should have been more careful. I should have told you to burn it if I had thought there was any danger of your leaving it about. It—it really does make things so very awkward! How am I ever to look any of them in the face again? If it had been in my official style I could have borne it better, but the personalities are too—too terrible. A man doesn't want to make enemies at my time of life. Do you suppose Maude or Eley will ever speak to me again? Never mind! Never mind! Only tell me how it happened." And Mark longed to make a clean breast of it. But to tell Mallinson the truth and bind him to silence would be only dragging Mallinson after him into the mud, and for the tenth time that morning Mark gave his stiff, curt version of the affair. It brought Mallinson to his feet. "Wynne not to blame? *You* take the blame? . . . No explanation to offer? But that is absurd! You must know how you came to lose it. I don't understand what you mean by an 'authorization.' You are not going to tell me that you intended Wynne to print that letter?"

Standing with his back to the wall, Mark swore inwardly that he would not speak, no, not till the investigation was over. In six months' time Mallinson should know all. So long as he, like Mark, was liable to be badgered in cross-examination, it was better for him to be able to say, "I wash my hands of Sturt. He will tell me nothing." Which was, in effect, much what Mallinson did say. . . . "But you ought to explain. You have

no right to refuse. No, Sturt, no: I can't see eye to eye
with you here. I suppose you're shielding some one,
but if it were your own brother you would not have any
right to shield him. You owe it to all of us as well as
to yourself to speak out."

When Mallinson had limped out of the study, Mark
laid his head down on his folded arms and groaned. He
was a proud man; till that hour he had never known
how deeply pride had struck its roots in him, pride in
his ancient name, in his unspotted personal honor. He
had never given any man a chance to accuse him of a
betrayed confidence or a broken word. But now? By
now the clubs and country-houses were humming with
the news of Mark Sturt's amazing indiscretion. He had
enough faith in his own reputation to be sure that many
of those who knew him would at least suspend judgment. There would be a rush for the later editions,
and their columns would be scanned for his disclaimer.
But when no disclaimer followed—when it was whispered that Wynne held Sturt's written authority—what
then? What would his own verdict have been? "Got
at," and a shrug of the shoulders. "Squared by the wire-
pullers. Press money probably—the Merridew gang."
The Merridew newspaper ring had corrupted bigger men
than Mark Sturt.

But, though he winced, he was not a bit the more inclined to explain himself. Society is no sentimentalist,
and in its rule of thumb judgments probability of fact
takes precedence of probability of character; if he could
bring himself to tell the ridiculous truth, all London
would laugh at him, and four-fifths of London would
not believe a word of it. A great wave of scorn and
healthy anger went over Mark as he reached that fortify-
ing conclusion. He defend himself? He, with the soldier's discipline in his blood, stoop to an excuse? He, a

Sturt, confess the slips of his private life to Wynne the journalist, or to Lauderdale's sneering secretary? "Never!" said Mark with glimmering eyes. Better set his back to the wall and fight it out; and in this frame of mind he rang for Henham and ordered a solid lunch and bottled beer. . . . Well: but it was hard luck to have to fight, and fight for his life, because once in thirteen years he had slipped as other men slip every day. That wild-cat Jenny!

> The gods are just, and of our pleasant vices
> Make whips to scourge us.

Mark startled Henham by laughing aloud as he shook out his table napkin. He had just remembered the vaunt on which he had gone to sleep overnight. "Why didn't I touch wood?" he reflected. He was impenitent, but he was not blind to the poetic justice of her betrayal. Done with Jenny Essenden, had he? Till his life's end Mark was not to have done with Jenny Essenden.

The day wore on. After lunch Mark determined to keep to his original plan of going down to Shotton, and he left the flat soon after two o'clock, directing Henham to summon him by telephone if any urgent message came from Mr. Mallinson, and swung off for Waterloo on foot to get a breath of air. The first man he saw when he turned into Victoria Street was Grayson-Drew, the Chief Whip, whirling past in an open car. Mark automatically raised his hat to his official superior, and Grayson-Drew put up two fingers in a stiff unsmiling acknowledgment. Mark swung round and stood for a moment following the car with his eyes. A foretaste, this, of what he had to expect? If he had not taken the initiative, Grayson-Drew would have cut him. Mark walked on with a glowing heart; he swore he would not take the initiative again. Well, what wonder if the party organizers were

in a rage? there must be dire confusion that day in the
Government camp. It would have mattered less had
Mallinson been less indispensable, or had his luckless
letter been less damningly and comically indiscreet. The
Liberal government could not get on without him, and
yet how was he to go on working with the distinguished
colleague whom he had described as suffering from golf-
ing degeneration of the brain?

Meanwhile, not desiring any more casual meetings till
his position should be defined and regularized, Mark got
into a taxi and was driven the rest of the way. But in
town, even in the week after Christmas, one cannot escape one's friends. When Mark had settled himself with
a pipe and the *Badminton* in the corner of a smoking
carriage, he saw coming up to the door another man
whom he had known more or less intimately on sporting
terms for the last ten years. French had put his foot
on the step when he caught sight of Mark buried behind
the tall magazine. He drew back swiftly and passed on
to another compartment.

It was a bitter, dark afternoon when Mark got out at
Shotton. The frost of New Year's Eve had never
thawed, and the country was masked in snow, feature-
less save where patches of wood, stripped by the sudden gale on New Year's night, stood up black and bare.
Overhead the clouds lay packed, rank on rank, no light,
not even a western rift, breaking through their black-
ened fleeces; thick and low they stooped over the land,
while all along the northern horizon copper-colored gloom,
dotted with grayish-white puffs of moister vapor, rolled
upwards like the smoke of war. There was no cab to
be had, and no car had come to meet him because he
had not named the time of his arrival, and Mark tramped
the twilit miles to Shotton in a frame of mind not ill
suited to his surroundings. "Think hard, Mark: think

like the devil." He remembered that caution as he turned
in at the gate. He had thought hard, and had believed
himself to have guarded every avenue of danger, but the
worst of it was that Mrs. Essenden had begun thinking
earlier.

Mark reached the house and let himself in by the open
door. Footmen came forward to take his hat and stick,
and Mark wondered whether they knew all about him;
no doubt the *Journal* was taken in the servants' hall.
He asked for Mrs. Ferrier; she was out driving with
Miss Archdale, but Mr. Ferrier and most of the other
gentlemen were in the gun-room. Mark nodded and
strolled forward, opening the door. ". . . I'd give a
year of my life to have seen old Maude's face. . . ."
Ferrier's dropped sentence and the hush which fell all
over the room told Mark that his own affairs had been
under discussion. Oddly enough, till that moment it
had not occurred to him that at Shotton, among his personal friends, in the circle that he had left not six and
thirty hours ago, he could suffer any embarrassment.

Through the firelit dark he recognized the more familiar figures; Charles Ferrier with his lean gypsy face
standing back to the hearth, his hands deep in his trouser
pockets; Roderick Earle lounging on a couch; Harry
Forester posted in the window-seat; Lawrence Sturt sitting with folded arms on the edge of a table, one breeched
and booted leg cocked over a neighboring chair. Mark
came into the room, and found that he had not the faintest idea what to say to any of them. He drew up, and
the color—a man's rare, heavy blush that seems to scorch
the skin under which it passes—went over his
face and neck from the line of his collar to the line of
his hair.

"Hullo!" said Ferrier, coming forward swiftly and
holding out his hand. "Here you are, Mark! 'Fraid you

had a beastly walk up from the station. We couldn't
send to meet you because we had no notion of the train."

"I expect it was a mistake for me to come at all,"
said Mark simply. "I have to apologize, Ferrier. Somehow it never struck me."

"Rot," said Ferrier, flushing, and, "Oh, rot!" said
Earle, getting unexpectedly off his sofa. "Come and
have a whisky and soda, Sturt—excuse me, Charles—
you've had a rough day."

Lawrence had not budged hitherto, but when the other
men gathered round Mark he too came forward, parting his way between them, and dropped his hand on
Mark's shoulder. "Get it over," he said in the deepened
tones that were his only betrayal of strong feeling.
"Come! the cat's out of the bag—we know the text, you
may as well let us hear the commentary. You never sent
that letter, Mark. Who did?"

"The letter to the *Journal?*"

"Oh, yes. Own up: don't be a fool!"—It was Lawrence's eternal cry, "Don't be a silly ass!"—"Oh, Mark,
don't shirk your fences! It isn't good enough; it simply
is not good enough. Defend yourself: you owe more
to the family than to—— Keep your own name out of
the mud and let the rest go to the devil."

Mark held his peace for a couple of breaths. He
knew what Lawrence wanted—no details, not even
Jenny's name. Every man in that room could have filled
up some sort of detail for himself. He was not even re-
quired to say "A woman betrayed me"; he had only to
say "I was betrayed." Lawrence himself would have
entered either plea without scruple; and indeed so would
Mark, so far as the traitress was concerned. It was
not pity for Jenny—for that matter, what would Jenny
care?—nor chivalry, nor any lingering sense of obligation to the life once mixed with his own that held Mark

back from speech, but sheer stubborn pride. He could stand any obloquy—and it was hourly becoming clearer to him that he would have a good deal to stand—sooner than confess how Jenny had fooled him.

"I have nothing to explain," he said quietly. "Wynne holds my authorization."

"To print Mallinson's letter? Wynne holds a permit from you?"

"He does, indeed."

"Were you drunk?"

"We'll defer this discussion for the present, Lawrence."

"Defer it as long as you like," said Lawrence.

He turned his back on Mark, took out his cigar case, and lit a cigar. Mark watched him in silence, a silence which none of the other men attempted to break. These men knew Mark—he was of their blood and class; they had knocked about with him for years in the loose intimacy of covert, moor, and camp, and they represented, not the unbiased cynicism of London, but the shrewd faith that is begotten by danger out of hardship—the careless and inarticulate freemasonry that will damn one man by a shrug of the shoulders and stand by another to the death. A word, and Mark could have had them on his side through thick and thin; but, as a point of personal preference, he would sooner have died where he stood than speak that word.

He turned again to Ferrier. "Really I'm very sorry: I wouldn't have inflicted our family squabbles on you if I'd foreseen them, but, as you know, it has all happened so quickly that I've hardly got my bearings yet. I'll say good-by, Ferrier; I shan't see you again for some months to come."

"Going off?" said Ferrier. "Dare say you're wise. Explanations are futile things. Better wait for the row to blow over." He hesitated, then went on with a visible effort. "All the same, if you'll forgive my saying so, none of us who know you will accept the crude statement of the case which is apparently all you're going to give us. Publicly, I suppose we shall be bound to take the facts at their face value; but, if it's any consolation to you, we all know there's something behind."

"Amen!" said his brother-in-law. "Although I'm not your brother and I haven't known you as long as Ferrier has, I should like, if I may, to endorse what Ferrier says."

"Thank you," said Mark awkwardly.

He shook hands with Earle, included Lawrence among the other men in a slight bow, and came out into the hall, followed by Ferrier. "I hear Dodo is out with Miss Archdale," said Mark, dropping into a more ordinary manner as soon as he was alone with Ferrier. "Have you any idea how soon they'll be in?"

"In half no time, I should say. Listen! aren't those wheels in the avenue?"

As he went to the door, Dodo's high dogcart drew up before it. Mark waited in the darkened hall, where no candles had yet been lit because of Dodo's liking for long twilights and firelights. He heard his own name in a brief exchange of speech between husband and wife. Then the two women came in together, Ferrier following, and Mark went slowly forward. He remembered afterwards the appeal of Dodo's upturned face, white and scared; but after the first preoccupied greeting it was not to Dodo that he addressed himself. He forgot Dodo, forgot Ferrier, forgot everything in the isolation of his rising fury.

"How d'ye do, Miss Archdale? So sorry to bother you when you haven't had any tea, but my time is short. May I see you for ten minutes?"

Maisie strolled over to the great hearth, slowly pulling off her gloves. She glanced up at him with her clear cold eyes, steady as a fencer's blade.

"Of course you may, Mr. Sturt. Don't go, Dodo: Mr. Sturt doesn't want to see me privately."

"Yes, I do."

She smiled and slightly shook her head.

"You'll remember that I have a right to insist."

"I'm sorry that I can't recognize any right of yours. I'm very sorry about—about everything; it's all most unfortunate, and I wouldn't willingly do anything to make it harder for you. But I won't see you privately."

"Are you afraid of me?"

"Do you think that likely?"

"I think you ought to be. I am a tolerant fellow, Maisie, and I have given you a long rope, but you came to the end of my patience two nights ago, here on that staircase. God knows what you meant by it, I don't. I swore to myself that evening that I would have an explanation out of you, or, failing that, cut my own way out of the tangle once for all. Are you going to refuse me an explanation?"

"Yes, I refuse."

"As you please." A door opened behind him; the men were coming out of the gun-room. Mark did not even turn his head to see who they were. He was desperate—strung up to the point at which a man does not care who hears what he says; but if he had been as cool as he seemed he would still have held on his way. "But in that case, since I'm not going till I've said what I came to say, you force me to speak before others."

She tried to escape towards the stairs. Mark stopped her. But he felt Ferrier's hand on his arm. "Mark, old fellow, you can't——"

"Let me alone," said Mark: "she is my wife."

He addressed himself again to Maisie. "Before you married me you gave me leave to make the marriage public if necessary. In my judgment, it has become necessary, because I'm going away to-night, and I refuse to leave you in your present absurd and anomalous position. It is not fitting that my wife should pass for an unmarried woman. To-night I shall send the dated announcement to the papers."

"Sorry," Maisie murmured with the old good-humored irony, glancing past Mark to Dodo Ferrier. "It is quite true. I married him last July."

"And if I were to die," Mark went on, "the truth would have to come out, because, though this fact does not seem ever to have struck you, men in my position don't get married without making settlements on their wives. So that I was obliged to take my lawyers into my confidence, last July. You wanted the marriage kept secret, for reasons which I didn't dispute then, and don't dispute now." Carefully and plainly, Mark scored his points for the benefit of the jury. "You have from start to finish acted, from a woman's point of view, in an open and honorable way; I don't grumble at anything, except, perhaps, your having forced me into this disagreeably public explanation. But your point of view is not mine. I ought to have protected you from your own ignorance."

"Thank you. All this happened six months ago. Why have you suddenly wakened up to your duty?"

"I can't imagine why I didn't wake up to it long ago. At all events I'm going to do it now. I dare say you think that after what has lately happened I ought to take myself out of your life with as little fuss as possible. I wish I could think so too: believe me, I should prefer it. But marriage is a bond that can't be lightly broken. It is a poor bargain for you, I know: you're richer than I am, and after selling my party I can't even offer you a decent name." He curbed himself; he was half mad with rage and pain, but he was not going to stoop to irony. "For all that, you are my wife. I came here to-night to ask you to leave Shotton with me."

"Here and now? Straight out with you into the snow?"

"Here and now," said Mark, holding out his hands. When Maisie laid her own in them he believed that he had conquered. He drew her towards him, looking down into her eyes with the strange gay smile of the man who has snatched victory out of defeat. "I'll give you ten minutes to get on your snowboots, Maisie."

"Ah! I shouldn't mind the snow."

"Well, will you come?"

"No." She added, so low that Mark himself barely heard, "Take Mrs. Essenden."

She made him gasp for breath, but he was too well drilled to betray by any definite sign how cruelly she had hit him.

"What do you mean by that?" he cried.

"But for that I would have come, Mark."

"Well, I am done," said Mark with clenched hands. "If, knowing what you know, you think you have the right—!" He broke off, and shrugged his shoulders. "That finishes everything. I have nothing more to say. But you'll not continue to pass under your maiden name. You'll acknowledge me as your husband. You'll sign yourself Maisie Sturt in future."

"Certainly, if you like."

"Good-by."

"Good-by, Mark."

At the door Mark turned, drawing himself up for a last glance. The hall was still pervaded by the silence of sheer astonishment. Dodo leaned against Charles Fer-

rier's arm, holding a handkerchief to her eyes. Maisie
stood by the fire, smoothing out her gloves, and looking
down with stern thoughtful glance into the gold and ruby
of the flames. In the background the white sharp face
of Lawrence Sturt jeered at him out of the shadows.
The same ironic commentary that had mocked him when
he looked up out of the pains of death to find his brother
kneeling over him in that fly-haunted pit at St. Éloi.
"O passi graviora," he could hear Lawrence saying, "for-
san et hæc olim. . . ."

But this was worse than that.

CHAPTER XVIII

THREE hours later Mark let himself into his flat, where he found Henham waiting.

"Any more people called, Henham?"

"No, sir. Well, no one to speak of. One or two gentlemen connected with the Press, that was all. I had a job to get rid of them."

"Oh, you're an invaluable fellow. Well, now get me something to eat, and then I shall want you to pack for me. I'm leaving town to-morrow, and I shall want you to stay on here for a bit and look after the place."

"Yessir."

"I shall probably be away a good long time. I'll arrange for you to draw your money as usual. I shall want my guns and fishing tackle."

"Yessir."

"If any one should turn up to-night, say I'm not at home."

"If Captain Sturt should come, sir?"

"I won't see him."

"Or Father de Trafford?"

"Nor him either."

"Or if—if a lady was to call, sir?"

"Good God!" said Mark, with a sudden burst of laughter, "if a lady calls, put the chain up."

Mark went into his bedroom. He was not one to collect litter, but no man can live seven years in a spot without gathering a few personal trifles about him; letters, memoranda, things of no value but for their associations. Mark had not much, but he came across a dozen photo-

graphs of Lawrence and some of his letters, and one note
from Maisie which he had discovered under a pebble on
the window-sill at Ushant one morning when he returned
rather late from a stroll to find the cottage empty. "Dear
Mark, *Don't* turn your steps towards the cove, I've gone
down there to bathe. Put some coal on if the fire looks
low, I've stacked on all I cd. but it's not a big enough
grate. M." Lawrence and Maisie's letters went together into the flames, and Mark stamped them down
with the heel of his boot. He had not much sentiment
left in him, but he had enough to be glad when they
were burned.

He returned to the living-room, where Henham was
waiting to serve dinner. Wonderful man, Henham! He
could not have expected Mark home that night, and yet
in forty minutes he had got ready an admirable meal,
with claret of the right temperature and Mark's favorite
hors d'œuvre. Between two courses, when Henham had
left the room, a point of recollection pricked Mark's
mind, and he rose at once and went to a cabinet by the
window. He had just remembered having left in it a new
automatic pistol which Bannatyne had recently sent home
to him, and which he and Henham had been examining
together. They had been testing the mechanism, which
was of a novel design, and Mark knew that they had
left the weapon loaded; a careless act, witness many a
coroner's inquest. Henham of course knew his way
about, but a loaded Browning is not a safe thing to keep
loose in empty rooms. But, when Mark went to draw
the charge, he stood weighing the toy in his hand with a
very odd expression. It was already drawn. At that
moment Henham came in with coffee and a bénédictine.
. . . Mark looked at him: not an eyelash flickered,
though he certainly saw his master standing by the open
cabinet with the unloaded pistol in his hand.

"There are a lot of other weapons on the wall, Henham," said Mark.

"Yessir," Henham agreed, sweeping a crumb from the table. "But they don't come so 'andy like."

Mark returned to the fire, his coffee, and a pipe. Henham retired in his own noiseless fashion, and Mark let his eyes rove over the stand of weapons that filled the length of the wall. There was every variety of cutting and stabbing implement, from the paralyzing poison-dart of the Tsavo jungle to the eight-foot spear of the Dyak, but there were no guns. Decidedly Henham showed judgment; the crook of a finger round a hair-trigger is a swifter and a neater trick than disemboweling oneself, say, with a Japanese sword. Mark's mind ought to have been fixed upon the wreck of his political and matrimonial career, but instead of that he found himself ruminating over Henham, and wondering whether there had ever been a Mrs. Henham or a little Henham junior. He did not know one single fact about Henham's private life—not even his Christian name.

The door reopened, and Henham himself appeared—but such a harassed and agitated Henham as Mark had never seen before. "I beg your pardon for disturbing you, sir," he panted out as respectfully as his breathless state allowed, "but there—there *is* a lady to see you, sir, and I—I couldn't stop her coming in——"

Mark was on his feet with a bound: he had a flying memory of Lawrence's cautionary note, and the thought struck him that it might be needed. "Where is she?"

"Sir, it's—it isn't Mrs. Essenden——"

It was not Jenny Essenden: it was Maisie Sturt.

She stood in the doorway, towering over Henham's shoulder: no wonder he had not been able to keep her out! She was in her sable suit again, cap and coat and fur-bordered gauntlets: but where had she been and what had she been doing? Coat and cap and skirt, every garment down to her gaiters and boots was powdered thick with snow; her jacket was unfastened as usual over her bare throat, and the snow had eddied in against her skin; a wreath of snow lay in the folds of her veil. Shutting the door on Henham's discomfiture, she came to the fire and began to strip off her out-of-door clothes, shaking into the hearth their white drifts, which the warmth of Mark's room was fast thawing into rivulets that dripped round her in a pool on the floor.

"Maisie!" said Mark, stupefied. "Is it you? How—how did you get here?"

"I motored."

"Motored up from Shotton? In an open car? You don't mean you drove yourself?"

"Yes; the last train had gone and it was a very bad night, and I couldn't drag a man out. I took my own little run-about that was stabled at the inn. What does it signify? I had powerful head-lamps."

"Your dress is saturated. You'll get rheumatic fever if you sit in those clothes."

He knelt to unfasten her boots: they were wet—the little run-about was not designed to face the storms of a winter night, and apparently the snow had drifted in round her legs all the way. Maisie let him take them off, while she herself removed the drenched cap and veil. Her hair was still dressed for the evening, a pearl comb set high among its shining puffs and coils; she had apparently flung on her furred suit over silk stockings and a white evening gown. "I shall be none the worse," she said. "You know I took no hurt when I got wet at Ushant, and then I was soaked to the skin. This is nothing to that, because my motoring clothes are so thick; see, I'll slip out of them—the silk is not wet underneath."

"Your bodice is wet." Sturt hurried into his bedroom and came back with a coat of his own. "Put this on over it. Why hadn't you the sense to fasten your collar?"

"I don't know. I never thought about it. Let me sit down by the fire."

Then he saw that she could hardly stand. He dragged up his own chair for her to sit in, and raked the coals to a blaze. Maisie leaned forward, stretching out her hands to the glow, nestling her bare shoulders into Mark's old coat as if she liked its roomy warmth.

"No coffee, Mark, thanks—no, and a bénédictine still less. Come here and let me say what I have to say."

He leaned one elbow on the mantelpiece and stood looking down at her, the other hand thrust into his pocket. His rather heavy, impassive face was keenly observant and attentive, but it expressed no feeling of any kind—neither anger, nor tenderness, nor admiration, nor even curiosity.

"You don't seem much moved," said Maisie, smiling faintly. "How do you feel—like having a gun accident?"

"Not a bit. It's a smash, certainly, but it will blow over; or, if it didn't, there are other countries in the world besides England. I still have our national resource of killing things."

"Do you think you'll have to resign your seat?"

"I shall not have to do so. I have already done so."

"You would, of course: I might have known that. But if you were nominated again would you stand?"

"Certainly, if Gatton did me that honor. But I don't think Gatton will."

"Lawrence thinks they will. He says you took a wise line in refusing to explain."

"Oh?" said Mark blankly. "I did not gather that opinion from Lawrence this afternoon."

"He lost his temper. But he said to-night, and Charles Ferrier agreed, that in the long run you'll score by it. No explanation is better than a lame defense. After all, the bribe theory doesn't cover the facts. Where is the bribe? You lose the chance of office and your seat."

"I see." Mark's tone was dry; he did not care to discuss his brother. When he remembered the scene in the gun-room, a desire to hit Lawrence ached in his arm like cramp.

"Of course I know who did it. She has smashed up your career out of revenge."

"How do you come to know anything about Mrs. Essenden?"

She passed by that question. "And, after all, it's not your career that you mind about, is it? It's the breach of confidence, the failure in honor towards Mr. Mallinson. I know how proud you are, and how sensitive about a thing like that."

"Am I?"

"Very: and deadly reserved, too, and rather shy, under the drilled manner. You've schooled yourself to go through with things, but you feel them acutely, and a stab like this, which touches your personal honor, is what you can least stand. Oh! outsiders won't see all that, but I'm not precisely an outsider, and—no more is Mrs. Essenden. She knows you through and through, that's why she chose this particular form of revenge."

"Sheer chance. She took the first weapon that came to hand."

"She could have struck twenty times before. She held her hand till she could strike right up under your armor."

Mark did not answer, but his expression remained no less coldly attentive and polite.

"And you're going away—when? To-morrow?" He nodded. "Where shall you go—Central Africa?"

"Central Africa?" Sturt laughed. "Oh, no—Central Africa is where you go to meet all your friends. I shall drop off the edge of civilization. I'm not keen on meeting my friends—although, as you say, the bribe theory doesn't cover the facts."

"I am very sorry about it all, Mark—very sorry."

"So you said to-night."

"I behaved very badly to you."

"Not at all," said Mark politely.

"And now you are not going to forgive me," said Maisie. She covered her eyes with her hand.

"Don't cry," said Mark. "It isn't worth it. You had much better have a bénédictine, it will pull you together a bit."

"I am not crying: and you needn't be afraid—I shan't make you any scene. Believe me, I am not one of the women who make scenes. I rather wish I were, you would probably understand me better if I did. Are you angry with me for coming here?"

"Certainly not. You seem to forget that you're my wife. You have every right to come here, and to say anything you like to me. What is it you want to say? You'll feel happier when you've gone through with it, and, for that matter, so shall I. It's getting late, isn't it? You must be tired."

"You hate me for understanding, you hate my coming here," said Maisie, turning her head away. "But it is not my fault that I'm here. I came under orders."

"Whose—Mrs. Ferrier's?"

"Would she meddle? No: some one who knows you better than Dodo or I do. Lawrence made me come: so, if you're angry—and I know you are, though you say you aren't—be angry with him."

"*Lawrence!*"

"We had a short explanation after you left. He waylaid me on the landing, and we had it out together in my room. I told him how I married you, and he told me about Mrs. Essenden's peculiar catholicity of taste. No, it wasn't a conventional dialogue: but Lawrence is not prudishly conventional, is he? He was angry, if you like. He said his usual motto was never to interfere with another man's horse, or his gun, or his wife; but that you and I were such fools that there was nothing for it but for some kind friend to knock our heads together."

"I recognize Lawrence in the turn of that phrase. He can always manage other people's business better than his own."

"He advised—I may say he ordered—me to come up by the first train to-morrow morning and confess to you; but I couldn't face a night's inaction."

"I owe him one for that," said Mark, smiling and giving a little twist to his mustache.

"Oh, I can't stand this," said Maisie under her breath. "I can't, Mark, I can't."

"If it will make things easier for you, I believe I know what you're trying to say."

"What, then?"

"That, feeling yourself partly responsible for the ruin of my career, you are prepared to let bygones be bygones and accompany me into exile. Isn't that the way of it?"

"More or less."

"Then, with all possible gratitude both to Lawrence and to yourself, I beg to state that I have changed my mind and I decline the honor."

The choice of words, the smile, the undisguised and

penetrating sneer brought Maisie to her feet. "Is that meant for an insult?"

"Anything you like."

"Well, you are pretty badly hit, then," said Maisie.

She faced him with her direct eyes and deer-like carriage of the head, as she had faced him long ago in the fields at Shotton. "And that is my fault; it was through me you fell into Mrs. Essenden's toils; but for me you would have gone on living the old, hardy life. Now you shall have the truth. You are a proud man, aren't you? I'm proud too. You haven't been very generous to me this evening. I don't wonder; you've had a great deal to chafe you to-day, and you're tired and out of humor, and the last thing you want is a scene of sentiment. Believe me, if it is disagreeable to you, it is—no less so to me. I must say what I came to say, not only because I promised Lawrence, but because it has to be said. I've done so very wrong—I've wronged you so deeply—that there's nothing left for me now but to put myself into your hands. I must—I must stand up to my punishment." She was on her feet, white as death, facing him in her silk and pearls and crushed tulle as he could have imagined her facing enemy rifles. "Will you—will you promise to hear me out—not to interrupt the tale? I can't—I can't finish if you do."

"I promise."

"Thank you. Haven't you often wanted to ask me why I married you?"

"Occasionally."

"Ask now."

"Why did you marry me?"

"Because I loved you."

"Because you—?"

"Because I loved you. Oh! don't—don't laugh, Mark, will you?" She cowered down, but only for a moment.

"There never was any other reason at all. I loved you, not better than my honor, as Mrs. Essenden said, but far better than my pride. Oh! no, you promised!" Sturt, deeply flushed, would have stopped her. "Have patience with me this once, you ought to know how you stand." She waited for a moment, struggling for quiet breath, while Mark fell back into impassivity; the firelight played on her slight foot in its clocked stocking, on her gleaming silks, on the white shoulders bare under Mark's serge coat. Outside, over the dark roofs of London, a north wind rushed along laden with snow, thundering in Mark's chimney and raving round his curtained windows. Had she headed her car, then, sixty miles into that blinding gale to face this harder firelit scene at the end of it?

"I cared from the first day I saw you, which you don't remember, but I do; Lawrence was telling me Andean tales under the beech trees, and you came up to us over the grass, and Lawrence said 'My brother.' And I said to myself, 'Heavens! am I going to care for that man?' It was a—a fatality, Mark. These things happen, don't they? It wasn't a girl's fancy. One could imagine a young girl falling in love with Lawrence, say, because of his extraordinary looks, or because of his reputation. But you're not Lawrence, and I'm not a young girl. It was a—a torment. One can't fight against one's stars. And you?—you were the only man in the house that never looked at me, though heaven knows I took pains enough to make you. You thought I was amusing myself, didn't you? You were out in that guess, my friend: but you drove me mad and I didn't always know what I was doing."

Sturt moved restlessly and kicked the brands together; she was trying him high.

"It was all done in that one evening, the evening Lawrence told me you were going to America. When I heard that, I think I went mad. Anything may happen in six months. You might have got killed—or you might have got married. Oh! I know now it was unpardonable. Heavens! when I look back to five months ago it seems to me I was nothing but a child. I knew things with my mind, with my intelligence, but I didn't see where they led. Inexperienced women don't. I never had the dimmest inkling of what Ushant would mean for you. I never thought I was doing you any wrong. I knew Lawrence and Dodo wanted you to marry me. I was blind with vanity, I suppose, for I never doubted—no, I don't think I once doubted that I could make you care for me if I could once have you to myself. Like a child, I wouldn't tell you any lies, but I told you half-truths. I offered you a week at Ushant, but it was in my mind that before the week was up I'd make you love me so that you would never let me go. Do you remember what I told you at Ushant?"

"About your brother?"

"Ah! you do remember." The shadow of a smile flitted through her eyes. "I'm glad—I don't want you to hate me. Then you'll remember I had not had much happiness in my life. I was very lonely; no, worse than lonely —solitary. I love my friends, but I don't find it easy to talk to them. I did long for some one to hold on to, some one I could touch when I couldn't talk to him . . . and I used to think . . . just to touch you, Mark, not saying anything. . . . Ushant was sin. I know that now. But I didn't know it then. I never knew till that first night in the cottage. I never knew what shame meant, till then. You put me to shame then, as you're doing now. But I'm yours, to take or leave."

"Here!" said Mark, holding out his arms. She came to him. "Leave you?—never."

"Lawrence was right, then? He said you cared for me."

"Lawrence was exceedingly right."

"And you don't despise a woman that has—?"

"Not a bit. I'm grateful for the honor done me."

"No satire, Mark: I can't stand it. Remember I'm dying of shame still."

"Die, then," said Mark with levity. "What do you want?—to be adored? So you shall be, but give me five minutes to get myself in hand again. I was mad with rage when you came into the room this evening. I've been mad with rage ever since that night on the stairs. I lay up to score off you."

"You did it," Maisie murmured.

"And now you want consolation—affection—what's the trick? What do you think a man's made of? Feel my heart. Now say you're afraid of me?"

"I'm not."

"Aren't you? You look as if you were. Sit down, I can't get at you properly. You can hardly stand, you know, and I seem to be half drunk myself."

He dropped on one knee beside her, taking her into his arms, and the chalice of love, so long desired, was at her lips. Questions framed themselves in Maisie's mind, and died there. "Do you love me more than you loved Jenny? How long have you loved me? Why did you say no at Ushant? Wasn't that because you cared a little even then, too much as well as not enough?" To some she already knew the answer; others must go forever unanswered, for Mark probably could not have answered them, and certainly would not if he could. Many a woman's love is woven in and out of such silence and renunciation, because some men will be bound by no chain but of their own forging, and they will not submit to questions; bitter-sweet, this certitude came to

Maisie as she drew down Mark's head against her heart,
and the tenderness of motherhood was in her eyes, for
in the depths of life, below passion, a woman bears her
lover as she bears his child, in pain and patience as well
as in joy.

Yes, he was hers: but he came to her in his unimpaired
strength and untouched pride, with thirteen years of
manhood behind him—years of war and trade and sport
and politics, years in which he had subdued dangers and
difficulties, and tasted strange experiences, and sinned
sins that to her were a name only; years in which he
had stood alone, never bending his will against his will,
never asking or giving a confidence. Yes, he was hers;
but for how long? Forever? He had gone from Ushant
to Normandy; were there to be other Normandys in his
life?

Sharp as the point of a sword Jenny Essenden's warning for the thousandth time pierced her, sharp as a bodily
pain at her heart; at Shotton and at Ushant she had
cheated him out of one prerogative of his manhood—
the chase, the conquest; and—oh, fool!—in her recklessness she had thrown away the armor that innocent women
wear as a guard against a man's light thoughts and easy
infidelities, not only her own dignity and reticence, but
the dignity of Mark Sturt's wife, the reticence traditional
among men and women who are trained to endure and
forego. Passion obliterates all things, but when passion
fades memory returns, and, though she knew that Mark's
lips would always be sealed, was it so certain that she
would not live to read a memory in his silence? Maisie
was not given to weeping, but the poignant tears of regret hung on her eyelids now: oh, that regret for what
we would undo if we could with our life-blood, but it
can never be undone!

Yet, he was hers; and as the swift moments ebbed,

and there was no sound in the quiet room but Sturt's deep,
hurried breathing and the rustle of her own dress when
he shifted his clasp, there came to Maisie a broader vision
of human life, which builds a nest in heaven out of error
and failure and even sin. What did she want, after all,
of armor against Mark? She was his own, to love or
hate, to hold or leave, to honor or scorn. For other
women, other ways of love : this way for her.

The clock was striking midnight, and the fire had
burned down to red embers.

"Oh, Mark, it's late !" said Maisie. She drew herself
slowly out of his arms and held him away from her : an
unknown Mark, half dazed, but with the white radiance
of passion still visibly lighted in his face. "Oh, Mark,
don't look at me like that ! I'm not worth it."

"Aren't you ?"

"Let us be sensible. I ought to see about a room at
an hotel. I wonder what your man did with the car
and my dressing-case? I suppose I can get in at the
Wharton."

"Get in at the Wharton ?"

"Why not? I must sleep somewhere, and my own
house is shut up."

"Oh, quite !" said Mark. He began to laugh. "Locked
doors—what? There's no key here, Maisie : come and
see."

She sprang to her feet. "Oh, Mark, I can't, I can't!
I—I don't feel a bit married. It's so long ago."

"So you think you'd like to go to an hotel ?" said Mark
with sparkling eyes. He stood up, stretching his cramped
limbs ; he was still in his rough homespun, and he threw
up his arms and straightened back his shoulders with
the easy vigor of the athlete. "Ouf! I'm tired." He
did not look it. "Don't you think you're rather young

to go without a nurse? You won't have any one to brush your hair for you to-morrow morning, and put your bib on and tie your sash. Ha ha! when you laugh and blush like that you look about fifteen and almost pretty.—My darling, you shall do absolutely as you like; but be generous, Maisie—I'm not made of putty, though you seem to think I am. And what's the odds, after all, if you're coming to Central Africa with me to-morrow?" Bending his head, he raised her hand gently to his lips. "Dear, if you can forgive the mess I've made of things, not only the hash I've made of my political career, but the rotten time I gave you at Ushant, and—and all that's happened since—if you can forgive all that, are you going to be afraid of me now, Maisie?—Recollect, you're giving up a lot. It'll blow over in time, as Ferrier said; but for the next year or two it'll be a toss-up between cutting London and being cut by it. Some of our side will never forgive me—never; I've made them look such fools. And I shall never explain. I split with Lawrence over that. They can think what they like and say what they like. Don't fancy I'm doing it to spare Jenny either. I could crush her, if that were all, with no more compunction than killing a fly. It's not for Jenny's sake, it's for my own."

"And mine," said Maisie. "Do you imagine I want it proclaimed all over London that Mrs. Essenden picked your pocket?"

"How on earth do you know that?"

"Aren't I clever? Anyhow, that is what she did: and I quite agree, my dear boy, that you had better hold your tongue about it. You don't come out of it at all well."

"Not at all. Maisie, did Mrs. Essenden go to see you?"

"Yes, she did."

"At Shotton?"

"Yes, the night Lawrence arrived. The night I met you on the stairs, dear."

"Oh, damn the woman!" said Mark between his teeth.

"Leave her," said Maisie. "In point of fact she is already getting her deserts, or some of them: Lawrence had it all out of me this evening, and I rather gathered from his manner that he proposed to go and see the lady himself. I said he'd better not, but Lawrence in a rage is a little difficult to influence. I couldn't cope with him at all, and if I were Mrs. Essenden I should get under the table. He is fond of you, Mark. I told him what she had told me of her little trick of reading your letters—yes, dear boy, she read them all—and I have an impression that he overtook me on the London road just south of Clapham. He started after I did, but he had a bigger car."

"En route for Jenny's?"

"I should say so, from his expression."

"I'll call quits with Jenny, then," said Mark with an unforgiving laugh. "Oh, there you are, Henham. This is Mrs. Sturt, your new mistress. She is going to stay the night, so we must see what we can do to make her comfortable. Will you bring her bag up and get her something to eat? You took the car to the garage?—that's right. You had better light a fire in my room. You won't mind roughing it for one night, will you, Maisie? It can't be more uncomfortable than we were at Ushant. Oh, and, Henham, I can't take Mrs. Sturt to Mr. Bennet's quarters. I shall want you to go round to Captain Sturt to-morrow—he's at Chelsea to-night—and tell him I want to borrow Longstone Edge for a bit. We'll shut the flat up and you shall go down with us and help me to get things shipshape."

"Yessir," said Henham.

"Longstone Edge, Mark?" Maisie repeated, docile but bewildered. "But—but—I thought you were going to Central Africa?"

"Did you?" Mark answered cheerfully. "So I gathered. I didn't. What a shame, isn't it? No, dear, I'm going to Gatton to do a little work."

CHAPTER XIX

THE riverside mission was thriving, and yet Father de Trafford was not happy.

He sat alone in his study, reading a book that he had read many times before when he felt depressed. It was a night of snow and storm, but the curtains were drawn, and the room, though sparsely furnished, was of warm and comfortable aspect, with its Turkey carpet, shaded lamp, and pleasantly fusty smell of leather bindings— a little too comfortable, in Father de Trafford's opinion, for the tenancy of a Catholic priest. He often longed for the severer life and harder penances of the monastic clergy. But his superiors told him he was doing his best work where he was, and so he stayed on at St. Casimir's, and consoled himself with the reflection that he could not have entertained MM. Athos and d'Artagnan in the blessed solitude of a cell.

It was late; the deep tolling from Westminster began to sound twelve, and the tale was taken up by St. Casimir's thin reiteration. Father de Trafford came out of the cellar of the *Lis d'Or*—out of the hams, the sausages, the olive oil, and the broken bottles—and pushed away his reading lamp; for a man who was obliged to take care of his health and who had a mass to celebrate at 7:15 a.m., it was time to go to bed. Yet he did not rise; he leaned his cheek on his hand and sat on by the fire, musing.

It was of Mark Sturt that he was thinking; Mark Sturt, the founder of the riverside mission, to whom the

priest had not spoken since parting from him on the
steps of St. Casimir's with that strange "Pray for me"
ringing in his ears. Not one day or night, not many
single hours had gone by him since then without a prayer
for Sturt's soul. Father de Trafford knew his London
well. Of the outside of Mark's life he knew as much
as Horton did, or any other male gossip who moved in
Jenny's set; and from it he had divined, with the strange
inward vision of the Catholic priest, who sees day by
day men and women bared to the dry light of the confessional, a good deal of Mark's inner history as well.
Not that Mark had ever gone near a confessional since
his connection with Jenny! but de Trafford had shriven
him in the old days, and could make a pretty shrewd
guess at the effect Jenny would have on a man of Mark's
temper. De Trafford read Jenny pretty clearly—Jenny
who had bathed him in penitential tears which dried up
soon after he let slip the word *Normandy*—and he had
regretted that indiscretion more than many sins. Slight
it was, and natural, for Normandy is wide, and Mark's
journey was indeed no secret, yet de Trafford guessed
that he had put the end of a clew into Jenny's hand.
"She diddled me," he reflected ruefully. Like Lawrence,
like Ferrier, and like Alfred Henham, when he read
George Mallinson's letter in his morning paper de Trafford was not slow to put his finger on the guilty party.
No evidence would have convinced him that Sturt had
committed a breach of confidence. In the aimless malice
of the trick he read Jenny's hand.

And what now? Where would it all end? Again and
again that day the priest had been on the point of going
to see Mark, and yet he did not go. He had an intuition that Mark would refuse to see him, and, after that
refusal, there would be a definite barrier where now
there was merely no bridge. If he wanted spiritual com-

solation, Father de Trafford reflected with his shrewd smile, Mark knew where to go for it; he knew, none better, that the doors of Holy Church are open day and night. If he wanted the counsel of this world, he knew equally well that all de Trafford could give as man to man was equally at his service. Mark was very sore, no doubt, very angry, savagely shy of his friends; but he would not doubt de Trafford. There was no need for the priest to go and say, "I know this is not your doing." Such faith is taken for granted in certain relations, and after twenty years. On the whole, the priest was of opinion that Sturt would not want to meet him —not yet, anyhow. "It looks like revenge," de Trafford reflected. "If the truth were known, I expect Mark has chucked the lady, and she is getting her own back." His thoughts, and indeed his speech, occasionally refused to wear clerical dress. "No, I won't go to him. But I wish the dear fellow would come to me. He won't, though—not yet." Nevertheless, when the door bell jangled suddenly through the sleeping house, he started to his feet with Mark's name on his lips.

His servant was in bed long ago, and all other lights were out. Taking a candle, de Trafford hurried into the hall and unlocked the door. Outside, darkly silhouetted against a street of glimmering snow, stood a very tall man in a heavy overcoat, who stretched out his bare hands to the priest as if he were flying for his life. Mark Sturt? No: Lawrence.

De Trafford drew him into the study and set him in a chair by the fire. Used as he was to the unforeseen, he was so excessively startled and shocked by Lawrence Sturt's appearance that he knew not where to begin: nor did he know in what capacity Lawrence had come to him—Lawrence who had never, within de Trafford's knowledge of his adult life, approached a sacrament of the Church. But when no word came de Trafford was forced into a question.

"Lawrence, what have you been doing?"

"Killing a woman."

"Ah!" said Father de Trafford under his breath.

He unlocked a cabinet, took from it a hunting flask three parts full of brandy, and poured out the spirit with no sparing hand.

"Drink this, and pull yourself together. Remember, what you tell me now is not under the seal of confession."

Lawrence drank it. As if it had given him a swift up-leap of strength, he rose to his feet and stood looking round the room till his eye lit on a tall crucifix that hung against the wall. Then with a step like that of a drunken man he reeled across to the prie-Dieu and fell on his knees. There was something terrible, something repellent to de Trafford's taste in his prostration. De Trafford thought to himself, "This agony won't last. How he has sapped his own manhood! I don't believe he has killed any one. I must stop this."

He bent over Lawrence and seized him by the arm. "Lawrence, get up: control yourself. Do you wish me to hear your confession?"

Lawrence raised his head, and before the blazing misery of his eyes de Trafford reconsidered his judgment. "Oh, de Trafford, save me! can you save me?"

"Save you from what?"

"From sin," said Lawrence: "from sin."

Over brow and breast de Trafford made the sign of the cross. "Confess to me then."

"Pray, Father, give me your blessing . . ."

There was no reserve about Lawrence Sturt's confession. Forth it all came, the sins of boyhood, early manhood, middle age: every sin that Lawrence could remember, and, beyond the limits of a slender code of honor, nearly every sin that de Trafford could suggest. But it was not altogether easy to understand. Even the timeworn leading questions, that had served to rack many a tormented mind into peace, de Trafford found in this case difficult to frame. When he reached the events of that night, Lawrence spoke so low, and he was trembling so violently from head to foot, that the priest could hardly follow him. He had gone late to Jenny's house . . . he had forced his way in . . . there was another man with her . . . there had been a row, and he had thrown the other man out. . . .

Poor Horton, who had paid his price for Jenny's favors after all!

"Oh, I suppose I didn't strangle her," Lawrence said with his imperishable gleam of humor. "You can't kill her sort. I tried to . . ." He looked down at his hands. ". . . But that was afterwards."

"After what?"

He shuddered again from head to foot, murmured a broken sentence which de Trafford barely caught, and fainted.

Wan dusk of snowlight, an hour before dawn, glimmered through St. Casimir's painted panes. Not many worshipers had gathered for early Mass, that winter morning; foremost among them knelt Lawrence Sturt, the light of the radiant altar striking down over his bare head. In the serene ecstatic splendor of his regard there was no trace left of last night's agony, and his lips moved in the rapture of the *Pange lingua.* As a matter of fact his absolution had been deferred; but that affliction could not lessen—nothing could have lessened—the glory of his mood. Meanwhile Guy de Trafford, not a little weary after his night of vigil, was robing himself in the vestry

for the sacrifice of the Mass. The delicate fair face of
the priest was overcast, as if the burden lifted from his
penitent had fallen upon him; as if on his fastidious
purity of spirit the grime of Lawrence Sturt's unedited
revelations had thrown a temporary stain. As he waited
for the clock to strike the quarter-hour, de Trafford
thought of many things: of Mark Sturt and his marriage,
whose complete history up to date he had not been able
to prevent Lawrence from betraying to him; of Lawrence and his headlong reformation; of the chaos reign-
ing in the Liberal camp; and of the little house in Green
Street, and its mistress, the *causa causans* of all these
changes.

"Mark will come back," he said to himself. "It will
blow over—much the sooner when the eccentric romance
of his marriage begins to get known. It will cost him,
say, a year's seniority, but he will come back to politics
in the end, and he will come back to us. One is sure of
my dear old Mark. And Lawrence? Him we shall not
keep. I don't think he will go to Green Street again."
De Trafford was not sure even of that. "But so long as
he keeps his splendid looks, and there are women in the
world of the Essenden type to tell him so, we shall have
no hold on Lawrence Sturt. So it all comes round again
to Jenny Essenden. Ah! I am wanting in faith. Why
should we not keep him, after all? He is ours now;
he would lie down on the rack with that wonderful smiling splendor in his eyes. Faint-heart that I am! is not
the grace of God stronger than the grace of Jenny Essenden?"

THE END

www.ingramcontent.com/pod-product-compliance
Lightning Source LLC
Chambersburg PA
CBHW030340020726
47493CB00003B/622